COLD STEEL

Paul Carson is a doctor based in south Dublin where he runs an Asthma and Allergy clinic for children. He has published a number of health books and, as well as writing for various medical journals, he was editor of *Irish Doctor* magazine. His first novel, *Scalpel*, was published in 1997 and spent seventeen weeks at number one on the *Irish Times* hardback bestseller lists. Dr Carson is married and has two children.

Also by Paul Carson

Scalpel

COLD STEEL

Paul Carson

ARROW

Published in the United Kingdom in 1999 by Arrow Books

3 5 7 9 10 8 6 4 2

Copyright © Paul Carson 1998

The right of Paul Carson to be identified as the author of this work has been
asserted by him in accordance with the Copyright, Designs and Patents Act,
1988

First published in the Republic of Ireland in 1998 by William Heinemann

Arrow Books Limited
Random House UK Limited
20 Vauxhall Bridge Road, London, SW1V 2SA

Random House UK Limited
20 Vauxhall Bridge Road, London SW1V 2SA

Random House Australia (Pty) Limited
20 Alfred Street, Milsons Point, Sydney, New South Wales 2061, Australia

Random House New Zealand Limited
18 Poland Road, Glenfield, Auckland 10, New Zealand

Random House South Africa (Pty) Limited
Endulini, 5a Jubilee Road, Parktown 2193, South Africa

Random House UK Limited Reg. No. 954009

A CIP catalogue record for this book is available from the British Library

Papers used by Random House UK Limited are natural, recyclable products
made from wood grown in sustainable forests. The manufacturing processes
conform to the environmental regulations of the country of origin

Typeset by SX Composing DTP, Rayleigh, Essex
Printed and bound in Germany by Elsnerdruck, Berlin

ISBN 0 09 927929 0

To my wife, Jean, and my children, Emily and David, for putting up with the stolen hours in the attic.
To my agent, Darley Anderson, in London, for his encouragement.
To my editor, Lynne Drew, at William Heinemann, for her astute and constructive criticisms.
To sales and marketing at Random House for their support.
Finally to my partner, Dr Conor O'Toole, for looking after my health.

Acknowledgements

The doctors
My thanks for technical advice to Professor 'Jack' Harbison, forensic pathologist to the Republic of Ireland; forensic psychiatrist Dr Art O'Connor; psychiatrist to the National Drugs Treatment Centre in Dublin, Dr John O'Connor; orthopaedic surgeon Paul McNamee and finally Dr Rory O'Donnell, haematologist.

The detectives
I am also grateful to Dr James Donovan, founder and current head of Ireland's Forensic Science Department who still carries the scars of an attempt to assassinate him. Thanks also to the members of Garda Siochana, Ireland's largely unarmed police force, who provided background information.

Prologue

Dr Frank Clancy, physician specialising in diseases of the blood, crooked a phone between right ear and shoulder as he scribbled notes on a patient chart in his office.

'Hi, Clancy here.'

A youngish female voice came back.

'Dr Clancy, this is the lab. We have a rather unusual blood film we'd like you to look at.'

Clancy flicked over a page and continued his hurried scrawl, glancing at his watch.

'What's so unusual?'

'There's no white cells. It's a full blood count and we're not finding any white cells.'

Clancy stopped scribbling.

'Full blood count?' he checked.

'Correct.'

'No white cells?'

'Definite.'

'At all?' Alarmed, incredulous.

'None.'

Clancy slipped the chart onto the desk in front and sat down slowly, disturbed by what he was hearing.

He shifted the phone into his right hand, thinking furiously. The absence of white cells was extremely serious, they were the body's vital defenders against infection. Without them no patient could survive. He ran a hand through his hair, then glanced again at his watch. Behind time as usual.

'I'll be down when I can. Get the medical history and any other blood screens.'

'Right away,' the girl replied.

'Oh,' Clancy cut back, 'leave details and ward number. I'd like to examine the patient myself.' His voice suggested urgency.

'It'll all be here in fifteen minutes.' Calm and efficient.

Clancy forced a grin and stood up. 'Okay, I'll be down soon.'

'Thanks, Dr Clancy.'

Frank Clancy pulled on his white coat and hurried out from his office to the bustling wards. He steered past a group of students squinting at films on an X-ray viewing box and along to his medical team waiting at the middle of a row of beds.

'Hi, sorry I'm late,' he announced, avoiding the disapproving frown of the ward sister. 'Where do we start? Who's going to tell me about this patient?' He picked up a chart and skimmed the tattered, dog-eared pages until he found the most recent entry, then nodded to his second in command. 'Off you go.'

As the monologue began Clancy's thoughts were already elsewhere. The telephone call worried him. Yet another patient on the wards deficient in white cells. That's two, maybe three in as many months. What's going on?

CONCERN GROWS FOR MISSING
US SURGEON'S DAUGHTER

Police are concerned for the safety of missing schoolgirl Jennifer Marks. The eighteen-year-old failed to return home yesterday and a search for her began late last night. Extensive inquiries failed to determine the teenager's movements after she left school yesterday afternoon. The search continued until after dark, when it was finally called off. Officers resumed door-to-door questioning at first light this morning.

Jennifer Marks is the only daughter of Dan Marks, the top US cardiac surgeon appointed head of this city's recently established Heart Foundation. He was unavailable for comment this morning.

Tuesday, 12 May, *Dublin Evening Post*
(morning edition)

CLICK.

A gasp filled the lecture theatre.

'It is not my intention to disturb you this morning.' Declan Kelleher, trauma surgeon at the Mercy Hospital, Dublin, stood at a lectern studying the tiered rows of third-year medical students. There was no mistaking the shocked expressions on each young face. A few had momentarily averted their eyes from the image on the screen behind him. 'However in trauma you often see the worst side of medicine, the blood and guts.' He paused, then half turned to the colour transparency on display. In his right hand a light source directed a tiny red blip onto the screen.

'Let's try and make out what we are looking at.' The red blip stopped at a bend on a limb. 'That's the knee joint,' he explained, then moved the blip slowly along the image, 'that's what's left of the lower tibia and fibula and ankle joint.' Whispers spilled down from the middle rows. At the back a much older man shifted uneasily in his seat and eased out his right leg for comfort. He did not look towards the front, eyes firmly closed, lids flickering. He listened intently to every word. Kelleher turned to face the group again and pressed a button on the lectern.

CLICK.

'Before we go any further, maybe we should remind ourselves what a normal lower limb looks like on X-ray.'

As a silver-grey image slotted into place, Kelleher trained the red blip. 'That's the femur, the large, strong bone that connects hip and knee joints. That's the knee joint itself and underneath you can see normal tibia and fibula, ankle joint, metatarsal bones and phalanges, what we recognise as our toes.'

He turned back to the audience. Most eyes were on the screen, the rest on him. His tall frame, with head of grey hair that always seemed combed into permanent disorder, blocked one or two and they craned to see past him.

'Let's look at that first slide and see how much damage this patient sustained.'

CLICK.

The transparency glided onto the screen and all eyes turned to inspect. This time none of the heads turned away, the initial shock had abated. The trainee doctors were learning to steel their stomachs as much as their nerves. In the very back row a set of eyelids momentarily flickered open then closed just as quickly. In that split second he saw everything and shuddered involuntarily despite the uncomfortable warmth of the room. The image was overwhelming. Against a green background of theatre drapes rested a leg. The slide captured a little of above-knee and all of the below-knee structures. The knee was bent at a thirty degree angle. From about two hands'-breadth below the knee the skin surface abruptly ended and was replaced by a mass of bloodied and bulging muscle and the distinct whiteness of freshly exposed bone. The visible bone was clearly shattered and slivers stood out like tooth picks.

'To be completely honest,' confessed Kelleher, 'I'm not sure what I can identify here.'

The red blip picked out a white shard. 'That might be part of the tibia.' The blip settled on a reddened mass. 'That could be gastrocnemius muscle, possibly part of soleus. I'm not sure which is which though.'

CLICK.

Another silver-grey image slipped onto the screen. As it did someone in the middle rows groaned loudly. 'Yes, pretty ghastly, isn't it?' agreed Kelleher as he inspected the result. The red blip shot up and rested on a structure picked up on X-ray. 'That's femur,' the blip slowly traced a path from normality to utter chaos, 'that's normal knee joint, that's the upper third of the tibia and fibula and the rest is broken, smashed, crushed bone.'

He turned back to the audience and scanned the faces. Most were still riveted by the transparency, a few heads bent as hands scribbled notes, one or two stared directly at him. He noted the lowered head at the back.

'As I said, I'm not in the business of shocking you, but in accident and emergency, you deal with what comes through the door, no matter how bad it looks.' No one spoke, pens paused, all eyes now directed at him. 'However I thought you might like to see how this patient fared, what was the outcome of that bloody mess we saw a minute ago.'

Kelleher flicked a switch on the lectern and the

theatre lights flashed on. Eyes were rubbed to adjust to the change, heads moved closer as comments were exchanged. Pens returned to paper and notes were made. In the back row the man shifted his leg again, using his left foot to drag the other back slightly. He massaged the lower part of his right leg through his trousers, grimacing as he felt a twinge of pain.

Kelleher raised a finger. 'I'd like to introduce the owner of that mangled limb. Can you come down to the front, superintendent?'

All heads swivelled.

A distinct Donegal accent answered. 'Yes, if you give me a minute.'

'I'd like to introduce you to Detective Superintendent Jim Clarke,' Kelleher said.

Clarke struggled out of the cramped seat and settled his single crutch carefully in front before swinging his right leg into the aisle. It hit the floor with a thud. He took his weight on the left leg to stand up, then slipped his right arm through the crutch guide and grasped the hand rest before moving any further. Each step down the aisle seemed painfully slow. The students could not take their eyes off the slightly stooped figure. He was slim, almost thin, and one inch above a full six feet in height. He wore regulation police uniform. Those near the aisle could see the pain that flickered across his face with each step. Near the bottom he stopped and pulled a handkerchief from his side pocket to wipe his brow. Then he brushed fingers through the bit of straggling hair still left after fifty-two years of life, trying to present a better image.

'I'm sorry, I'm a bit slow on steps.'

'Take your time,' encouraged Kelleher as he pulled

a chair closer to the lectern. He unclipped the microphone from his jacket lapel and held it until the other man had settled again, then handed it to him.

'Superintendent Clarke,' Kelleher explained, 'is a senior member of the Serious Crime Squad.' Clarke looked at the rows in front and smiled awkwardly. He seemed embarrassed, like someone about to be given a medal at an awards' ceremony and not sure how to handle the occasion. 'On 25 July two years ago he was admitted to this hospital with the injuries you saw. I was on duty and involved in his immediate management.' Kelleher half turned. 'He's here to relate how those injuries came about.'

Clarke acknowledged his comments with a slight nod.

'Also with us,' continued Kelleher, 'is Dr Patrick Dillon.' A tall, heavily built man stood up from one end of the front row and faced the audience. He was wearing neatly pressed flannel trousers under a navy blazer with a white handkerchief in breast pocket. He unfolded a pair of glasses and slipped them on, then shielded his eyes against the theatre lights. His hair was dark and slicked back in a duck tail.

'Dr Dillon,' explained Kelleher, 'is a forensic psychiatrist, someone who deals with the criminally insane. He has trained in secure psychiatric units where staff are taught self-defence and carry Mace spray on the wards. He has also worked in Broadmoor, the main British hospital for such offenders. He has just been appointed head of the forensic psychiatric department at Rockdale Hospital in County Meath and can be called upon to assist police with their assessments of certain serious crimes.' Kelleher was reading from notes on the back of an

9

envelope. 'As part of this series of early morning lectures,' he went on, 'I wanted you to consider trauma from angles other than medical management. Look behind the scenes, as it were.' He paused briefly. 'Often in casualty departments we see criminal violence. Rape, stabbing, shooting, bludgeoning. Severe, deliberate inflicted injuries. Frequently we ask ourselves "Who could do such a thing?" You're about to hear how one such event happened, then have the background explained.' Kelleher nodded towards Dillon and sat down in the front row to listen.

Patrick Dillon moved to the lectern and scanned the faces in front. 'Psychiatry,' he began, 'is the study and treatment of disorders of the mind.' His voice was quiet yet distinct, with a slight English accent. 'Most psychiatrists spend their working lives dealing with conditions such as depression, anxiety states or schizophrenia. The forensic psychiatrist deals with the criminal mind. More importantly he deals with the criminal but mentally abnormal, those whose acts of violence, often murderous, cannot be presented to the courts in the usual manner.' The audience was gripped, attention unwavering.

'My work,' continued Dillon, 'involves psychiatry and criminality, two of the most intriguing fields of human behaviour.' His voice became hard and deliberate. 'I look into the mind of the murderer.' The words chilled and Jim Clarke turned sharply.

'Occasionally,' Dillon went on, 'I am asked to provide a psychological profile, a characterisation if you like, of the person most likely to be involved in specific crimes.' He slipped his glasses back into a side pocket. 'After we've heard the superintendent's story,' he finished, 'I will attempt to explain the mental status of the criminality involved in his case.' He stood down and moved to the side.

Clarke shifted slightly on the chair and eased out his right leg with the top of his left foot. He reached over and rested the crutch against the lectern, wiped his brow with his handkerchief, then paused to collect his thoughts. And control his emotions. He'd had to go over this so many times he could have recited it in his sleep. But each retelling was just as difficult, the pain almost as intense, the horror as real.

'I was on survcillance duty in Blackrock, south Dublin,' he began, 'in an unmarked squad car.' His voice sounded weak despite the microphone and students at the back leaned forward to hear. 'There was myself and one other officer. We'd been following a Dublin drug baron for months, watching collection and delivery patterns, mapping distribution networks.' He stopped and nodded towards the glass of water resting on the lectern, noticing a few sympathetic smiles flicker along the front row. The glass was passed over.

'We were parked outside a pub along the seafront,' he continued. 'A black transit van pulled in and drove very slowly to an empty corner, well away from the rest of the cars. It looked out of place immediately, as though the driver had chosen that exact spot for a reason. We checked with headquarters and learned the number plates were false. The driver left the van without locking it and walked towards the pub. My colleague waited three minutes, then followed on foot. I stayed in the car watching. I noticed a young couple sipping on beer cans a little way away but didn't pay much attention.

They were laughing a lot, as if caught up in their own company.'

For a brief second he was back in the driver's seat, wondering whether to sit tight and wait or check the van. He could almost hear again the static on the radio, smell the sea, hear the waves crashing on rocks behind the high wall barely twenty yards away.

'I got fed up waiting. That was my only mistake, I got fed up waiting.'

The van was clean, only empty boxes, stacked one on top of the other in a neat pile and pushed against the driver's side panel. It had taken him less than ten minutes to open and check each one. As he made his way back he noticed the young couple had gone.

'I can't remember what I felt first. I do remember turning the key in the ignition, then there was a sudden bang and I felt pain in my legs, or maybe it was the bursting in my ears. I really can't remember.'

He stopped and looked up. The lecture theatre was silent, not a hand moved, not a pen scribbled. 'The next I remember was being dragged from the car and someone screaming, that and the noise of an ambulance siren. There was a mask over my face and a voice shouting to take deep breaths.' He wiped a handkerchief across his brow and took another sip of water.

Kelleher looked at the audience, noting their absorbed attention. He adjusted the sound on the microphone.

'A pound of explosive had been planted under my seat, wired to the ignition.' Clarke sipped on the water again, then took a deeper quaff, as if trying to drown his voice. He placed the glass down carefully at his feet, taking time so the audience wouldn't see the shake in his hands.

The emotional pain was palpable and Kelleher decided to interrupt.

'Superintendent Clarke's physical condition was very poor when he arrived in casualty. He'd lost a lot of blood, was hypotensive, lapsing in and out of consciousness. The right leg was in a poor state, the left leg relatively unscathed even though he'd sustained a fracture of the tibia. Priority was to stabilise and get his blood pressure up. Then he was taken to theatre to have the right leg amputated, it wasn't considered viable.'

Kelleher dimmed the theatre lights and began flicking slide after slide onto the screen as he explained the surgical reconstruction of the right leg. One transparency picked up wires and screws where the decision to amputate had been changed and an orthopaedic team worked throughout the night, pulling shards and slivers and pieces of bone together. A vascular surgeon joined at the halfway stage to protect the blood vessels.

'Fortunately the nerve supply to the limb remained reasonably intact,' Kelleher continued, dropping medical labels that slipped over the head of the man sitting in the seat beside the lectern trying hard to remain detached from the discussion.

'Did you find out who did this?' a red-haired girl in the second row interrupted. Clarke's head dropped slightly and he massaged the damaged leg. He squinted at the questioner through the darkness, her face lit by the projector light.

'Yes. His name was Christy O'Hara, a well-known

hit man. He went into hiding but was shot dead in a gangland feud.'

'Was anyone else involved,' the same girl pressed.

'Three months later, while I was still in a ward upstairs,' an index finger pointed roofwards, 'the investigating team discussed possible suspects, those most likely to benefit from my death. It took four hours to go over the list.' Someone near the back whistled softly and a few giggled nervously. Clarke ignored them. 'We narrowed the group to seven. Finally an informer came forward with the name. Jude Kennedy, the drug baron we were shadowing.' No one spoke, the theatre silent again. The pointer in Declan Kelleher's hand threw the red blip aimlessly against a side wall.

Clarke cleared his throat and reached for the glass at his feet. Against the microphone the noise of the water trickling down his throat sounded above the tiered rows. He set the glass back and looked up. 'He's also dead, taken out in a dispute over territory.'

'Great,' someone muttered and Clarke allowed a terse smile.

Declan Kelleher stood up and motioned the forensic psychiatrist back to the lectern.

'Perhaps, Dr Dillon, you might explain what drives men to murder in cold blood? What is the mind-set of the hit man? What is the psychiatric background? How can you help the police, say, in a murder investigation?'

Dillon listened to the questions, lips puckered, eyebrows creased. He didn't speak for almost three minutes, then adjusted the microphone to his height. 'The ruthless hit man is almost certainly a sociopath. In cold blood and without remorse, he kills for money. Those who send him on such missions and pay for the results are equally evil, equally devoid of remorse. My role in police investigations is to assess the type of crime. Is it a frenzied attack with multiple injuries or a single bullet to the back of the head?' The lecture theatre was totally silent. 'The type of attack,' continued Dillon, 'reflects the mind of the attacker. When I advise the police I explain the specific characteristics of each event; the crime, the likely murder weapon, the crime scene, et cetera.'

The eerie silence was broken by the noisy opening of the only door at the back of the theatre. Everyone turned to the tall figure filling the frame, coughing for attention. A hand waved into the darkness. Clarke reached over and lifted his crutch in the air to show where he was sitting. Down the steps bounded Moss Kavanagh, Clarke's full-time minder and part-time driver. Six foot three with cropped black hair and the squashed face of a front row rugby player he rolled a mobile phone from hand to hand as he bent down and whispered.

'Boss, you've gotta go. They've found the Marks girl.'

Clarke examined the other man's face.

'Where?'

'She's lying in some park in the east of the city.' The whispers were caught on the microphone and Clarke enveloped the tiny device in his right hand.

'Alive or dead?'

'Dead.'

'Jesus,' was as much as Clarke could muster as he struggled to his feet. He motioned Dillon to follow.

The body was discovered at 7.46 that morning.

A jogger had tripped over a pale and still white leg

that stuck out from undergrowth. He'd stumbled and dislodged the earphones on his Walkman, causing him to stop to readjust. While he fiddled with the earpieces he glanced back. For almost two minutes he didn't move, barely able to believe his eyes, barely able to trust the rational explanation for what they were seeing. Then he edged closer, twice looking over his shoulder to see if anyone else was around. There was no one. The park was deserted apart from a few magpies strutting across dewy grass, the only sound coming from their raucous screeches as they criss-crossed one another's paths. Going as close as he dared, he made out two very pale, wax-like legs, one slightly bent, the other more or less straight. The legs were attached to a body, face down, partly hidden by twigs and leaves on which spiders had spun dew-dropped webs. As he parted a branch, the early morning sun glinted and danced on the droplets before the delicate lattice work collapsed. The legs were female, he immediately decided, as he also spotted a skirt hitched up to the waist. He knew within seconds those legs, like the rest of the body, were lifeless and wasted no time running for help. He glanced at his watch as he ran.

The first squad car arrived at 8.23, as recorded by the young policeman who climbed over the green spiked railings surrounding the park and followed the jogger to his discovery. As he strode along the wet grass he fired off questions and the jogger, a forty-year-old balding accountant, a good six inches smaller than his sudden companion, did his best to answer. His replies were cautious, not wanting to give the impression he was personally responsible

16

for the body being there in the first place. At 8.35 the body was officially reported to police headquarters as that of a female with clothes in a state of disarray. At 8.37 there was an additional finding. A knife was imbedded in the back of the body, somewhere around the middle of the right upper-chest area. The officer added that the knife was imbedded to the hilt. A minute later he added in a slightly flustered voice he now had a collapsed jogger and asked for an ambulance to be called.

'Clear that group back from the railings. Find out where the keys to the gates are and get a couple of the uniformed lads to patrol the perimeter.' Detective Sergeant Tony Molloy was protecting the crime scene, waiting for the forensic team to arrive. He was tall but paunchy with a bald pate and fluffs of grey hair above both ears. Aged forty-six, he moved with the ease of a man who'd done this many times before, clear instructions, few hand movements, quiet words rather than shouts. Those under his control lost no time, their movements casting weak shadows in the early morning sunlight.

'Don't anyone go near the body and don't let one of those bloody birds near.' The magpies had fled their quiet haven, only a few squawked from surrounding trees which were coming into full leaf after the harsh spring weather.

Sandymount Park in east Dublin was two acres of square ground. There were mature trees, a mixture of sycamore and chestnut, blocking the green itself from nearby houses and apartment complexes. The central uncut grass lawn was used mainly for ball games, two coats as goals and someone taking penalties, or frisbee throwing. The park was sealed off from the road and back gardens that abutted its edges by a six-foot-high green spiked railing that screamed for a lick of paint. Scattered randomly, or so it would appear to anyone with gardening expertise, were clumps of bushes and small trees. At the south edge, where the body had been found, thick undergrowth flourished. There was a sad-looking wooden shelter about thirty yards from this spot. The wood had rotted in places and graffiti covered most of the remaining paintwork. Inside the shelter were a number of empty beer cans, cider bottles and cigarette butts. Molloy had noted these when he peered in earlier. He'd also spotted a bloodstained syringe.

'Seal off that shelter,' he ordered and a yellow crime-scene incident tape circled the wooden structure in minutes.

Molloy was a born worrier. He worried about his health, his pension, about the weather, about the way the country was going, everything. When he wasn't worrying, he worried he had nothing to worry about. As he checked the description of the missing Jennifer Marks with headquarters, he quickly sensed he'd have a lot more to worry about than usual.

Two uniformed police officers arrived at the Marks'
house just after ten o'clock that morning. Dan Marks
had waited downstairs all night beside the telephone.
He had disconnected the two lines upstairs so as not
to disturb his invalid wife.

'Dr Marks?' The policemen were both tall and
gangly, young, one red-haired, the other dark. They
held their peaked caps at their sides, and were
sombre-faced.

'Yes.'

The red-haired officer spoke first, in slow,
deliberate tones. 'I'm afraid we've come about
Jennifer.'

Dan Marks went into denial mode. 'Yes, yes. Have
you found her?' Desperate. 'Is she all right?'

'I'm afraid the news isn't good.' The dark-haired
officer turned away slightly to avoid eye contact. His
colleague continued. 'The body of a young girl
answering Jennifer's description has been found in a
park about two miles from here.'

The slow, clear, deliberate delivery of information
continued. Time found, clothes worn; immediate

observations toned down significantly to conceal the awful truth. Marks listened for about four minutes, then pushed the door closed.

'Annie, they've found Jennifer.' Dan Marks stood at the half-open door leading into his wife's bedroom.

There was a silence and in the gloom of the bedroom Dan Marks could just about make out his wife. She sat in a wheelchair staring at the closed curtains pulled across the windows.

'When? When do they want us?'

'Annie, if you don't want to . . .'

'When, you bastard! I said when?' The scream shook Marks and he gripped the door frame.

'As soon as they let us know we can go there.' His voice was heavy with pain.

'Where is my daughter, where are they taking her?'

Dan Marks could barely speak the words. 'The morgue. They'll call us from the morgue.'

'Well, get yourself ready,' Annie Marks snapped as she dabbed at her eyes in the dark, 'I've been waiting all night for this. I'm ready.'

'I'll come back when I hear more.'

There was an unintelligible grunted response.

Dan Marks started to close the door then turned. 'Annie, I'm sorry.'

'Leave me alone, you bastard. I don't want your snivelling tears. Do you hear?'

He closed the door gently to drown out the sobs.

It had all begun so differently eight months earlier.

'Good afternoon, ladies and gentlemen. Thank you for coming along.'

Dr John Regan, Minister for Health in the recently

elected government, addressed the gathered media from a podium. The large hall in government buildings was full to overflowing and Regan glanced around, assessing the turnout. He was well satisfied. There were eight TV crews, each with their own station reporters. He noted two major US networks, as well as CNN and Sky. In another corner the BBC, two European crews he couldn't identify and the national station RTE. A TV crew from Boston had pushed to the front, checking angles. Slumped in chairs around the room were print and radio reporters, some gossiping while others scribbled in notebooks. Just as well I ordered the big hall, thought Regan. It was an impressive turnout and he knew the journalists would mention that in their reports.

Behind him was an empty table covered in green cloth with bottled water and glasses on top. Four empty chairs were pulled back awaiting occupancy. Two feet behind the chairs large screens carried government propaganda with photographs of the winning election slogans and logo: *A New Government For A New People*. Smiling faces of the 'future of Ireland: its young people' with John Regan shaking hands, looking concerned, head thrown back and laughing, wiping away tears, kicking a football. The images were strong and positive. Ireland with the youngest population in the European Union needed to brush away the cobwebs of the past and concentrate on the future. The slogans had won the day and the government swept into power with a handsome majority.

At thirty-three John Regan was the youngest ever Minister for Health. Born into a poor working-class home in Dublin's inner city, Regan had fought his way to the top on the streets. Drive, ambition and an incisive brain won him a place at university where he had been a student radical, campaigning against privilege and class distinction. His choice of medicine as a career surprised many, though all agreed he had enough ruthless dynamism to carry him to the top. But the tedium of hospital medicine and lack of promotion frustrated. A politically charged Regan left the wards to stomp the campaign trail. Despite angry protests from opponents about intimidation from his handlers, Regan cruised to victory in the election.

He was in office only two weeks when he stage-managed the first confrontation with a medical profession he secretly loathed. He announced all public hospital appointments would no longer carry the right to private practice. There was uproar within the ranks of the consultants, used to doubling and sometimes trebling their incomes with private work. Next he published the official salaries of the consultants and their estimated extra private fees. There was public outcry at the excesses. While the consultants went into a huddle to plan their strategy, Regan played his trump card and announced the establishment of a Heart Foundation. This was to be an international heart disease research and treatment centre based at Dublin's Mercy Hospital ('already a centre of medical excellence').

The Mercy Hospital had been created on a green field site in 1994, amalgamating five of the older inner-city Dublin hospitals. The first few years after its opening had been difficult, but the petty rivalries and jealousies that bedevil many medical institutions soon burned out. The institution became a recognised nucleus of medical excellence with special interest in cancer research, diagnostic radiology and respiratory diseases. Regan's intervention was a bold and daring move. The government promised thirty-five million pounds to establish the Heart Foundation. Fifteen million pounds would be provided by Irish tax payers, while the balance was guaranteed by the European Union, a community initiative designed to counter North American dominance of medical research. The EEC money was conditional on regular reviews and appraisal of results from the Foundation. At the time Regan said he anticipated international interest in the project. 'It will be the envy of the world.' He hoped Irish doctors would be at the top of his appointments. He knew they wouldn't. His project was snubbed from the beginning and looked certain to collapse. But Regan had laid his plans carefully. After a decent delay of six weeks to allow the local medical fraternity an opportunity to come around, he flew to Boston and arrived back with the scalps of the 'Dream Team', three heart specialists committed to establishing the Foundation. They had been lured from their positions at Springton hospital, one of the most prestigious medical institutions in the United States.

It was an audacious and courageous coup. The people loved it and the government's rating shot higher in the polls. Regan's personal profile was established. He had taken on the might of the most formidable trade union in the country, the medical profession, and left them gasping. And he had captured twenty million pounds of EEC grants. Even Dublin's gossip columnists were silenced. Throughout the election campaign they had made much of

Regan's single status, occasionally printing unsavoury rumours about his private life. He was now untouchable, the nation's favourite son. Today was the culmination of many months' work, a vindication of all his effort.

'As you know we're here today to meet the medical specialists from Boston now under contract with our government to develop the proposed Heart Foundation,' Regan began when the audience had settled. He looked the consummate politician, tall and broadshouldered. For the occasion he'd chosen a beige Armani suit over dark blue shirt and bright yellow tie. His short black hair was swept back severely, emphasising his broad forehead. Unmarried, Regan's looks meant he was sought after by many women. He was wearing his concerned face which could just as easily turn vicious and angry if provoked.

'You'll see in the press release a brief summary of their backgrounds, hospital appointments and research work to date. After you've had a chance to read this I'm sure you'll agree we are very fortunate to have such high calibre talent here in Dublin.'

He paused and allowed his gaze to drift around the room. Cameramen fiddled with lights and lenses, Dictaphones were held up in the air to capture every word.

'I'm going to introduce each in turn and at the end we'll throw the meeting open for questions.' He looked down, noting the cynical posturing and bored expressions of journalists who'd attended too many press conferences. Wait'll they see what I've got. They'll be hanging out of those chairs by the end.

'First I'd like you to meet Dr Stone Colman, biochemist and internationally recognised expert in the field of cellular changes in heart disease.'

A door to the side of the podium opened and a rather bookish looking man stepped out and smiled nervously. Regan glanced at the press release detailing Colman's background, age, appointments and research work. He looked up and smiled encouragingly. Stone Colman was medium height, forty-four years old and dressed in a rather sagging, crumpled dark brown suit. His ginger hair was tight crew cut giving him a military air which his slight stoop marred. He moved quickly and sat down at the table, immediately opening a bottle of mineral water and pouring a glass to almost overflowing. He looked ill at ease in such a public arena.

'Dr Colman will continue research on the cellular changes that occur in the immediate hours after heart attacks. In particular he will seek to identify the mystery chemicals we believe trigger off fatal heart rhythms.' Regan noticed some of the journalists scribbling. 'It's all in the press release, boys,' he rebuked. 'Next I'd like you to meet Dr Linda Speer, internationally renowned cardiologist.'

Onto the podium, walking like a model in a fashion show, came Regan's showpiece, brains with beauty. Linda Speer was thirty-five years old but looked ten years younger. She wore a fashionably cut navy jacket over long grey skirt and white cashmere roll-neck. She walked confidently over to Stone Colman who smiled and set a glass in front, lifting a questioning eyebrow. She declined with a flick of her right wrist, allowing the audience a glimpse of gold bracelet, then sat down. Regan watched as one or two cameramen zoomed for better views. Linda Speer crossed her legs and allowed a polished Gucci high heel to dangle provocatively off her toes, then swept a hand through her short blonde hair, pulling it away from her face.

Regan smiled to himself as he watched the shoe rock back and forth. This girl's got class. 'Dr Speer is both an adult and paediatric cardiologist and is particularly keen to expand the paediatric heart surgery programme in Ireland. If you look at page three of the press release,' paper rustled all round the room, 'you'll see the statistics of our current heart surgery programme and waiting list. Since modern trends suggest children with congenital heart disease should be operated on in the first twelve months of life, we are failing many young patients by delaying surgery beyond their first birthdays.'

Regan turned to look at the upturned face of Linda Speer who was listening attentively. 'Dr Speer believes we can halve the current waiting list inside a year as soon as our new centre's up and running. Isn't that right, Linda?'

The beauty with brains smiled and a perfect white flash stunned the audience. She mouthed a slow 'yes' at Regan and he felt a slight stirring in his groin. He coughed to distract himself and turned back to the journalists.

'As you know, this government was elected to represent the future of Ireland, our young people. If we cannot provide adequate medical services for our youngest members, our babies, then we fail the electorate who voted us into power.' A few in the audience smiled at the party political broadcast, the rest carefully read Speer's CV. Regan was sure they would note she was divorced with no children. He knew one or two of the cockier journos would wonder about their chances.

'Finally, I'd like you to meet Dr Dan Marks.' The side door opened again and into view strode the icing on the cake as far as Regan was concerned. Dan Marks was two inches above six feet, with the build of a man who'd played American Rules football for years. His curling hair was totally grey, long at the back. He wore an off-white linen jacket over navy T-shirt and denim jeans with the sort of trainers middle-aged men choose to hide their advancing years. His face showed a healthy tan, courtesy of a recent cardiology conference in Florida where he'd delivered a paper in thirty minutes and spent the rest of the week at the poolside. Marks stopped halfway to the podium, looked down at the audience and bowed slightly. A ripple of laughter reached his ears and he smiled broadly before sitting down.

'Dr Marks is an internationally renowned cardiac surgeon,' Regan went on smugly, 'and has a patient list that reads like the *Who's Who* of celebrities. Before he left Boston he carried out a triple bypass on Senator Bill Hall of Alabama before moving to theatre two and replacing a damaged mitral valve on top chat-show host, Marvin Hanna.' He waited to allow these feats of glory to sink in before continuing, 'And I'm told he went out that afternoon and played an almost perfect eighteen holes of golf.' Regan started to laugh at his brilliant aside but stopped short as he noticed the impassive faces in front of him. Dan Marks was whispering into Linda Speer's left ear, ignoring all else.

'Dr Marks is second-generation Irish-American, his parents coming from County Mayo. He's particularly pleased to be coming *home*, as he told me last month, and his wife and eighteen-year-old daughter have been living in Dublin for the past six weeks.'

'And loving it,' Dan Marks shouted, catching Regan off guard. 'Absolutely loving it.'

That was how the media came to meet the 'Dream Team'. The nation watched and marvelled as the press conference was assessed on the main television current affairs programme that evening. The trio looked confident and relaxed, self-assured. Their New England accents impressed and many commented they could have been straight out of central casting, *ER* meets *Dallas*. John Regan was so at ease in their company. Ireland went to bed that night glowing in the warmth of a strong 'feel good' factor.

The TV, radio and newspapers made much of the three specialists over the subsequent weeks. The tabloid *Daily Post* ran profiles of the group and their backgrounds, filling pages with direct quotes: 'inadequate facilities' . . . 'poor career structure for junior staff leading to low morale' . . . 'lack of commitment to training among senior staff'. These open criticisms of existing cardiology facilities in Ireland were so scathing the Dream Team had more enemies than patients by the end of the first month. The social editor of the *Evening Post* featured Jennifer Marks' first day 'at the exclusive Holy Rosary Convent all-girls' school in Dublin's southside' where 'the emphasis is more on producing young ladies than career girls'. She included a list of the socialites, celebrities and academics who had spent their schooldays at the convent, many providing over-the-phone quotes on how wonderful it had all been.

Linda Speer was the subject of a long profile in a *Post* weekend colour supplement. She told reporters she was part of a 'cardiology team of excellence' and wanted the unit to stay together for the next two years to continue research they had already begun. What she failed to mention was the money. Speer had grown up in a hand-to-mouth existence, one of five children abandoned by their father. In a run-down neighbourhood of north Boston her mother had struggled to rear the children, sometimes juggling three jobs at a time for extra money. Like John Regan, Linda Speer never wanted to go hungry again. She despised the ignominy of poverty.

The report mentioned she'd married young while in medical school, but not that she'd abandoned her husband less than three years later when he didn't match her drive and ambition, merely that it 'didn't work out'. Since then she'd concentrated on her career but, as she confided to the reporter, gender was still a drawback. At crucial interviews the male-dominated medical profession often chose one of their own rather than a younger, brighter woman. She admitted, with unusual frankness for a doctor, that the Dublin position was a different route to her ultimate goal. Linda Speer wanted real success, power and wealth. She knew this was unattainable as a practising doctor, or not at the levels she aspired to. The research Ireland was willing to fund was her ticket to fortune.

A short piece in the medical press claimed Stone Colman was ready for a career move and that Regan's centre offered advancement in establishing his personal international profile. Colman was known to be ambitous but the report suggested he'd peaked in Boston and needed a fresh challenge. He was quoted as 'delighted' with his share of the promised budget, knowing how tight finances were in the Mercy hospital. 'I can confirm that over one million pounds of the promised EEC grant is earmarked for laboratory work alone,' he was quoted as saying. 'While this sum may sound generous it is no more than adequate for my department. Indeed it is no more than one would expect for a large hospital laboratory,' he'd added pointedly.

The *Post* also ran an EXCLUSIVE on the Marks family: 'Wheelchair-bound wife, Annie, once an aspiring neurosurgeon but now stricken with the devastating wasting disease multiple sclerosis. She is cared for by doting husband Dan, who administers her Interferon therapy himself every day.' There was a happy smiling family portrait, taken outside the front door of the new Marks' residence, a three-storey Victorian splendour in Dublin's embassy belt. 'MARKS MANSION' ran the headline with a photo underneath of a laughing Jennifer Marks, pretty face, slim build, one hand on her mother's wheelchair the other pulling back her long dark hair. She was wearing a T-shirt with its logo clearly visible: I LOVE IRELAND.

'The All-American Girl' ran the by-line.

3 *10.30 am*

'Joe, over here. Get shots of all that group. Don't let them see you. Get close-ups.' Jim Clarke clutched the hand grip on his crutch tightly as he motioned a uniformed officer closer. 'You, yes, you, over here. Stand beside me and pretend you're talking with us. Keep your back to that crowd,' he nodded at spectators gathered at the park railings. 'No, don't look round, keep looking at me. Let Joe rest his camera on your shoulder and stay as still as you can.'

One of Clarke's trademarks was the number of photographs he ordered in major investigations.

Clarke, Kavanagh and Dillon reached Sandymount Park within twenty minutes of leaving the hospital. (It was official policy to include the forensic psychiatrist in high-profile murders and occasionally the inspection of crime scenes was delayed until he arrived.) The park was already sealed off and, in a weak breeze, yellow incident tapes fluttered from precisely placed self-standing stakes. There was about twenty yards between body and nearest tape. A strategically devised corridor allowed all movement to and from the centre of attention without disturbing evidence. Five white boiler-suited forensic specialists were inspecting sites of immediate attention, two conversing and comparing notes as they stared down at a patch of trampled grass near the wooden shelter. A spiked stake with a yellow tip marked an area of blood-staining, three more lead directly to where the body lay. Clarke scanned the scene, counting the number of uniformed and plain-clothes officers and immediately contacted headquarters for another squad car. The sun had climbed higher in the sky with only an occasional cloud challenging. The magpies had fled.

Joe Harrison, the tall, bald and bulky forensic photographer on duty, switched lenses and began clicking, a spare Nikon resting on his ample belly. He zoomed and panned and shot off a thirty-six-roll film within seven minutes.

'Finished?' Clarke asked, wiping his forehead with a handkerchief. His uniform was overheating his body. Harrison, a man of few words, nodded, then ambled towards a shout from inside the secure zone.

'Now,' Clarke directed the young officer whose shoulder had been turned into a tripod, 'grab those three over there and split into twos and move as discreetly as possible to the opposite ends of the rails. Get out onto the road.' The listening head craned closer, anxious not to miss a word. 'As soon as you're over don't let anyone up or down. Close in on that group watching. Get every name and address and how they came to be here at this hour. Okay?' Clarke couldn't help but feel his age as he inspected the intense young face listening.

By five minutes past ten the road running alongside Sandymount Park was sealed off at both ends and all traffic, pedestrian and motorised, diverted to side roads. A few minutes later the group of onlookers began dispersing as they noticed blue police uniforms approach. The same group was kept waiting in line as notebooks were produced and details taken. Clarke looked on approvingly. Beside him Moss Kavanagh rolled his mobile phone from hand to hand, his tall head like a lighthouse beacon. Patrick Dillon had joined a group gathered in a huddle yards from the undergrowth, heads locked in deep conversation. Satisfied, Clarke wiped his brow and shook the numbness out of his damaged leg before limping towards the body.

'A touch of cold steel this morning, superintendent.' Dr Noel Dunne, the state forensic pathologist stood waiting in the middle of the taped corridor, twenty feet away from the undergrowth. He was a tall, paunchy man with a magnificent steel-grey beard and moustache that merged with his equally steel-grey head of hair. The end result almost covered his face, masking any expression. His eyes darted from side to side as he spoke, taking in every detail of the park and its surroundings. Despite the warmth of the morning he wore a Donegal tweed suit and Viyella shirt set off badly by a dark blue linen tie. He was something of a living legend within the force with a wealth of stories and humorous anecdotes that flowed like whiskey when the occasion demanded. The usual demanding occasion was murder.

'Knife in her back to the hilt,' he muttered as he made notes on an A4 page attached to a clipboard. 'Your men tell me she's the missing Marks girl.' It was more statement than question. 'Is that why our friend

Dillon's here too?' Dunne grinned at his psychiatric colleague. 'Looking for the mind of our murderer?' he teased.

Dillon was humming softly and said nothing. Humming was his own peculiar way of dealing with unpleasant situations.

From somewhere a framed photograph was stuck into Moss Kavanagh's large hands and he glanced at it quickly before handing it over. Clarke and Dunne studied the face smiling out from the frame, then turned and stared at the spot Joe Harrison was photographing.

'The description given out last night fits exactly,' Dunne said gloomily. He stopped to shout instructions at one of the white-suited forensics. 'And she's certainly got three silver studs in her left ear lobe.' Clarke looked at him. 'She's lying belly down,' explained Dunne, 'but the right side of her face is flat on the ground. I could see the left ear lobe. Three silver studs.' He pointed at the photograph. 'Just like you see in the picture.'

Clarke squinted closely and noted the tiny silver dimples on the ear of the smiling girl.

'Three silver studs,' muttered Dunne as he moved off, 'just like you see in the picture.' He paused briefly and turned back. 'And if it is her,' he added unhappily, 'there's going to be hell to pay.'

The sun now commanded clear blue skies without a cloud in sight. The warm May day had clothes sticking by the time the pathologist and his team completed their inspection of the murder scene. The body lay where it had been discovered, examined but not moved. Clumps of earth from beside and around had

34

been lifted. Tufts of grass were trowelled, twigs and branches snipped. Brown evidence bags built up at the end of the taped corridor. As plastic protectors were slipped and secured around the feet and hands and head of the body, in the wooden shelter a bloodstained syringe was slipped into a cardboard case. The beer cans and cider bottles and cigarette butts were teased into separate containers. Everything was recorded and detailed. There was an air of weary resignation as the fourteen men and three women went about their work. Another body found, another murder recorded. But secretly each knew this one was going to cause ripples. As if to reinforce their thoughts a helicopter whirred into view with a television crew hanging out the side. The chopper blades almost drowned out conversation, the only relief coming from the cooling effect of its downdraught.

Just after two that afternoon the body of a young female was gently lifted and carried across Sandymount Park to a waiting hearse where it was laid in the 'shelf' compartment. From the nearest-allowed vantage post, a battery of press cameras recorded the movements. Protected by squad cars front and back, the hearse slowly made its way through the afternoon traffic and the short journey across the River Liffey to the city morgue on Dublin's Store Street. A few of the older neighbourhood residents blessed themselves as they watched the cortège leave.

'I'd say she got stuck there.'

Noel Dunne, Jim Clarke and Patrick Dillon stood at the edge of one of the yellow incident tapes. Only Dillon seemed less troubled than the others by the violent images. A small number of the investigation team gathered to listen, their shadows casting irregular lines. All eyes were fixed on a ten-by-twenty foot patch of heavily trampled green with divots lifted where red blood had clung to green tufts. The park was tended only occasionally and the grass had grown long and straggly. Its flattened surface stood out like a map.

'There was a thick pool of blood at that first stake,' Dunne motioned his clipboard towards the yellow tip. 'Then a sort of trail,' he moved the clipboard in an arc, 'to there.' Another yellow tip marked the next stage of the murderous journey.

Patrick Dillon made notes in a pocket book, his large frame contrasting with the slightly hunched pathologist. He interrupted. 'I'd say something happened at that point, something different.' All eyes switched to him. 'The body seems to have been laid down for a while. The grass is flattened again and there's more bloodstaining.' He scribbled on a corner of a page and went on, 'You can almost see the trail where her feet were dragged.' Dunne and Clarke followed the pointing finger. 'Then she was dumped. Like a sack of coal.'

For a moment no one spoke, each to their own thoughts but all trying to imagine the scene.

'There are no footprints,' Dillon added pointedly. 'Someone's gone to a lot of trouble scuffing any footprints.'

A very deliberate sweep of the earth had fudged all traces where the murderer had stood and walked. Dillon went down on his hunkers, resting chin on upturned hand. His attention was concentrated on one small area close to where the body had lain. 'He must have dragged her head first, hands under armpits.'

'He?' Clarke cut in.

'I'd say it's a "he". It usually is, isn't it?' Dillon looked towards Dunne for confirmation.

'Aye,' agreed the pathologist wearily, 'in Dublin murder is almost always a male activity.'

Dillon stood up slowly and arched his back, then reached into a side pocket for a Dictaphone, fiddling with its buttons.

'Any idea what time she died?' Clarke asked.

Dunne scanned scribbled notes. 'I'd say around ten last night. Her rectal temperature's down to 26C. Her body's cold and stiff. Allowing for the warm night and the light clothes I'd go for ten, no later than eleven.'

Dunne began putting away his clipboard. 'I'll see you in the morgue.'

Clarke watched him trudge heavily between the incident tapes, a man worn out by repeated contact with violent death.

'I'll follow you in an hour,' he shouted at the hunched back. A hand went up in the air to acknowledge.

Patrick Dillon dictated his immediate observations into the pocket recorder, then flicked it off. 'I'll have a preliminary report as soon as I can.'

Moss Kavanagh's mobile phone went off in the middle of the first on-site conference and he moved away so as not to disturb. The phone had an unusual ringing tone, like a cartoon jingle. Clarke had nicknamed it 'looney-tunes'.

'Yes?'

'That you, Mossy?'

'It is. That you, Barry?' Barry Nolan was crime reporter for the *Post* group of newspapers.

'Aye, what's happening? Is it definitely the Marks girl?'

Kavanagh swivelled on one foot to make sure he wasn't being overheard. 'I can only confirm we're not looking for her any more.'

'What happened, Mossy? I heard she was found with a knife in her back, can I print that?'

'You could print that all right.'

'Anything else? Was she raped?'

Kavanagh noticed the group breaking up. 'Nothing yet. Ring me tonight and I might have something more.'

'Ah fuck, Mossy, how am I gonna make the last edition?'

'I'll give you an exclusive on the PM for the morning, okay?'

'Jaysus, I love you, Mossy, d'ye know that?'

'Bugger off,' advised Kavanagh. He pushed the OFF button.

4

Micko Kelly didn't know he had blood on his hands when he finally awoke to the high-pitched screech of the drug-addicted baby in the next flat. It was just before three that afternoon and he was still lying on his flea-infested mattress. He reached one hand out, eyes half closed, and searched until he felt a small plastic bottle. He shook and listened for the comforting rattle, flicked open the lid and slid out two Rohypnol tablets. Gathering as much spit as he could, he swallowed them in one go then reached out again until he felt a large plastic bottle. He shook it until he sensed the comforting roll of liquid inside. One-handed, he twisted the cap off and took a deep swig on the methadone, coughing as he felt it burn his throat. He pulled himself half upright and took another swig, rinsing his teeth and foul-tasting mouth before swallowing. He noticed the blood for the first time and splayed his fingers out to see how much. The staining even covered the tattoo on each knuckle. He slumped back onto the filthy pillow and pulled both edges over his ears to drown out the screeches.

'Fuck off,' he screamed, pounding the thin walls.

'I'll slit that child if ye don't shut the bastard up!'

The screeches only intensified. In a violent rage Kelly fumbled under the mattress until he grabbed the handle of a wide-bladed Bowie knife. He made for the door.

'I'll kill that wee bastard!'

The screeches were momentarily muffled.

Kelly slumped back onto the mattress, moaning. He was still holding the knife. He squinted at the dark staining on his hands and tried to remember how he'd got home. It wouldn't come. His mind was a blank. He struggled unsteadily to his feet, leaning against the wall as he stood up fully for the first time in over sixteen hours. He felt dizzy.

Kelly was six foot three and once weighed fourteen stone. That was in his early twenties. Now aged thirty-three he was down to eleven and still dropping. His hair was unwashed and lay in dank matted curls over both ears and along the top of his shoulders. He was unshaven and hadn't attempted a cut for days. He was still in the same clothes he'd been in for the previous four days, a stolen navy blue tracksuit bottom and stolen white Marks and Spencer T-shirt. His mind was fogged, his vision slightly blurred, his mouth dry and unpleasant. He was in a foul, vicious temper. He noticed bloodstains on the T-shirt and ran his hands up and down vigorously as if trying to shake the discoloration away. With one hand he pulled the T-shirt off, threw it angrily into a corner and staggered to the cracked and chipped hand basin in the corner of the room. Resting his right elbow against the wall in front he peered at the reflection in the dirty half mirror stuck above the basin with glue. *Fuck it.* The vision was not good, not even to Micko

Kelly who'd spent many years squinting at mirrors watching his face disintegrate. The hand-clutching-dagger tattoo over his left eye was sagging, reflecting his recent weight loss.

The screeching started again and he flicked on a stolen Black Sabbath CD on his stolen CD player and turned up the volume. Then he pissed into the plastic bucket beneath the sink and tried again to remember the night before. It still wouldn't come. He started washing the blood off his hands and glanced at the bloodstained T-shirt lying in the corner. For a minute he ran wet fingers across his face and jaw, testing he hadn't anything broken. Then he lit up a prepared silver foil containing heroin and inhaled deeply.

Outside in the corridor he heard loud angry voices and doors slamming and screams and curses and the baby started screeching again.

'I'll kill that fuckin' child, I fuckin' will,' he promised and turned up Black Sabbath. He slumped down on his backside, opened a Mars bar and began munching. His brain was fogging even further and he felt himself slipping as he drew on the last of the foil. He smiled a little, munched some more then began a fit of coughing. A hand reached out and pulled back the ring on a stolen can of Pepsi. He sipped on the opening.

Where am I gonna get some scag today? I'm right outa everythin'. Fuck it, I'll havta get out.

The bloodstained T-shirt caught his eye again.

In the outside corridor a seventeen-year-old drug-addicted mother wheeled her six-month-old baby down to the stairwell that led to street level. The baby had been born addicted to heroin courtesy of his mother's habit. They lived in an inner-city tenement called Hillcourt Mansions. This had the reputation as Dublin's toughest and most drug-infested hot spot. It was a three-storey flat-roofed 1950s design, twenty units on each level overlooking a central concrete courtyard, two stairwells to the ground at each end. Before heroin fully took over it was merely a petty-crime area, handbag snatching, mugging, drunken brawling. After the city's surge in hard drugs 'the mansions' had become a vicious, dangerous complex. Doctors refused to go into it and the police only in numbers and not for long. Hillcourt Mansions was hell on earth, an urban desolation of graffiti, used syringes and crack houses.

Kelly had a single room along a narrow corridor in one of the shared flats and spent most of his time lying on a filthy mattress on the floor, spaced out in a multi-drug-induced stupor. He had no other possessions apart from the stolen CD player and discs. In one corner rested a tin waste bin quarter-full of dirty syringes and small clingfilm sachets that once contained heroin. A selection of knives, flick and fixed-bladed, wide and slim, were usually hidden under the mattress. More often than not they were bloodstained. The room was a pit, a flea-infested, urine-stinking dump.

Micko Kelly couldn't care less.

5 *3.30 pm*

'I'm sorry to disturb you, Mr Nolan, but I have something important to tell the girls.'

Sister Concepta Downes stood at the front of classroom six of the Holy Rosary Convent in Blackrock. The school was four miles from Sandymount Park. Slightly behind her Detective Sergeant Tony Molloy watched and waited. Sister Concepta wore standard nun's uniform, navy veil across the middle of her hair allowing tufted grey fringe in front, long heavy grey skirt and white blouse, with grey cardigan. A wooden crucifix hung around her neck and she fingered it nervously. She was barely two inches above five feet and was dwarfed by the tall policeman.

'This is a policeman, a Sergeant Molloy. He would like a word as well.' Her words were directed at the French teacher, Gerry Nolan, but loud enough for the class to hear. Nolan was a good-looking man in his early thirties, dressed in slacks and linen jacket with dark blue shirt open at the neck. He moved away from the blackboard and leaned against a radiator.

'I'm afraid I have dreadful news,' the nun began, choosing her words carefully.

Molloy inspected the faces behind the desks. There were twenty-two girls, aged around seventeen to eighteen years, all with the healthy complexions of good breeding and careful diet. There were a few black and oriental faces, probably from the embassies he decided. The girls were dressed in school uniform, grey skirts, white blouses, navy ties. Beneath the desks he spotted regulation navy blue tights and black, sensible shoes. There wasn't a pair of trainers anywhere. The overwhelming impression was wealth and privilege, the sort of girls ferried to school in BMWs, Volvos and Mercs, not old bangers like the '90-registered Toyota Corolla Molloy's wife used for their three children.

'I'm afraid Jennifer Marks is no longer with us.' The words hung in the air and puzzled glances were exchanged around the classroom. 'She's dead.'

There was a sharp intake of breath and the expressions changed suddenly to shock and disbelief. Gerry Nolan muttered a quiet 'Jesus Christ'.

'I'm not going to say any more, I know this is a terrible shock for all of us,' continued the nun quickly, 'but Sergeant Molloy wants to know if any of you were with Jennifer, God rest her soul,' she crossed herself, 'yesterday after school.'

As one all heads turned to a dark-haired girl sitting two desks from the back and near the window.

'Also,' Sister Concepta added, 'I was wondering if Joan Armstrong,' now looking directly at the centre of attention, 'would come with me immediately? I know you and Jennifer were close friends.' She forced a reassuring smile towards the girl.

Joan Armstrong seemed to be struggling to put on a brave face.

'Yes, sister.'

Molloy noticed her hands shaking slightly as she stood up. Her face seemed drained of colour.

'Now, sergeant, is there anything else you'd like to add?'

'Thank you, sister.' The deep voice was a stark contrast to the nun's quieter tones. Molloy hitched at the belt on his trousers and allowed his gaze to glide slowly around the room. He frowned. 'I'm sorry to bring such dreadful news, but this is no ordinary event.' He stopped, wondering how to go on. He decided to call it straight. 'Sometime late last night Jennifer Marks was murdered.'

A girl in the front row turned white and began to slide in a faint. Gerry Nolan rushed and grabbed her head before it hit the floor. Sister Concepta was quickly at her side, loosening her tie, lying her in the prone position. The rest of the girls in the class appeared numb, senses reeling. The nun urged Molloy to continue while she cradled a tousled blonde head in one hand. Joan Armstrong sat back heavily in her chair, breathing deeply.

'If any of you,' Molloy said quickly, 'know anything of Jennifer Marks' whereabouts yesterday please tell your teacher,' he glanced over at Nolan who nodded vigorously, 'and he will take details. All will be followed up later.'

The girl who had fainted was slowly coming round, muttering loudly, wondering what had happened. There were a few nervous giggles. Molloy decided this was a good time to get out and opened the classroom door, holding it ajar. Sister Concepta followed. A very young and frightened-looking girl was in tow behind her.

'Let's go down to my office,' the nun suggested.

Molloy had left Sandymount Park for the convent just after three that afternoon. Jim Clarke started immediate house-to-house inquiries, hoping to catch as many as possible before memories dulled. Molloy drove the short journey to Blackrock, tuning in to the latest radio broadcasts, noting the story was already the main news item. One station had interrupted its chat-line to discuss developments and the airways quickly filled with listeners' dismay and disgust.

This is gonna make waves, he thought as he drove into the immaculately kept school grounds. This is gonna make big waves. He could feel his stomach tighten and began chewing an antacid.

'At what time exactly did you and Jennifer split up?'

The three, Molloy, Joan Armstrong and Sister Concepta, sat in the principal's office, a large, bright airy room full of religious books and school time-tables. The nun sat behind her desk, while Molloy placed himself beside the schoolgirl. Armstrong worried him immediately. She was tall, about five nine, he reckoned, and more mature-looking than her years. Despite the school uniform there was no disguising the gentle curves and slopes. Her jet-black hair was pulled back severely and held in a clasp at the back. He could imagine the tresses let down and hanging loose over shoulders in some tight outfit at the Saturday night discos. Her face held slight traces of acne camouflaged by cosmetic. She was pretty rather than beautiful, with full lips that would look provocative when reddened.

Before he had gone to the classroom, Sister

Concepta briefed him on what to expect. What she had to say was not for Joan Armstrong's ears.

'The two of them hung around a lot, they were great pals.'

He sensed immediately the nun wasn't much pleased by the friendship.

'They are . . .' she'd corrected herself immediately, 'rather, they *were*, very alike. Mature, precocious and a bit too showy for my liking. They even looked alike, almost sisters. Same hairstyles and clothes, same foul language. I may as well tell you I wasn't happy with most of their habits.'

'Like what?'

'Well, I know for a fact they smoked, it's strictly forbidden here,' she added in a disapproving voice, 'and they were in and out of pubs every weekend.'

Molloy couldn't stop himself interrupting. 'Ah God, sister, this is the nineties. Most young kids their age are in pubs at the weekends.'

Sister Concepta had cut across immediately. 'I know that, sergeant, I'm well aware of that. It's the type of pubs they frequented that worried me. And,' she added thoughtfully, nibbling on her lower lip, 'it worried their parents, too.'

Molloy encouraged her to continue.

'Joan's father is in banking. He's about sixty, a tall grey-haired man, always wears a pin-stripe suit. The perfect bank manager, conservative and subdued. Joan is his third child and I think she was a bit of a mistake, if you know what I mean.'

Molloy fixed a smile at this insight.

'The other two children,' the nun continued, 'are boys, late twenties, early thirties. Both in banking like their father.' Sister Concepta obviously approved of the boys. 'Joan is a pea from a totally different pod. She has tormented both parents since the day she was born. She's rebellious, difficult, disobedient and a born liar. Totally at odds with her father most of the time.'

'What's his name?' Molloy interrupted.

'Harold, Harold Armstrong.' The nun waited until this was added to Molloy's notebook. 'I know they were delighted when Joan teamed up with Jennifer. I mean everyone thought the Markses such a *respectable* family. Friends in the government and all that.' The sarcasm suggested the Marks family had not impressed Sister Concepta. 'I can tell you, sergeant,' voice low, strictly confidential, 'their delight quickly soured when they discovered the girls actually fed off one another. They became notorious.'

'How?'

'Well,' the nun disclosed, 'Joan's father found out she was drinking when she came home from a friend's party with speech slurred, clothes in a state of disarray. I believe she was banned from going out for a month but sneaked away the next weekend.'

Molloy suppressed a grin.

'But after certain information came my way,' Sister Concepta was triumphant, 'I took the issue into my own hands. I rang Harold Armstrong myself.'

Molloy looked up from his notebook. 'About what?'

'I wasn't completely sure but I felt I had to let him know my fears.'

'About what?' Molloy pressed.

'Joan was taking drugs. She might have thought she was experimenting, it was only harmless fun. But we have two past pupils addicted to heroin and that's how they started.'

Molloy held up a hand. 'What'd he say?'

Sister Concepta frowned. 'All he wanted to know was where the money was coming from.'

'Do you know?'

'No. I confronted her and she lied as usual.'

'Are you sure?'

The nun nodded. 'She blamed everything on Jennifer Marks. She claimed Jennifer's parents give her loads of pocket money.' At the other girl's name Sister Concepta crossed herself again.

'But you didn't believe her?'

'I never do, sergeant. I never do.'

'About five or maybe a little after five. We took the train from Blackrock and got off at Sydney Parade Avenue.'

'Was Jennifer in good spirits or did she seem down or preoccupied in any way?'

'No. She seemed normal, you know, like, just her normal self.' Joan Armstrong's voice lifted an octave and she glanced towards her headmistress. Sister Concepta had her head bowed, as if in prayer.

'Did you notice anyone following or did anyone strange talk to you on the train?'

Armstrong put on her thinking face. 'No, no. I mean, I wasn't really looking, you know, like, it was just a normal schoolday, you know. I mean, we weren't paying attention to anyone and, like, I don't remember anyone sort of looking at us.' Her voice was strained.

Sister Concepta reached across and took one of the young girl's hands in her own. She squeezed it reassuringly. 'I telephoned your mother, Joan, and she knows we were going to ask you to talk with

Sergeant Molloy. She particularly asked me to tell you to make *sure* you tried to remember everything.'

'But I am, sister, I am.' The protesting voice sounded less than convincing.

'Good girl, Joan,' the nun soothed, 'good girl.' She withdrew her hand.

'So the last you saw of Jennifer yesterday was sometime around five o'clock, after you got off the train at Sydney Parade Avenue?' Molloy decided not to be heavy-handed. He was interviewing the girl without her parents and didn't want to create a problem if he had to come back to her later.

'Yes. She went off towards Ailesbury Road, like the way she always goes, and I went down Park Avenue like usual. I mean, that's what always happens.' The nervous flicking of the head, the slight shake of the hands suggested otherwise.

'But she couldn't have gone to Ailesbury Road, could she?' pressed Molloy. 'She ended up in Sandy-mount Park. That's over a mile away in the opposite direction.'

Armstrong shrugged nervously. 'Yeah, it's really weird, like, you know. I mean, I don't know how she could have got there, like it's miles out of the way.'

'No idea, no idea at all?'

'No, none.'

'She's lying, sergeant. I can tell. I'm over thirty years in teaching and I know when someone's lying, believe me. That's Joan Armstrong's lying face.'

Twenty minutes of asking the same questions in as many different ways hadn't shaken the girl's version of events. Molloy let her return to classes. Sister Concepta's expression was hard as granite.

50

'Maybe she's worried about saying too much in front of you, sister?' Molloy offered.

The nun looked at him strangely. 'I hope that's all there is to it, sergeant. But I don't believe it is.'

The trail was picked up in the first hour. One of the forensics spotted a smear of blood on a spike of railings that surrounded Sandymount Park. It was near the edge where a red brick wall marked an outer perimeter. Scuff marks suggested feet scrambling to gain a foothold, the blood suggesting a bloodstained hand grabbing the spike for support.

'Yeah, he was a big bollox all right. About six foot, maybe a bit more.'

Star Sign Cabs was based on a first-floor office along one of the nearby roads. There was always somebody leaning out of one of the windows watching the world go by. Cigarette butts lay in small pockets on the pavement beneath the vantage point.

'He was lolling along the footpath heading towards town.' One of the cabbies, a small fat man with bald head and Coca-Cola-bottom glasses was feeling important as he recalled the man who had staggered past the offices around ten thirty the night before. 'Raggedy sort of a mangy dog look about him. He was in a whitish-coloured T-shirt and there was something on the front, you could see that as plain.'

Something?

'Yeah, like a big stain.'

Do you know what colour it was or where he'd come from or where he went?

'Nah.' Emphatic. 'Nah, I watched him as far as that Indian takeaway down there,' a finger poked in the general direction, 'then he disappeared behind a big truck parked along the side of the road.'

Around eleven o'clock a driver coming back to base had seen someone similar, 'Running about like a chicken with its head cut off. Christ, he was going around in circles, then shot off down the road. Big ugly-looking bastard, mean-looking. Totally spaced out if you ask me.'

He'd also been spotted by a bouncer in a pub along Pearse Street and a pizza delivery boy on a motorcycle remembered him vividly.

'He nearly ran straight inta me. Fuckin' wired to the moon, so he was. Shirt covered in blood.'

Blood, are you sure?

'Fuckin' sure. Either that or he missed his big mouth with the ketchup.' The delivery boy was so disgusted as he recalled the near accident he cleared his throat and spat a blob of phlegm onto the road. He was a small wiry youth with a thin face, reeking of cooking oil. 'And he had a tattoo on his head.'

On his head? You said he had long hair, how do you mean a tattoo on his head?

'On his forehead, ye dick.' A nicotine-stained finger went up to a spot above the delivery boy's left eyebrow. 'There.'

What was the tattoo like, did you get a good look at it?

'Are ye jokin' me? Get a good look at it!' The voice rose with incredulity. 'A big bastard covered in blood, wired to the moon and staggerin' about the place like a drunk and ye think I'm gonna start examinin' his face? On yer bike.'

But the scraps were helpful; taken along with all the other sightings and descriptions, a picture was forming.

5.00 pm

Dr Frank Clancy sat at his desk in the basement of the
Mercy Hospital, deep in thought. The basement was
the nerve centre of the hospital's laboratory and
pathology work. Each day specimens of human tissue
were brought there to be sliced, inspected and micro-
scopically examined. Samples of blood, urine, sputum
and faeces, along with swabs from outside and inside
the body were analysed and reported. Grasped firmly
in Clancy's right hand was a quarter A4 page with an
FBC (full blood count) result on patient Harold
Morell, ward three, four levels above.

As consultant haematologist to the Mercy Hospital
Clancy was in overall charge of interpreting and
advising on the many blood results churned out from
the wards every day. He was a young man, just turned
thirty-eight, with a shock of curly black hair. At six
foot three, his boyish face was easily spotted around
the wards. He had trained in Dublin, London and
Chicago before being appointed to the prestigious
consultant position three years previously. He
frowned as he scanned the results for the sixth time in
as many minutes, then turned to the PC in front of

him and began tapping on its keyboard, pulling himself closer to the edge of the desk. He typed in MORELL first, then HAROLD, followed by the same patient's date of birth and address. FILE NUMBER 276DE149 flashed on the screen. Clancy clicked on the OPTIONS button, then chose HAEMATOLOGY. Within seconds all of Harold Morell's blood results appeared in chronological order. Clancy began scrolling to find the very first recorded FBC, a basic analysis reflecting his blood level and a count of the many sub-divisions of cells necessary to fight infection, allergies et cetera. It looked normal, dated 23/04/90 when Morell had first attended the out-patient department of the Mercy Hospital. Clancy checked to see what clinic he had been booked under. CARDIAC flashed on the screen. Next he scrolled slowly along the many blood tests ordered on Harold Morell in the years since. It took almost thirty minutes. They all looked basically normal, a rise in his white cell count reflecting an infection during one in-patient stay the only blip in an otherwise stable haematology pattern.

Clancy sighed and leaned back in his chair. He turned again to the blood result now lying innocently on the desk beside the PC, pulled a pair of reading glasses from the breast pocket of his white coat and perched them on his nose. Harold Morell's blood picture had changed, suddenly and dramatically. Dangerously and recently.

Clancy stood up, stretched and yawned, and walked slowly to a bench on which rested a row of microscopes. He sat down in front of one, flicked the light source and a tiny, intensely bright beam trained on a blood-red smeared glass slide set in place under the lens. Clancy slipped off his glasses and squinted down the eyepiece. With one hand he moved the slide about underneath, with the other he focused. Each time he shifted the slide a different view of the blood cells appeared. No matter which way it was moved the underlying picture was the same. Harold Morell's blood was severely depleted in white cells, those vital to fight off even the most trivial infection. There was an almost total absence of neutrophil polymorphonuclear leucocytes. He removed the slide and replaced it with a different one, this a bone-marrow smear.

Earlier, in ward three above, Clancy had sat behind Harold Morell as the gravely ill patient lay on his side in his bed with the curtains drawn for privacy.

'You're going to feel a boring pain in your lower back now, Mr Morell,' he'd warned as he positioned his patient.

'Go ahead, doctor, do whatever you have to do.'

Morell had sounded weak and resigned. Gone was the strength of voice that had ordered men around building sites. He'd been a foreman and site inspector for years, a tall, burly man with hands like shovels.

Clancy had scrubbed to sterile standards, then donned surgical gloves and face mask and carefully swabbed Morell's lower back with antiseptic. He'd glided his trained fingers along the patient's back and upper pelvis, feeling for bony landmarks. Finally satisfied, he'd mentally marked the entry point and quickly injected local anaesthetic. The long point of the needle had dispersed the anaesthetic along most of the skin and immediate underneath tissue, down to bone. Next Clancy had slowly inserted the sharp-pointed, stainless-steel wide bore trochar until its tip met Harold Morell's pelvic bone.

'Okay now, Mr Morell, steady yourself.'

He'd sensed the older man stiffen in the bed. Slowly and delicately the trochar was turned until it bored through solid bone.

'Jesus Christ,' Morell had grunted through gritted teeth.

By the time he'd felt the pain it was all over. The trochar had passed right through bone and into marrow. Soft, treacly liquid had seeped out to be collected and analysed. It was this same marrow Clancy was now inspecting. There was virtually no evidence of the early forms of the white cells. Having few white cells in peripheral blood, that which could be drawn from a vein, was bad enough. But no sign of regeneration of white cells in marrow, the power house of blood formation, was even more ominous.

'Agranulocytosis, no doubt about it,' Clancy murmured to himself.

Agranulocytosis was the medical term for an almost total lack of white cells in peripheral blood and bone marrow. Some doctors preferred the alternative label, neutropaenia, for the same condition. Clancy always opted for the longer version. He thought it sounded grander.

He picked up a Dictaphone and began recording his findings. As he spoke he flicked the pages of Harold Morell's in-patient chart. Morell was a sixty-one-year-old male with a seven-year history of angina, a condition of narrowing of the inside bore of the arteries around his heart such that it became momentarily deprived of sufficient blood from time to time. When this happened Morell had experienced pain and a sensation of tightening in the chest. He'd been admitted to the Mercy Hospital for tests, then further investigations and finally a coronary angiogram. Here a special dye had been injected into Morell's heart arteries to highlight their calibre and detect any sign of narrowing.

Clancy looked at the entries in the chart, noting the procedures that had been performed by cardiologist Linda Speer. He studied her findings: *'Stress ECG showed ST depression in the inferolateral leads. While not diagnostic these changes suggest underlying ischaemia.'* Next came the coronary angiogram result: *'Immediately after injection of the right coronary artery the patient experienced acute cardiac pain with ST elevation. Treated in the usual way with atropine, nitrglycerine and sub-lingual nifedipine. The pain settled after about six minutes. Critical coronary artery disease found involving principally the mid portion of the left anterior descending artery and mid portion of the right coronary artery. There is 50% stenosis in the proximal portion of the circumflex artery. Left ventriculography confirmed normal left ventricular function.'* Then her final recommendation: *'I have discussed this patient with Mr Marks with a view to coronary artery bypass.'*

Morell had been sent home to await a suitable slot on the cardiac surgery operating programme but became suddenly unwell with unstable angina within a week and readmitted as an emergency. Clancy turned to the operation notes on Morell's chart.

Pre-operative diagnosis: *Unstable angina pectoris, recent anterior myocardial infarction within 12 hours, streptokinase therapy. All secondary to three vessel coronary artery disease.*

Operative procedure:	*Urgent CABG × 3 (LIMA to LAD, VG to RCA3, VG to OM1)*
Surgeon:	*Dan Marks*
Anaesthetist:	*W. Carter*
Assistants:	*N. Dowling and L. Speer*
Perfusionist:	*L. Moloney*
Complications:	*Re-sternotomy for bleeding*
Notes:	*Harold Morell was admitted with a small anterior infarction where he was given streptokinase with a good result. Operated on later the next day, some 16 hours after admission. Three grafts placed, he has excellent distal vessels. In the immediate post-operative period Mr Morell bled a lot and the operation site was re-explored. Nothing important discovered and the bleeding settled. It may have been due to the thrombolytic therapy. Postoperative recovery uneventful.*
Discharge Drugs:	*Adizem 120mgs daily: D/N Aspirin 300 mgs daily.*

A thought flickered as Clancy read. Linda Speer had assisted at the operation. That was unusual. Cardiac surgeons preferred fellow surgeons during operations, men and women with similar technical skills. Speer was certainly a world-class cardiologist, expert at examining and interpreting cardiographs, heart scans, angiograms and such like. Surgeon she most certainly was not. Clancy mulled this over, then dismissed his reservations as old-fashioned. He recognised more than anything else the notes reflected a straightforward and uncomplicated heart operation.

Harold Morell's pre-, intra- and post-operative treatments and management were excellent, of the highest international standards. Indeed he'd made such good progress he'd been discharged home after six days and scheduled for a follow-up angiogram three months later. Unfortunately he'd had to be readmitted as an emergency only four days previously when a simple throat infection had turned unaccountably life threatening. In the admitting ward, Morell had been been feverish, sweating and shivering violently. He'd been prostrate with the illness and almost succumbed but for the timely intervention of intravenous antibiotics. As he'd rallied the treating doctors had started to delve deeper into the illness and discovered his rare and unusual blood disorder. That's when Frank Clancy had been called in.

Clancy flicked to the drugs treatment page in the chart. His lips puckered as he read. Morell was only on a standard anti-anginal tablet, Adizem 120 milligrams once a day, and D/N Aspirin. Clancy knew D/N Aspirin was routinely used in post-operative heart patients, it 'thinned' their blood thus allowing it flow more easily through narrowed arteries. D/N was the manufacturing pharmaceutical company's shorthand for day/night, their product a slow-release aspirin that maintained therapeutic levels in the bloodstream twenty-four hours a day. D/N Aspirin, a USA product, was not in the Mercy Hospital drug formulary but still a recognised and acceptable pharmaceutical agent.

Clancy turned to the daily notes, searching for any other drug regime that might not have been entered into the pharmaceutical therapy pages. There was nothing. An unusual reaction to a treatment drug was the most likely explanation for Harold Morell's sudden and life-threatening blood picture. Yet, puzzled Clancy in the gloom, the medication he's on couldn't cause agranulocytosis. He sat back again, taking his glasses off and pinching the bridge of his nose. He looked aimlessly around the laboratory, as if somehow there might be an explanation for Morell's sudden blood change hiding behind the test tubes.

'Agranulocytosis,' he muttered to himself, 'that's the third case in as many months.' He spun the swivel chair round and around. 'What is going on?'

Clancy glanced at his watch and groaned. He was an hour behind time at least. He knew he'd be home late, his wife glaring at the clock, the dinner probably burned as usual.

Frank Clancy was married to a pretty brunette, Anne, six years his junior. They'd met at university where she'd been reading modern languages and he'd been swotting on pathology. They'd ended up studying each other and married within a year. Anne had followed him on the post-graduate training rounds of London and Chicago. She'd had their first child, Martin (aged eight), in England and the second, Laura (aged four), in Seattle. They'd gone there for a medical conference, only Anne went into early labour. Laura was born during the break between a lecture on leukaemia and a slide show on marrow transplants. The Clancy family had returned to Ireland when the

60

Mercy Hospital position had been offered. Anne Clancy was delighted with the thought of a stable unit at last. But work pressures caused early tensions. Frank Clancy was a workaholic. He roamed the hospital wards later than most colleagues, made himself constantly available for worried telephone calls from his team. Anne and the children came to resent the late-night discussions on spiking temperatures or mismatched blood transfusions. Clancy had recently made a solemn vow to scale back on his workload. As usual things weren't working out to plan.

He heaved a resigned sigh, then turned to the PC on the desk. Fingers itching, he typed in AGRANULOCYTOSIS, followed by SEARCH, followed by 01/01/97 THROUGH TO 13/05/98. He waited as the hard disk memory ticked over. Then, onto the clear blue screen two names flickered:

Mary Hyland.

James Murphy.

This was followed by their addresses, dates of birth, next of kin and first attendances at the Mercy Hospital. Clancy remembered both patients vividly, could even see their faces in his mind. Each had been transferred to his care as they re-presented to the hospital. Each had developed a sudden and unexplained agranulocytosis. Both had finally succumbed to recurring infections, living only weeks from onset of initial illness.

Clancy then typed in the question he most wanted answered, which clinic they had originally been booked under:

CARDIAC

CARDIAC

'I thought so,' he muttered.

7 *6.02 pm*

'Put her on the central table.' Noel Dunne, the state pathologist, was directing operations in his 'office', Dublin's city morgue.

Rush-hour traffic had built up outside and horns blared as tempers flashed in the late afternoon heat. The morgue itself was a relatively small building, sixty feet wide and two hundred feet long, tucked in behind the coroner's office on Store Street in the north inner city. There was a police station next door and Dublin's main river artery, the Liffey, flowed to the sea a quarter-mile further south. The building was over one hundred years old and reeked of history. Inside its white-tiled walls generations of the dead of Dublin had been brought to be inspected and dissected, their cause of death determined. The bludgeoned, the bombed, the burned, the drowned, the shot, the strangled and stabbed had been laid on one of the autopsy tables in the central room. Those bodies fished out of the Liffey or the sea or discovered after days in the open were laid in a back room, the 'stinker's room'. The door between these chambers creaked with winds that draughted under ill-fitting frames. The roof of the morgue was wire-strengthened opaque glass that allowed plenty of natural light.

Three white-marble dissecting tables were anchored to the floor in the middle of the main autopsy room, six feet from one another. The marble was lipped to prevent spillage and there was a short hose attachment at the top of each while a sink unit and swivel tap formed part of the bottom. There were overhanging fluorescents to light up the gloom when business continued well into the evening. In the old days an open fireplace had heated up the cold but this had been bricked over and wall-mounted electric units took the chill out of the air when needed. If the Dublin city morgue could speak, its voice would have had that rich gravely growl of a lifetime of Guinness, whiskey and cigarettes. But the walls were silent, the secrets of the dead safe.

The body of Jennifer Marks was laid face down on the central autopsy table, the handle of the knife still sticking out.

'Okay, Joe, get as many shots as you need of her back.' Dunne was walking slowly around the table, eyes darting behind beard and moustache as he took in the dreadful scene. Behind followed forensic photographer Joe Harrison.

FLASH! The first shot in the roll was an overview with knife handle sticking out like a landmark.

The autopsy room was crowded. Apart from Dunne and Harrison there were three white-suited forensics and a fingerprint expert. Resting against a bench two plain-clothes detectives attached to the case looked on impassively.

Surgically gloved hands began removing the

clothes from the young and stiff and cold body. First came her white Nike trainers.

'You can see grass stains on the heels of those trainers,' muttered Dunne.

FLASH! The trainers were caught.

Next came each navy blue ankle sock, gently teased off the stiff feet and placed on the nearby empty autopsy table. There, evidence bags waited to be filled.

'There's blood on those socks.' Dunne was scribbling on his autopsy chart.

The black panties were eased down and inspected for semen stains. The short black skirt came away next and it too was scrutinised for blood, semen and grass stains. Leaves, dirt, bits of gravel and cobwebs clung to the fabric. It was carefully laid separate from the others.

FLASH! The bare lower torso and legs were captured on film.

'Take a close-up of the blood smears on the side of her legs,' Dunne ordered and four flashes lit up the room.

A pair of razor-sharp scissors were produced and the black T-shirt stuck by blood to skin was cut, the line of incision well away from the entry wound. Carefully protected by two sets of overlapping surgical gloves, Dunne peeled the T-shirt in separate segments. FLASH! The room lit up again as Harrison's Nikon captured the sight of the naked back of a young woman lying on a cold white-marble autopsy table with a knife buried in her back to the hilt. For a moment no one spoke. Then the pathologist collected himself and walked around the table dictating immediate findings, directing further angles for Harrison's Nikon.

Jennifer Marks' body lay as it had been found, right cheek down, left side of face and lifeless eye looking sideways. Her long black hair lay in a tangled and blood-matted mess with bits of earth, leaves and cobwebs clinging. Her left ear with the three silver studs was clean. The hair was now carefully combed, traces of dirt and leaves and cobwebs placed in separate evidence containers, sealed and labelled. All finished it was time to turn her over.

'Okay, Joe,' Dunne ordered as he switched to a different A4 page and began scribbling, 'get a close-up of the handle. Four different views.'

As Harrison chose his angles, Jennifer Marks' wax-like fingertips were blackened and pressed to collect their prints. The handle of the knife sticking out from her back was of an unusual type, small and narrow with a hemp grip. It measured four inches from end to hilt.

'I doubt I'll get any prints off that,' muttered the fingerprint detective.

FLASH! FLASH! FLASH! Pause. FLASH! The hemp-covered handle was captured on film.

The knife was pulled from inside the body with a slurping sound. A trickle of dark blood oozed at the entry site.

'Nasty piece of work,' muttered Dunne. He held the dagger by the merest edge of its handle. The blade was narrow and slim, six inches long and double-edged, tapering to an unusually long final point. Blood clung the full length. FLASH! FLASH! Harrison caught the murder weapon before it was eased into a cylindrical cardboard evidence box, sealed and labelled.

Four sets of gloved hands lifted and turned the

body so that it now lay face up. The stiffening of rigor mortis made Jennifer Marks look like an athlete about to take off from starting blocks. One knee was slightly bent, the other held straight. Both arms were bent at the elbows. The signs of hypostatic lividity, the pooling of blood due to gravity after death, was fixed in the face and neck and abdomen. Just as Dunne began recording his external inspection of the front of the body, the tapping of Jim Clarke's crutch echoed off the marble floor. It was followed by the heavier steel-tipped steps of Moss Kavanagh. They moved to within a few feet of the autopsy table. For a few brief seconds Dunne and Clarke exchanged glances then the man with the steel-grey beard and moustache and equally steel-grey head of hair began recording his findings of death.

Clarke reached into a side pocket and fingered a pair of rosary beads. It was a ritual he had developed over the years since moving to the serious crime division. He was a religious man, a weekly Mass attender in an era when going to Mass was considered old-fashioned, still believing in his God despite bearing witness to inhumanity on a daily basis. He always prayed for the souls of the deceased he had to deal with, no matter how violent and cruel and criminal their lives might have been. He looked at the lifeless eyes of Jennifer Marks as they stared at the opaque glass above. Bits of dirt clung to the side of her face that had lain so long against ground. Clarke began silently reciting the Sorrowful Mysteries of the rosary. '*Hail Mary, full of grace . . .*'

'There's bruising around the throat,' Dunne interrupted his note-taking and pointed an elbow in the direction under inspection. '*. . . the Lord is with* *thee . . .*' 'There is indistinct marking on the side of her left neck.' Dunne directed the Nikon. FLASH! The marking was captured. Harrison changed lenses and zoomed closer. '. . . *blessed art thou amongst women . . .*' FLASH! FLASH! FLASH!

'There are defence injuries on the hands.' All eyes stared at the deep cuts, one so deep tendons had been exposed. '. . . *and blessed is the fruit of thy womb, Jesus . . .*' 'There are two stab wounds in the left chest,' Dunne placed a gloved hand on the body and felt for bony landmarks, 'one in the sixth intercostal space, mid-axillary line. The wound is V-shaped suggesting the knife was twisted.' '. . . *Holy Mary, mother of God, pray for us sinners . . .*'

The clipboard was laid down and Dunne studied the second wound closely. Clarke's silent prayers continued.

'There is another stab wound two inches below the left clavicle beside the left sternal edge.' He paused and changed glasses again. 'The second wound shows bruising at the edge.' He stood up, arched his back and groaned loudly. The onlookers grinned, glad of any diversion. Clarke continued to finger his beads, '. . . *now and forever, until our death . . .*' 'Well, he certainly didn't hold back,' Dunne announced to no one in particular. '. . . *Amen . . .*'

'She has three silver studs in her left ear lobe, a tattoo over the nipple of her right breast in the shape of a butterfly.' He squinted closer, 'Professional job, I'd say.' He lifted the left arm as much as the stiffness would allow and inspected. Then he laid it down, the limb sinking as if in treacle.

Dunne walked to a side press and started pulling at drawers until he returned with a thick-lensed magnifying glass. He bent slightly and peered at the inside of the same elbow and grunted. 'Needle tracks here.' He handed the lens to one of the white boiler-suited forensics, 'Have a look.'

The other man squinted, moving his head up and down until he had the best focus. 'Absolutely,' he agreed. 'No doubt about it.'

Clarke paused in the middle of a *Glory be to the Father* to inspect, surprised at the finding.

Dunne scribbled on his clipboard and drew an arrow to the mark. His eyes wandered further, 'There's a silver ring in the umbilicus,' then further again, 'an old appendix scar.' The eyes continued their inspection. *'Our Father who art in heaven . . .'*

A sudden 'looney-tunes' ringing on Kavanagh's mobile phone mercifully broke the oppressive atmosphere and everyone sighed with relief.

'Boss,' the big man mouthed. 'It's the parents. They're outside.'

It was Dunne who suggested meeting Dan and Annie Marks first. 'He's a fellow doctor, a colleague,' he explained as he slipped off surgical gloves and climbed out of his protective clothing. 'It's the least I can do.'

Clarke readily agreed. He'd had to do it so often in the past he was relieved to have someone else to break the news. Also he'd heard rumours of the wheelchair-bound wife being shielded from the public eye by her husband. He wanted to see why.

Dan Marks sat on a steel and wood chair beside a chipped formica desk in the small office that acted as waiting room. His wife, Annie, was slumped in a wheelchair beside him. Her face was pale and drawn, eyes red-rimmed and damp. Once dark hair, now flecked grey, was pulled back tightly, revealing flabby, sagging cheeks and wrinkled eyes. She looked much older than her thirty-nine years.

'Dr Marks, my name is Noel Dunne,' a comforting and condoling hand was stretched but not accepted. 'I'm the state pathologist.'

'Take me to my daughter,' interrupted Annie Marks. She ignored everyone, her gaze fixed firmly on the door between office and inner chamber.

'I'm afraid . . .' began Dunne, hoping to cushion the horrific vision awaiting inside.

'I am a doctor, too,' snapped Annie Marks, eyes still on the door. 'I know what death looks like. You have a body in there that is probably my one and only child. Spare me your well-meaning words.' The voice was hard and cold, clipped and definite.

Dunne looked towards Dan Marks. The other man just shook his head. He seemed crushed. He wheeled his wife through the door and across the marble floor towards the central autopsy table. The audience moved back, averting their eyes. The body lay face up, now covered from feet to neck with a thick green surgical drape.

'Lift me,' snapped Annie Marks and for a moment her husband started to plead then cut his own words short.

He slipped the brakes on the wheelchair and came behind, placing both hands under his wife's armpits. His tall athletic body took the strain with ease. One detective started forward to assist but a grasping hold from Dunne restrained. Unsteadily, Annie Marks was lifted to a standing position. She gripped the edge of the white mortuary table with both hands, swaying slightly. She gazed down at the lifeless face, eyes moving from side to side, as if committing the vision to memory. Her left hand brushed a wisp of blood-matted hair away from the dead girl's forehead, then she slumped back heavily and started to sob, her control gone.

'It's her, oh my God, it's her.'

'She was stabbed three times, twice in the front of the chest and then in the back.'

In the courtyard outside the morgue Moss Kavanagh was relaying the final post-mortem findings to Barry Nolan, chief crime reporter for the *Post* group of newspapers.

'The knife was left in her back, buried to the hilt.' Kavanagh paused, imagining Nolan scribbling furiously at the other end of the line. He walked in a brisk circle to stop his legs cramping.

'Any definite leads?'

'Nothing yet, no suspect.'

'Anything else?'

'I've enough to take the whole front page if you really knew,' said Kavanagh, looking around, anxious to make sure no one was listening. 'I'm only gonna tell you enough for an exclusive, not enough to hang me.'

'Fair enough,' Nolan agreed readily.

Kavanagh was only too aware of recent grumbles from prominent politicians about leaks to the media. 'She might have been into drugs. I can't say any more than that. She may have been messing with drugs and got hurt.'

'Was she raped?'

'Nothing obvious.'

'Anything more?' Nolan asked.

'That's as much as you're getting, Barry. There's plenty more, but it'll have to come later.'

'Ah Mossy . . .'

Kavanagh flicked off the mobile phone. He hadn't mentioned needle-tracks. Deliberately he hadn't mentioned Tony Molloy's discovery.

'Are those her clothes?'

Molloy had arrived as the autopsy was ending. He hated everything to do with the morgue, the sights, the smells, the sounds, the confrontations with death. He usually busied himself with routine work and had this worked out to a fine art, slipping in when he knew most of the cutting and sawing and weighing of organs was over. Even then he spent the time poking at forensic material.

'Are those her clothes?' he repeated, his usual worried features deepening.

Jennifer Marks' pants, skirt and bloodstained T-shirt lay on a spare autopsy table. With the tip of a biro he pushed at a grass-stained Nike trainer. 'Was she wearing these?'

Noel Dunne ignored the questions and continued scribbling on his clipboard. One of the white-suited forensics, a tall balding man with pock-marked face, moved closer.

'Yeah, that's all we brought back.'

Molloy wasn't happy. His nose was within an inch of the black skirt, scrutinising it, then he moved to the T-shirt, then to the trainers, then back to the skirt.

'She certainly wasn't wearing those at school.' He related his visit to the convent, what he'd learned, what he felt he hadn't learned and what he'd sensed. He pointed his biro at the collection of clothes and trainers. 'They're very strict about uniforms. There's no way she would have been allowed into classes in that gear.'

One of the detectives flicked through a notepad. 'She didn't go home after school. Maybe she changed somewhere?'

Clarke rested his crutch on a bench and leaned his back against it for comfort.

'Everything that was found is here. There is no other clothing,' he said.

Molloy poked at the skirt with his pen, turning it over, then inside out. 'What's this?'

The tone of the question stopped everyone. One by one they gathered. The inside hem of Jennifer Marks' short black skirt had been cut right round. Traces of blood, now brownish-rust in colour, clung to the rent stitching. In one area a sharp-edged stain was visible.

'Get me the knife,' ordered Clarke and the hemp-handled murder weapon was slid out of the evidence cylinder. With gloved hand Clarke placed its tip over the stain. It matched perfectly. No one spoke for a moment.

'What was he looking for?' Noel Dunne asked the question running through everyone's mind.

8 7.12 pm

'Have ye any scag? Come on, Jimmy, I'm dyin'. I need a hit.'

Micko Kelly was back on the streets. The ache in his limbs and belly grew by the minute, the craving even faster. He felt disorientated and unsteady yet his legs carried him towards the usual haunts. The streets were busy as shoppers and drinkers lingered in the warm evening sunshine.

'Waddye lookin' for, Micko?' A weasel-faced youth in dirty denims with cloth cap pulled firmly down on his head shuffled nervously up and down the pavement outside a pub in Dublin's Moore Street. He held a mobile phone under his jacket.

'Scag, Jimmy. I'm dyin', Jimmy, come on, don't fuck me about. Have ye any scag?' He flashed a knife handle tucked into his tracksuit waistband. 'I'll carve ye if ye fuck me about.'

Jimmy backed off. The handle looked blood-stained. 'How much have you got?'

Kelly pulled a wad of recently mugged twenty-pound notes from a side pocket. 'Gimme a hundred.'

Jimmy dialled, then walked away, mumbling into the phone. Within ten minutes a lean, tough-looking denim-clad thug with four silver rings in both ears strode straight up to Micko Kelly and stuffed a brown paper bag under his left arm. As fast as his shaking hands would allow, Kelly passed five twenty-pound notes over.

'Yer lookin' great, Micko,' lied Narko, the dealer. 'Need anythin' else?'

'Nah,' growled Kelly. He began his tortured journey back to Hillcourt Mansions.

'Waddit you give him?' asked weasel-faced Jimmy, head bobbing from side to side as he checked for police. His bloodshot eyes blinked repeatedly, unaccustomed to the brightness of the sunlight. Jimmy preferred the dark.

'Fuck all. A bit of scag and a ton of bakin' soda.'

Kelly had been sold the hitter's nightmare: white powder containing about three per cent heroin and the rest sodium bicarbonate.

'Did ye see the sight of him?' said Narko. 'He's on his way out. No point wastin' good scag on him, he's headin' to the moon big time.'

Jimmy whined. 'He'll fuckin' kill me when he finds out.'

Narko grinned and a mouth of rotten teeth showed. 'Don't worry, Jimmy, I look after me customers, don't I? Micko doesn't look like he's gonna be a big spender much longer. Time to find new markets, time to look for new clients.'

Weasel-faced Jimmy loved that sort of talk, it made him feel important, like a real businessman. He smiled. The smile didn't improve his looks. Then he remembered the knife and began worrying. The smile disappeared. 'I'm tellin' you, that's one mean bastard. He'll come after us when he finds out.'

Narko spat onto the footpath. 'Fuck him, let him try.'

Kelly barely made it back to his room, passing three other junkies along the corridors eyeing him up and down, wondering whether he was 'carrying'. They let him pass as he started to heave and vomit. Inside he flushed tap water into one of the syringes he'd pulled out of the waste bin, trying to clean dried blood away. The urgency of the fix took over and he pulled the brown paper bag from under his waistband and set up a hit. His hands shook violently. He sensed within minutes Jimmy and Narko had sold him shite.

'The fuckers, the fuckers. I'll kill the bastards.' But the pains were coming fast, his head was already covered in sweat so Micko pulled all the syringes out of the waste bin and set up as many fixes as he could. He knew there was some scag in the powder and knew he hadn't the strength to look for more.

One by one seven syringes full of a dirty-looking fluid disappeared into a vein, the only one that hadn't collapsed. He staggered over to the hand basin to splash water on to his face and glanced into the broken mirror. His dank hair was soaked, his face drawn, his eyes showed a tinge of yellow behind the bloodshot veins.

He felt awful. He looked a wreck. He cursed viciously and angrily, swearing he'd kill Jimmy and Narko when he had strength back. He even sat down and chose a wide-bladed knife, practising his lunges on the mattress. Stuffing began falling out.

*

'That looks like him, righ' enough.'

At police headquarters a photofit image was shaping up. The pizza delivery boy was being made to feel as important as he ever would in his life, sitting at a desk surrounded by seven of the investigating team while the many variations of a face were offered.

'Nah, not that, thinner,' or 'Yeah, that's good, maybe longer hair,' and 'Ah Christ, nah. Nah, not like that at all. Nah, it was more like above his left eyebrow, know worra mean?' A nicotine-stained finger shot up to the exact spot above his own eyebrow. The smell of cooking fat and the slow, deliberate way he was milking the occasion irritated. Behind his back a fist threatened to take his head off at the shoulders.

'Have yiz a fag?' A reluctant and begrudged Sweet Afton was offered and the full packet taken. 'I think we're gettin' there,' proclaimed the delivery boy as he lay back in his chair, blowing smoke rings into the air. 'I think we're gettin' there. Defin'ly.' He grinned at everyone. 'Defin'ly.'

Just after eight thirty the final image was faxed to the news desk of the national television station in Donnybrook on the southside of Dublin. Page two of the fax contained a detailed description. As the delivery boy made his way back on to the streets, fifty pounds richer for his efforts, the editor of the *Nine O'Clock News* set aside an extra three minutes for the murder report to include the photofit picture and description.

'Are you absolutely sure about this?' she double-checked with Jim Clarke over the phone.

He sensed her concern, acutely aware that on one previous occasion a photofit had been flashed onto the nation's screens accompanied by the wrong background briefing.

'This is a strong lead,' Clarke confirmed. 'The man was seen by eight different witnesses heading away from the scene of the crime. He was also seen in the company of the victim around the time we believe she was murdered.'

In fact two separate sightings had been reported by residents of a nearby apartment block. Each had heard voices, then shouts and curses, coming from the park late the previous evening. A man had now been sighted *inside* the park, *in* the company of Jennifer Marks *and* around the estimated time of death. This suspect's trail had been followed from Sandymount, through Ringsend, then along Pearse Street before disappearing down one of its many side alleys towards the River Liffey.

On his flea-infested bed in Hillcourt Mansions, Micko Kelly was gulping down methadone dregs and swallowing the last two Rohypnol tablets he could find. In desperation he topped up this multi-pharmacy with a number of unknown tablets stolen from another junkie he'd once discovered lying in a coma. By the time he lapsed into an hallucinatory stupor, still drawing on a joint, Kelly's blood was carrying heroin and its legal substitute methadone, as well as Rohypnol, Valium and cannabis. He had also rubbed traces of cocaine powder off old tin foil along his gums.

Micko Kelly knew how to enjoy himself.

'Police have confirmed the body found in Sandy-mount Park early this morning is that of missing schoolgirl Jennifer Marks.' The sombre-faced newsreader sat upright in his chair behind the wide *Nine O'Clock News* desk. 'The eighteen-year-old was apparently stabbed to death sometime around ten o'clock last night and police are anxious to contact a man seen in the vicinity at that time.' The photofit flashed onto the nation's screens. 'He is described as being between six foot and six foot two inches in height, of slim build, with long dark hair that covers his ears and shoulders. He is between thirty and thirty-two years old. His face is thin and he has a tattoo above his left eyebrow. When last seen he was wearing a white T-shirt, black tracksuit bottoms and dirty white trainers. The T-shirt may have been stained with blood. He was last seen running in the immediate north of the city along Pearse Street. If anyone knows this man or knows of his whereabouts, they should contact their nearest police station or the incident room at police headquarters so he can be eliminated from the inquiry.'

The news item continued, outlining Jennifer Marks' background, her father's medical career and Dream Team appointment. The piece ended with immediate comments from colleagues at the Mercy Hospital accompanied by publicity photographs of Dan Marks in operating theatre greens talking to grateful-looking patients. For many, Ireland's image as a low-crime environment was shattered that night for ever. Here was a top cardiac surgeon, encouraged to leave Boston and head up a heart foundation, now with his only offspring brutally murdered. Everyone wondered how the government would respond.

John Regan, minister for health reacted immediately. As the news bulletin ended he picked up the telephone in his office at government buildings and began dialling. His face was white with fury and he gripped the handpiece so fiercely he felt it might shatter. With his free hand he flicked the remote control, turning off the small TV tucked in one corner of the room.

'Did you see the news?'

At the other end of the line Paddy Dempsey, Minister for Justice, turned down the sound on his TV set. 'Yeah, that you, John?'

'This is a disaster for the government.'

'I know, I know.'

'We better move fast. I'll call a press conference, get all the main movers together. Could you be there?'

'Absolutely. I'll start ringing and get the usual crowd to turn up. We'll present a united and determined front.'

'Good man, Paddy. I'm going over to Dan Marks right now to let him know how shocked we all are. I'll assure him the full weight of the Justice Department will be brought to bear on this case. We'll crucify the bastard who killed this girl.'

'Keep your cool,' advised the Minister for Justice. 'Don't say anything rash.' Regan had a reputation for sudden and violent outbursts. He'd been cautioned before about shooting from the hip.

Regan hung up and immediately began dialling five of his closest media contacts. There was no point wasting a good photo opportunity.

9 *10.05 pm*

Moss Kavanagh drove Jim Clarke home to his house in the Dublin suburb of Crumlin after the *Nine O'Clock News* bulletin finished. Kavanagh was very upbeat about the sightings of the bloodstained suspect and Clarke tried to respond but the pain in his leg was too intense. He found it difficult to concentrate and ended up scrunching four analgesics inside thirty minutes. When he let himself inside the front door of his small red-bricked terrace house the smell of cooking greeted, making his stomach rumble. He felt hungry for the first time even though he hadn't eaten since breakfast. The many painkillers he'd had to swallow throughout the day often dulled his appetite and he was a stone in weight lighter since the bombing.

'You look drained, Jim' said his wife Maeve, a small brown-haired woman six years younger than her husband. She scanned his face anxiously.

'I feel it.' His edginess was obvious.

'Katy,' Maeve shouted over her shoulder as she tugged the uniform off his back. 'Your dad's home. Give me a hand.' The sixteen-year-old with long ash-blonde curls always eased her father's tension with a winning smile.

'Hi, dad,' she greeted with a peck on his cheek. 'How do you like my hair?' She was nearly as tall as her father and pirouetted in front of him, grabbing his uniform as it was thrown at her. 'Didn't cost much,' she added hastily, aware that expensive hairstyles were frowned upon. Her father had come from farming stock where a haircut was a pudding bowl over the head and rapid, jerky snips from a pair of badly sharpened scissors in their mother's hands. 'Nora Mallon did it as a nixer.'

'Katy,' her mother scolded, 'don't annoy your father with that nonsense.'

The light banter, the ritual of helping off with the uniform eased Clarke back into family life, enabling him to put aside the tragedies and horror of his work, and cope better with his damaged limb.

'I'll get the hairdryer.' Katy skipped up the stairs allowing her parents a few moments intimacy. They hugged briefly but tightly, their contact important, a couple who had nearly lost each other. They knew emotional pain deeper than most and grasped at any comforting physical contact, frightened it might never come again.

'Any news? Do you know who that fella is we saw on the TV you're all looking for?'

'Not yet.'

As she grilled with questions Maeve led her husband to an armchair in the front living room and eased him down. A TV with the volume on low rested awkwardly on a small table in the corner. Maeve helped him slip off his heavy navy trousers, baring bony knees, exposing his scarred and deformed leg. Olive oil had been warming for about an hour and lay in a baking bowl.

'Katy, did you find it? It's in the back bedroom.'

The young girl skipped down the stairs and bounced in, hairdryer held high. 'Got it first go. You might make it easier and leave it in the same place.'

Clarke grinned at her spunkiness and winked. Katy winked back and plugged the dryer in.

'How's the leg?' she asked, frowning as she noticed purple blotching along the scarring. 'God, it looks awful blue tonight, dad.'

Her mother shot a look that would kill. 'I'll get your father's dinner, you look after his leg.'

Katy nibbled her lower lip anxiously. 'Yes, mum.' She wondered where to start. She flicked the dryer on and played the warm breeze up and down, turning the heat up full as she watched a healthier pink colour slowly push away purple. 'Is it hurting?'

Clarke was squinting at the headlines on the evening paper. He hated looking at the leg, secretly wishing it had been amputated, resenting how it had taken over so much of his life, bitter its pain was twisting his personality.

'No, that feels much better.' He glanced at his watch. 'Just another two minutes then you can rub in the oil.'

A tray was set on his lap and a glass of white wine stuck in his hand. As he sipped and felt the warm glow, Clarke relaxed. He was hungry and felt quite pleased with himself. I'm still alive. You bastards are dead and I'm still alive. He laughed silently as he recognised the thoughts. I'm still alive.

As the ritual of heating and oiling his leg ended, the pain ceased. Clarke mixed gravy into his potatoes, cut up chicken, added a few carrots and peas and took a mouthful. He sipped on the wine and chewed contentedly. A blanket was thrown over his legs and

Katy sat at his feet, one arm resting on the good knee, while Maeve sat behind massaging the back of his neck. They watched a late news bulletin on Sky and discussed the report on Jennifer Marks' murder. Katy laughed with delight when a clip momentarily caught her father in a head-to-head with the forensic team.

'God, dad, you look very important.'

Clarke pinched the side of her arm making her yelp and there followed a good-humoured shouting match between all three. It was much the same every night, almost a ritual. Clarke and his wife dreaded the day when someone would come and take their daughter away. They hoped it would be a friend and in love, not an enemy and full of hate.

Later as he lay in bed with his leg propped under three pillows, Clarke cursed the men who had destroyed his life. His restlessness was such that he slept alone always, needing the extra space to thresh about. Pain usually kept him awake for hours, brooding, praying, plotting. He found it hard to switch off and often watched the early morning light filter through the bedroom curtains. He turned over and stared at the digital clock. Outside, in the distance, a burglar alarm beeped intermittently.

'Run, Jimmie, run. Come on, ye boy ye, run.' Recently his disturbed dreams carried him back to the family farm in north-west Ireland. He was the middle of five boys, but the one with the strongest and fastest legs. 'Come on, Jimmie, come on! You're well in front, come on!' He'd won so many races, cross country, sprints, middle and long distance. He'd even learned the skills of hop, skip and jump and in one memorable year represented his school in seven separate events.

'There's no doubt about it,' his mother had laughed when he came home with a clutch of medals. 'You're the fastest thing in the parish.' They nicknamed him Roadrunner.

He was fourteen years old the day his father walked him proudly along the wet country roads from the bus stop in the village to their farmhouse. One hand rested on his son's shoulder, the other held a gold medal, a trophy won at a national event against stiff competition. In his dreams he relived that home-coming, the delighted shouts in the kitchen, his mother's excited tears. Then a dart of pain would waken, bringing cursed reality. He always tried to go back to sleep immediately, wanting to jump into that warm, deep pool of his youth, recapture happier days, feel the strength in his legs. But the ache denied escape and he would massage the scarred flesh for comfort. He cursed the murdering bastards who had plotted his death. In blacker moments he cursed the doctors for saving his life. At the Mercy Hospital he'd turned his face to the wall and willed an eternal sleep. It was only Katy's sobbing and anguished voice that brought back the fight in him.

'You've got a child to rear,' Maeve begged one morning. 'We've got our girl to look after. Quit this self-pity, stop wishing you were dead. Fight back. *Get the bastards.*'

He'd never heard such anger in her voice.

Getting the bastards became his motivating force and he left hospital sooner than the doctors advised. But revenge was foiled by other thugs, his attackers taken out elsewhere and Clarke had to channel his energies into work. He quickly gained a reputation as a man driven. He followed all leads, looked up every dark alley, peered into the depths of every criminal activity. He wanted results.

As he lay on his bed, restless for comfort, the image of Jennifer Marks' body lying on the cold white-marble slab flashed in his mind. She was only a slip of a girl, he thought, barely eighteen. It won't be long before Katy's that old. God, what'll *she* be up to then? Nothing, he consoled himself. Nothing much anyway, her mother has her well reared. She's a good girl. Maeve is a good woman, a good wife and a good mother. Katy is a credit to her. He remembered Noel Dunne bending over, inspecting the stiff left arm, 'Needle tracks here.' What if she *was* injecting herself? She was still only on the threshold of life. She hadn't done anything to deserve such a dreadful death.

Some bastard had snuffed a young life. He'd have to be caught. He'd have to pay.

From that moment Jim Clarke took Jennifer Marks' murder personally.

He reached over and pulled the mobile phone beside him, his only bedfellow most nights. He dialled and waited.

'Hello?'

'This is Superintendent Clarke.'

'Yes, sir.'

'Who's that?'

'Officer Grimes.'

'Are you at Sandymount Park?'

'I'm in a patrol car alongside it this minute.'

'Anything happening?'

'No, sir, the area's still screened off. There's been no one up or down the road all night.'

'You sure?'

'Certain.' Clarke knew by the sharpness of the answer Grimes wasn't sure.

'Check again. Get details of anyone who goes near that area.'

'Right, sir.'

'Do it now, right away.'

'Yes, sir.'

Clarke pressed the OFF button and waited. He watched five minutes tick away on the clock, then redialled. Grimes answered again.

'Did you see anything?'

'No.' The voice echoed surprise.

'Get out and look again.'

'Right away, sir.'

Clarke lay back on his bed and willed sleep forward. He lifted both arms up in front, clasped hands and then slowly let them drop at a ninety-degree angle from his body. It was one of his relaxation exercises. As they settled on the bed the tips of his right fingers brushed against the aluminium crutch where it rested against the bedside table. Without looking, he locked fingers around the frame and lifted it so that the hand grip was just above his face. He squinted in the gloom until he could see tips of tiny bolts at the edge where grip abutted main frame. He held the frame firm in his left hand and then slipped his right hand along the hand grip until the tips of two fingers felt the bolts. He pressed and turned at the same time. The hand grip moved slightly. The fingertips left the bolts and the hand now fastened around the grip firmly. He turned it one hundred and eighty degrees and pulled back. The grip separated from the main frame. Fingertips moved to two separate bolts on the side and pressed. With a sudden 'shush' a four-inch, double-edged, sharp-pointed blade shot out. He admired the steel, turning it around, catching light from the street, watching it glint and dance. Satisfied the spring mechanism was working he reversed the manoeuvre and the blade disappeared back inside the hand grip. It was then reattached to the aluminium main frame, turned until it snapped firmly into place and the crutch returned to the bedside locker.

He peered at it before closing his eyes. It looked like a crutch, nothing more, nothing less. In the gloom he smiled. For a man who'd been caught once and nearly killed, Clarke was taking no chances on a second encounter. He knew his reliance on the crutch put him at a disadvantage in any violent confrontation. He'd had it specially modified and the blade inserted on a tight, strong steel spring mechanism. 'My little surprise,' he'd grinned when the final result was handed over. 'My own cold steel.'

On the road alongside Sandymount Park, Officer Grimes longed for the comfort of his squad car. He was tall and thin and his uniform hung loosely, barely keeping him warm. He cursed silently as he peered across the railings at the darkness inside, noticing the crime scene incident tapes fluttering gently in the late breeze. The air was now cool and lights from a nearby block of flats threw an orange glow along one side. He walked slowly up and down, yawning and stretching, squinting at his watch, wishing his shift was over. He stopped and leaned against the railings, allowing his weary eyes to peer into the darkness. For the briefest of seconds he thought he saw a shadowy figure move among the undergrowth.

He dismissed it as a trick of the lights.

10 9.30 am, Wednesday, 13 May.

'Okay, settle down. Let's get started.'

It was the first briefing of the day. Jim Clarke looked tired and drawn and tried to drag his straggling hair into shape as he waited for silence. He was in full uniform, trousers freshly pressed by Katy before she'd left for school, jacket carefully brushed by Maeve. Moss Kavanagh stood to his right, big hands resting against the back of a chair, mobile phone in the OFF mode. He had discarded his jacket and was in a short-sleeved shirt.

'Some information's come in over night and it looks like we have a strong lead.'

A murmur of satisfaction rippled. The investigating team of twenty detectives was squeezed into a small room, some gathered around a table, others with backs resting against the walls. It was uncomfortably warm. Behind Clarke sat Tony Molloy, on his lap three thick, bound books. Behind yet again and slightly to the left sat the Minister for Health, John Regan. Beside him was the Minister for Justice, Paddy Dempsey. Regan's Hugo Boss suit made Dempsey's tweeds look like a bad buy from a car boot sale. Their features contrasted just as starkly, Regan handsome and confident while Dempsey had thick lips, broad nose and coarse skin. Police Commissioner Donal Murphy looked on from the side. A one-time army commandant, he was a tall man with tight grey crew cut and dressed in full navy blue uniform with gold-braided epaulettes.

'I'm going ahead without Dr Dunne,' announced Clarke.

Puzzled looks were exchanged. Noel Dunne, the state forensic pathologist, rarely sat in on murder conferences. However the presence of the politicians and commissioner suggested this was no ordinary investigation. A flipboard was stuck in a corner with *Jennifer Marks* scrawled in thick black felt-tip on top of the first page. Underneath crime-scene photographs were pinned. A map of the area scored with red marker highlighted Sandymount Park, undergrowth and body position. A portrait photo was stuck with blue tack to the bottom right-hand corner.

'Jennifer Marks went missing the night before last,' began Clarke. 'When she didn't turn up by seven thirty her mother rang for help.' He paused, very much aware the main movers in the subsequent train of events were in the room. 'The duty officer suggested two hours late for an eighteen-year-old wasn't that unusual,' he went on, 'and advised she give it a bit longer.' Murmurs of agreement rippled. 'Mrs Marks wasn't happy and rang her husband. He rang his own contacts and a search was ordered around ten o'clock.'

'Can I come in on this?' John Regan stood up suddenly. 'I'd like it put on record that Dan Marks rang me,' he snapped, 'and I immediately rang the

Minister for Justice. Thanks to him a search party was mobilised. Just as well too, in light of what was discovered.' He sat down sharply, his expression reflecting his anger. The designer clothes and bright tie belied his black mood.

A door at the back opened and in bustled the burly figure of the state pathologist, Noel Dunne. He had given in to the unseasonable warm weather and was dressed in a light linen jacket over navy slacks. He acknowledged the audience, then squeezed beside those clustered around the bottom of the table. He held a brown manila folder in his right hand.

Clarke used the interruption to press ahead, ignoring Regan's outburst. 'We've had a number of sightings of the man described on page eleven.' Heads turned towards neighbours with knowing glances. 'You can see his photofit.' All eyes switched to the charcoal and pencil image. 'One name keeps cropping up in this,' said Clarke, settling a collection of faxes on the table. The room fell silent. The government ministers strained forward to hear better. 'A convicted killer and drug addict called Michael Leo Kelly, better known as Micko Kelly.'

Kelly's most recent mug-shot was now stuck beside the photofit. The likeness was uncannily accurate. Apart from leaner looks the photo matched the photofit.

'Let's get the bastard!'

The sudden interjection from John Regan took everybody by surprise. He was on his feet again, face white, fists clenched, shaking agitatedly. 'You know who this is, go get him.' Dempsey tugged at his jacket, urging him down. Regan pulled away. 'What's holding you back? You all seem to know everything about this bastard, why don't you get off your arses and go after him?' The fury in his voice, the unaccustomed profanities surprised and an embarrassed silence descended.

'With respect, Mr Regan,' Commissioner Murphy interrupted quietly, 'your remit does not extend to running the affairs of my department.'

Paddy Dempsey buried his head in his hands and stared at the floor. Regan rounded angrily and only his colleague's timely intervention saved another outburst. He was dragged down in his seat, seething.

'Kelly squats in Hillcourt Mansions,' Clarke went on, unruffled, 'and that's a hell hole. It's full of drug addicts, dealers and pushers. At the first sign of a squad car there'll be a riot.'

Noel Dunne listened, an amused smile on his face. Clarke sensed he had enjoyed seeing Regan put in his place.

'Also we don't know which flat he might be squatting in. We can't knock down every door in the place.' He half turned towards Regan, 'These crack-heads are often armed and wouldn't think twice of going at us with dirty syringes, knives, broken bottles or even guns. I'm not prepared to risk that confrontation. The papers would have a field day.'

The noise of chairs scraping interrupted and without as much as a nod or word, John Regan slipped out of the room.

Clarke ignored the distraction. 'Dr Dunne, would you fill us in on the post-mortem findings?' He sat down.

'Certainly.' Dunne flipped open the folder resting on the desk in front.

'Okay, let's start with fact,' he began, twirling his

moustache as he scanned the pages, 'and get on to conjecture at the end.' He slipped three pages back into the folder and shuffled the rest into order. 'The girl had taken alcohol, I won't know how much until toxicology gets back, but when I opened the body bag in the morgue there was a strong smell of alcohol. She had needle tracks suggesting intravenous drug abuse. That'll come back with toxicology.' His voice was monotone, as if reciting a traffic report. He paused for a moment while he squinted at a note on the page margin. He loosened his tie and opened the top two shirt buttons, flapping the opening to cool. 'I'd say the first wound came from the left side with some force, the track of the blade penetrating her left lung and bronchus. The main airways contained frothy blood-stained mucus.' A few grimaced as they listened. 'The second stab wound was fatal as it almost transected her aorta.'

Dunne explained. 'From the moment that blood vessel was sliced the girl more or less exsanguinated. Her blood pressure would have plummeted, the blood supply to her brain would have ceased and she would have been brain dead within minutes.' The conference room fell silent. All thoughts were on the photograph of the smiling young dark-haired girl staring at the camera and the dreadful way her life had ended. 'She must have fallen to the ground at that point,' continued Dunne in the same monotone, 'as there was considerable blood at the scene. Then she was dragged, face up, heels along the grass, to the undergrowth. There are bloody hand-prints under both arms.'

Dunne laid down the page he had been reading and flicked through four more, squinting until he came to the next notes of importance. He fiddled inside his jacket pocket until he found a pair of half-moon glasses and perched them on the end of his nose. He suddenly noticed they were smeared and wiped the lenses on the end of his tie.

'She must have been laid on her back,' he continued, this time without squinting, 'as there was dirt, cobwebs and a squashed insect clinging to the back of her clothes.'

'Dr Dunne,' Clarke cut in, 'the girl must have been dying by then.'

'Not dying, superintendent,' Dunne said very deliberately. 'Dead.'

'So those defence wounds you mention in your report must have happened earlier?'

'I'd say just before the first stab wound,' Dunne volunteered, glasses on his nose as he flicked back over pages. 'There was bruising around the throat and scratch marks suggesting her assailant gripped her by the throat.' Here he reached across and placed his left hand around the neck of the detective sitting on his right. The younger man smiled weakly and massaged at the skin when the grip slackened.

'She was tearing desperately at that throttling hand and trying to ward off the swinging knife at the same time. The blade caught her grip, cutting deeply.' Dunne's right hand went up in the air and came across sideways in an arc. 'The first wound penetrated lung, followed afterwards by that fatal upper chest wound.'

'But why did he stick the knife in her back?' Molloy wondered out loud. 'She was dead by then.' Dunne half smiled and began stuffing his glasses back into the inside pocket of his jacket. 'That one's for you, sergeant. I'm only here to tell you what he did, not why.'

The two men exchanged wry grins, the first time Molloy's face had lost its worried look.

Clarke interrupted again, reading from the report. 'What's the bit about the IUCD?'

Dunne leaned back in his chair and explained. 'An IUCD is a contraceptive device placed inside the womb.'

Anxious not to miss anything Clarke pressed harder. 'Any other significance?' Catching up with Dunne after he'd presented a report was notoriously difficult.

'Well, it suggests the girl was sexually active,' said Dunne. 'These devices aren't usually put inside the womb in someone so young.'

Clarke made a few notes as he listened then smiled across the table to confirm he had finished.

Commissioner Murphy coughed for attention. 'Let's take a break,' he suggested.

11 10.15 am

'Could I have a word with you?' Dr Frank Clancy stood in the doorway of heart specialist Linda Speer's office in her specially furnished top-floor suite.

Among the many petty jealousies and professional rivalries that dogged the Mercy Hospital nothing matched the anger and resentment stirred by the money and attention lavished on the 'Dream Team'. Within one month of the announcement of their appointments the top floor of the hospital had been cleared and renamed: 'HEART FOUNDATION'. New equipment for such procedures as angiograms, echo-cardiography, radio-isotope scanning et cetera had been installed, even though most being replaced were still good. A new, specialised laboratory was created immediately outside the intensive care unit for post-operative patients. On the same corridor a state-of-the-art coronary care unit was constructed with every diagnostic and resuscitative facility necessary. 'The proximity of the laboratory to these two nerve centres of cardiology,' Minister for Health Regan had announced to a glowering hospital audience on opening day, 'will allow Dr Stone Colman to analyse within minutes the biochemical and cellular changes occurring in an acute myocardial infarction.' Standing slightly behind Regan, the Boston trio listened attentively. Dan Marks' Florida tan had faded in the sunless Irish winter yet he still looked his casual and supremely confident self. Beside, and whispering occasionally to him, Linda Speer wore a linen blouse and beige slacks under grey checked jacket. Biochemist Stone Colman leaned against a wall listening and grinning. He'd kept his ginger crew cut and fondness for crumpled suits, but seemed more at ease than at his first public appearance. 'It will also,' continued Regan, purring with delight, 'permit monitoring of similar changes in the post-operative period of patients undergoing heart surgery.' His beaming expression was in stark contrast to the discontented audience, many of whom were being asked to scale back their budgets. The liver transplant team, the paediatric asthma research team, the geneticists, all knew only too well how much money was being lavished on Regan's cardiac unit. The three Boston specialists had become loathed throughout the hospital. Not that they seemed to care, neither mingling nor socialising with their colleagues. Apart from government sponsored cocktail parties they kept to themselves, engrossed in their work and vital results they knew they would have to produce to justify the massive budget following their wake. If they had private lives they were well-guarded secrets. No one ever spotted them out on the town.

Linda Speer did not shift her head one inch from her work when Frank Clancy spoke. 'I'm sorry, I can't. I'm busy.' She sounded irked by the disturbance.

Clancy glanced around the office, admiring the rosewood furniture, subdued lighting, green leather sofa and small drinks trolley tucked discreetly in one corner.

'I'd like to talk with you now, if you don't mind,' he pressed.

Speer gave him a jaundiced look, making Clancy feel even more uncomfortable. He sensed how poor his dress code was compared to the Gucci wonder in front.

'Who are you?' she snapped, eyes back on the paperwork.

'My name's Frank Clancy. I'm the haematologist here.'

'So?'

'I'd like to talk to you about a problem I have.'

'I hope it's a medical problem,' grunted Speer, still not looking up, 'otherwise I'd suggest you check if the social workers are still in the house.'

Clancy ignored the cheap jibe. 'No, in fact, it's about one of your patients.'

Speer stopped writing and turned around. 'And what,' she said slowly, her accent more exaggerated than usual, 'would you be doing with one of my patients?' One eyebrow cocked up. The tone of the question almost suggested sexual impropriety and Clancy had to clear his throat to hide his discomfort. He noticed a smile curl at the edge of Speer's lips.

'It's about a sixty-one-year-old man called Harold Morell,' explained Clancy, reading from the patient's chart which he'd been holding all the time. 'Perhaps you remember him?'

Speer shook her head dismissively. 'No I don't, get on with it.'

Clancy looked at her in surprise, then continued. 'Well, Mr Morell had a triple bypass operation up here about four weeks ago. Everything went very well, and . . .'

'They usually do,' Speer cut across sharply. 'When our first six months' results are published next week you'll know just how well our work is going.'

Clancy tugged at the glasses in the breast pocket of his white coat nervously. He'd read in the national press that a cheque for twenty million pounds, EEC money, would be handed over to John Regan at a government press conference on Wednesday, 20 May. He'd planned to be out that evening. He knew he wouldn't stomach all the crowing.

'Yes, I'm sure we will. However there's one problem bothering me.'

'And you want me to help?' Speer's attention was drifting, Clancy sensed that. Her eyes had started to wander.

'Well, there's something I thought you might be able to shed some light on, certainly.' Clancy moved closer and set Harold Morell's chart down on the desk, quickly turning the pages. A whiff of expensive perfume reached his nostrils.

'Is this a cardiac problem?'

'No.'

'Anything to do with cardiology?' Speer's stare was now boring into him.

'No.'

'Well, what the hell are you doing here?' she snapped, the cultured accent now turned hard. 'I've a mountain of work to do.' She waved a gold-bangled arm across a pile of charts.

'Well, you see,' Clancy tried again, 'the patient

started out in this department and . . .'

'Where is he now?' Speer snarled in exasperation. 'Don't tell me he's down in the dermatology wards. I know nothing about skin diseases.'

Clancy lifted the chart onto the paper she was working at. 'No,' he said quietly, 'he's in my department, in haematology. He's seriously ill. He's got agranulocytosis.'

Speer squinted at the chart for no more than a minute. 'He's deficient in white cells, right?' she asked.

'Yes. In his case deficient in both peripheral blood and bone marrow.'

'That's a haematology problem, though, isn't it, Dr Clancy?' Speer was beginning her dismissal mode.

'Yes.'

'And you're the haematologist, right?'

'Yes.'

'Well,' she closed over the folder and handed it back to Clancy, 'shouldn't you be back with *your* patient?'

Clancy refused the implied dismissal. 'I need to know why Morell has developed this,' he said calmly, eyes fixed on Speer. 'And I need to know why there have been three such rare blood disorders in this hospital in as many months.'

'You're the haematologist, Dr Clancy, with the greatest respect that *is* your job.'

'Indeed it is, Dr Speer, no one knows that more than me.' Clancy decided to treat Speer with the same contempt he was getting. 'But what's puzzling about these cases is they were all in this cardiac unit for one procedure or another about four weeks before their blood disorders set in. I was just wondering about any link? That's what a haematologist is supposed to do. Look for causes as well as treat.'

Speer lifted Harold Morell's chart as if it was a piece of dog dirt and flicked through until she reached the pages dealing with in-patient stay and cardiac procedures. She dropped it and returned to her paperwork.

'His cardiac procedures were standard. Routine stress ECG, followed by angiogram, followed by triple bypass surgery. His post-operative phase was completely uneventful.' She picked up another chart and began turning its dog-eared pages. 'What happens to these patients after they leave here is none of my business.'

For a moment Clancy was stunned. The dismissive manner in which Speer was treating his query was bad enough, but her total indifference to the patient's final outcome shocked.

'I find that attitude quite extraordinary,' he said, barely able to control himself. He'd heard about her legendary coolness, her attitude towards patients, looking on them as merely interesting pieces of pathology which she could work on and turn around. 'But,' he continued bitterly, 'to think you can dump your patients out of this department,' he pointed towards the outside offices, hands shaking with rage, 'and then not want to follow them up is quite extraordinary.'

Speer continued at her paperwork. 'Think what you want. That's your problem, not mine.'

Clancy was not to be outdone. 'Well, it's more than just my problem, Dr Speer, a great deal more.'

Speer turned around slowly.

'The other two patients, a Mary Hyland and a

James Murphy,' Clancy was reading from a slip of paper he'd pulled from a side pocket, 'both developed a sudden and dramatic and fatal agranulocytosis within six weeks of being discharged from this great cardiac unit.' He couldn't keep the anger out of his voice. 'I'm wondering this: what therapy were they on? What drugs, cardiac or otherwise, were prescribed that could have shocked their peripheral blood and bone marrow so violently?'

Linda Speer listened without blinking. 'Apart from drug therapies, what else can cause agranulocytosis?' she asked.

'Radiation or cytotoxic or antimetabolite therapy,' Clancy rattled off quickly, 'severe infections or sometimes associated blood disorders such as leukaemia.'

'Did you ...' Speer began but Clancy cut in immediately.

'None of those conditions apply.'

Speer dangled a shoe off the tip of her right foot, brow furrowed as if deep in thought. 'Isn't there an idiopathic form, where we don't ever find a cause?' The question was offered more by way of helpful explanation.

'Yes, indeed there is,' agreed Clancy, 'but three cases of idiopathic agranulocytosis in the past few months is stretching coincidence too much, wouldn't you say?'

'Well,' sighed Speer as she stood up and stretched, the gesture implying the discussion was over as far as she was concerned, 'you're the haematologist, Dr Clancy. This is your department.'

Clancy walked to the door and leaned against it. Speer glared at him angrily. 'You're not going to try and hold me here until I solve *your* problem, are you?'

Clancy ignored the taunt. 'Were there any other drugs prescribed for these patients? Drugs maybe not entered into their notes?'

Speer slowly sat down, her eyes now as cold as ice. 'What exactly are you getting at?' The Boston accent was clipped and hostile.

Clancy flicked through Harold Morell's chart until he came to the drugs treatment page. 'I see you use D/N Aspirin rather than the usual hospital formulary product?' He stopped and waited. No answer or explanation was offered. Linda Speer stared at him with a mixture of contempt and rage. 'I'm not that familiar with D/N Aspirin,' Clancy persisted, 'and was just wondering why you use it when we have equally good products in the hospital pharmacy here?' He raised his eyebrows quizzically.

'Because,' hissed Speer, her face twisted with irritation, 'that is what we used successfully in Boston. That's the aspirin we found gave the best sustained therapeutic levels compared to its rivals. That's the aspirin we've been using for the past five years and, as you must know yourself, doctors tend to stick to the products they know best.'

'But,' pressed Clancy, unpreturbed, 'D/N Aspirin isn't available in Ireland. I checked myself.'

'We brought our own stock supplies with us,' Speer screamed, the cool façade finally shattered. 'God-damn it we brought a few boxes of the stuff with us. Jesus Christ, Clancy, get off my fucking back and go and do some work or I'll have security throw you out of here!' She stood up, and pulled the door open violently. A gold-bangled arm waved to the corridor. 'OUT!' she ordered.

Clancy gathered Harold Morell's notes up slowly, then paused, face furrowed. 'How exactly do you spell your second name?' he asked innocently.

Linda Speer was thrown momentarily. 'S . . . P . . . E . . . E . . . R,' she said in her strong Boston tones, then mocked by repeating the letters phonetically. 'SSS . . . PPP . . . EEE . . . EEE . . . RRR. Speer. Happy?'

Clancy brushed past her. 'S . . . P . . . E . . . E . . . R,' he repeated slowly and thoughtfully, shaking his head as if puzzled. Then he looked back at the cardiologist and smiled. 'Such an ordinary name for such an extraordinary woman.'

Linda Speer was left speechless with rage.

Outside in the corridor, Clancy was stopped by Stone Colman. His office door was open wide. The smaller man held a hand up. 'Wow, man. What's going on? What the hell's all the shouting about?'

Linda Speer came out. 'It's okay, Stone. Dr Clancy was just making an asshole of himself and I put him right.' She waved dismissively. 'It's no big deal. Leave it.'

Colman eyeballed Clancy. 'Lighten up,' he advised. 'This is a hospital, not some shanty house.'

Clancy walked away. He turned back at the lifts. Speer and Colman were deep in conversation.

During the coffee break Police Commissioner Donal Murphy had kept to himself, ignoring the small knots of conversation. In the earlier exchanges he'd contributed little to the discussion, apart from putting John Regan in his place. But he was a worried man. He had been last into the incident room, a deliberate decision as he had little time for overt political interference and wanted to see if any other government stooges might turn up. He knew this was going to be a high-profile investigation and wasn't surprised to find three TV crews waiting outside even before the conference had begun. News bureaux from Boston had been telephoning for comments since early morning. There would soon be a media pack following every move. He suspected Regan was milking the occasion, self-promotion wouldn't come much easier. Copy and photos of the Minister for Health personally involved in the murder investigation was a campaign manager's dream. Regan, he decided, would do all in his power to protect his own reputation and also his greatest asset, the 'Dream Team'. Jennifer Marks' murder could destabilise the Heart Foundation, dash his ambitions and put him back at the mercy of Ireland's home-grown doctors. John Regan, consummate politician, Armani socialist and media darling could be crushed by the murderous act of a small-time knife man and drug addict. Murphy knew Regan would want Micko Kelly's head on a plate. And fast.

'What else do we know about Kelly?' the commissioner asked. 'How dangerous is he? How easy would it be to lift him without starting a riot?'

Murphy was acutely aware of the operational difficulties. Hillcourt Mansions was a no-go area and had been picketed by Concerned Parents Against Drugs on many occasions. A number of the picketers were subsequently attacked by drug dealers, unhappy their main customer base was coming under so much attention. The picketing stopped and the mansion residents got back to their daily business of shooting up, then going into the city to rob and mug to pay for their habit. The mansions also had its own early warning system. The crackheads took turns guarding the only entrance wide enough for patrol cars or arrest vans. At the first sign of a blue uniform dustbin lids were banged against walls and within minutes the concrete jungle would reverberate to the clanging of tins and shouts of abuse. Rocks would be thrown at anything moving in the courtyard, toilets would be flushed with an unusual frequency as drugs were discarded. Hillcourt Mansions was the least likely place to start a conflict. No, decided Murphy, this would have to be thought through carefully.

'He's very dangerous,' explained Molloy, opening one of three thick files resting on his lap.

The team eased themselves into whatever comfort

they could find. Some doubled up on the small seats. The air stifled despite all the open windows. The police commissioner motioned for one of the chairs to be vacated and sat down. He slipped off his jacket, resting it over the back. 'Go on,' he ordered.

'Kelly is a small-time criminal,' began Molloy, skimming through the sheets. 'His family lived in a tenement before being rehoused in the suburbs. They brought their social problems with them.' He stopped briefly to flick over more text, 'He's the third of four boys and three girls. The father is dead, fished out of the Liffey after a drunken spree. The mother tried to pull the rest together and keep them out of trouble.' A hand at the back pushed a window open further and distant traffic noises filtered inside the crowded room. 'Kelly developed a reputation as a knife man after he pulled a few petrol station jobs brandishing Bowie blades. He was caught on video and arrested. He was out on bail awaiting trial when he got into an argument with,' here Molloy searched until he found a name, 'Dinny Johnstone from Finglas, another druggie. They started fighting and Johnstone ended up dead on arrival at hospital. Kelly had stabbed him twice, one cut right into the heart.'

'Anything else?' Murphy asked. His expression hadn't changed but he was analysing, processing, deciding.

'He did ten years for that but got involved in drugs again while in gaol.' Molloy closed the file. 'There was a raid one weekend and his cell was turned upside down.'

Murphy wiped beads of sweat from his hairline. 'Did they find anything?'

'The usual, packets of heroin, syringes, tin foil with

crack cocaine, a few uppers. Nothing to set the place apart.'

'So what's the big deal?' Murphy's eyebrows shot up.

'Well, Micko kind of took the raid personally,' Molloy explained. 'He bided his time until he had one of the warders cornered in the print workshop, then pulled a makeshift knife and nearly cut the hand off him. Two others held him down while Micko sawed away. He was seven hours in surgery having it stitched back.'

'Jesus,' someone whistled.

'So he's a hard man.' The commissioner echoed everyone's thoughts.

'Yes,' said Molloy, 'and he's become meaner. Dirty syringes and knives are his speciality. He's a heroin addict and wouldn't think twice about cutting your throat if he needed money for a fix.'

The door opened and a young blonde secretary squeezed in. Every male eye in the room admired her, delighted with the pleasant distraction. The girl searched the faces until she spotted Clarke. Someone whistled softly, then stifled it. She handed two fax sheets over and they were passed across the table. Clarke read through quickly, then turned back to the first page. He frowned.

'Okay,' he announced. 'According to witnesses Marks and her friend Joan Armstrong did not get off the train at Sydney Parade. They both waited until the next stop and left together. They were seen later in Balfe's pub in Ringsend.' Balfe's was a notorious drug hangout, a dump where many dealers plied their trade and took their orders. 'Micko Kelly and Marks were seen leaving together sometime after six thirty, heading in the direction of Sandymount Park. There's no mention of the Armstrong girl being with them.' He stopped and held the second page at a slight distance to make out the smudged print. 'Marks was carrying a bag. She was not dressed in her uniform.'

Murphy stood up slowly and began edging towards the exit. He carried his jacket over his shoulder. Before he opened the door he turned back. 'It's over to you now, Jim. I'd say we go for Kelly. But for Christ's sake don't start a riot.'

'I want the word on the streets immediately.' Clarke rested one hand on the grip of his crutch. He wiped a handkerchief across his face and back over his hair. It only made him look more bedraggled than usual. 'We want Kelly. If he's seen, get him. We mustn't force him underground. If he gets wind we're after him he could hide for weeks.' Notepads fanned perspiring faces. 'Put out feelers among the scag-heads, find out where exactly he's shacked up and does he use the same room all the time? Use any favours you're owed. Knock a few heads if necessary.' He noticed he was breathing heavily, the adrenalin rush pounding him on. 'I want him by tonight.' He stopped, face set rigid. 'Otherwise we'll drag the bastard out at dawn tomorrow.' A cheer filled the room.

'Talk to the Armstrong girl again,' Clarke pulled Molloy aside. 'Call after school while one of her parents is at home.' Molloy craned his head closer. 'Say you've learned where Jennifer went to after she got off the train. Don't mention Balfe's pub or anything to do with Kelly. Just say you'd like her to think real hard in case there's anything she may have forgotten. Leave it at that.' From outside came the whirl of cameras clicking. 'There's more to this than messing with drugs. There was no reason for her to lie. She's hiding something.' He blinked at the sunlight streaming in through the open door. 'And find Marks' schoolbag and clothes.'

The search for Micko Kelly began just after midday. Around inner-city police stations faxes and phone calls bounced back and forth. A number of unmarked cars and plain-clothes officers positioned themselves in the narrow streets and alleys around Hillcourt Mansions. Mobile phones kept each in contact.

Known dealers, junkies and informers were pulled aside and quizzed about his whereabouts. Did you see Kelly today? When did you see him last? Where did you see him last? What is he shooting up? Where does he get it? Where does he go when he's desperate? The information slowly filtered in and was relayed to Clarke as he waited at police headquarters. He'd despatched Moss Kavanagh onto the streets to work the prostitute scene. Many of the girls were on the game to feed their heroin habit and knew the drug scene backwards. The offer of a few clean twenty-pound notes without the usual discomfort opened mouths. More information came in than Clarke had hoped for. Everything except the whereabouts of Micko Kelly.

At that time, now after seven in the evening, Kelly was setting up a massive fix in the room he hadn't left all day. The junkie mother with her junkie baby had done him a favour and gone out on the streets and bought him seventy pounds' worth of crack cocaine, two deals of heroin and sixteen Rohypnol tablets.

She'd also bought two tablets she was told were Ecstasy. In return he'd given her seventy recently mugged pounds and a bag of cannabis. The two felt well pleased with the transactions, Kelly even forgetting his threats to slit the screeching child's throat. They went to their respective rooms to while away the night in a drug-induced stupor.

13 7.45 pm

Frank Clancy was in ward three checking on his patients. The duty sister stopped him before he reached Harold Morell. 'He's not great,' she warned. 'He's spiked a temperature again, his mouth is severely ulcerated and he's had three rigors in the past hour.'

Clancy took the bedside chart and studied the basic thirty-minute observations. Morell's vital signs were ominous, high swinging fever, fast heart rate, low blood pressure and poor urinary output. He walked slowly to the special isolation unit outside the ward where the seriously ill man had been moved. Morell lay slumped on high pillows, cannulae in both nostrils delivering oxygen, drips delivered fluids and antibiotics into each arm. A long tube drained urine from inside his bladder. The man lying on the bed was a mere shadow of the big, strong builder of better days. Clutching his right hand was his wife, a tall, plumpish woman with streaked grey hair. Her face was wracked with worry and strain, she wrung and unwrung a once white linen handkerchief. The moment Clancy looked at his patient he knew he was going to die. He moved closer to the side of the bed, avoiding Morell's wife's questioning stare.

'Harry,' he half shouted into the man's left ear. Harold Morell opened his eyes briefly, moistened his lips and tried to speak, then shook his head. 'Harry,' Clancy pressed, despite his patient's weakness, 'I need to ask you about the tablets you were taking before you came into hospital.' Morell nodded a fraction. 'I know you were on Adizem and D/N Aspirin, weren't you?'

'Yes, he was, doctor,' Mrs Morell cut across. 'I always look after his tablets, he can be so forgetful.'

Clancy turned to the woman. 'Is there any chance he took more than what were prescribed for him? You know, by mistake, maybe he got confused?'

'No, doctor.' Mrs Morell was emphatic and Clancy sensed a woman well on top of such matters. He'd come across patients who wouldn't have known a tablet from a bar of chocolate, others who read the instructions incorrectly. Mrs Morell was not of that sort. She seemed like a woman who guarded her husband's health with strict vigilance.

'I always keep them inside a small pillbox and only put out each day's dose. The rest are kept in the medicine cabinet.' She spoke with a flat north Dublin accent.

Clancy smiled at her attentiveness and fiddled with one of the drip sets to give him time to think. 'Were there just the two tablets?' he asked, now adjusting the nasal cannulae.

'Oh yes,' replied Mrs Morell, emphatic as ever. 'The pinky-blue capsule for his blood pressure and the little blue one for his blood.'

112

'You don't happen to have them with you?' Clancy was now adding a useless note to the bedside chart.

'No, I'm sorry, doctor. I didn't think you'd need them. They're at home.'

Clancy smiled at her before he left the room. 'Perhaps you'd bring them in with you when you visit tomorrow?'

'I will, doctor, I'll make a knot in my handkerchief to remind me.' She tied the knot immediately. 'There,' she held the handkerchief up, 'I won't forget.'

'Thanks very much. Bring them all. Don't leave any behind.'

'I won't, doctor,' promised the diligent Mrs Morell.

Clancy took the ward sister's elbow and walked her to a corner. 'Louise,' he said quietly, rummaging in the pockets of his white coat, 'would you order those two files up here for me, please?'

The sister took the slip of crumpled paper and read the scribbled names. 'Mary Hyland . . . James Murphy?'

Clancy nodded and directed her attention to the chart numbers he'd written beside both. 'They're both dead,' he added, glancing round to make sure no one could overhear, 'so the notes should be in the DECEASED section in medical records.' The ward sister's eyes never left the names. 'See if you could get them here for me by tomorrow. I've a mountain of paperwork to deal with before I go home. Tomorrow would be great, if you could manage it.' He forced a hopeful smile.

As the troubled blood specialist began sifting through a series of test results on his other patients, above in the Heart Foundation offices Linda Speer was on the phone. The door to her suite was locked and the blinds were drawn.

With no sign of Michael Leo Kelly by ten thirty on the evening of Wednesday, 13 May, Jim Clarke made the operational decision to storm Hillcourt Mansions at dawn the next morning. He left Molloy and Kavanagh in charge of selecting the snatch squad and exact location of the suspect.

Back home he slumped into bed and tried to sleep. But sleep would not come. The pain, the drive to arrest Kelly, the possibility of closing the case in one dramatic swoop pumped his adrenalin. He tossed and turned all night, watching the digital clock flick the minutes towards dawn.

At police headquarters, Molloy and Kavanagh could not sleep either. They had drawn up a list of twenty-six men and primed them for the morning raid. As they played poker into the small hours, smoking and gossiping, they kept an eye on the clock, itching to get on. Kavanagh sneaked away for five minutes to tip off *Post* crime correspondent Barry Nolan.

'We've codenamed it "Operation Storm the Barricades",' he gleefully informed. Nolan spent the rest of the night cramped in the back of a mini-van near the mansions. He brought three cameras, two with telephoto lenses, and enough film to capture a small war. He'd earlier agreed a hefty fee for a separate report to the *Boston Globe*.

At her home in the Dublin suburb of Sandymount, Joan Armstrong was wide awake. The needle tracks on her arms were more difficult to camouflage than she'd expected. She hadn't been able to get near the phone without being overheard. Then Tony Molloy had called to the house at six thirty. His parting words were heavy with menace. 'Maybe there's something you've forgotten, Joan? I'm going to call again tomorrow. Maybe you'll have remembered something by then, no matter how small. Okay?' She'd had to change her sweat-soaked pyjamas twice already, and the night was quite cool for a change.

In his flea-infested room in Hillcourt Mansions, Micko Kelly was asleep. The sleep was disturbed by unusual and distressing dreams. Kelly rocked on the mattress. In his drug-induced mania he found fire-breathing animals following him, reaching out to grab his arms and legs. He screamed for help. On a heap in the corner, undisturbed from the moment he'd discarded them, lay his blood-spattered trainers and bloodstained white T-shirt. If Hillcourt Mansions had gone up in flames Micko Kelly couldn't have cared a damn. The dragon had Micko and the dragon was in control.

In New York, the city that never sleeps, the price of Cynx Pharmaceutical shares rose to $17.22, up $1.82, after unexpected buying from an unknown European source.

14 *5.30 am, Thursday, 14 May –
'Operation Storm the Barricades'.*

'The gloves are needle-proof. They're awkward but
safe, that's the main thing.' In a small quadrangle at
police headquarters, Tony Molloy was briefing his
twenty-six-man snatch squad. The grey light of dawn
was edging over nearby Georgian buildings while
vans loaded with morning papers played 'skip-the-
red-lights' on the streets outside. The smell of roasted
malt from Guinness's brewery hung in the still, cold
morning air. Distant burglar alarms vied with barking
dogs as wake up calls.

'There are needle-proof jackets and leggings as
well. They'll itch but you won't be in them for long.'
Molloy looked over his squad. They're tough-
looking, right enough, he thought. Most had crew cut
hair, physical bulk with intimidating faces. All were
above six feet tall, he'd insisted on that. Ten were
from the élite Rangers Command, trained in anti-
terrorist and urban conflict duties. The ten would split
into two groups of five. The first would go in after
Micko Kelly, the other five would protect the outside
landing of the tenement complex. The rest of the
squad would disperse to strategic positions along both

stairwells, blocking any attempt to get up or down. Molloy didn't want a melee with his men being attacked with every conceivable weapon imaginable.

'The moment we're inside the courtyard it's enemy territory and you better believe it. I don't want any Rambo antics. Don't taunt or intimidate, don't rough anyone unnecessarily. Our job is to get Kelly and nothing else.' He stared at the impassive faces in front, knowing full well some would love to get stuck into the scag-heads. They were so psyched up they'd have stormed an army barracks just to vent their pent-up aggression.

'Kelly mustn't be hurt. I want one man for each arm and leg and one for his head. Don't let him bite. Carry him face down. Don't put anything over his mouth to stop him shouting. He's going to be taken immediately to a holding centre for questioning.' The cold air frosted at his lips as he spoke. He noticed the rapid breaths of the snatch squad. The more he briefed, the more psyched up they were becoming. He sensed he'd have to let them off the leash soon. 'It's important he's not hurt in any way.' No one spoke. 'He'll be paraded before the press and I don't want a mark on him.' The squad listened silently. 'As soon as he's out there'll be a forensic team after you to bag any evidence. They must be protected. We need evidence, understand?' The silent heads nodded.

'Okay,' Molloy ended, 'get into that gear. We're outa here at six exactly.' He checked his watch and motioned the men to do likewise. In the morning gloom twenty-seven handwatches fixed the time at five forty-eight. Twenty-six men moved inside a training shed and began donning protective gear. Not a word was exchanged, not even eye contact made.

The silence was intimidating. Molloy murmured into a walkie-talkie and within minutes heard the gentle rumble of four transit vans. They pulled up in front of the shed, front and back windows protected by steel mesh. The vans were black with POLICE painted in large white lettering on both sides and roof. Four drivers sprang from the front cabs as one and slid the side panel doors open. The doors were so well greased the action was noiseless.

'Okay, let's go,' Molloy ordered and the group split. All were wearing black riot helmets with visors flicked up for the moment. All were dressed in needle-proof jackets and leggings underneath black tracksuits. All held onto their black needle-proof gloves, waiting until the last moment before donning.

6.00 am

The doors slid shut and the four vans drove out onto Harcourt Street where Jim Clarke sat waiting in the back of his unmarked squad car. Moss Kavanagh sat in the driver's seat. The left-side passenger door was open and the running figure of Tony Molloy soon appeared. He jumped inside just as Kavanagh edged the car in behind the convoy.

'They're ready,' he announced grimly, 'and as keen as mustard.'

Clarke leaned forward, his bad leg pushed to one side for ease. 'You warned them not to rough him up?'

Molloy didn't turn, his eyes fixed on the back of the last black van. 'I did, don't worry, I did. They know exactly what to do.' He twisted the rear-view mirror with his right hand. 'We'll be in and out in ten minutes,' he promised. 'Ten minutes.'

The convoy sped rapidly through the deserted streets, along St Stephen's Green and down Dawson Street, past the Mansion House. Pigeons and magpies fighting among litter bins scattered in their wake. Clarke hadn't felt so keyed up for years and clutched tightly onto the hand rest of the car door. In the rear-view mirror he could see Molloy's worried frown and turned to look out the side window. Shuttered shop fronts flashed past as the convoy turned into Nassau Street, picking up speed as it headed towards the Hillcourt Mansions complex. One mile before, a black-windowed, steel-reinforced police car with the forensic team pulled out from a side road and followed in line.

6.15 am

They reached the entrance to Hillcourt Mansions in good time with no traffic delaying. All engines were switched off as the convoy glided noiselessly inside. The tenement was deserted with only the litter of takeaways, tin cans, bottles and drug dealing blowing aimlessly in the breeze. The courtyard was surrounded on three sides by run-down and graffiti-covered flats, with two end stairwells. There wasn't a movement along the corridors, the scag-heads asleep or comatose.

6.18 am

The van doors glided open and from inside sprang the

snatch squad. Clarke watched from the safety of his car, parked in a slewn-across fashion at the entrance, blocking any getaway. He wound the window down quickly lest his breath mist the view. Twenty-six black-uniformed figures raced across concrete to their pre-arranged positions. The Ranger Command unit was at the head and the lead five were already on the second-floor landing, eyes scanning door numbers as they rushed. One stopped suddenly and motioned his colleagues forward. Each checked the number and location and a final nod agreed the target location. Micko Kelly's whereabouts had been betrayed the night before for twenty pounds, less than he spent on an average hit. As the door crashed off its hinges the first dustbin lid alarm sounded.

6.23 am

Kelly was already awake. He was sitting half upright on the mattress, fumbling for a fix. All night in his mind he had battled with demons and lost. His brain was in turmoil, he felt shaky and agitated. His eyes could barely register the bits and pieces scattered around the room. He felt invisible. He lifted one hand up and waved it in front of where he sensed his eyes might be. He couldn't see it. *I'm fuckin' invisible.* His ears registered the sudden crashing of the flat door, the high-pitched wailing of the drug-addicted baby, the curses of the drug-addicted mother as she tried blocking the outside corridor with her wasted body. He scrambled for a knife but couldn't find one. The demons were back, larger than ever. They were inside the room and coming towards him. He watched with a mixture of mesmerised horror and intense fascination as the black-suited figures came closer. He stared as the black-uniformed arms and black-covered hands reached out for him. But Kelly felt invisible. *They can't see me, they can't take me, I'm invisible.* He started to grin, the half cocked, stupid-looking grin of a man not sure what was going to happen next and believing it couldn't happen to him. Hoping. The first grip shook him to the core. He started roaring.

6.25 am

'Get the bastard.' Two commandos grabbed his long, dank hair and pulled his head back severely. Two sets of eyes drilled through visors. 'Open your fucking mouth and your head comes off.' Just as Kelly's first roars disturbed the junkies in the flats to the side and below, his arms and legs were up in the air, his torso spun violently, his face suddenly staring at the ground. He was out and over the flat door where it rested on the floor in the outside corridor. His passage was so quick and forceful the drug-addicted mother was knocked over and stamped by the charging feet. Her screaming curses were suffocated by a rough hand as she was thrown inside a toilet and the door pulled shut. As Kelly was carried into the weak morning light the forensic team pushed inside with evidence bags. The second five commandos positioned themselves to protect. They stood like aliens from another planet with the darkness of their uniforms and visors, their physical bulk, their batons drawn and ready.

The first junkies to spill out along the corridors and corners stopped and stared for minutes, uncertain what was happening. The contrast was stark. Wasted faces, dishevelled clothes, bewildered expressions. Then shouts further along alerted them. This was a raid. Heads craned over the landing walls, taking in the sight of Micko Kelly being carried across the courtyard while another six black-suited henchmen protected, their movements jerky and agitated. Already a small group of the flats' residents on the ground floor had spilled out, shouting abuse. They started edging closer. Rocks were thrown, the cacophony of the bin-lid alarm urging on the crowd. The first scuffle had already broken out as one of the braver challenged the team protecting the forensic squad. A baton snapped sharply across his head, drawing blood and curses. His howls encouraged more outside and within minutes the complex was teeming. Battle had commenced.

Clutching their now full evidence bags the forensics rushed onto the landing and the protection of the commandos. Crab-like, the unit edged and bludgeoned their way towards the stairwell, dodging rocks and bottles which rained on them from all sides. As they passed a flat door it would suddenly burst open and a hand clutching a dirty needled syringe would jab down. Nothing penetrated. Uniforms were cut, spat on and grabbed, but nothing gave way. The protective underlay held fast. Within minutes they were down to ground level and crouching together for the final sprint along the concrete nightmare.

'Go,' urged Molloy over a megaphone. 'Everybody back in the vans.'

The black uniforms edged towards safety, followed at baton's distance by the angry mob. Tempers were fraying all round, blood was boiling. The bin lids continued to beat their jungle rhythm, more rocks and bottles were hurled through the air. The court-yard had become a riot zone. The snatch squad could see only angry, bloodshot eyes; see knives and syringes drawn. They flailed at the grasping hands. The sudden noise of police klaxons momentarily stunned the mob, allowing the squad to leap to the safety of the vans. Thirty-six minutes after the doors had slid open they slammed shut again and the convoy screeched out the entrance and away from the baying horde behind.

6.54 am

Micko Kelly was officially cautioned and placed under arrest. He didn't understand a word being said.

The convoy sped through early morning traffic, sirens scaring all in front and leaving traffic chaos in its wake. One of the unit clutched an unopened can of Heineken. 'Jaysus they had the goat up right enough,' he smirked, 'throwing full cans of beer.' The others grinned.

At a pre-arranged point one van and one car peeled away and headed towards the holding centre. Inside the van a bemused and frightened and shaking and agitated and *how the fuck did they get me, I'm invisible?* Micko Kelly lay face down. His feet and arms and head were restrained by rough, strong hands. His forehead never once bounced off the floor along the pot-holed side roads, the grip on the back of his neck vice-like. *What the fuck's goin' on?*

Just after eight o'clock on the morning of Thursday, 14 May, while bright sunshine lifted the city mood, Kelly was brutally thrust into a single holding cell on level two of Bridewell Gaol. The cell had been cleared earlier and nothing, not even a blanket or pillow remained. As the steel door slammed closed, Kelly crawled into a corner and slumped down on his behind. He drew both knees up to his chest and rested his chin. He dragged his arms over his head and pulled them down tightly. He was shaking violently and felt agitated. He was sweating and his own smells began to irritate. His teeth were chattering. He was beginning to feel withdrawal symptoms. His belly ached with gnawing pains.

Jimmy, where are ye? I need some scag, quick. Don' fuck me about, Jimmy. I need a fix badly. Have ye any scag?

But there was no Jimmy. There was only the silence of the cell and the torture of his drug-destroyed mind. Micko Kelly was in trouble. Again.

'I want to see Arnie Leeson.' Jim Clarke stood at reception of the Forensic Science Laboratory in Dublin's Phoenix Park. He'd followed the forensic team like a tracker dog, not letting them out of his sight.

'You're up bright and early.' Arnold Leeson, director of the laboratory, was a tall, lean man in a scientist's white coat, breast pocket bulging with pens and bits of paper. His thinning hair was totally grey. He glanced at the flustered group and decided this was no time for pleasantries. 'What's going on?' His voice had dropped from welcoming lilt to growling business-like. 'What's in the bags?'

The Forensic Science Laboratory occupied one level of a new office complex beside older Victorian buildings. There was plenty of natural light from windows overlooking playing fields. Each department had different functions, one dealing with narcotics, others with firearm patterns, another with trace evidence such as fibres, blood and semen. As Clarke followed the team along the corridors, he noticed bulging evidence bags strewn inside the many corners. Finally they reached a sealed door which was quickly unlocked. Inside was a small, well-lit room with worktop benches. Jennifer Marks' clothes had been laid out, markers identifying the case number. A space had been created to allow note-taking and a Dictaphone lay in the middle. An opened box of surgical gloves was propped awkwardly in a corner, one latex finger poking out provocatively. Clarke quickly scanned the clothing then closed and locked the door. Further along another empty room awaited Kelly's belongings. Inside the evidence bags were laid down and their seals broken.

'I want to see clothes and shoes,' ordered Clarke. Onto the bench slipped a heavily stained T-shirt. Next came tracksuit bottoms and finally two pairs of trainers. There was no mistaking the blood-like stains on one. 'How long to get DNA profiling?' he asked.

'A week, maybe a day earlier if I push it,' Leeson offered.

'Push it.' Clarke squinted at three separate cardboard evidence cylinders. 'Open those.'

The seals on the cylinders were broken and onto the bench slid three knives. One was a long, wide-bladed Bowie knife, the second a narrower, stiletto blade. The third was a pearl-handled flick knife. The stiletto blade had old blood clinging.

'Bit of a connoisseur,' Leeson grunted. 'What's he been up to?'

Clarke didn't answer. He inspected the clothing and trainers, squinting as he got closer, imagining them laid out on the oak-panelled bench of some courtroom in the months ahead.

'What's he done?' pressed Leeson.

'Murder,' said Clarke finally. 'We lifted him for the Marks girl stabbing.'

Leeson's eyebrows shot up. 'The surgeon's daughter?'

Clarke nodded.

'He'll swing for that,' Leeson exclaimed, now caught up in the excitement. 'If John Regan has his way he'll hang.'

Clarke pursed his lips thoughtfully. 'We better make sure we've got the right man then, Arnie.'

Leeson flicked at the bloodstained shirt and trainers with a pen. 'It's all there. If the DNA matches you have him.'

Clarke's brow furrowed. 'Could you start on this today?'

Leeson started to protest. 'I've a mountain of work waiting out there.'

'I know you have,' agreed Clarke, 'but nothing that'll make as many waves.'

'How'd it go, boss?' Moss Kavanagh waited beside the lift.

'Fine,' lied Clarke. 'All we need is the DNA result.' He looked away, most uneasy. He hadn't seen any cobwebs clinging to Micko Kelly's tracksuit. He hoped forensics would.

15

Dr Frank Clancy had been angry from the moment he'd checked into his office on level three of the Mercy Hospital.

'What do you mean you can't find them?' he barked at the medical records secretary after reading the message left on his desk. FILES ON PATIENTS MARY HYLAND (115CD346) AND JAMES MURPHY (224CD579) CANNOT BE LOCATED.

'I'm sorry, Dr Clancy,' a timid female voice answered, 'but we've searched everywhere. They're just not where they should be.'

Clancy took a deep breath. Relax, you're not gonna get anwhere by shouting.

'Did you check in the DECEASED section?' He tried a more soothing tone this time. 'You know both patients are dead?'

'Oh yes, that's where I've been all morning,' the timid voice explained. 'I've been down there since I came in.'

'Well,' he suggested calmly, 'perhaps they were never put into the DECEASED section. Maybe they're still in the live register?'

'I checked that too, Dr Clancy. They're not there either.' The timid voice now sounded bolder. 'The computer search states they were definitely refiled under DECEASED, but they're not in either section, dead or alive.'

Clancy mulled this over. 'Filed somewhere else by mistake?' he offered hopefully.

'We're all looking, Dr Clancy, I can assure you. This has never happened before.' Timid voice sounded genuinely concerned. 'It's very strange.'

'Maybe,' Clancy took a final shot in the dark, 'someone has the files out?'

'Well, that's what we think. But the rules on removing files are very strict.'

'Yeah,' grunted Clancy, 'I know that.'

The Mercy Hospital, like every medical institution, had a tight protocol on handling patient files. The ever-present threat of litigation meant no files were ever destroyed, those over ten years without new entries or where the patient had died, were stored in a specially constructed annexe at the back of the hospital. The air temperature in this unit was controlled to prevent damp and decay. Lawyers hungry for past mistakes had been known to dig back as far as twenty years. Not being able to produce a file, or one that was falling apart and practically useless, did not look good in court. All files were protected and preserved. More importantly, access to old or DECEASED records involved filling out a request form, signing for file removal, and a double-check when the file was returned. The pages were counted, numbered and identified. In this way no one could alter records, perhaps putting a better gloss on their clinical or operative notes in advance of an impending law suit. Clancy knew only department heads had keys to the record storage annexe for out-of-hours access.

'Well, keep looking,' he ordered as he hung up.

His morning worsened soon after.

'I just don't understand it, Dr Clancy. I'm sure I had all Harry's tablets safely in the medicine cabinet.' Harold Morell's steady and sound wife stood in the door of his office trying to explain her loss. He listened to her uncertainty with sinking heart. 'I know I had enough until his next out-patient visit, I know it.'

'When was that due?' Clancy asked.

Mrs Morell produced a small black diary and scanned its tatty pages. 'Next month, Friday, 12 June, at ten in the morning,' she read. 'Cardiac out-patients with Dr Speer. She always gives out the tablets.'

Clancy's wandering attention suddenly focused. 'She gives the tablets out herself?' His voice rose. He knew the only drugs dispensed through the hospital came from its pharmacy on the ground floor.

'Oh yes. She gives a prescription for the angina tablets, the pinky-blue capsules, and we get that at our local chemist. His other tablets, little blue ones, we pick them up here. Always just enough for two weeks. I have to come back myself every fortnight and collect the next supply.'

Clancy sat upright as he listened, the office empty apart from himself and Mrs Morell. 'And,' he asked as casually as he could pretend, 'who gives you the tablets each time?'

'Dr Speer herself. She's such a lovely lady, isn't she? Not like some of the consultants you meet here.' Mrs Morell looked around conspiratorially, then whispered, 'Some of them think they're God Almighty. Not Dr Speer, she's a real lady.'

'Yes,' murmured Clancy, brow furrowed in thought. 'A real lady indeed.'

'That's why I'm puzzled, Dr Clancy,' Mrs Morell complained. 'I know I had enough on standby. They just weren't there when I looked.'

'You couldn't have put them somewhere else, could you?' The question was more in hope than expectation.

'No, that's definite. I never put them anywhere else.' The woman clutched at her handbag anxiously.

When Mrs Morell left he turned to the computer screen in his office and began typing on the keyboard. First he brought up the file on Mary Hyland, noticing she *was* classified as deceased. Next he searched for personal details and wrote down her address, telephone number and next-of-kin. Then he scrolled through the file, noting she had been a Mercy Hospital patient for thirty-four years, first attending at the age of twenty-nine with a skin complaint, then again in her fifties with a gall-bladder infection which was successfully treated with antibiotics before she underwent surgery for gall-bladder removal. There was a twelve-year gap before she reattended with chest tightening, 'especially on exercise'. This was to be her penultimate hospital experience. She was referred to the newly opened cardiac unit and came under the care of Dr Linda Speer. Clancy's ability to determine what happened from then on was limited. Only basic details were transferred from the traditional handwritten chart notes: diagnoses, important medical and/or surgical procedures, drug therapies, adverse drug reactions, et cetera. The daily record of clinical progress, observations such as blood pressure, temperature, heart and respiratory rates were still only available in the chart. The missing chart. Still, Clancy was able to access her drug regime and surgical procedures. *Stress ECG, coronary angiogram, bypass surgery recommended.* He scrolled further. *Crescendo anginal episode associated with slightly raised cardiac enzymes. Urgent single vessel bypass: surgeon Dan Marks.* He looked for the operative assistants. Linda Speer's name appeared again. What the hell is she doing assisting at operations? He reread the cardiac notes. Another patient with a pre-operative ischaemic episode forcing an early bypass procedure. Clancy leaned back in his chair wondering at the significance, if any, of the sequence of events. He stared at his wife and two children smiling out from a photograph perched in one corner of his cluttered desk. He was so pre-occupied he didn't even blow them the usual kiss.

Aware he was letting his morning ward rounds and medical student teaching slip even later than usual, Clancy returned to the PC screen and accessed the drugs' regime for Mary Hyland. He scrolled past the earlier prescriptions and honed in on her recent admission entry. Capoten 12.5 mgs b.d. and D/N Aspirin 300 mgs daily had been the only drugs prescribed. Capoten was a standard, uncomplicated treatment for raised blood pressure. D/N Aspirin seems to be Speer's favourite drug, he thought as he wrote down the exact date it had first been used. He noted the time span of only six weeks from Hyland's heart operation and her subsequent readmission with agranulocytosis. Then he closed down the Mary Hyland file and typed in JAMES MURPHY, file number 224CD579 and waited. He inspected his nails as the hard disk whirred. Suddenly a red warning asterisk flashed on the screen, accompanied by FILE 224CD579 CURRENTLY IN USE. Clancy stared at the screen for almost three minutes before repeating the exercise. The same result: red warning asterisk and FILE 224CD579 CURRENTLY IN USE. He stared intently at the screen again, before playing with various combinations of the same patient's name, address and date of birth to access the file. The red warning asterisk and FILE 224CD579 CURRENTLY IN USE message flicked up each time. Who the hell's going through that file at *this* moment? And why?

He dropped his head, heart racing and tried to think things through sensibly and logically. What is going on? The two standard charts I'm looking for are suddenly and mysteriously missing, now one of the computer files is being used by someone else in the hospital. *And this is a dead patient!* Alarm bells rang. Feverishly he clicked back onto the Mary Hyland file, typing as fast as his fingers would flick. The red warning asterisk suddenly appeared, followed by FILE 115CD346 CURRENTLY IN USE.

'Jesus Christ,' he swore out loud. Beads of sweat were forming on his brow. He was just about to wipe at them with the sleeve of his white coat when the telephone rang.

'Dr Clancy. We found those files.'

The news threw him momentarily and he listened into the earpiece without speaking.

'Hello? Hello, is that Dr Clancy?' The timid-voiced girl was back again.

'Yes, yes. Sorry, I'm terribly sorry,' Clancy mumbled, his mind in overdrive. 'I was working on some tests,' he lied.

'Sorry to disturb you, doctor, it's just you seemed so

keen to get these files I thought I'd ring you immediately.'

'No, no. I'm delighted you rang. Where were they anyway?'

There was an embarrassed pause. 'Down in the annexe all the time. Someone had pushed them so far back I couldn't see them for ages. It was only when we took a whole shelf down that I spotted them.'

'But why,' Clancy wondered out loud, immediately regretting his words, 'would those be the only two files pushed out of sight?'

Timid voice didn't answer. Then: 'I don't really know, Dr Clancy. I thought you'd be glad we found them at all.' She sounded aggrieved and Clancy apologised immediately for his discourtesy.

'Look, I'm terribly sorry. Of course I'm delighted. Thank you very much for all your work.'

'Shall I bring them up to you?'

Clancy glanced at his watch and groaned. He was more than an hour behind. 'No. Do you have a safe for storing documents?'

'Yes.'

'Put them in there until I get down later. Don't let anyone else touch them, okay?'

'Right, doctor,' agreed timid voice.

Clancy stood up, straightened his tie in the reflection of the glass separating office from the wards, then grabbed a pile of charts and set off to start his rounds. As he left the red warning asterisk on his computer screen disappeared.

'*Look at me, Michael.*' The voice had a siren-like, entreating timbre.

The cell in which Micko Kelly lay slumped was ten feet long by six feet wide. There was a single hard bench on which to lie but nothing else inside the tiny room. No blanket, no pillow, not even a thread on the mottled marble floor. There wasn't as much as a bucket for a toilet. The walls were ten feet from floor to ceiling and one held a two-foot square barred window a few inches below ceiling level. The glass was of thick, shatter-proof variety. A single light fitting recessed into the centre of the ceiling was positioned such that no one could access it. In the past prisoners had been known to electrocute themselves and the newer fittings made such attempts impossible. An eight-foot high, three-foot wide steel door was the only opening to the corridor. There was no handle on the inside of the door. A spy-hole was strategically located at eye-level so that warders could squint inside, ensuring the occupant was present and alive and not attempting suicide. The walls of the cell were covered with graffiti, names and dates of previous prisoners' incarcerations and their comments on warders, gaol and society generally. Hardly a word was spelled correctly. Profanities were the norm. Everything was a *fucken* this or due to a *fucken* that. There was high praise for ecstasy, crack cocaine, scag and uppers and downers. The cells had held many connoisseurs of the drugs' trade in Dublin and beyond. One scrawl reflected a Jamaican on remand for smuggling.

On the door, about ten inches below the spy-hole, an elaborate drawing of Jesus Christ had been created. Since all prisoners were searched and anything sharp or capable of writing with confiscated, this etching was remarkable as much for its existence as its detail. The style was traditional: Jesus with long, shoulder-length hair, eyes subdued and compliant, looking slightly down and to the right. He wore a thick beard and moustache. His lips were rather thin, his eyebrows bushy. A crown of thorns rested firmly on his head and drops of blood had been scratched to mark where thorn tips pierced scalp. One hand, the right, had been etched in a forgiving pose and in the left chest area a heart with a cross on top had been lovingly created. Another crown of thorns circled the cross and the heart could be clearly seen bleeding as well. The final image, though scratched and shaky and overshot here and there, was excellent. It was the face of a suffering, yet forgiving Jesus Christ. Underneath the letters *OUR SAVIER* had been scratched. The total space of this creation was about eighteen inches square. It had obviously been there for some time as other graffiti had been painted over, their scrawling and scratches now barely visible. But the image of the suffering Jesus had been left untouched.

'Michael, look at me. I have a message for you.' The voice was more feminine than male, soft and beseeching, gentle and seductive.

'Check that bastard every five minutes,' the duty sergeant ordered from the moment the steel door had slammed shut on Kelly's back. 'Nothing's to happen to him, understand?' Three warders assigned to level two of the holding centre nodded. They weren't sure who exactly was in the cell or what he had done but the commotion that greeted his arrival warned they were dealing with a 'celebrity'. They agreed to check the holding cell every three minutes. Prisoners had rather ingenious ways of committing suicide between five-minute checks.

'What's he doing?' asked the sergeant after the first squint through the spy-hole.

'Nothing much, just curled up in a ball in the corner. He's hardly moving at all.'

'But he is moving?' The question reflected his immediate alarm.

'Definitely. I could see him running his hands through his hair.'

The sergeant heaved a sigh of relief and entered the exact time and observations in a large log book. The entry was in longhand, wide loops and swirls written with a fountain pen.

Three minutes later: 'He's yawning a lot and sneezing, but still stuck in that corner.'

Three minutes later: 'He's picking at his clothes as if he was pulling balls of fluff off them.'

Had he moved apart from that?

'Nah, still stuck in that corner.'

Three minutes later: 'He must have a bad cold or

something, he's sneezing a lot and his eyes are streaming.'

The duty sergeant was not impressed.

'Fuck him.'

'Look at me, Michael. This is your Lord God, Jesus Christ. I have a message for you.'

Micko Kelly's first sign of drug-induced insanity was the voice inside his head. He shook it from side to side, trying to rid himself of the utterance, frightened to look up. He had seen the image etched on the cell door immediately he had been thrown inside but had not looked towards it since. He pulled his legs against his chest and drew his arms closer and tighter over his ears and head. *Fuck off, fuck off!*

'He's up and wandering around the cell, gibbering to himself.'

The duty sergeant entered the observation. 'He's no shoelaces or anything?' he asked anxiously.

'There's nothing in there to hang himself with,' the warder replied. 'He's no notion by the state of him. He had a big stupid grin on his face when I looked.'

This annoyed the duty sergeant no end, aware of the charges being prepared against his prisoner. 'The bastard,' he growled as his loops and swirls finished.

'Michael, the devil is coming. He is outside this room. You must not let him take you.'

Kelly was now staring with a fixed fascination at the image of the suffering Christ. He *could* actually see the blood, bright red, dripping from the piercing crown of thorns on head and heart. He *could* actually see the thin lips of Jesus Christ move, the thick eyebrows bob up and down. He *could* actually hear the siren voice, the soft lilting, feminine beguiling, entreating and beseeching words. And he *could* see, clearly and powerfully, the piercing gaze of the suffering Christ as the eyes lifted from their downward stare to hold his own gaze. Micko Kelly was having an *experience*, the drug abuser's worst experience, hallucinations.

'The devil is coming to take you to hell. You will roast and no one will hear you. I can hear his footsteps. I can smell him. Don't let him take you, Michael.'

'I won't, I fuckin' well won't,' screamed Kelly as he sweated and shook and stared wild-eyed at the cell door. Goose pimples formed along his arms and legs and body. He heard the spy-hole slip over and noticed an eye squinting in at him. It was the devil's eye. The devil had come to take him. The devil was looking at him, sizing him up, planning how to snatch him. 'You won't fuckin' well get me, you fucker.' His screams penetrated the cell door and the watching warder began to worry about his charge. He went back to the duty sergeant to report.

'When the devil comes you must kill him.' The lips moved rapidly, the drops of blood poured like rain, the intense stare of the suffering Christ penetrated. The image left the cell door and entered the space between door and corner where Kelly lay sweating and shaking. The forgiving hand was now shaking violently, threateningly. The holding cell began to feel as hot as the fires of hell.

'When the devil comes you must kill him.'

'I will,' whispered Kelly, a feeling of impending doom sweeping his body like a branch in a violent storm. 'I'll kill the fucker before he gets me.' His body shook and sweat poured off his brow and face and trunk. His heart pounded inside his chest. His nose was blocked and he sneezed repeatedly. His eyes were streaming.

'The three of you better open up and check him. Make sure he doesn't bite, he's on drugs.'

The warders exchanged tired, resigned glances. 'That's all I need,' one complained angrily.

They donned protective gloves and marched along the corridor. From adjoining cells they could hear curses and shouts and crying, but nothing like the baying coming from Kelly's room. The sound was like that of a wounded animal, an animal caught in a steel-toothed trap, waiting to be snatched by a hunter. It was like the howl of an animal gnawing through its own flesh and bone to release its paw. The warders stopped and listened.

'Sounds like some mad dog,' one of them grunted.

'The devil is coming. Kill him.'

The noise of keys in the lock alerted and Kelly prepared to do battle. He crouched down on his hunkers in the furthermost corner from the door. The toes of his feet coiled, ready to pounce. He gripped the side of the bench with his left hand for support. The devil wouldn't take him without a fight.

'Get up, you mangy bastard,' the first warder into the cell ordered. He took two steps inside, his colleagues only inches behind. He noticed the froth on Kelly's lips, the wild stare in his eyes, the insanity. He recognised the features seconds too late.

The image Kelly saw was of a cloven-hoofed, black-faced demon with horns on the front and sides of his head. There was fire pouring from the demon's eyes, his tongue a coil of flame. The demon was laughing as his wrinkled chicken-skinned, sharp-pointed claws reached out.

'Get up, you bastard,' ordered the warder.

'He is the devil. Kill him.'

Kelly sprang like a leopard after prey. His long finger-nails raked the warder's face, his teeth sank into bare skin folds where the shirt collar lay loosely open.

'Aaagghh!' the warder screamed, flailing furiously at the lunging figure. 'Aaagghh!' he howled again as he felt nails rip flesh from his face and teeth sink into his neck. He felt the warmth of his own blood streaming down his neck as he slumped onto the marble floor.

'Get off, you bastard,' shouted the second warder as he tried to prise Kelly's jaws open. But Kelly held firm. He had the devil in his mouth, could feel fire quench between his teeth, feel relief as the demon's strength ebbed in his grip. He felt the serpent convulse. As baton blows rained on his head and shoulders, the insane Micko Kelly looked up at his tormentors. The bloodstained froth around his mouth, the wild staring eyes, shocked. There was no mistaking the expression in the mad, glazed, yellow-tainted eyes. It was of an animal with prey locked in its jaws, savouring its dying moments. Kelly only slackened his bite to laugh, an animal-like hysterical wail that echoed along the outside corridor, silencing every cell.

'Sweet Jesus,' the duty sergeant couldn't believe his eyes. The general alarm had been sounded and from all corners of the gaol warders rushed towards level two. Their first sight of trouble was an unconscious,

140

blood-covered and still bleeding uniformed figure being dragged away. 'Oh sweet, merciful Jesus.'

Two warders stood over Kelly's cowering body, batons poised for another onslaught. He had crawled back into a corner, mouth and face covered in blood, lips frothing and foaming. Blood and flesh clung to his nails. He was laughing and crying intermittently, running his hands up and down his legs and arms as if checking they were still attached to his body. He giggled nervously, then his expression hardened when he spotted the sergeant. Another serpent had entered the room.

'The devil is back.'

There was barely enough time to slam the steel door shut.

11.17 am

'I don't believe it.' The voice at the other end of the mobile phone was agitated and shouting. 'Slow down, for Christ's sake,' Moss Kavanagh pleaded.

The squad car was stuck in late-morning traffic along Dublin's quays. In the back seat Jim Clarke was oblivious to the conversation. In the front Tony Molloy stared at the back of a bread van. 'What's the matter,' he asked, half listening.

Kavanagh held the car's progress in a reasonably straight line with an elbow, flagging with his other hand not to interrupt. Molloy transferred his frown from the bread van.

'Who's there?' snapped Kavanagh. More agitated shouts came down the line. 'I don't believe it.' The voice at the other end suggested it was time he did.

'Where are they taking him?' More shouts. Kavanagh flicked on the car siren and pulled out to overtake a row of banked-up cars. He swerved narrowly past the edge of an open drain, almost knocking a workman off his feet, ignoring the shaking fists and curses.

In the back seat, for the first time, Jim Clarke began to pay attention. 'What's up, Mossy?'

Kavanagh glanced into the rear-view mirror. 'You're not going to like this, boss.'

The prison doctor had been shocked when he pushed past the group gathered outside Micko Kelly's holding cell. The first two warders were pacing nervously, gripping and ungripping their bloodstained batons. Four others stood at the ready, equally agitated. All jackets were off in the heat of the confined space, ties pulled down, collars open. They waited at the open door. Inside the cell was the duty sergeant, a large man with straining belly and turkey chin. He mopped repeatedly at his brow, speaking slowly and gently. On the hard bench sat Kelly. His ankles were manacled and chained with only twelve inches movement between them. His hands were ensnared to a thick, leather belt that had been pulled tightly around his waist. The back of the belt was clipped to a bolt hole on the bench. The end result immobilised him totally. Over his face a leather mask had been pulled and straps from the mask were attached to the leather waistband. He had little head movement. The leather mask was a thonged open-lace type creation. Behind the thongs, darting wild eyes flickered.

'Why does he need the muzzle?' snapped the doctor.

At the sudden change of noise, from quiet and

142

calming, to loud and angry, Kelly began to shake. He rocked his head, shook his legs and tried to stand up. He moaned. The restraining belt only frustrated further and he snarled a rasping, snorting noise that chilled those listening. The sergeant ushered the doctor out and the two engaged in angry exchanges, both trying to keep their voices low. As events were explained, the doctor's body language changed from enraged to stunned, from stunned to professional, from professional to caring. He walked cautiously back inside and began untying the muzzle, slipping the mask over and away from Kelly's entangled hair. Behind the sergeant watched warily, hands ready to pull the smaller man away from harm.

'Mr Kelly, my name is Dr Hamilton, I am the prison doctor.' The voice was reassuring. There was no hint of threat or rebuke. 'I have to talk with you, do you understand? I'm going to call you by your first name, Michael, is that okay?'

Kelly's eyes stared but didn't register. The doctor's accent was Dublin, yet light years away from Kelly's territory. Cultured and educated versus deprived and drugged.

Hamilton noted the vacant gaze, the yellow tinge in the whites of the other man's eyes. 'Michael, do you know where you are?'

Pause. The eyes flitted, the froth-stained lips trembled.

'Michael, do you know why you are here?'

The gaze moved to an inch of the doctor's nose, yet seemed to fix about six inches further back.

Hamilton noted this too. He glanced down and for the first time spotted the blood on the floor. 'Michael,' he said, 'do you know what day it is, why you are

143

here? Do you know who these men are behind me?'
He pointed towards the duty sergeant and warders.

'This man has been sent by Satan. Kill him.'

'Do you know who you ar . . . aaaagghhh!'
Hamilton just missed the lunging teeth by inches. He
felt the heat of Kelly's breath, felt froth as it flicked
across his own face, sensed the madness of the mind
that wanted to take him. 'He's fucking insane,'
snarled the professional Dr Hamilton as he wiped
Kelly's saliva off his own lips. 'Strap him up again.'

The muzzle went back over the struggling head.

1.45 pm

That afternoon, while people basked in the warmth of
the sun, opening shirts and blouses to catch any
breeze, the muzzled and manacled Michael Leo Kelly
was carried along level two of the Bridewell holding
centre. There was one warder to each limb, one to
hold his head and one supervising in case of trouble.
Kelly's saliva drooled onto the floors. He was wearing
the same clothes he had been arrested in, denim
jeans, black T-shirt and black trainers.

It was many years since he had taken two journeys
in a vehicle on the one day but just before two o'clock
on the afternoon of Thursday, 14 May, he was
transferred by secure van to Rockdale Hospital for
the Criminally Insane.

17 2.53 pm

'Dan, I wanted you to be the first to know the police have arrested the man we strongly suspect to have killed Jennifer.'

John Regan sat in a front lounge of the Marks' mansion. Beside him on the sofa was his special advisor and spin doctor in the Department of Health, a reedy looking young man called Flanagan. Sitting opposite, composed and attentive, Dan Marks held both hands clasped together. His eyes were fixed at some spot on the polished rosewood coffee table between the three men. He was unshaven and wore an open-necked check shirt over denims.

'He was arrested early this morning.' Regan was unaware of the events that had occurred earlier, unaware that as he was speaking the man 'strongly suspected' to have murdered Jennifer Marks was stuck in a traffic jam on the north side of Dublin, awaiting transfer to the state's main criminal psychiatric hospital. 'I spoke with the Minister for Justice before I left government buildings and he told me the commissioner was in continuous touch with the investigating team and well pleased with

145

progress. They feel confident this is the man involved.'

Regan had left government buildings forty minutes earlier in a three-car cavalcade with sirens blaring. He'd looked grim-faced climbing into the back of his black-windowed, chauffeur-driven Mercedes. He hoped the waiting photographers and camera crews would catch his mood exactly. Another group waited as he stepped out from the Mercedes in front of the Marks' Victorian mansion, 'no-commenting' as he strode firmly towards the front door. They'd been tipped off by Flanagan and he made sure Regan knew which were local and possibly important, and which were international and vital.

'The government is treating this dreadful event extremely seriously. We are still completely shocked. Stunned.' He paused to see how he was progressing.

Dan Marks lifted his head slowly. His eyes were red-rimmed and Regan could sense deep sorrow through the professional composure. 'Thank you, John, I appreciate you coming like this.' Marks' voice had lost its usual strength. He sounded defeated, almost weary.

'How is Annie taking this?' Regan asked, uncomfortable with the warmth of the room and the overwhelming sense of gloom.

Marks shook his head sadly and his gaze dropped again. 'Not very well at all, John. I've had to sedate her she's become so agitated. It seems to have affected her multiple sclerosis, her hand and leg movements were very rigid this morning. I gave her something strong. She's upstairs asleep.'

Regan grasped at the opportunity to appear helpful. 'Would you like me to arrange a nurse to come in and help for the next few days?'

Marks came back quickly. 'No, not at all.' He was emphatic. 'That won't be necessary. I think we're better left to grieve alone, thanks all the same.'

The spin doctor Flanagan interrupted, 'Perhaps we could arrange for someone to come in for a few hours during the day and help with cooking or cleaning?'

Marks shook his head agitatedly. 'No, no, no. That won't be necessary. We get on much better on our own, any outsiders might just upset Annie. She's very temperamental and this has really tipped her over the edge.' Marks' voice was suddenly back to its usual strength, his manner determined. 'I'm sure we're best left alone.'

Outside in the sunshine Flanagan briefed Regan before they walked to the Mercedes.

'Don't say anything other than the investigation is progressing rapidly. You were calling on Dr Marks to keep him up-to-date on events. Keep it tight, voice slow and steady, eyes fixed on one questioner only.' He acknowledged a waiting reporter with a brief nod. 'Let the cameras move after you, don't try and follow them and don't let anything distract you from the questions. The US media have taken a huge interest in this so choose your words carefully.'

Regan looked downwards, seemingly admiring Flanagan's high-polished black shoes. 'This could be as big here as the Louise Woodward trial in Boston.'

Flanagan brushed a piece of fluff off the back of Regan's jacket. 'Tell them we offered the Marks family every possible facility.' He interrupted himself, 'No, better still, say Dan and Annie Marks, not the Marks family. Okay?'

Regan nodded.

'Don't say he refused.' Flanagan paused and

looked at the cluster of photographers and reporters outside the garden railings. 'Why do you think he was so goddamn adamant about not letting anyone in there anyway?'

John Regan began walking along the gravel path and to his next photo-opportunity. 'I don't know. He certainly doesn't want anyone in that house other than themselves.' He put on his serious, concerned face, the one he reserved for difficult occasions and funerals. 'Good afternoon, ladies and gentlemen, I've got time for a few questions.'

3.42 pm

Frank Clancy clutched the charts of Mary Hyland and James Murphy to his chest. He practically hugged them. With a few lame excuses to his junior staff and ward sister he disappeared inside his office on level three of Mercy Hospital and locked the door. Breathing rapidly and feeling slightly shaky he sat down and rested the charts on the desk in front, turning each over, staring at them. He knew the contents could be disturbing, unsettling, yet he couldn't bring himself to read too quickly. It was as if he wanted to savour the moment. He thought over the previous few days' events, his discovery of the third case of agranulo-cytosis, his confrontation with Linda Speer and his concern that someone was interfering with patient records. Clancy worried some type of drug therapy was the cause of his three patients' blood problems, yet what he knew had been prescribed appeared standard. Except D/N Aspirin. But even that was quite standard in the States, although he was disturbed at the unusual

148

manner this product was being distributed. The 'little blue tablet', as Mrs Morell had described, was being issued directly by the treating cardiologist. Most unusual, thought Clancy as he flicked at the edge of the first chart. Yet he was just as concerned about making a fool of himself, of jumping to the wrong conclusions and bringing the wrath of the Dream Team on top of his head. Equally he was very wary of confronting Minister for Health John Regan. He knew how much tax-payers' money, personal time and effort Regan had committed to establishing the Heart Foundation. For Clancy to bring this house down he recognised the need to be on very sure ground. He could see a minefield ahead, accusation and counter-accusation, losing his job, legal action against him, the hospital up in arms. No, he decided firmly, I need hard facts, then decent legal advice.

He opened the first chart, that of the deceased Mary Hyland, registered number 115CD346, and began reading. The chart itself was a thick, maroon-coloured, cardboard-backed, ring-bound mass of dog-eared pages. The front cover held the patient's name, address, registered number and known drug sensitivities. The back was also maroon and listed the various speciality clinics the patient had ever attended. Clancy noticed DERMATOLOGY, GENERAL SURGERY, CARDIAC, then the final tick, HAEMATOLOGY. He couldn't help feeling guilty his was the last department Mary Hyland had attended and he had been unable to save her life. He turned the pages slowly, ignoring the dermatology and general surgery entries, stopping at the cardiac clinic writing. He recognised Linda Speer's copperplate style immediately and painstakingly followed every step of Hyland's progress. Symptoms, investigations, clinical observations, results, pre-surgery condition, sudden deterioration and emergency rescheduling of her coronary artery bypass procedure. Everything appeared straightforward. He turned to the special pink-coloured page where prescribed drug treatments were recorded. His heart skipped a beat and he stopped to fetch his glasses. He tried to peer through them and found his hands shaking. His mouth felt suddenly dry. There was no mistaking the entry: Capoten 12.5 mgs b.d. Nothing else. No D/N Aspirin.

Rummaging quickly through his pockets he pulled out a tattered piece of paper on which he'd recorded the data from the computer files. There it was, exactly as he'd read it off the screen, Capoten 12.5 mgs b.d. *and* D/N Aspirin 300 mgs daily. He glanced again at the drug entry on the pink page in the chart. It did not match the computer data. Quickly Clancy flicked through the rest of the pages until he came to the operation notes, this time written in a different hand, probably Dan Marks he decided. He scanned the scrub assistants and found Linda Speer's name. Almost without thinking he reached for the telephone and dialled the operating theatres.

'Sister,' he said innocently, determined not to raise undue suspicion, 'it's Dr Clancy from haematology here. I wonder if you could help me with a few queries?'

The theatre sister at the other end warned she had very little time. 'We're just about to start an aortic valve replacement,' she said sharply. In the background Clancy could hear the clatter of instruments on stainless-steel worktops, the clip-clopping of wooden theatre clogs on tiles, the occasional shouts of instructions. He could almost feel the buzz of the busy cardiac theatre.

'This will only take a minute,' he reassured, anxious not to lose the contact, 'but I was wondering if Dr Speer – you know the one I mean, the cardiologist?'

'Yes, I know who you mean.'

'Does she assist at all cardiac operations?'

There was a brief pause. 'No,' replied the theatre sister, obviously mulling the question over. 'Now that you mention it. As far as I can recall she only asks to scrub for coronary artery bypass procedures.'

'Never valve replacements, resection of aneurysms, anything like that?' The words sounded so innocent, the question so uninteresting.

Another brief pause. 'No, definitely not.' Then the sister added, 'I can tell you she does ask to be notified when any patient on the bypass waiting list gets into difficulty and needs to be operated on urgently. Those are the only cases she scrubs for. Is there a problem, Dr Clancy?' she asked. 'Anything coming out from here you're especially worried about? I've watched her assist and she's very good.'

Clancy hurried to reassure there were no problems, no problems at all.

'She works very closely with Stone Colman on these cases though,' the sister added helpfully. 'He takes a blood screen before, during and immediately after surgery and every four hours during the intensive care stay.'

Clancy flicked quickly to the page on Mary Hyland's chart where the cardiology blood results were stuck in place. He noticed immediately there was nothing there ordered by Stone Colman. 'Any idea what he's analysing?'

'No, I'm sorry, Dr Clancy, I'm no help to you there. I mean, there's ongoing research in this department all the time. Perhaps they're involved in that.' Over the line Clancy heard a shout and more clip-clopping of clogs. 'I'll have to go. They're calling me to scrub up. If you need any more information leave a message and I'll get back when there's more time, okay?'

She hung up, leaving Clancy staring into the earpiece, no wiser than before. He considered ringing one of the other nurses on the cardiac operating team but decided against, certain his queries would get back to Speer. Caution, he urged himself, proceed with caution. Through the partially opened venetian blinds on his office window he looked to the ward outside, noticing the nursing and medical staff going about their daily chores. Patients were being examined, charts consulted, blood samples taken, observations monitored. He thought about dropping the whole paper trail and forgetting everything. You're losing the run of yourself, you're seeing conspiracy where probably none exists. Back off before you stir up unnecessary trouble. He studied his watch. It was now almost four thirty and he estimated he was ninety minutes behind time. He had a lecture to prepare, more blood films to inspect in the laboratory and three new patients requiring his immediate attention. He decided he needed time to think things through.

4.37 pm

'Rockdale?' Jim Clarke's face was white with fury.

'When?' He was in the Bridewell holding centre looking for his arrest.

The duty sergeant had explained earlier developments. He was still trying to stop himself shaking. 'About two o'clock. The prison doctor ordered the transfer.' The sergeant had set out the sequence of events and had the log book open in front to confirm each detail.

Tony Molloy scanned the entries, frown deepening as he read. 'Could you not have waited until I got here?'

The sergeant hitched at the belt on his trousers and ran a hand along his sweat-covered shirt collar. 'You don't understand, he's fucking insane. He nearly killed one of my men. We couldn't have kept him. He was a danger to himself as well as everybody else.' His voice rose to shouting level. 'He was like a mad dog. The doctor couldn't wait to get him outa here.'

Clarke shouted angrily. 'Could he not have given him something to calm him down?' The pain in his leg was making his temper even more frayed than usual.

'Ask him yourself,' the sergeant snapped. 'Hamilton had him out of here so fast his feet never touched the ground.'

Clarke spun on his heels and limped to a bench, fuming and cursing. 'Damn Hamilton,' he snarled. Molloy and Kavanagh exchanged glances. 'Mossy,' Clarke growled through clenched teeth, 'ring control and see if there's anything new on that girl's bag and clothes.'

Kavanagh moved to a quiet corner and began pressing buttons. 'Nothing, boss,' he announced.

'Tony,' Clarke stood up awkwardly, 'call on Joan Armstrong and put the pressure on. We've got to find that school bag.' He started towards the stairs leading to the street entrance. 'Mossy,' he beckoned, 'you and I are going for an afternoon in the countryside.'

18 *4.17 pm*

'Have you been here before?' Moss Kavanagh sounded uneasy. He was driving along the two-mile stretch of pine-tree-lined roadway to Rockdale Hospital for the Criminally Insane in County Meath. County Meath was north of Dublin, the hospital an hour's drive from the city centre. The heat outside had reached twenty-six degrees. Inside it was over thirty and both Clarke and Kavanagh were perspiring heavily. They had shed jackets, revealing heavy sweat stains on both shirts. Clarke sat with his back against one door. His hair was matted down with wetness. All windows were open to catch the breeze and he gazed idly at the green countryside and rolling plains. April had been a wet month, late May warm and sunny, the combination producing a rush of growth in grass and hedgerows.

'I have two other arrests,' said Clarke.

'What are they in for?' Kavanagh sounded anxious to keep the conversation flowing and Clarke grinned as he sensed the younger man's discomfort.

'Murder. Both went to trial but they were as mad as hatters.'

Kavanagh slowed more than seemed possible as he negotiated a large pothole. He gently pressed the accelerator, skewering wheels onto the grass verge. 'What'd they do?' He flicked the windscreen wipers and pressed screen fluid into action to clear away collecting midges.

'Funnily enough,' said Clarke, now taking an interest as he spied the walls of the institution in the distance, 'both were family homicides. One fella slit his father's throat because he said someone on the radio told him to do it.'

Kavanagh gulped and spun the steering wheel sharply to avoid a sheep standing defiantly in the middle of the driveway. He blared the horn and the sheep bounded into a patch of long grass to the side. 'What about the other?'

The granite walls of the main buildings loomed ahead. Clarke craned forward and leaned against the passenger seat, chin resting on folded arms. 'You wouldn't want to know about her, Mossy, it'd put you off women for life.'

Kavanagh almost drove off the road as he spun around to look. 'Her?' he said incredulously. 'A woman?'

'Of sorts,' grinned Clarke, 'a woman of sorts. She smothered her four children in the middle of the night after she'd discovered her husband was having it off with some young thing.'

Kavanagh slid the car into neutral, keeping the engine idling. 'This isn't one of your sick jokes, is it?'

Clarke shook his head. His gaze was directed at the last yards of driveway ahead. 'Certainly not, Mossy. When the husband came home she smashed his skull in with a hammer and sat in the house for three days, surrounded by the corpses.'

Kavanagh shifted into first gear and let the car drift forward. 'Jesus,' he complained, shielding his eyes from the sun. 'What a way to spend a lovely afternoon.' He braked gently in front of large steel-barred gates. 'How do we get in?'

Rockdale Hospital for the Criminally Insane was located on a fifteen-acre plot along flat plains of valuable farming land. The institution was surrounded on all sides by a thirty-foot high, six-foot thick concrete wall. There was only one entrance, a thirty-foot gap in the wall across which a twenty-foot high steel-barred gate was pulled. The gate was operated by a two-man unit located in a tiny stone cottage barely visible from outside.

The original building had been a poorhouse in the 1880s, then an 'asylum for the demented'. The government of 1906 had bought over the buildings and an extra ten acres to create a secure institution for the violent but insane. The buildings were upgraded in 1956 and recreational facilities added in 1983. However Rockdale, more or less, was still the same institution built at the beginning of the century. Most of the stonework was original, some of the attitudes of the locals in the nearest village five miles away no different. 'The Rock', as they called it, would always be the 'serious madhouse'.

Kavanagh beeped the car horn and within minutes a tall, heavily built security guard appeared. He stopped inside the bars and noted the car registration and occupants. Then he shouted for identification before going back inside the cottage. Clarke and

Kavanagh waited and sweated. The distant sounds of farm animals broke the eerie silence, the buzzing of bees as they bounced along wild flowers the only distraction. The guard came back and began pulling at the gate. With a deceptive ease it opened in the middle and was drawn wide enough to allow the car through. The guard motioned to stop while he double-checked identities and registration.

Kavanagh watched every move, eyes darting as he took in the scene. 'They're very tight on security, aren't they?'

On the inside of the outer walls and stretching as far as the eye could see, razor wire was attached to the top ten feet of concrete. The afternoon sun glinted off the steel. Inside again a separate steel and barbed-wire fence encircled the outer perimeter wall, separated from it by a distance of about thirty feet. At one hundred-feet intervals flood lights and security cameras were trained on the inner grounds.

'When that electronic gate opens fully,' the guard pointed towards a second gate in the inner security fence, 'you can drive in. Go to the blue door at the front entrance of the grey building on your left.' He leaned in through the passenger window, scrutinising the occupants closely. 'I've rung ahead to let them know you're coming.'

Kavanagh mumbled his thanks and started forward.

'Better wait a minute,' cautioned the other man, following on foot. 'Don't go through until it engages fully.' He rested a hand on the open driver's window, waiting for the gate to settle, then leaned in again. He was grinning broadly. 'Otherwise you might start off a security alert. We wouldn't want that, would we?'

His voice had a lilting country accent. 'Not after the fun we've had already with Jack the Ripper.' He laughed at his own joke, watching as the car edged past onto newish tarmac.

The heat was stifling, the air still with midges gathering in clusters around the open windows. In the rear-view mirror Kavanagh watched the outer and inner gates close over. He shifted into second gear. The new tarmac ran for three hundred yards, the tiny strip broken only by signs directing to smaller slip roads. DELIVERIES . . . RESIDENCE . . . GYMNASIUM . . . LIBRARY . . . MAIN HOSPITAL.

'Do you know there's a fifteen-foot swimming pool, a fully equipped gymnasium and a good library here?' Clarke amazed himself as he remembered the facilities.

'Really?' said Kavanagh.

Clarke sensed his partner was still uneasy. 'Yeah, and they're hardly ever used from what I hear,' he continued. 'The doctors told me the inmates spend all day staring at the television. It doesn't matter what's on. *The Simpsons, Sesame Street*, news, ice hockey. If it moves and makes a noise they'll watch it.'

The main grey building came into view and the car was parked in a bay marked for staff.

'Let's go.' Clarke eased himself gingerly out of the back seat. They left their jackets and walked to the blue front door. From a distance it looked like a standard door to any building except for the scratch marks around an overly large keyhole. The marks extended almost eighteen inches in a semicircle around the lock. Both men stepped back to take in the Victorian splendour. The institution had grey granite walls and narrow windows with high-pointed roofs and slate tiles.

Kavanagh located an old-fashioned press bell and pushed. Nothing happened. They wiped sweat from their faces and swatted at the clustering flies. Kavanagh made to press again when the door was pulled open and a young, fresh-faced girl stood in the entrance.

'Are you the policemen?' Two heads nodded. 'Come in, Dr Dillon will be with you in a minute.' She pulled the door wide enough to permit one entrance at a time, then produced a bundle of heavy-duty keys and locked it. There was a similar pattern of scratch marks on the inside. 'Sit there.'

The policemen were directed to a wooden bench immediately inside the entrance hall. Without another word the girl walked inside a clear-glass office and picked up a phone. Clarke noticed Kavanagh grinning at him.

'Sure it'll be something to tell the wife,' he said.

Kavanagh's eyes wandered along the cool white-tiled floor. 'Not in her condition,' he growled. His gaze stopped at the next door on the level. There were scratch marks around its lock. 'The baby's due soon. I don't want her going into early labour from fright.'

The gloom of the entrance with its narrow barred windows added to the oppressive atmosphere. Keys turned in a lock and a door opened. Forensic psychiatrist Patrick Dillon walked into the hallway. He was dressed in navy slacks and a white, open-neck, short-sleeved shirt. A pair of glasses peeked out of his breast pocket. He closed the door behind and locked it.

He smiled and the gesture lightened the moment. 'I'm sorry to have kept you waiting but it takes a bit of time to come down through the wards, locking and unlocking each door.' In his right hand there was a circular steel-band cluster of heavy-duty keys. The group shook hands briefly. 'You've come to see your Mr Kelly.'

'I've come to take him back,' said Clarke.

'There might be a problem with that.' Dillon sounded as if he was describing some mechanical complication.

'Why?'

'I could spend all day trying to explain this in medical terms,' Dillon warned. 'It's better you see for yourself.' He walked to the office and began conferring with the girl, their heads locking momentarily as they flicked over paperwork. Finally he came back to the entrance hall. 'Before we go upstairs I'd like to make a few things clear.' Dillon was slightly smaller than Kavanagh and his head bobbed as he talked. 'This,' he explained, 'is a hospital, not a prison. My job is predominantly to help my patients regain their sanity or control the distress of their insanity.' Kavanagh glanced briefly at Clarke but the other man ignored him.

'The rooms here may look like cells but the doors are open most of the time to allow patients to wander freely along the corridors.' Kavanagh's mouth dropped. 'Within certain limits, of course,' Dillon added hastily. 'The inmates are delighted with anything that breaks up the daily routine and may become intensely interested in you.'

He turned the key in the first door. The three walked silently along a narrow corridor towards yet another door with large lock and scratched surface.

'Visitors often comment on the rather strange, staring expressions they find here.' Click, twist, turn. Another door was opened. Click, twist, turn. It was locked again. 'The patients look but you get the uneasy impression their gaze is about six-inches distant. When they talk their minds could be miles away. This may be due to their psychiatric condition or the drugs we use.' They stopped at another door. A large key was selected. 'Any questions?'

Clarke rested his back against the corridor wall. Kavanagh shook his head.

'This is a very quiet institution,' continued Dillon. 'There are rarely any violent incidents. We do not use batons, straitjackets or any restraining device. Our staff are trained to deal with any unpleasant incidents with minimum force.'

Kavanagh watched the key turn in the lock. 'Thank God for that,' he said.

Dillon grinned. 'I'm afraid Kelly was the exception to that rule.' The door opened and a heavy barred steel gate confronted. Dillon waited for a four-minute security lock to activate. A small TV camera beamed down. 'This is the maximum security ward.'

The first thing Clarke noticed was scuff marks on the walls. The corridors they had walked were clean and bright with good natural light through the heavily barred windows. The paintwork was unscratched. Inside the maximum security ward the paintwork was of a similar texture and colour, but at about waist level here and there distinct scuff marks could be seen.

Dillon noticed Clarke's uneasy inspection. 'Kelly's handiwork,' he explained. 'And we've only had the place painted recently,' he added glumly.

At the sound of their voices a head appeared out from one of a strip of open doors along the corridor. The head was followed by the body of a small, red-haired man.

'Dr Dillon?' The voice was loud and strident. He waddled closer. 'Are you going to let me out in the sun at all? I'd like to get outside.' He noticed Clarke and Kavanagh. 'Are you here to talk to me?' he barked. 'Are you from the newspapers?' He confronted Clarke aggressively. His voice was slightly slurred, making his country accent indistinct.

Dillon intervened and lead his patient back to the main nurses' station where a white-coated male attendant waited. The small red-haired man was then talked back into his room where he lay on the bed and restored his gaze to the ceiling.

'Strangled his sister, his mother and the family dog,' said Dillon.

As they passed each cell Moss Kavanagh squinted inside. Most of the inmates sat or lay staring at the walls or ceiling, some muttering to themselves. The rooms were clean and reasonably spacious. Many had pin-up photos while others carried popular football stars. In one cell religious posters covered all available space, on the window sill there was a cluster of religious statues. From the far end of the corridor a baying roar erupted. The howl came from behind a closed door above which a green light glowed. Two attendants waited outside. The scuff marks on the walls here were at head level. Slivers of broken glass lay on the floor. The glass was of the wire-reinforced variety.

Dillon flicked at a shard with the tip of a shoe. 'Look at the TV monitor.'

On the wall an eighteen-inch security monitor glowed. A still picture flickered. Clarke peered at the screen, his face scrunched up. Using a remote control Dillon changed the view. The crouched figure of a body could be seen in one corner of a small room. Another button was pressed and sound clicked on. An animal like moan came through.

'That's your arrest, superintendent,' said Dillon. 'That coiled-up ball of humanity is your suspect.' The grunting and groaning ceased. The crouching figure unrolled and Micko Kelly suddenly sprang into the air, hands flailing. 'He's chasing the light bulb in the centre of the ceiling,' the psychiatrist explained. 'This is the only padded cell in the hospital. It's a ten-by-eight room. The walls are fourteen feet high and eight inches thick, heavily padded with a bottle-green cloth which does not make climbing easy. In the ceiling there is a solitary green bulb for light. A TV camera is recessed out of sight.'

Dillon pressed another button and a different image flashed up. Kelly was stripped to his underpants, his bare legs and lower back now visible. The camera caught him trying to scramble towards the light source. The sight and the sounds chilled despite the warmth of the corridor. Dillon pressed another button and the floor came into view. He used a roll-top joystick to zoom and the lens picked up a mattress with a blanket on top. The blanket was pulled to the side of the bed.

'He's wet himself again,' he said. 'We'll go in and sedate. Then he's into the secure cell.'

The waiting attendants nodded wearily.

Dillon turned to Clarke. 'The predominant colour in that room is bottle-green. Psychologists claim it's a calming colour.' He grinned. 'On the one occasion I asked to be left inside with the door locked it did nothing for my anxieties.'

Clarke managed a weak smile.

Dillon flicked at the joystick. 'Patients are put into this room when they become a danger to themselves or others.' The TV image changed. 'Kelly scored top marks on both.'

The group looked up at the monitor. Inside the padded cell Micko Kelly lunged again at the ceiling. For a split second the lens caught his demented face, the froth at his mouth, the eyes of insanity. Clarke watched with a mixture of fascination and horror. Then he spun angrily on one heel and tapped his way back along the corridor, frustration and exasperation threatening to boil over.

'I haven't examined him completely yet.' Back in the cool of the white-tiled entrance Dillon was explaining events. The three sat on the wooden bench. Dillon held a manila folder with the name MICHAEL LEO KELLY written in thick felt-tip pen on one corner. 'He came in manacled and muzzled. The staff thought they had him settled. They were removing the chains when he went berserk. It took six to restrain him and he put up one helluva fight by all accounts. The orderlies are trained in restraint techniques. I believe that went out the window. It took brute force to subdue him.'

Clarke fiddled with a button on his shirt.

'He was quite psychotic,' Dillon added for good measure.

Clarke's eyebrows shot up. 'Meaning what?'

The psychiatrist scanned an entry in the folder. 'He

was hearing voices and seeing visions. Very aggressive. His shouting disturbed the other patients.'

Clarke leaned against the bench. 'What do you make of all this?'

Dillon came back immediately. 'It may be some time before he regains his sanity. No one can question him until I feel confident he has recovered.' He ignored Clarke's deepening scowl. 'I will keep you informed on any progress.' He tucked the chart under his arm and stood up. 'Unlocking his insanity is the key to your prosecution.'

'Joan, you had better come inside to the study. Your father's waiting.'

Joan Armstrong arrived home from school to find her mother fretting at the front gate of their two-storey red-bricked house in the south Dublin suburb of Sandymount. She noticed her father's black Lexus parked in the driveway. He was rarely home before seven most evenings. She sensed trouble.

'That policeman who called yesterday is here. What have you been up to?' Mrs Armstrong, a small plump lady with thinning hair clutched and unclutched a lace handkerchief. She dabbed at the corner of one eye.

'Nothing, mum, nothing,' blurted her daughter. 'Like, I don't know what he wants.' Her hands shook as she slipped off her uniform jacket and hung it in the tiny press inside the front door. Her mother watched anxiously, then ushered her into the study with a silent wave.

Harold Armstrong was the perfect bank manager. A tall, grey-haired man, his dress code matched his temperament and personality: conservative, subdued,

167

dull and boring. Joan was his third child and, as Sister Concepta had so astutely observed, a mistake in every sense of the word for him. She was born when he had least wanted another child, being ill-prepared to start parenthood again. She had been nothing but trouble, rebellious, insolent, defiant and a compulsive liar. Her behaviour had become more disturbing as she moved into the late-teenage years. 'Where is she getting the money?' Armstrong had snapped during one of many arguments about his errant daughter. She'd been discovered drunk yet again. 'I'm too old for this,' he'd complained. 'I'm out of touch with her generation.'

The most worrying development had been the telephone call from Sister Concepta warning about Joan's involvement in the drugs scene. As Armstrong listened his stomach churned. 'She's only just turned eighteen and thinks she knows it all,' the nun had said scornfully. 'She knows nothing.' Armstrong agreed. 'Thank you, sister.' Joan was grounded for another month and there was an inquisition as to how she was getting money to buy drugs. Nothing new came to light.

Less than two months later the body of Jennifer Marks was discovered in Sandymount Park. Harold Armstrong was shaken to the core. Rumours spread as to how and why she had been killed, all involving his daughter. As soon as Tony Molloy rang to arrange a second meeting Armstrong decided to turn Joan over to the police and let them sort her out. He hoped the experience would frighten her back to respectability.

He sat at his writing desk in the front study. At his side Molloy chewed on an antacid, his usual worrying frown in place.

'Hi, dad,' Joan greeted nervously and sat down in the only other free chair, strategically placed to face both men.

Armstrong ignored the greeting and immediately got down to business.

'Joan, Sergeant Molloy wants to talk to you again.' He let the words sink in for a moment. 'I want you to be completely honest with him. You can discuss everything on your own. Neither your mother nor I will be listening.' He stood up and walked out, closing the door firmly behind.

Molloy inspected the young girl sitting opposite, eyes fixed on her lap, both hands gripping the sides of the chair to stop them shaking. She seemed so vulnerable, not the precocious young lady any more. He looked around the study, noting family photographs inside silver frames, one of Joan at her first communion, small girl in white-veiled dress, hands clasped together as in prayer. He looked back at the grown-up version.

'I'm not gonna spend all day with this, okay?' His voice was hard, eyes drilling into the averted stare opposite. 'You spun me a pack of lies the other day and I know it.' Joan Armstrong looked up and Molloy sensed her fear immediately. 'You did not get off the train at Sydney Parade Station, you and Jennifer Marks went on to the next stop at Ringsend, didn't you?' A subdued head nodded. 'So maybe you'd like to tell me what really happened? I have statements from a number of witnesses, including school pals, so don't try and hide anything. We know everything, all I need is confirmation. Okay?' He pressed the ON button on a microcassette. 'Start from when the two of you got off the train at Ringsend.'

Trembling hands went up and Joan Armstrong untied jet-black hair from the clasp at the back of her head and shook her tresses free. She pulled them back again and replaced the clasp.

'We went to Balfe's pub to score dope. Jenny was heavy into dope and I often went with her, like, you know, sort of to keep her company.' The voice was weak and defeated and Molloy snapped back immediately.

'Don't bullshit me, Joan, you can feed that sort of crap to your parents but don't try shoving it at me. I don't give a damn if you smoke dope or not, understand? But don't insult my intelligence with that innocent "I was only keeping her company" line.'

The girl's façade collapsed and she shook violently as the words poured out.

'We went into Balfe's pub and waited for Jenny's contact to turn up. She had this fella who supplied whatever she wanted and they always met there.'

The 'you know' and 'like it's really weird' phrases had gone, Molloy noticed. She can't wait to clear her conscience, he decided.

'There was this big-head with a tattoo on his forehead waiting to score as well and she started messing with him.'

Molloy cut across, 'What do you mean "messing"?'

'She'd grab at his drink and swig some of it, snatch a drag on his cigarettes, that sort of thing.'

Molloy turned his microcassette tape volume up. 'What'd he look like?' A perfect description of Micko Kelly followed.

'I left about six. I was late already and I had to go. Jenny stayed on drinking with the head.'

'Had she scored anything?'

'No. The usual contact didn't turn up. The head she was with gave her something, I don't know what. I told her I was going but she said she would go home on her own later.'

'And you left her in the pub with this big fella with the tattoo on his forehead?'

'Yeah. Honestly.'

Balfe's pub, Joan Armstrong confirmed, was a popular meeting place for young kids looking for drugs. Dealers from the inner city had migrated to the more affluent suburbs, getting better money for their trade and less hassle from the police. The pub had been one of Jennifer Marks' favourite haunts. Joan Armstrong's too. They'd often gone there after school and at weekends.

'Where would you go to smoke or drink? Or did you just sit and smoke your heads off in the pub?' Molloy was scribbling notes as well as recording.

'No, we usually went to the park.'

Molloy's head shot up. 'What park?'

'Sandymount Park.'

Molloy stopped scribbling and looked directly into Joan Armstrong's eyes. He noticed the fear had left, the uncertainty replaced by the confidence of truth. 'Did you use the park regularly?'

'Yeah, most weekends, sometimes after school. There's an old wooden shelter there we used to sit in.' The voice was stronger now.

Molloy scanned past notes as he turned the cassette over and pressed the ON button again. 'When Jennifer Marks' body was discovered she wasn't wearing her school uniform.'

Joan Armstrong didn't wait for the question. 'She

changed in the toilets in the pub. We always did that so we didn't stick out. You know, little convent girls in a pub full of junkies.'

'What did she do with her uniform?'

'Like we always did, stuffed it inside our school-bags.'

Molloy noted the 'we' rather than 'she'. 'But we didn't find her schoolbag in the park.'

'I know.'

Molloy's eyes shot up, surprised. 'Waddye mean you know? Where is it?'

'I'd have to show you. I'm sure it's hidden where we always leave our gear.'

'Show me.'

Joan Armstrong's parents were relieved as they watched her climb into the back of Molloy's car. They were relieved it was unmarked.

'I'll have her back in half an hour,' he advised, his frown replaced by a grin for a change. 'We're getting on famously.'

Harold Armstrong even managed a weak smile in response.

5.55 pm

Dr Frank Clancy was rubbing his glasses against a corner of his white coat. He breathed on the lenses to moisten, wiped again, then shoved them back on his nose. With little enthusiasm he flicked at the dog-eared pages of the charts on his desk. He'd reviewed the facts as he understood them while studying an acute leukaemic blood film in the laboratory. Like a barrister in court he'd mentally argued the pros and cons of the conspiracy theory. Then, to grab back lost time, he'd passed the lecture commitment to his registrar, second in command on the haematology medical team. No matter how aggressively he presented the case 'for', instinct shouted 'not guilty'. Fear of the consequences if he read the situation wrong troubled him greatly. This is a legal minefield, he reminded himself. Don't step on a bomb and expect not to get hurt. He began leafing through patient Mary Hyland's chart, stopping when he reached the pink drugs page. His fingers played with the edge of the paper as he stared at the sole entry: Capoten 12.5 mgs. He was about to turn when he noticed the difference between the page he was holding and the rest in the chart. It looked new. Quickly Clancy flicked through all the recent entries. Each page was dog-eared, the look of being well used. There were ink smudges, rushed handwriting and scribbled notes along some margins, even thumb-prints. But when he returned to the drug entry pink page its cleanliness, its straight edges, its lack of dog-eared corners suddenly hit him. Unsettled him. Very gingerly he parted the pages beside and eased the ring binding. There was no mistaking the barely clinging torn edge. It was pink. Someone had removed the original page in a hurry. Someone had interfered with Mary Hyland's chart.

Frank Clancy mopped at his brow with the sleeve of his white coat. *Someone's trying to hide something.* Checking through the venetian blinds that he was not going to be disturbed, Clancy parted the ring file and teased out the edge of pink paper, placing it carefully inside an envelope. He closed the file over and returned to the pages where the post-operation notes had been entered. The handwriting varied depending on which of the heart surgery team was examining and recording. Some of the writing was clear, some barely legible. Now and then he could distinguish Linda Speer's copperplate from the others. But the entry he was looking for, the one clue he needed to piece together the jigsaw forming in his mind, eluded. Until he spotted the Tipp-Ex. A note had been written in the white daily record pages, a continuous handwritten observation of Mary Hyland's imme-diate condition when transferred from intensive care to standard ward. Alongside her blood pressure, temperature, pulse and respiratory rates the examining doctor had written: *continue Capoten 12.5 mgs b.d. . . .* , there then followed a small Tipp-Exed space. By looking at the other side of the page through his desk light, Clancy was just about able to make out the concealed entry: *. . . and D/N Aspirin 300 mgs daily.* Without closing Mary Hyland's chart, he flicked open the maroon cover on the second, that of patient James Murphy, and hurried through the pages until he reached the most recent cardiac pink drugs page. It too looked brand new. Parting the ring binder slightly he uncovered the remnants of another torn-off pink page. Like Hyland, according to the chart he was reading from, James Murphy *had not* been on D/N Aspirin. But just as with Mary Hyland, he *had been* on D/N Aspirin 300 mgs daily when Clancy had scanned the drugs on the computer screen. Someone was deliberately changing the drug treatment schedules, but in such a hurry they were leaving vital evidence.

He turned to the PC on the desk in front and accessed both patients' records. This time there was no red asterix warning the file was in use. Even before he reached the drugs records he sensed something would have been altered. He was right. According to the existing files on both patients there was no record of either having been prescribed D/N Aspirin. Clancy leaned back heavily in his chair and stared at the blue screen. His heart was racing and he was perspiring heavily. He felt his chest rise and fall rapidly.

What is going on?

He glanced at his watch. It was almost six ten in the early evening. He did a quick mental calculation. Six ten in the evening, Irish time. That was around noon Chicago, USA, time. Clancy had trained in Chicago and knew his old hospital had an emergency Drugs Assist programme for queries. This allowed treating physicians and casualty doctors to call direct for immediate information on any particular drug. It could mean the difference between life and death for someone being treated for a drug overdose, or a patient on the wards with an unusual medical problem possibly related to prescribed medication. One telephone call and the latest data on all legal and illegal, doctor-prescribed or just 'over-the-counter' pharmaceuticals was available within minutes via the hospital data bank. He scanned the telephone book, picked up the phone and began dialling.

'Drugs Assist helpline.' The broad mid-western accent lifted his spirits immediately. Clancy almost cheered, he felt he was back in Chicago.

'Hi,' he said, not certain whether to tell the nurse-aide where he was ringing from. The line was so clear he might only have been two blocks away. 'My name is Dr Frank Clancy and I'm calling you from Dublin, Ireland.' He decided on half truths.

'Hi there, Dr Clancy. What can we do for you here in Chicago?' The voice was friendly and accommodating.

'Well, it's a simple problem, really,' began Clancy. 'I'm looking after a patient from the US who is on a drug we don't have in our formulary.' He was making it up as he went along, it was easier than explaining conspiracy theories. 'I was wondering if you could identify the drug in particular and whether there are any known side-effects recorded against it?'

'No problem, Dr Clancy. Just tell me all you know and I'll do an immediate search.'

'D/N Aspirin. Could you give me a physical description and side-effect profile.'

'One moment.' Even over the transatlantic line Clancy could hear the tapping on a keyboard. 'Here we are,' the nurse came back within two minutes. 'D/N Aspirin: comes in one strength only, three hundred milligrams. It's manufactured by Cynx Pharmaceuticals in Boston, comes as one preparation only, a slow-release, once-a-day version.'

'Do you have a physical description of it?' pressed Clancy. 'You know, what it actually looks like?'

Tap-tap on the faraway keyboard. 'Yes, sir, it's an oval-shaped yellow tablet, scored down the middle on both sides. Letters CP on one side only.'

A voice suddenly echoed in Clancy's head. Harold Morell's plump and careful wife's description of his medication: 'the pinky-blue tablet for his angina'. Clancy knew that was Capoten 12.5 mgs, he had recognised the description immediately. It was the second tablet, the 'little blue one' that wasn't fitting in now. The D/N Aspirin being prescribed and handed out personally by Linda Speer was not matching its description in the US National Pharmaceutical Formulary.

'I'm sorry,' Clancy sounded as confused as he felt. 'Could you repeat that?' His pen was pressed and ready to record.

'Yes, sir. An oval-shaped yellow tablet, scored down the middle on both sides. Letters CP on one side only.'

'You sure?'

The friendly voice suddenly hardened. 'Dr Clancy, it's my job to be sure. People don't ring me for information and expect me not to be sure.'

'Oh God, I'm sorry,' Clancy mumbled. 'It's just that your description doesn't fit in with what I've got here.'

'Then you ain't got D/N Aspirin.'

Clancy stared at the earpiece, speechless.

'Are you still there, Dr Clancy?'

'Yes,' said the haematologist, his head spinning.

'Do you still want the side-effect profile?'

Clancy stared at his written description of D/N Aspirin. 'No, it's okay, that won't be necessary, thank you very much. I think you're right. I ain't got D/N Aspirin.'

'Have a nice day and say "hello" to Dublin from me.'

6.10 pm

'Turn left here and take the second left again.' Joan Armstrong sat slumped in the back seat so no one would see her. She allowed no more of her head up than necessary to give directions. 'Now go down this road to the T-junction and take a right.'

Molloy drove past red-bricked terraced houses, apartment complexes, cricket greens and small shop clusters selling anything from videos to Chinese takeaways. The roads were a mixture of wealth and second-rate wannabees.

'Do you see that disused electricity meter box about halfway down the road?' Joan Armstrong was sitting higher, straining past Molloy's neck.

Molloy slowed to a crawl and let a motorbike courier shoot past on the wrong side. 'Where?' He spotted it and swerved to the other side of the road and parked beside. He glanced up and down, there was no activity. A graffiti-scarred nameplate said Mercers Road. Underneath it rubbish lay scattered from a burst garbage bag. A dog nosed at an empty packet of crisps.

'Quiet here, isn't it?' he said.

'That's why we use it.'

Molloy turned and grinned. 'Where's the bag?' he asked quickly, not wanting his grin to defuse the gravity of the situation.

'Inside it.'

'Inside that meter box?'

'Yeah. Look in there, I'll bet that's where she stuffed it. That's where we usually hide our bags.'

Joan Armstrong watched from the car. Molloy poked at the rusty lock on the meter box with the top of his biro and the doors parted easily. He pushed one door open fully. The schoolbag sat innocently in one corner. It looked untouched. A spider had spun a web that covered the upper flap. He slipped on a pair of surgical gloves and went to the boot of the car and removed a large evidence bag. The schoolbag was slipped inside. The meter box was checked again carefully, inside and out. There was nothing. Molloy looked up and down. There was no one on the road, no one at any of the windows of nearby houses, no one to witness the small piece of drama being enacted on the quiet slip road in Sandymount in the warmth of the evening sun. Only the spider whose web he had destroyed.

'Why here? Where's Sandymount Park?' The locality was well off Molloy's beaten track and he was unsure of his bearings. He sat in the driver's seat, door open for air. Joan Armstrong was slumped down again in the back seat. A van sped past, much too fast for the road but Molloy ignored it.

'There's a gap in the wall at the very back of the park used by heads. You can reach it from here.' A finger pointed past Molloy's left ear. 'You go down to the end of this road and take a right. You'll see three big granite rocks with the name of the apartment block there. You can squeeze past the rocks and there's a narrow path that goes along the side of the park. It's only a few minutes from here.' The finger changed direction and Molloy's head swivelled to follow. He still wasn't sure of his co-ordinates and turned the engine on, allowing the car to glide slowly to the end of the road. There was a newish looking two-storey block of flats in a cul-de-sac to the right. The road ended after about one hundred yards. The granite rocks stood out like fallen meteorites. 'THE PALMS' was chiselled into one. Molloy squinted at the apartments and decided he couldn't have thought of a less appropriate name. He climbed out of the car, squeezed between two of the boulders and discovered the narrow path. Brushing dust and grit off his clothes he returned.

'Where did she get money to buy drugs?'

'From her parents.' Joan Armstrong's voice changed again, from confident to unsure. 'They're filthy rich,' she added for good measure. 'You know, like, it's really weird, they just gave her whatever she wanted.'

Molloy was too preoccupied wondering what was inside the schoolbag to challenge. He squinted at the girl in the rear-view mirror. The head of jet-black hair was low, the provocative lips were being nibbled. The make-up was not concealing the anxiety. He decided she'd had enough for one day.

'Great girl,' he beamed as he left her back at the house. 'She's been a great help.' The Armstrongs forced weak smiles as they ushered their daughter inside.

7.35 pm

DID PSYCHO JUNKIE KILL JENNY?

Jim Clarke scanned the *Evening Post* headlines and quickly read the report underneath Barry Nolan's by-line. Inside, four pages were devoted to the dawn raid on Hillcourt Mansions ('Dublin's notorious drugs' flashpoint, where junkies rule the roost') and the arrest of an unnamed male 'in his thirties, well known to the police'. Nolan described how 'the suspect' had been first taken to the Bridewell holding centre and then to Rockdale Hospital for the Criminally Insane. The account carried photographs of Hillcourt Mansions, photographs of the cortège screaming away from the tenement buildings and a file photograph of Rockdale. There followed a list of the more notorious inmates at the hospital and their crimes. Clarke twisted the paper into a side pocket of his jacket and stared out at the slow-moving traffic along O'Connell Street, Dublin's main traffic artery.

'You better take me home, Mossy, my leg's killing me.'

Moss Kavanagh glanced at the pain-racked face in the rear-view mirror and pressed the accelerator.

'Your father's like a bear, for God's sake don't say anything to annoy him.' Clarke's wife Maeve was fussing in the kitchen trying to get a meat pie heated. She poured a glass of white wine. 'Take that to him and talk to him for a minute 'til I get his dinner.'

Katy took a furtive sip and carried the rest to her father. Clarke was lying on the couch, one eye on the television news, the other on a blister he'd just discovered on his damaged leg. The early evening news lead with the arrest of the still-unnamed Micko Kelly on suspicion of being involved in the murder of Jennifer Marks. A quick flick through the channels confirmed the story was being carried on most networks. Clarke took the glass without a word and knocked it back. Katy made a face and went back to the kitchen to fill up again.

'His leg looks awful bad tonight, mum,' she whispered as she fiddled inside the fridge for the wine bottle.

Maeve made a low shoosh. 'I know. Don't say anything to him though, it'll only upset him more.'

Katy poured a full glass and took another furtive sip behind her mother's back. Without turning, Maeve growled at her.

'Don't you touch another drop. That's all I've left

and with the mood he's in he may as well have the whole lot.'

Katy grinned and took a deeper sip, topped the glass up and went back inside the sitting room. The tension was unbearable and she slipped upstairs to her room and took up a book.

Clarke ate his dinner in silence, drank the best part of three-quarters of the bottle of wine and groaned his way to bed. He neither spoke nor acknowledged his wife or daughter. Inside his room he inspected the blister. It had got bigger, now at least an inch in diameter and full of dark blood. The leg ached unbearably and he knocked back two more painkillers despite the warning they shouldn't be taken with alcohol. He slumped back and was asleep within minutes.

20

'I think you should come out now.'

Dr Patrick Dillon, consultant forensic psychiatrist at Rockdale Hospital for the Criminally Insane, was standing outside the institution's one and only padded cell. Beside him in the corridor were three warders and two medical students, both female. Dillon had gently eased the lock and opened the cell door. It was later than he would have liked but Micko Kelly's increasingly agitated behaviour had delayed his hand. Dillon had finally sedated him with an intramuscular dose of Clopixol Acuphase.

'This is a fast-acting major tranquilliser,' he explained to the students. 'It should start to work in about twenty minutes. I'll leave him an hour, maybe a little longer before we open the door again. He should be a lot calmer.' The students listened attentively, scribbling notes. 'He's been settled in the corner for the past forty minutes. I'd say we coax him out now.'

Dillon's voice was calm and quiet, deliberately so as Kelly had been one of the most disturbed patients seen for some time. Word of his attack at Bridewell had reached the hospital. No one was prepared to take any chances. Already a special holding cell had been prepared.

'I think you should come out now. You're getting cold and it's late.'

Kelly's head lifted as he searched for the voice. For almost five minutes he didn't stir and no one approached. His eyes had a glazed, distant look and he blinked occasionally and slowly, as if wiping the lenses clean. Those watching had been warned not to make any noise or sudden movement. All stood still, breathing softly.

'I'm coming in now,' Dillon murmured as he inched into the padded cell. Behind, the warders followed.

The medical students watched intently, notepads put away. They were allowing their senses to record and observe. This was human drama at its sharpest, nothing that could be learned from a textbook.

Kelly's hair was matted down with sweat. A hand went up as if to ward off the approaching figure.

'It's all right, Michael, you're safe now.'

The hand went up again, fly-swatting movement, and Kelly stared straight at Dillon. His eyes moved slowly as if his brain was barely registering. Dillon knelt down. Kelly recoiled. 'Fuck off.' The rebuke was half-hearted.

Dillon took a hand and held it firmly. 'Try and get up. You're getting cold.'

The thick walls of the institution always kept the corridors and rooms warm after the summer sun. Inside the padded cell no heat penetrated. Dillon placed one hand firmly on an elbow, the other on a wrist and dragged Kelly to his feet. He stood unsteadily, eyes rolling, mouth opening and closing as he chewed on the side of his tongue. Dillon lead him into the corridor. Kelly stood shivering, eyes shielded from the sudden brightness. He rested one hand against a wall. The small group of onlookers stepped back.

Kelly looked thin and malnourished. His ribs were too obvious, his hips carried little meat. His legs were spindly and his long dank hair was dishevelled. His eyes were vacant and distant, hands moving as if through treacle. Dillon held an elbow and escorted his patient along the corridor, stopping when Kelly stopped, allowing him to take in his surroundings. His staring gaze reflected astonishment, bewilderment, incomprehension. Twice he tried to shake off the gripping hand.

'I want you to come into this room.' Dillon steered the weak frame towards the holding cell.

Kelly stopped at the door and squinted at the single bed in the centre of the floor. Beside was a small hand basin and lavatory. The walls were clean and unmarked, only barred windows reflecting prison status. He allowed himself to be guided inside and slowly laid on the bed. He lay on his back and stared at the ceiling. The tiny room filled up. He continued to chew slowly on the side of his tongue and occasionally yawned, a long, open-mouthed yawn that exposed poor dental hygiene.

'Angela,' Dillon addressed one of the medical students, a pretty blonde with hair tied in a bun. 'I'm going to examine him now. We have to rule out any physical cause of this psychosis. Perhaps you'd record my observations?'

Micko Kelly's hospital chart was passed over and Angela clicked a biro into action. Dillon slipped on two pairs of surgical gloves, one on top of the other.

'There is infestation with head lice, this involves the beard as well.' He stopped. 'We're going to cut your hair and shave you.'

Kelly's eyes rolled and he mouthed an answer no one could make out. One of the warders moved to the top of the bed and produced a pair of scissors. Within minutes the lice-ridden hair and beard lay in a small cardboard box.

'Burn that,' ordered Dillon. 'The nose shows marked mucosal swelling and there is conjunctival hyperaemia with icteric changes.' Dillon directed the students to the yellow tinge of jaundice in Kelly's eyes. 'Open your mouth.'

Kelly obliged, eyes rolling as he watched. Dillon made sure his hands were well out of the way.

'There is poor dental hygiene.' Experienced fingers now glided along Kelly's neck. 'There are no glands enlarged.' The fingers ran along shoulder and arms. 'There are needle-track sites at both elbows with vein thrombosis. The nails are very long.' Clip, clip. The nails were cut. 'Sit him forward.' A stethoscope was placed on chest. 'Lungs clear, heart sounds normal. You can lay him back again.' A blood pressure reading was recorded. 'He has significant gynae-comastica.' Dillon explained the significance of this. 'He has an almost female distribution of fat over the breasts.' Heads craned to inspect. 'That suggests long-standing liver disease.' Dillon's fingers continued to explore Kelly's abdomen. 'The liver is enlarged and extends to five fingers breadth beneath the right sub costal margin. The edge is hard and irregular. There are spider naevi on the trunk and abdominal skin surfaces.' Hands now examined Kelly's groin and slipped underneath his underpants. 'There is testicular atrophy.' Dillon double-checked. 'It's quite marked in fact.

In the corridor outside the clinical findings and suggestions on management of patient number 1142, Michael Leo Kelly, were being discussed.

'He presented with a violent, aggressive paranoid psychosis,' began Dillon. Out of the corner of an eye he watched warders coming and going from the holding cell. 'He has a history of drug abuse. That strongly suggests this is a pharmacologically induced event. He also shows signs of chronic liver failure. According to his prison file he has hepatitis B and C.'

'Might that explain his psychosis?' the bun-haired blonde asked. 'Maybe this is a toxic reaction because of his impaired liver?'

Dillon thought this over. 'It's a possibility. We'll do a full blood count, liver and renal function tests and toxicology report for alcohol and drug screen. We'd better re-check his infective hepatitis status.'

He stopped to check the holding cell. Kelly lay as he'd left him, staring at the ceiling, eyes vacant and glazed. He was yawning large, open-mouthed yawns and continued chewing on the side of his tongue. Dillon returned to the students.

'He's much calmer, easier to manage. We'll have to treat him carefully, fatten him up, get him back to health, physically and mentally.' He remembered the earlier conversation with Jim Clarke. 'Then he'll be crucified.'

'Dr Clancy, how are you?' The man at the door in the west Dublin suburb of Blanchardstown squinted at Frank Clancy in the gloom of a low-wattage light. 'God, but you look awful tired. Would you like to come in for a cup of tea? It's very late, you must be exhausted.'

Clancy declined. He was in a hurry. After discovering the deliberate and hastily disguised changes in the medical charts and computer records of both Mary Hyland and James Murphy, he was sure something crooked was going on at the Mercy Hospital. He wasn't exactly sure what or why. His conversation with the Drugs Assist nurse in Chicago had thrown him completely. He now believed it was not D/N Aspirin that was being dispensed to patients. *But what was?* What was the 'tiny blue' tablet each of the three patients had taken that could possibly have caused their blood disorder, agranulocytosis? There was only one way of finding out. To get hold of one of the tablets. Which was why he was standing on the doorstep of Ned Hyland's small cottage in Blanchardstown. He'd rung earlier and explained who he was, certain the late Mary Hyland's husband would remember him only too well.

'Ah, Dr Clancy,' Ned Hyland had greeted over the phone, 'delighted to hear from you again. I can't tell you how grateful I am for everything you tried to do for Mary, God rest her soul.'

Clancy had listened politely, keeping the conversation general and simple. Then he'd slipped in a few questions about Mary Hyland's drug treatments before she'd been admitted for the last time to the Mercy Hospital. 'The "little blue" ones, do you remember them, Ned?'

'Indeed and so I do. Dr Speer gave them out herself every Thursday. I had to go and collect them from herself personally.'

This was all Clancy needed to hear. 'Is there any chance,' he'd asked casually, 'you would have any of them left? Maybe you threw them out, most people do. I was just wondering if you might have held on to any, though?'

'The little blue ones?'

'Yes, the little blue ones.'

'Faith and I do, Dr Clancy.' Ned Hyland had a wonderful country way of making every sentence sound like a major statement. 'I never throw anything out. Medicines are too damned expensive to be dumping. I was going to leave them back to the hospital for any deserving soul who mightn't have the money to pay for them. Just didn't get round to it yet.'

'So you still have them?' Clancy pressed.

'Up in a wee box in the spare room.'

'Could I call over and collect them?'

'Ah, sure don't you be bothering yourself with that. You have a hundred and one more important things to do. I'll drop them over to the hospital myself, tomorrow.'

'It's all right,' lied Clancy, 'I'm going out your way later tonight. I'll call in.'

'Fair enough, Dr Clancy. I'd be delighted to see you.'

Which he was. He had the box containing the 'little blue' tablets on a table just inside the front door and opened the lid with a great flourish. 'There they are. I'm sorry there's only the five left.'

Clancy picked up one carefully, turning it round. Without his glasses and in the poor light he could barely make out the lettering etched on one side. It was CYN. On the other side were the letters XP.

'Perfect,' he murmured, heart racing with excitement. The gloating face of Linda Speer flashed in his mind. 'Thank you very much.'

Ned Hyland beamed in the gloom. He was delighted to be of any help to such an important man. 'They must be fierce expensive tablets.'

Clancy started to leave, then stopped. He turned back. 'Why do you say that?'

'Well, I had some other fella ringing me about an hour after you did, asking about those very same tablets.'

'Did you tell him anything?' Clancy couldn't keep the anxiety out of his voice.

'Just that you were coming to collect them, that's all. I said you might be able to spare him one.' Hyland stopped. Clancy suddenly seemed very agitated. 'Did I do wrong, Dr Clancy? Should I not have said that?'

Clancy forced a confident smile and shook the other man's hand firmly. 'Not at all, Ned, not at all.

Probably one of the other doctors trying to beat me to the post in my research.'

Ned sighed with relief. 'Good man yourself, Dr Clancy, you run with it first. Pip the other bastards before they get out of the traps.'

Clancy chuckled in the dark as he made his way back to his car. He clutched the small box firmly in his right hand. 'I will, Ned,' he shouted back. 'I'll be collecting my winnings before they've even marked their cards.'

Hyland closed the door, laughing quietly at the racing banter. Three minutes later he heard a car start up and rev off at high speed. 'Hoors,' he muttered to himself. 'Bloody joyriders, I'll bet.' He turned on the television to watch the midnight news.

The weather broke overnight. A deepening Atlantic
front swept in over the hills and valleys of Kerry and
west Cork. Angry, rain-laden clouds, coiled in
swirling masses, were pushed over the countryside by
force-eight winds. As if venting rage, loud and violent
thunder claps rattled window frames and sent farm
animals scurrying into huddles. Lightning flashes lit
up skies and fields, warning of the deluge to come.
The ensuing rain poured down in sheets, over quiet
country roads and lanes, upon green fields and dark
bogs. It drilled at the earth and dragged dust from the
headstones of the hundreds of thousands of graves
around the country. The storm reached Dublin
around five o'clock in the morning. Great swirls of
wind sparked mini tornadoes among high-rise buildings, scattering the litter of the rich among the
rubbish of the poor. The rain filled gutters and down-
pipes, overflowed storm drains and dragged away the
flecks of blood still clinging to blades of grass in
Sandymount Park. By six o'clock all remaining traces
of the murder of Jennifer Marks had been washed
away.

Just as the weather broke on the nation's capital, the blood-filled blister on Jim Clarke's leg burst.

'Wake up, Jim, your leg's bleeding.' The first Clarke knew of the day was his wife's gentle shaking. He had slept uninterrupted, the first time in weeks, had not moved from his on-back position. Next he became aware of the still sleeping body of his daughter Katy, snuggled beside him. Distressed at her father's pain the night before she'd crept in for a last-minute kiss only to find him asleep. She'd eased her own body into the bed and lay down, one arm around his waist. They had slept like that all night. Maeve had checked before she went to her own bed and left them undisturbed.

'Jim, wake up.'

Clarke lifted his head groggily and looked down at the foot of the bed. He was still disorientated from the night before. He tried lifting his leg and it moved without the usual pain, but the bloodstaining was very obvious. 'Ah Christ,' he cursed.

'Don't move any more,' cautioned Maeve as she fussed to clear blanket away from undersheet. Still Katy slept on, one arm clinging to her father's chest. Clarke leaned over and kissed her gently on the forehead.

'I've rung the hospital and they want you in before nine o'clock. Dr Kelleher said he'd see you himself.'

Clarke showered with a plastic bag over his leg, breakfasted in silence while he waited for Moss Kavanagh to collect him. He was kept waiting only five minutes in the casualty department before he spotted the tousled grey hair of his treating doctor bob towards him.

'Overdoing it again?' Kelleher asked.

'I've got a job to do, Declan. We're under a lot of pressure with this Marks girl murder.'

Kelleher lifted the damaged limb above waist level and inspected it closely. 'That's a dreadful business, right enough.' He waited to see if the oozing stopped. It did. 'Are you resting this?' Clarke ignored the question. 'You're going to have to look after this better, there's an ulcer forming.'

Clarke's silence was deafening. Kelleher called a nurse and left instructions on treatment. Before he left the examination cubicle he leaned down and whispered into Clarke's ear. 'John Regan's on the war path. He's ordered all of the top floor to a press conference.' He grinned mischievously. 'God help anyone turning up here today with a heart attack.'

10.00 am

'Good morning, ladies and gentlemen. Thank you for coming at such short notice.' Minister for Health Regan was back in the same large hall in which he had held his triumphant news conference eight months earlier. On the podium behind Regan sat Dan Marks, Linda Speer and Stone Colman, each dressed in black. Their sombre faces were in stark contrast to the glamour and buzz of the first appearance. The backdrop of government slogans was missing. Regan had dressed appropriately, muted charcoal single-breasted suit, usual bright tie replaced by a narrow black linen effort.

'I will not dwell on Tuesday's dreadful event.' He turned and looked towards Dan Marks. 'Other than to say the government will bring to justice the man who murdered Jennifer Marks. We have arrested a suspect. He is securely locked up. He will feel the full vigour of the law.' His voice was loud and commanding, his demeanour that of controlled anger. 'We offer our sincerest condolences to Dan and Annie Marks on their tragic loss.' Dan Marks looked up to acknowledge. 'We are,' continued Regan, 'very aware of their immense burden of grief, a pain shared by all in this room and throughout the country.'

He scanned the audience. The hall was almost full, a mixture of journalists and TV network reporters. There was an impressive US East Coast presence. The rest was a mixture of Mercy Hospital cardiology staff and government supporters hounded from their desks to swell the numbers.

'This government is determined to continue the work of the Heart Foundation.' He paused and clenched the lectern tightly, whitening his knuckles. 'Let me confirm the team of specialists behind me are determined to stay and complete what they have begun.'

The hall filled with unrestrained applause, the acclaim starting from the enthusiastic hands of Regan's advisor, Flanagan. The TV cameramen zoomed in on the Dream Team, catching tight, resolute expressions.

'We will go on.' Regan had to shout to make himself heard above the applause. 'We will not be beaten.'

Dr Frank Clancy listened from a corner at the very back of the hall. He had squeezed in as the news conference began and edged his way out of sight behind a TV crew. Throughout he kept his head down, chin resting on chest. As the first hands started clapping, he slipped out again. 'This government is determined to continue the work of the Heart Foundation.' John Regan's determined pledge worried him. There was no doubt of the government's continuing and total committment to the hospital project. If anything Jennifer Marks' murder seemed to have firmed Regan's resolve.

As he stood on the wet pavements trying to flag a taxi, Clancy began fretting again about his conspiracy theory. Careful, Frank, he cautioned himself. This could blow up in your face. You need more facts. Time to rethink strategy. He just caught a glimpse of the dark figure shadowing him as a hackney pulled up.

'We've gone through almost as much as you gave us.' Arnold Leeson, director of the forensic science laboratory, sensed the impatience on Jim Clarke's face immediately he spotted him at reception. He decided to get his retaliation in first. 'We're swamped with work,' he added as he signed a form stuck in front of him by one of his surgically gloved assistants.

'I'm not here to put any pressure on,' lied Clarke.

Leeson flicked off another few signatures, ending with a grand flourish. 'Thank God for that. Both the Minister for Justice and the Minister for Health have been on the phone looking for a preliminary report on Kelly.' He noticed Clarke's alarmed expression. 'Don't worry, I gave them nothing. We won't have much until after the weekend,' he added. 'Can you not wait 'til then?'

Standing just behind Clarke, Moss Kavanagh shook his head.

'What about the bag brought in yesterday? Can we check that?' asked Clarke.

Leeson opened the heavy-duty door separating reception from the main activity centres inside. Clarke prodded Kavanagh ahead with the tip of his crutch.

'Molloy's been in since nine waiting for you,' said Leeson. He let the door shut after them.

They gathered inside the small room set aside for material collected from Jennifer Marks. The space was cramped and Kavanagh had to stand in the corridor. He peered over the backs of the assembled group. Tony Molloy sat on the one high stool, forehead creased, jowls sagging. Arnold Leeson squeezed into a corner and clipped a microphone lead onto the pencil-filled pocket of his white coat. The other end was connected to a microcassette in a side pocket. He lifted a clipboard and slid a fresh A4 page into place. Molloy offered Clarke his seat and the two swapped.

'Okay, gloves on before you handle anything,' Leeson warned. Two pairs of surgical gloves were snapped onto impatient hands. 'Open it up.'

The seal was broken on the evidence bag and Jennifer Marks' school satchel slipped onto the bench. All eyes fixed on the bulging green canvas with leather straps. There was a flap at the back pulled over and buckled in place at the front. On the canvas the letters JENNIFER MARKS U6A had been carefully written with thick black marker. The outer margins of each letter were traced further with red marker. RADIOHEAD was written in longhand with black marker along a side flap. There were two side pockets, each buckled down. Traces of cobweb clung to the leather straps and green canvas at the front.

Clarke lifted the bag and inspected bottom, sides and back. 'It's very light.' He looked at Leeson. 'I'm opening it.'

The buckles rattled as they were released and the

flap was peeled back. On the inside more black marker picked up loyalty to Bon Jovi. The side pockets were opened and their contents recorded. The left pocket held an opened box of ten Tampax Regular sanitary tampons. Inside the same pocket were two biros and a pencil. The ink on one of the biros had leaked and the Tampax container had ink-staining on the bottom. The right pocket contained small change, an opened twenty packet of Benson and Hedges cigarettes, a lipstick, an eye-shadow pencil and a compact with face powder. Clarke flipped the cigarette carton. It looked half full.

Leeson scribbled each detail on his clipboard. 'Okay,' he suggested, 'start with what you've opened and I'll record. Left pocket.'

Surgically gloved fingers turned the ink-stained Tampax packet around. The outside looked un-remarkable apart from the ink-wet bottom.

'There are five tampons, four still inside their sealed protective paper,' began Clarke. 'All look clean.' He tipped the box up and onto the desk slid four sealed tampons and one unsealed white circular cardboard cylinder with cotton-wool tampon show-ing. The cylinder was four and a half inches long and half an inch in diameter, its thin retrieval cord poking out. Clarke squinted inside. 'Looks okay to me.'

Leeson's lips puckered. 'Open it.'

Clarke unscrewed outer cardboard from inner sheath and the two separated. A small packet of clingfilm wrapped tightly around white powder had been forced inside. The cotton-wool tampon had been carefully trimmed to allow space. The end had been left in place to leave the impression of standard tampon.

'See what I mean?' said Leeson. 'If you knew the ingenious ways kids have to hide drugs nowadays.'

Molloy's frown deepened. He poked at the clingfilm package with the tip of a biro. 'Looks like heroin.'

Leeson leaned over and inspected. 'I'll get it analysed over the weekend.'

Kavanagh poked his head in and complained. 'Weekend? You guys do no work at all. What's wrong with working all night?'

Leeson scowled at him, then nudged Clarke. 'Check the fags.'

Gloved fingers teased twelve cigarettes onto the workbench. They were pronounced standard. Three rolled cigarettes, their ends curled to a fine point, contained the unmistakable mix of leaf tobacco and crumbled cannabis.

'Bag it.' Leeson handed over an envelope.

'Quite a start,' said Molloy.

Leeson pulled a non-committal face. He scratched the side of his nose with an edge of clipboard. 'For a convent socialite, yes. For your average eighteen-year-old scag-head probably less than I would expect. What we get and where it's hidden reveals an art form in deception. If the same crowd could only use their brains more usefully they'd be better off.'

Molloy grinned. 'Then you'd be out of a job, Arnie, wouldn't you?'

Leeson ignored him. 'Go on, see what's inside the schoolbag.'

The bulging green canvas was pulled together at the top by a leather thong threaded through loops. The ends had been tied in a knot. It freed easily. A navy jacket lay at the top. Underneath was a white blouse, navy blue tights and finally, a pair of black 'sensible' shoes. Each was lifted and inspected before being laid in a corner. Pockets were turned out, seams felt, but nothing found. Clarke's gloved hands reached in again and out came a navy tie, navy skirt and one very lonely looking school exercise book.

'Real swot, wasn't she,' observed Kavanagh from the door frame.

All attention was on the skirt. Molloy poked at it with a gloved finger. 'Moment of truth.'

Leeson pushed forward, allowing Kavanagh to squeeze in further. The tiny room was now uncomfortably warm and ties were loosened for comfort. Clarke slid the skirt across the workbench. 'You do the honours.'

Molloy inspected the outside material. It looked clean and fresh. The waist had been turned up three rolls to allow a higher hemline. A button had come off at the top and a safety pin held two ends together. He turned the skirt inside out and glided his fingers along the lower hem.

'There's something here.' His voice rose slightly. 'There's something here.'

The hem had been opened for about nine inches and stitched back. The restitching was amateurish, the thread a different colour and looped poorly. 'Cutter.'

Leeson reached for a pair of fine-pointed scissors from inside his side pocket. With two snips the inside hem was exposed. Molloy probed with his little finger and gently eased out a clingfilm wrap.

'What's in it?' Leeson was struggling to see over Clarke's shoulder.

Molloy searched for the outer edge of the wrap.

'Dunno yet.' Finally he snipped a corner and squeezed.

Four small, square blue tablets dropped one by one onto the bench top. Two landed face up. Their upper surface was clearly scored. D117C. The other two were turned over and a different marking showed. CYN.

'Any idea what that is, Arnie?' asked Clarke.

Leeson picked up one of the tablets and peered at it with the naked eye, then under a pair of reading glasses. 'Never seen this type before. I'll take one and have it analysed. It won't be . . .'

Kavanagh finished the sentence. 'Ready before the weekend. I'll let you know on Monday.'

Leeson turned on his tormentor. 'Do you know, if you weren't such a big bastard I'd kick you in the balls.'

Molloy looked up from the bench. 'Kick away, Arnie. It's the only bit of activity they'll be getting.'

The banter lightened the moment and all agreed to take a break. They were about to leave when Molloy upturned the canvas schoolbag. Onto the workbench fluttered a roll-your-own cigarette paper. Written on it were the words EENIE-MEENIE-MINEY-MO. Over MO, and encircling the letters, a heart had been drawn. An arrow had been drawn through the heart. The arrow was a crude attempt at an erect penis.

'Bag it,' ordered Leeson, 'it might mean something, it might be just juvenile humour.'

Clarke flicked through the school exercise book. It was Jennifer Marks' French homework. It was obvious she had been no language scholar. The blue handwritten text was spattered with red biro corrections. Each second page reflected a new day's work. 'SEE ME AFTER SCHOOL' was marked in large red biro at irregular intervals.

The door was locked and the four men shuffled along the corridors making small talk. Clarke had two of the mystery blue tablets inside his jacket. He patted the pocket.

'We're working on some of her clothing.' They were stopped at a locked door. Leeson swiped a security card. 'Follow me.'

The biology section of the forensic science laboratory was four rooms on the west side of the main building overlooking playing fields. The workbenches were topped with microscopes, chemicals, scattered paper and one fume cupboard. In another corner one large funnel-shaped stainless-steel vat had a stainless-steel coat hanger hanging over its upper end. Over the hanger a bloodstained dress was draped and a white-coated technician was painstakingly brushing its surface, watching as dust and fibres dropped and slid to collection plates below.

'Here,' directed Leeson and Clarke hobbled towards a broad worktop. Behind it a young and very pretty dark-haired girl in a white coat was working. 'We're checking the black skirt,' explained Leeson. He waved the girl to continue.

On the bench Jennifer Marks' black skirt was laid, outside surface up, seam carefully cut to allow full width stretched. The white-coated girl set a large sheet of blotting paper on top and wet it with water from a spray gun, careful to shield her eyes. She leaned heavily on the paper from end to end, then side to side, ensuring good contact.

'Okay,' she announced, brushing her hair away from her face, 'another thirty seconds.'

The blotting paper was laid in a fume cupboard and sprayed with Brentamine fast blue B. The cupboard was closed and a switch pulled. The girl waited, one hand resting on the bench.

'Something's showing.'

The cupboard was opened and the white square lifted back out. On one six-inch irregular patch a splattering of purple-red blobs showed.

'Can you see those stains?' the girl directed a gloved finger. 'There's another about an inch above.' The gloved finger moved higher. 'Those are semen stains.'

Clarke turned to Leeson. 'What happens now?'

Leeson's face puckered. 'She'll stain that patch with H&E for cells and spermatozoa. Then a sample will be collected for DNA profiling. We'll be able to use the PCR, polymeraze chain reaction, rather than single-locus probes. That way I'll push for a quick result. I'll clear everything else and move this case up. I'll tell you what we've got on Monday.'

When Frank Clancy had been going through medical school he prepared for exams by interviewing himself and asking the most difficult questions possible. Later, before he presented research papers at conferences, he used the same technique to anticipate hostile queries from the floor. Clancy liked to keep on top of events, disliked situations outside his control. He had a keen analytical mind and would often spend hours in his attic at home toying with new theories on disease processes. His standard protocol was to type everything on a PC, print and read through during the day, then review at night. He consulted with hospital colleagues in different disciplines, inviting their comments on patient management and treatments, and disease progression probability. While he welcomed suggestions and advice, in the end all decisions were his alone. Frank Clancy was his own man.

On the afternoon of Friday, 15 May, Clancy was troubled, unsure of himself for the first time in many years. He sat at his desk on level three of the Mercy Hospital, his dark curly hair reflected in the clear glass of the office window. His head was bent, he was deep in thought. Fingers played with the keyboard of the PC in front. He had created a file, code name GRANNY, for his assessment of the deaths from agranulocytosis. He'd typed in the two previous deaths, those of James Murphy and Mary Hyland and their possible link with the cardiology centre on the top floor. Then he'd added the latest details of his patient on the ward, Harold Morell. Then he made six quick telephone calls.

'Hi Gerry,' he spoke to Gerald Hanson, Head of Haematology in Barton's Hospital in north Dublin. 'I'm doing a little research on agranulocytosis and was wondering if you could help?'

'Fire away.'

'Have you noticed any unusual clusters of cases recently, you know, a sudden increase in patients turning up in the wards with this problem?'

Hanson didn't need to consult any files. He came back immediately. 'No, haven't had a case in the past year in fact.'

The same trend was reported from hospitals in the southern city of Cork, Galway on the western seaboard and Belfast in Northern Ireland. For good measure Clancy rang haematology centres in London and Edinburgh. No one was aware of an unusual recent cluster of the rare blood disease.

Type, type, type. The information was entered into GRANNY.

By five thirty Clancy had placated his ward sister who had been hovering around waiting for late decisions on treatments before the weekend. He'd asked his registrar to deal with most of his patients and rang his wife to let her know he'd be home later than usual. He hung up quickly to avoid her wrath.

Then he picked up the telephone again and dialled long distance.

'Drugs Assist Helpline.' It was the same broad mid-western accent, his nurse contact in Chicago on the assist line for queries on pharmaceutical products.

'Hi there,' said Clancy. 'It's me again. Dr Frank Clancy ringing from Dublin, Ireland.' He sounded embarrassed.

'Well hello, Dr Clancy. You're getting to be a regular customer. What can I do for you this time?' The voice was just as pleasant as before and Clancy relaxed a little. He was becoming keyed up with the paper chase.

'You're not gonna believe this,' Clancy started, 'but that patient I was on about has produced another tablet we can't identify. I was hoping you could do a search for me.'

'No problem, Dr Clancy. Just give me as much detail as you know.'

'Well, it's not a lot,' Clancy apologised.

'Tell me what you have. We can only do our best.'

'Okay,' Clancy drew a deep breath. 'Small, square blue tablet. Letters in capitals on both sides.'

'One moment,' the nurse interrupted, 'I'm typing as I go.'

'One side has C,Y and N. The other side has capitals, slightly smaller.' As he spoke Clancy was inspecting one of the tablets Ned Hyland had given him the night before.

'And what are the letters?' asked Chicago.

'X and P.'

'Anything else?'

'No, that's all I have.'

'One moment.' In the distance the sound of keyboard tapping could be heard.

Pause.

'Nothing on colour description. I'll try on letters.'

'Thanks.' Clancy began chewing on his thumbnails, a nervous habit he'd given up in his teens.

Pause.

'Nothing on letters either. Hey, you've really got me on this one, Dr Clancy. Let me try one other approach.' Tap, tap, tap on the faraway keyboard.

Pause.

'Well, would you believe it, I don't have anything on that product. Are you certain it's from the USA?'

'As far as I can be sure of anything,' said Clancy.

'It's definitely not one of the pharmaceutical products licensed for use in this country.'

Clancy's pen hovered over a blank pad, ready to record any information.

'Still there, Dr Clancy?'

'I'm still here. I'm thinking.'

Pause.

'Let me go into the pharmaceutical companies' logos,' offered Chicago. 'Maybe it's an experimental product not yet licensed.'

It clicked in Clancy's mind immediately. 'That's it,' he exclaimed excitedly. 'That's what it is. Do a search on that, please.' He was begging.

'Okay,' laughed Chicago. 'One moment.'

Pause. Tap, tap, tap.

'Something's coming up.'

The pen in Clancy's hand pressed against the blank pad.

'Nothing on the actual product, just the manufacturing company.'

'Give me anything you've got.'

'Capital letters CYN on blue tablet background is used by one company only. It's their trademark. They don't manufacture in any other colour.'

'Who are they?'

'Cynx Pharmaceuticals.'

'Know anything about them?'

'Just headquarters and telephone, fax and e-mail addresses. They have an assist line for problems with their products.'

'Where is Cynx based?' asked Clancy.

'Boston. Would you like the exact address?'

Boston. Clancy leaned so far back in his chair he almost fell over. Then he pushed forward to scribble the details coming down the line.

'Would you like me to contact Cynx directly and ask about this tablet?' the nurse offered.

Clancy nearly had a heart attack. 'No, no, no. Most certainly not.' He had difficulty controlling his anxiety. 'I'll call them myself,' he lied. 'Thank you so much for all your help, you're a gem.'

'We try to help, Dr Clancy. That's what we're here for.'

The line between Dublin and Chicago went dead leaving Frank Clancy staring yet again at the ear-piece. He was stunned.

Tap, tap, tap. The information from Chicago was entered into GRANNY. Clancy inserted a disc and backed up the file through the A-drive. He printed what he was reading from the screen and folded the two A4 pages into a side pocket. Then he went into File Manager and deleted GRANNY. He was taking no chances.

He glanced at his watch, it was now after six. Time

to see a few patients before going home. He lifted a batch of charts and went onto the wards. As he was examining a young man in the middle of a row of beds he heard the distinct sound of John Regan's voice. He turned sharply and sighed with relief when he realised the noise was coming from a television. He walked closer to listen. It was a news coverage of the earlier press conference. Seeing Regan again unsettled Clancy and he returned to his patient quickly to escape the image.

By contrast Jim Clarke was impressed. He sat on an armchair at home nursing a glass of wine and scooping great lumps of lasagne into his mouth with a fork. He flicked channels with the remote control and there was Regan again, on the BBC and Sky bulletins. The stations reported the international interest on events in Dublin. Maeve came into the room from the kitchen and topped up his glass.

'Very determined is our Dr Regan tonight.' Maeve was no great lover of the government.

'I think he looks gorgeous,' jeered Katy. She was sitting on the floor at her father's feet. 'All the girls in our class think he's a real hunk.'

Clarke looked closely at Regan, seeing him now through different eyes. 'Waddyou think, Maeve? Do you think he's a hunk?'

Maeve paused on her way back to the kitchen and wiped her hands on a tea towel. She inspected the screen, seeing only a few seconds of the end of the press conference. 'I'd say he'd chew you up and spit you out if you crossed him. He'd have young girls for breakfast.'

Clarke winked at Katy, noticing her scowl. 'I think

you're right. I don't see a hunk, I see a right pratt.'

Katy stood up. 'You're just jealous. He's still got hair and you've hardly any. Nah-ne-nah-ne-nah-nah.' She barely escaped the swipe from the tip of the crutch.

25 10.26 am, Saturday, 16 May.

'Something's come in. Might be important, might be useless.' Tony Molloy's indigestion was playing up after a heavy breakfast. He chewed on an antacid. Clarke, Molloy and Kavanagh were in the incident room at Sandymount police station. Along the walls A4-size glossy photographs were hanging. There were three rows, ten photographs to a row. The shots were of the group of onlookers gathered at the railings on the morning Jennifer Marks' body had been discovered. Clarke edged along, staring closely at each print. 'One of that group gave a false name and address,' Molloy explained. He scrutinised a different set on the desk in front of him.

'Are things moving on this?' asked Clarke.

'Yeah. Everyone's back on the road, three sets of photographs each, putting names to faces.'

Clarke sat down. 'Any word on Kelly?' he asked hopefully.

'Nothing.' Molloy grimaced as a belt of wind-pain hit. 'I spoke with Dillon earlier and he says Kelly's still away with the birds.'

'Did he use those actual words?' Clarke sounded surprised.

'Maybe I'm not quoting him exactly,' confessed Molloy, 'but that's the gist of what he said.'

Moss Kavanagh grinned. He was leaning against a wall at the back of the room. 'Any word from the Marks family?'

'Nope.' Molloy popped another antacid. 'I've been ringing the house and hospital all morning. No one answers or returns the calls. Dan Marks is operating. A nurse told me they're trying to catch up with lost time since he went out of action after Jennifer was found. Said it has to be finished before the news conference.'

'What news conference?' asked Clarke.

'When the EEC grant is handed over next Wednesday,' explained Molloy. 'Twenty million pounds goes into John Regan's hands if the results from his Heart Foundation look good.'

Clarke eased himself to his feet. 'Time we called on them.' He picked up two faxes from the toxicology laboratory. They were the latest reports on Jennifer Marks. 'Let's go.'

The drive to the Mercy Hospital took less than an hour along Dublin's traffic congested quays. For most of the journey Moss Kavanagh scowled behind the fumes of a large articulated truck bearing computer parts from Dublin port. Its belching diesel blocked the struggling sunlight. Just before noon Clarke and Molloy climbed the stone steps of the front entrance. They left Kavanagh in the car admiring the nurses. All around was the buzz of the hospital complex. Ambulances drew up at Accident and Emergency, their sirens killed only when green-suited aides rushed out with a stretcher. White-coated laboratory assistants and blue-uniformed nurses scurried along highly polished corridors, some clutching blood samples and specimen bags. Sitting along the same corridors, huddled in worried groups, friends and relations of patients waited for the nod from a doctor that things were going well, were steady or had deteriorated. The smell of disinfectant touched all corners. Pyjama-clad patients occasionally poked their noses out from the wards, looked up and down, then returned to their beds, resigned and depressed. Occasionally the nervous laugh of a child bored with waiting broke the subdued atmosphere.

As Clarke hobbled to the lifts he tried to suppress the memories of his own weeks in the same wards two years previously. He recalled the many anxious looks cast in his direction. 'I hate bloody hospitals.'

Molloy grinned and punched a call button. Lights signalled the lift's descent to ground level. When the doors opened Clarke noticed immediately the Heart Foundation was highlighted in gold emboss. It was set apart from the names and descriptions of all other wards. An elderly man shuffled in and stood beside them. He was wearing a dressing gown that had seen better days. His face looked pale and drawn, cheekbones straining skin. He was talking to himself.

Clarke felt he knew the Mercy Hospital more than he would have liked. Yet he was taken aback when the doors opened on the top floor. It had the feel of a luxury five-star hotel. The corridors were wider and brighter, the flooring thick linoleum with multi-coloured, eye-catching designs. The walls were papered in marigold with a heavy navy stripe pattern. The nurses passing along had a different dress code. Instead of a faded blue uniform with starched white headband, on this level each girl wore a tight-fitting white dress held together at the front with bright red buttons. It didn't take Clarke long to decide the girls had been chosen as much for their looks as their nursing skills. Image was all important.

They asked and were directed to a long corridor at the end of which the Boston specialists had their offices. They passed a number of three- and four-bedded open wards. Inside patients were connected to ECG monitors with green traces blipping across screens. Some had tubes running into the veins, others had tubes draining their bladders. Clarke winced at the sight of the urinary drains and hurried past.

They were soon outside the new laboratory, close to the operating and intensive care areas. The walls here were thick see-through glass with horizontal venetian blinds dipped for privacy. Peering inside Clarke could just about make out microscopes, Petri dishes, rows of bottles containing blood, urine and other samples. Paperwork covered almost the whole of one bench and printers whirred and stopped, then whirred again as results came through. He counted seven white-coated lab attendants. A notice warned those passing further to be silent as they were entering the post-operative areas.

Molloy crunched a final antacid. Both men were surprised how much noise there was in this section. Instructions were being shouted over the loud beeping of cardiac monitors. Around a slight curve they arrived at the four-bed intensive care unit. The ward was full, their occupants surrounded by medical technology. Tubes entered the chest area and bright red blood could be seen draining into collection bottles. Thin wires connected to ECG monitors. Face masks carried the hiss of oxygen. Colour-coded lines transferred information on the patients' oxygen saturation, respiratory and heart rates. The technology of recovery and intensive treatment was overwhelming.

Each patient was being supervised by an individual nurse and two looked up as they noticed the detectives staring in. One silently waved a biro, warning them away. The two shuffled guiltily past until they reached the Dream Team offices. Again the walls to the corridor were thick see-through glass, shielded by slim horizontal venetian blinds. There were three beech doors, each with its own identifying polished brass plate. Dr Stone Colman, Dr Linda Speer, Dr Dan Marks.

Clarke squinted through a gap in the blinds and noticed the suites had connecting inner doors. Molloy took the initiative and knocked on one.

'Come in.' The voice had a distinct New England accent.

Clarke thought Dan Marks looked taller than his TV image. His shoulders seemed broader and he had large hands with long, delicate fingers. He was dressed in theatre blues, cloth cap on head, mask tied around the back of his neck but pulled away from his face and hanging loosely. He was writing a note on a chart in front and stood up as the two men entered.

'Yes? What can I do for you?'

'Dan Marks?' Clarke began.

'Who are you?'

'I'm Superintendent Clarke and this is Sergeant Molloy. We're investigators on your daughter's murder case.'

Marks slumped back down on his seat, body

language suggesting he was less than pleased by the interruption. 'What do you want?'

Clarke pulled a chair closer to the desk and sat down. Molloy elected to lean against a wall.

'We've been trying to reach you,' said Clarke, 'but our calls have not been returned, no messages left.'

Dan Marks pulled his face mask off with a snap and leaned heavily on the desk in front. He tugged the cloth cap away and ran a hand through his curly grey hair.

'What do you need with me or Annie now?' His voice was quiet, contained. 'We've suffered enough. I've been told you've arrested the killer, that he was covered in blood.' His voice rose slightly. 'A well-known and dangerous criminal, I believe.' He looked directly at Clarke. 'What use are we to you now? We need peace, time to grieve.' He leaned heavily on the desk and three charts fell off the edge. No one moved to pick them up.

'Dr Marks,' Clarke interrupted, 'Jennifer's toxicology result showed she was using heroin and cannabis.' He held up a fax with the details. 'Do you know where she got those?' He waited. There was no immediate answer. 'Have you any idea where she got the money to pay for them?'

If Dan Marks was surprised by the questions he didn't show it. He rested his chin on both upturned palms and looked from Molloy to Clarke. 'I'm sorry, I have no idea. I can't think straight since this happened but I really don't know where she got those drugs.'

Clarke flipped open a notebook and flicked through several pages. 'One person we spoke with,' he said, 'suggested Jennifer got all her money from her family, you and Mrs Marks I presume. The exact question was: "Where did she get the money to buy drugs?" Answer: "From her parents. They're filthy rich. You know, like, it's really weird, they just gave her whatever she wanted." Quote, unquote.'

'Who told you that?' asked Marks.

'I'm sorry, I can't reveal any names.'

Dan Marks' features changed from subdued to angry. He leaned across the table and fixed on Clarke. 'Let me put the record straight. Jennifer was never an easy girl to look after, I admit that. Like many kids her age she experimented with drugs, always soft. I checked that out in Boston.' He half-turned in his chair so he had Molloy's full attention. 'I have a wife confined to a wheelchair with multiple sclerosis. Annie's ability to be a proper mother was destroyed from the day Jennifer was born. I've had to do everything in our house since then. I changed every dirty and wet diaper. I walked the floors when she had colic or earache. I bought her clothes, her shoes, got her hair done. I even bought her sanitary towels when she reached that stage. I know everything about my daughter.' He stopped, as if choked with emotion, yet when he spoke again his voice was hard. 'Jennifer never received a nickel or a dime from myself or Annie we didn't know about.'

Molloy cut across. 'Can you think where else she might have got money?' He sounded unconvinced.

'I can't. But instinct tells me she got mixed up with someone who led her astray.' Marks turned to Clarke. 'There was some girl she was very friendly with, Jane or June or something . . . Armstrong. I never liked that girl, never liked her simpering, middle-class family. Why don't you ask her?'

218

Clarke flicked to a different page on his notebook. 'We've already checked with Joan Armstrong.'

'And?'

'She was very helpful. But we don't think she had the money to buy heroin and cannabis. Even in Dublin they're not cheap.'

The door into the office opened and a nurse walked in. She immediately apologised for interrupting. Dan Marks cut her short.

'It's okay, sister, these gentlemen are leaving anyway. What's the problem?'

The nurse smiled nervously, sensing the tension in the room. 'They're ready in theatre two. The chest's open and the veins have been harvested. They're just waiting for you to start the bypass.'

'I'll be right there,' Marks' voice was calm again. He stood up, pulled the cloth cap back on his head and tucked straggling hair under. 'If you don't mind, gentlemen, I'm going. Even in this time of grief my work must continue. I was away for three days and one of the patients on our waiting list died. I have to keep going.'

Clarke was surprised how the other man could maintain his composure under the circumstances. 'You're holding up well, I hope?' he asked.

Dan Marks adjusted his cloth cap and teased at the knot on his face mask ties. 'I've learned over the years to compartmentalise my life. I only deal with what I can change. Events outside my control I leave behind. I'm not the sort to take to the bottle or weep every time I hear a sad song. You don't get to my position in medicine by being faint-hearted. Jennifer's death has left a deep void. But don't expect me to wear my pain on my sleeve.'

As Clarke and Molloy made their way back to the lifts, the connecting door between Dan Marks and Linda Speer's office closed softly. Inside her own suite Speer was trembling. She lit a filter-tipped menthol cigarette and poured a finger of Southern Comfort, quaffing half in one go. Nibbling anxiously on her fingers she paced the floor. She twisted the slats on the venetian blinds fully closed and checked the clock on her desk. Making sure all doors were locked, she picked up the phone and dialled.

26 *3.17 pm*

Frank Clancy's house was burgled sometime between twelve thirty and three o'clock that afternoon. He'd gone out to the park with his wife and two children at noon, making a big effort to enjoy some quality time. He'd kicked a ball, played chase, pushed his four-year-old daughter Laura on the swings, sat her on his lap and went down a slide until he ripped a pocket on the back of his trousers. He went out of his way to discuss with his wife Anne the trivialities of family life. How the kids were getting on at school, the cost of orthodontic treatment, the hassle to get into town and buy school clothes. He was lightening up, enjoying himself. He was even forgetting conspiracy theories.

They stopped for lunch at a McDonald's and Clancy forced himself to eat Chicken McNuggets. He vowed never again. On the way back in the car they talked excitedly about where to go for the two-week break he was due in August.

'Disneyland,' screeched Laura from the back seat.

'Yeah, dad, Disneyland,' cheered eight-year-old Martin. He was squashed up beside his sister, leafing through a Manchester United soccer team magazine.

'No,' said Anne firmly. She always sat in the back with the kids to make sure they stayed belted up. 'Florida's too hot. Maybe when you're both a bit older.'

The children started booing. They were still booing when Clancy drove into Greenlea Road in the north Dublin suburb of Clontarf where they lived. There was a police car outside their house and neighbours gathered in small groups. The burglar alarm was whoo-whooing loudly.

'Stay in the car,' Clancy ordered. He felt his mouth go dry, his stomach turn over.

The children started crying when they spotted the blue uniforms. Anne cuddled them to her chest, trying to distract.

'Come on,' she coaxed. 'Let's sing together.' They started with 'Rudolph the Red-Nosed Reindeer'. Clancy was led inside by one of the officers, a big man with a moustache, his cap halfway back on his head.

'They cut the wires to the alarm at the back,' he said. 'Then forced a window. They haven't taken much from what I can see. Must have been scared off by something.'

Clancy rushed from one room to another. The kitchen was untouched. The front living room where most of the family valuables were on display seemed intact. The Waterford glass decanters and chandelier, the silver canteen of cutlery, a wedding present from his last hospital colleagues and worth a tidy sum, all were undisturbed. Three paintings, two watercolours and a very expensive rural scene in oil, still hung on the walls. He noticed his wedding photographs, personal graduation photograph and framed photographs of the children were missing. He sprinted upstairs, checked the bedrooms and decided they had been ignored. Heart racing he scrambled the ten steps to his study in the attic. It had been turned over. The PC monitor lay smashed in one corner, small filing cabinets were upturned and pages scattered around the floor. The hard disc had been smashed, its heavy plastic casing now in pieces, the information it contained destroyed. The drawers on his desk had been pulled out and their contents strewn. He tore at the paperwork, kicked away file holders, scrambled at books dumped from their shelves. His briefcase was missing. GRANNY was gone. And with GRANNY two of the blue tablets Ned Hyland had given to him.

'Anything taken?' asked the policeman. He was standing behind, scratching at his head. 'They've turned this room over rightly. Do you keep any cash or valuables here?'

Clancy was on his knees, stacking books and papers to one side as he assessed the situation. 'No, just research notes and hospital information. No use to anyone.'

The policeman pushed a book out of the way with the tip of a shoe. 'You're not missing anything valuable?'

Clancy stood up. He spotted the photographs. They were propped up against a skirting board in a corner, partly covered by a file. The glass had been smashed, the prints removed and sliced in two. He knew not torn in two but sliced with something sharp as the edges were razor clean.

'No,' he said quietly, 'nothing valuable. Nothing at all.'

The officer started down the stairs again. 'It's odd, I can tell you. Sneaked in the back after cutting the alarm but walked out the front and set it off.'

Clancy wasn't listening. His mind was in overdrive. He had his two-page printed copy of GRANNY and three of the blue tablets hidden at the hospital. For the previous twenty-four hours he'd sensed he was being shadowed, felt he was being watched. Now he knew. And they, whoever they were, were trying to frighten him off. Now they also knew what information he was working on. What if I persist? Will they do more than ransack the house? What will they be prepared to do to stop me?

4.33 pm

'You're taking a helluva risk here.' Tony Molloy was half-turned in the front seat of the unmarked squad car, talking to Clarke. They were parked outside the Marks' Victorian mansion in the fashionable Dublin 4 district. Kavanagh strummed nervously on the steering wheel. 'Dan Marks is well in with the government. He could make life difficult for you.'

Clarke stared at the well-kept lawns and full-leafed trees in the front garden. Dan Marks' response concerned him. It was not that of a grieving father. Parents usually swamped investigators with information, most of it trivial and useless. Marks, by contrast, had given little away. What he had talked about didn't match up with what was known about his daughter Jennifer.

'I'm going in.' Clarke stepped outside and forced the opening passenger door back. Molloy looked up, surprised. 'On my own.' As Clarke hobbled up the drive he noticed a curtain move in a ground-floor room.

Annie Marks opened the front door by a remote control button attached to her wheelchair. 'What took you so long?'

Clarke was immediately confused. He kept his back to the woman to give himself time to think and pushed the door tightly shut. 'I'm sorry?'

'You're the policeman I met at the morgue?'

'Yes.'

Clarke thought Annie Marks looked worse than at that first meeting. Her hair was now totally grey and straggling, almost unkempt. Her face was bloated, blood-red eyes sunk deep. She was wearing a high-neck black dress, black stockings and black shoes. Her fingers played with the control panel on the armrest of the wheelchair. There was a strong smell of whiskey. With a flick she manoeuvred the chair in a half-circle and with the slight purring of an engine she moved into a large room at the front of the house. Unbidden, Clarke followed.

The room was sparsely furnished, two armchairs, one three-seater sofa and a single small walnut-veneer table in the centre on which rested old medical magazines. There were no paintings on the walls, no sideboards with photographs or glassware. There was little to make the room feel part of a home. The curtains were half-pulled and a beam of weak sunlight struggled in. The atmosphere was oppressive. Musty, unused. Clarke sat on the sofa.

'Mrs Marks,' he began, 'why did you say "what took you so long"? We've been ringing for days trying to make contact.'

'Have you spoken with him?'

'Your husband?'

'Yes.'

'We spoke at the hospital this morning.'

'What did he tell you?' Annie Marks' New England twang sounded less than educated. Clarke sensed a mixture of alcohol and anger.

'Not a lot. Nothing we didn't know.'

Fingers flicked on the controls and the wheelchair sped to a different corner of the room. Clarke found himself staring at Annie Marks' back. Just as suddenly the chair spun around again and was propelled rapidly forwards, stopping only feet away from Clarke. The woman's eyes bored into him.

'He's trying to hide everything.' Her voice had taken on a witch-like tone, the black dress reinforcing the image. Clarke half-expected her to begin cackling. 'He's been doing that for years, denying everything, turning a blind eye when it suits him. But I know it all.' She flicked the controls again and the chair reversed. 'This,' Marks slapped an armrest, 'has been my tomb for the past eighteen years. Since the day I gave birth. I am the living dead.' She stopped, breathless from the outburst. Clarke began to understand why Dan Marks kept his wife out of the public eye. She was mentally unstable.

'Let me tell you a few facts.' The words were spat angrily. 'One or two things you'll never hear from my talented and beautiful husband.' She stopped and a crooked smile flickered. 'He is talented and beautiful, isn't he?'

Clarke nodded glumly.

'Quite a handsome man?' Pure venom.

Clarke shrugged.

'My husband knew little about his delightful daughter. Wasn't aware what she was getting up to. He was never around. He was too busy saving lives or screwing the pretty juniors on his team. He barely noticed her.' The outburst was interrupted by a fit of coughing. 'He barely knew he had a daughter, let alone a wife. We were mere appendages, accessories. He wanted to go to the top, he was a driven man. But from the day I became a liability, he abandoned me.' Her breathing now came in rapid, short bursts. 'Not physically, oh no,' the voice raised an octave, 'that was too risky in Boston medical circles. But emotionally I no longer existed.' She stopped, agitated and trembling. Clarke noticed an involuntary shake in her left arm. One side of her face had a slight droop. 'He neglected that child. She was too much like hard work. While he was out socialising I was left to bring her up.'

Clarke was addled. The conflicting accounts confused. 'Mrs Marks,' he cut across, 'Jennifer was using heroin and cannabis. Do you know where got the money for those drugs?'

The cackle Clarke had been dreading slowly began. From deep inside a guttural snigger surfaced. Half-suppressed by a fit of coughing, it changed to a disturbed laugh.

'She earned every dollar on her back.' The coughing became so violent Clarke stood up to help but was waved away. 'I knew one day she'd end up dead in a ditch.' Annie Marks crowed with the delight of a dreadful secret shared. 'She got there on her back.'

The words echoed in Clarke's mind for the rest of the day.

Joan Armstrong wore a bright red cloth headband in her hair. She stood in front of a long mirror in her bedroom admiring her figure. She was wearing tight denim jeans and a long-sleeved red blouse. Her eyebrows were darkened, her lips reddened. She could hear her parents moving about downstairs. They were going out to a bankers' dinner. She reckoned they wouldn't be home before midnight. Harold Armstrong's rules had been announced and Joan knew them by heart. Until he decided otherwise Joan was allowed out two nights a week, Saturday and Sunday. Never on her own. 'You have important exams coming up,' he explained to a sullen face that morning. 'You should be studying.' Joan offered a winning smile. 'Yes, dad.' It didn't work. 'Don't you "Yes, dad" me,' her father snapped. 'That means nothing, young lady, and I know it.' Another 'Yes, dad' was offered, this time without the false smile. 'Your mother and I are going out tonight.' In the background Mrs Armstrong dabbed nervously at the side of her mouth with a lace handkerchief. 'I've asked Andrew to stay with you.' Andrew was one of the beloved sons. Joan couldn't stand him. 'He'll wait until we get home. If you want to go out, Andrew will go with you.' Joan's sullen face changed to angry scowl. 'That's the way it's going to be, young lady, until you learn sense.' Joan immediately protested. Harold Armstrong silenced her with a wave of a hand. 'Those are the rules.'

Andrew arrived just as the parents were leaving. He was clutching a bankers' handbook which his father nodded at approvingly. Andrew was a tall, thin man in his early thirties. He was due to sit banking exams in two weeks. He didn't much mind the 'baby-sitting' exercise, it gave him a chance to escape the drudgery of his own marriage and get a few hours uninterrupted study. He was less than pleased when Joan announced she wanted to go out at nine o'clock.

'At this hour?' he complained. Joan's eyes rolled to heaven. 'Where do you want to go?'

'Just down to the pub to meet a few friends.'

Andrew marked the page he was reading. 'All right. Only for a short time.'

'Sure.'

Joan took him to the Black Bird public house along the seafront at Sandymount. It was loud and smoky, with a small band playing. Andrew didn't last long. The noise deafened, the smoke irritated his eyes and made his asthma flare.

'Is there anywhere else we can go?' he spluttered. His token beer was untouched.

'Nah, this is great.'

Andrew peered through the gloom and smoke. 'Where are these friends you're supposed to meet?'

'Get a life, Andrew,' taunted Joan. She knocked back her lager. 'They don't surface 'til after eleven.'

Andrew checked his watch and cursed. 'I'm not staying in this dump for another hour.'

Joan looked at him with mock dismay. 'Oh, come on, Andrew, you're being really weird, like. We're not going home yet. It's Saturday.'

'You can bloody well stay on your own,' snapped her brother. 'I'm going back. Make sure you're home within an hour, d'ye hear?'

'Only an hour?' Joan wailed.

'An hour and a half at the most. If you're not back

by eleven thirty you're in trouble.' Andrew leaned over and shouted against the background din. 'And you can't afford to be in any more trouble.' He left, not before pointing at his watch from the pub entrance.

Joan waited five minutes. At ten thirty-seven she was back on the streets. Hurrying. She stopped every now and then, pretending to tie laces, making sure she wasn't being followed. She spotted the Goon driving behind. She glanced at her watch. Ten forty-five exactly. As arranged. The Goon pulled over to the side of the road and waited while traffic passed. It was getting dark and over Dublin bay heavy rain clouds were building up. The Goon flashed the car lights once. Joan took off her red headband, pulled her hair back with both hands, then placed the headband inside her jeans. The car lights flashed again. The code had been passed.

'Mo says you're not to ring him again,' the Goon sat in the driver's seat, Joan Armstrong was slumped well down in the back, out of sight. The Goon was Joan's supplier. He was a tall, bulky man in his fifties, coarse-skinned with nicotine-stained moustache. He was wearing black leather trousers and jacket. Even his T-shirt was black. He had a silver identity bracelet on his left wrist. It dangled loosely as he draped his arm over the back of the seat. He dropped a small clingfilm packet of white powder over his shoulder. It landed on the floor and Joan Armstrong scrambled for it. The Goon smiled. 'Hungry?'

'Fuck off.'

'Mo wants to know what happened to Jenny's bag?'

In the back seat Joan Armstrong was twisting the cloth headband around her upper arm. She slapped at the veins on the crook of her elbow.

'Fuck Mo,' she snarled. The craving for the fix was too much.

'Mo won't like it if that's all I have to tell him.' The Goon turned around. He was holding a fresh needle and syringe.

'Gimme a minute.' The voice was desperate.

A small ampoule of sterile water was handed over and within minutes the needle tip was inserted.

'Slowly, Joan,' cautioned the Goon. 'Don't rush it.' He reached across and released the makeshift tourniquet. He watched the young girl's eyes glaze. 'Where's the bag, Joan?' His voice was gentle, almost soothing.

'Gimme a minute.' Half the heroin had disappeared.

'WHERE'S THE FUCKING BAG?' The Goon was over the seat, one hand restraining the plunger. 'WHAT HAPPENED TO THE BAG?'

'The police have it,' screamed Joan Armstrong, tears brimming. 'They won't leave me alone. I had to give them something.'

'Fuck it,' snarled the Goon. Joan Armstong's shaking fingers flushed the rest of the heroin into her body. The Goon gunned the engine alive. 'Mo's not going to like this, Joan.' He looked in the rear-view mirror noticing the girl lolling like a rag doll. He reached into a side pocket and emptied a small bottle of vodka over her blouse and jeans.

Joan Armstrong was home by eleven thirty. She slipped up the stairs with a quick shout to her brother. Her head was spinning and she had to grab at the rails to stop herself falling. Inside her bedroom she stripped quickly and stayed naked. It was an old trick she'd learned to keep her family out from her room.

Her blood hadn't stained the red blouse much. That's why she'd chosen it. She dabbed at the needle point with the red cloth headband. She felt on another world, exquisitely warm and comfortable, ecstatically happy. She slipped in between the sheets and lay on her back, relishing the sensations. She even forgot the Goon's angry threats.

27 *Sunday, 17 May.*

It was raining heavily. Dark grey clouds hung low over the city of Dublin, forcing mist onto the hills and high ground. The temperature dropped and the outdoor thermometer on fashionable Grafton Street barely registered twelve degrees centigrade. The unseasonal weather dampened spirits and those who planned holidays wondered at the wisdom of staying in Ireland. Winter sweaters were taken out and pulled on for comfort, even indoors. The police were kept busy with another spate of drug-related incidents. Those who couldn't afford their fixes mugged for the money. Those who could afford beat up those who approached looking for money. Those who controlled the supply and demand beat up those who had fallen behind in payments and made threats against those they worried might slip into debt. On the streets dealers made contact and deals were done. The usual mixture of adulterated heroin was injected in blind alleys by men and women, young men and young women, even by children. The drug barons dined in the best restaurants stepping over huddles of human misery lying on the pavements craving a fix. Business was business, supply and demand. If the scum wanted drugs they would provide them. If they didn't do it somebody else would and why lose a steady market to some outsider?

In Rockdale Hospital for the Criminally Insane Micko Kelly was coming down from his drug-induced psychosis. The sedatives and anti-psychotics were kicking in, he was less disturbed. The voices inside his head persisted but were less intense, less strident, less angry, less demanding. He was still suspicious of everyone and lay staring at the ceiling in his cell for hours. He was unaware that outside the barbed- and razor-wired walls of the hospital his name was on everyone's lips. MAD DOG KELLY had even been scrawled on one of the walls of Hillcourt Mansions. The newspapers were reporting his arrest and detention, how he was the only suspect in the murder of Jennifer Marks. Without naming him he was being described as JUNKIE KILLER and his past exploits, in and out of prison, set out for all to read. The nation now knew whom to hate, the government knew whom to blame. Micko Kelly was being set up. He was in a gaol of sorts, even if it was really a hospital. A lunatic who couldn't defend himself. A junkie with a history of crime and violence. The scum of the earth to many in the country. No one would give a damn if he was locked away for ever.

Journalists and TV crews followed the funeral cortège that left the Marks' mansion in Dublin's embassy belt, passing through the unfashionable Dublin 1 and 3 districts to the crematorium in Glasnevin on the north side. There, at three o'clock, the corpse of Jennifer Marks entered an incinerator to be turned into ashes. The ceremony was private, only close colleagues and family friends allowed inside the small building. Outside, in the pouring rain, TV crews from Ireland and across the world wiped repeatedly at their lenses so as not to lose their shots. Photographers snapped at anything in a black overcoat while tabloid journalists tried bribing the drivers of the cortège limousines for scraps of gossip. Standing watching, rain streaming in rivulets down his face, was Joe Harrison, the forensic photographer attached to the investigation. Even on a Sunday Jim Clarke would not let up and had ordered photographs of those attending the cremation. As the first flashes of lightning lit up the dark skies, Harrison rewound the spool on his Nikon. In his side pocket he had three rolls of exposed film. He looked down at his soaking shoes and decided he'd done enough.

5.17 pm

Frank Clancy was trying to decide which lies to tell.

Doctors lie often. Sometimes they lie to patients about their illnesses. They lie to lawyers to protect their reputations when some operation has gone horribly wrong. Occasionally they lie to colleagues about treatment results, indifference to wealth, their golf score, the size of their overdraft. Mostly doctors lie to their marriage partners. And they have a wide range of lies to choose from. That late-night emergency operation is just as likely to have been a blonde medical student hoping to advance her career on her back. The conference which would be dull and boring and too hot for the kids might mean the blonde is going instead. She was better in bed than anticipated.

There were no base motives behind Clancy's lies that afternoon. He wanted first to protect his wife and children. He moved them to Anne's mother. She lived twenty miles away and up a narrow country lane. Clancy reckoned no one would find them there.

'Look,' he lied, 'it's only for a couple of days. I have to present this paper at a hospital conference on Tuesday and I'll be like a bear trying to get it together in time. Why don't you take the kids to your mother and I'll collect you on Wednesday. I'll take the rest of the week off and we'll spend it together.'

It had happened so often in the past Anne didn't see through his deception. She packed the bags. Clancy drove the family to the Mercy Hospital and parked in a secluded car park. On the way he checked the rear-view mirror. He saw the heavy black car shadowing. It wasn't a model he recognised. With more lies he arranged for Anne and the children to be collected by taxi and taken out a side entrance. He watched closely, ensuring the cab wasn't followed as it left. He kept looking from his office window on the third floor until it disappeared over a narrow bridge across the River Liffey. He only relaxed when he decided it hadn't been tailed. In a filing cabinet in the basement laboratory he retrieved the three blue tablets and two A4 sheets of printed documentation from GRANNY. He made two copies of the pages and slipped each inside thick brown envelopes. Then he placed one of the blue tablets into each envelope, sealed and sellotaped them heavily. One envelope he addressed to the hospital administrator, the second he addressed to his personal solicitor. Then he stuck all three up his jumper.

He looked at his watch. It was almost seven thirty. He checked his pockets. Credit cards, cash, car keys. He left the keys in the filing cabinet in the basement laboratory. He had a holdall at his feet containing changes of clothes. Satisfied he slipped up through the wards to the on-call rooms. These were reserved for doctors staying in the hospital overnight when on duty. Being Sunday there would usually be a spare room and he soon located one. It was small with only a single bed and wash basin. The bathroom and shower were shared and further along the corridor.

Clancy made one telephone call, making sure Anne and the children had arrived. 'Don't bother ringing me until after Tuesday,' he advised. 'I'll be working on this paper all the time and the hospital don't like personal calls.' The lies came easily, but his heart ached. Still, he consoled himself, once I have all the information I can come out in the open. I need the final pieces to this jigsaw. Two more days. Before that press conference on Wednesday.

8.30 pm

Jim Clarke was frustrated and angry. Very annoyed. He sat in the front living room, TV on but sound at zero. Maeve had sensed the signs and was avoiding him. Katy had gone out for the day and was planning to stay overnight with a friend. Clarke had tormented her with questions as he'd listened to her get ready. Where are you going? Why won't you be home? Who's the friend? Does your mother know her?

What are her parents like? Should you not come home anyway? Katy left the house half in tears, relieved to be getting away from the oppressive atmosphere. As he chewed on his dinner and sipped on his sixth full glass of wine in ninety minutes, Clarke's frustration grew. There was something very unusual about Jennifer Marks' murder and he couldn't put his finger on it. No matter how much he tried to relax and put work out of his mind, the conversations with Dan and Annie Marks kept coming back. What sort of a dysfunctional family are they?

'There's a call for you.' Maeve was standing at the door. She made a face to show her displeasure. 'It's the commissioner.' Clarke's eyebrows raised quizzically.

'Jim, sorry to disturb you.'

Clarke said he wasn't being disturbed in the least.

'I need to talk.'

Clarke knew by the tone of Donal Murphy's voice that Sunday was more or less over. He leaned against the kitchen table holding the wall phone. Maeve scowled at him from the door and he waved her away.

'This Marks' case is taking a life of its own.'

Clarke stiffened. 'What do you mean?'

'Our Minister for Health John Regan and his hunchback colleague Dempsey are giving off-the-record briefings to journalists.' Murphy's dislike for the justice minister was well known. 'They're saying enough to stitch Kelly up like a turkey at Christmas.'

'Like what?'

'That he was covered in the girl's blood. That he was discovered in a room full of knives, all of them covered in blood. That he's insane and wouldn't know what he did that night.'

Clarke waited for a pause. 'They're not far off the mark.'

'I don't care. If the civil liberties crowd get to hear of this there'll be uproar.'

Clarke knew Murphy as level-headed and courageous, a man who'd stood up to previous ministers when political interference threatened.

'Things don't look good for Kelly,' he came back. 'His T-shirt was covered in blood, there were knives in the room and he has gone clean mad. You heard about his attack on the warder?'

'Yes.'

'Well, at this stage I'd put money on him being charged and convicted.'

'So would I, but I'd like to know we have a watertight case.'

'I agree,' said Clarke. He reached across and flicked on the kettle.

'When do you think you'll have the forensics?'

'Leeson said he hoped to have something by tomorrow.'

'Hoped, only hoped?' Murphy's voice raised an octave.

'They're snowed under with work. I know he's doing his best.' Clarke was prompting the reaction. He got it.

'I'll get them working on this throughout the night.'

'That would be great.'

'I want to review this tomorrow at ten. Everyone involved.'

'Right.'

'We need to know where we're going. There's huge interest from the US in this story. There was a travel agent on the news tonight complaining of cancellations from North America because of the negative publicity. I want this wrapped up soon.' The phone went dead.

Clarke poured a liberal measure of whiskey into a thick tumbler and added boiling water. He threw in a few cloves and stirred with the handle of a fork. He sipped carefully, staring at the darkness outside. Raindrops tap-tapped on the skylight. Don't torture yourself, he thought. Kelly did it. Leave it at that.

28 Monday, 18 May.

Frank Clancy woke at six thirty. He showered but did not shave. Under the hot spray he cut at his thick black curls with sharp surgical scissors. He groaned when he saw the end result. At the front his hair was jagged edged, at the back it stuck up. He hadn't time to improve the cut. He didn't care. He wanted to change his image, be less easily identified. Confuse the shadow. By seven he was down in his office on level three, unrecognised and undisturbed. He wore denims, white T-shirt under low-neck cable-knit sweater, white trainers. Over the sweater he had pulled on a loose-fitting linen jacket. He looked more pop star than haematologist. Especially with the hairstyle. He created a fax, simple and direct.

MUST MEET *YOU* AS SOON AS POSSIBLE TO DISCUSS MEDICAL PROBLEM OF MUTUAL INTEREST. WILL CALL YOUR OFFICE LATER TODAY. DO NOT, REPEAT, DO NOT REPLY TO THIS FAX.

He double-checked the address number from the medical directory and sent the page down the line. Then he picked up the phone and rang reservations at

Dublin airport. After five minutes haggling and switching of flights he booked himself on a Delta Airlines direct to Boston, leaving at two that afternoon. He hung up, then rang his ward sister, one hand on the phone, other pinching his nostrils.

'Louise, it's Dr Clancy.' Louise sounded half-asleep, Clancy as if his nose was blocked. 'Sorry to disturb you but I need to pass on some information.' There was just the right amount of nasal twang. Louise told him she was listening. 'I've picked up a dreadful flu,' he snorted loudly and coughed, 'and won't be in for a couple of days.' Louise told him how sorry she was to hear this. 'Thanks. I'm going to switch the phones off and take to the bed so tell the team I won't be contactable.' Louise said she would. 'I've left two large brown envelopes in the bottom drawer of your desk. If you don't hear from me by Wednesday morning would you make sure they are sent out?' Louise repeated the instructions to be sure she'd heard them correctly. 'One can go by courier, the other in the internal post.'

He hung up and looked out the office windows. Breakfast was being served, patients were being shaken awake. The nursing roster was changing, fresh-faced girls replacing the tired night shift. What am I doing? This unit is full of ill patients and I'm playing private investigator. I'm a doctor, not a detective. My work is here, on these wards. He suddenly felt alone and vulnerable. I'm up against the might of the government. One suspicious doctor against the system. This is stupid, plain stupid.

He slumped back, physically weary and mentally exhausted. Then he saw a note stuck on his PC monitor. HAROLD MORELL DIED LAST NIGHT. The arrogant smiling face of Linda Speer flashed in his mind. I've gotta see this through, it's too important.

He picked up his holdall and checked the corridor. When he felt sure he wouldn't be noticed, he teased open the door with the tip of a trainer and slipped away. He took the service stairs to avoid meeting colleagues, dodged through the kitchens to the ambulance bay on street level and hitched a lift into the centre of Dublin. The ambulance driver couldn't stop himself smirking at the hairstyle. On O'Connell Street Clancy jumped out at a set of red lights and hailed a taxi.

'Take me to the airport.'

The cab driver kept one suspicious eye on him as he turned the car around. 'What'd you do to your hair?'

Clancy inspected himself in the rear-view mirror. He looked so ridiculous he had to laugh.

10.00 am

The meeting was held in room twenty-three, fourth floor, police headquarters in Harcourt Street, two miles from the city centre. Outside rain poured down from leaden skies while inside six men sat around a circular table trying to shake drops from shoulders and hair. Commissioner Murphy was dressed in full uniform, white shirt with navy tie, navy slacks and jacket with gold epaulettes. The cuffs showed the appropriate number of stripes. He sat at the middle of one side of the table with his back to a window. A large flip chart with the Jennifer Marks' murder scene diagrams and photographs was positioned in one corner. Opposite was Arnold Leeson, director of the forensic science laboratory. He was wearing slacks and sweater. To his right was Dr Patrick Dillon, forensic psychiatrist to Rockdale Hospital for the Criminally Insane. He had dressed in a charcoal pin-stripe two-piece suit with white shirt, stiff collar and university tie. In his breast pocket half an inch of white handkerchief poked out. Jim Clarke sat beside the commissioner with Tony Molloy worrying to his right. Moss Kavanagh leaned against a wall. The introductions were brief, most knowing one another by reputation.

'This investigation has got off to good start,' Murphy began. 'Within a remarkably short time we've arrested the main suspect. If we did as well as this elsewhere I'd be delighted.' The audience did not respond. 'However in their haste to close down unwelcome publicity certain government ministers are directing leaks to the effect the case is as good as closed. The word going out is Kelly is as guilty as hell, mad as a hatter and safely locked up in the hospital for the seriously mad.' He paused. 'So I suppose we should all go home and put the kettle on.' A few amused smiles flickered.

Murphy stretched his long fingers out and ran the palms of his hands along the highly polished table surface. He seemed to examine a particle of dirt on his jacket sleeve and brushed at it.

'Well, I'm not happy. What's good for the government isn't always good for the police. If this rumour mongering continues I can see us going through hell in the courts. Kelly can't be declared guilty without understanding what he's being charged with.'

There was a murmur of agreement.

'He's become the centre of attention for media from all over the world. Since that attack on the warder, he's been branded a cross between Hannibal Lecter and Attila the Hun.' More smiles flickered. 'Dr Dillon,' Murphy continued, 'told me when I spoke with him last night that the hospital has been besieged by cameramen and reporters.'

Dillon cut in, 'We had three TV crews hanging out of helicopters yesterday. Laying aside the breach of security, the noise unsettled many of my patients.'

Murphy came back, 'And that's not something we'd relish, a riot in Rockdale.'

Dillon shifted in his chair and spoke again. 'Two of my staff have been contacted by tabloid reporters looking for background. One was offered £5000 to take a photograph of Kelly in his cell.'

Angry mutterings erupted. Murphy's hand went up for silence. 'Before this gets totally out of control,' he said, 'I want to know what we're dealing with. I'd like to sleep easier in my bed, not haunted by thoughts of courtroom challenges further down the line.' He looked at each in turn for confirmation. Satisfied, he started separating fax reports. 'You've all read the toxicology report?'

Yes by five.

'Okay, she had heroin, cannabis and alcohol in the blood. The vaginal, rectal and oral swabs are negative.' Murphy scanned another fax. 'The markings on her neck were old and not relevant.' He looked up. 'That's all new information to hand.' He leaned back in his chair, kneading his forehead with the knuckles of his right hand. 'Okay, Arnie, what do you have?'

Arnold Leeson shuffled paper, forensic reports and

two faxes. 'Right,' he started, 'let's begin with what you want to hear. The blood on Kelly's tee shirt, tracksuit bottoms and trainers is that of Jennifer Marks. The PCR test has confirmed that without any doubt.'

The commissioner sighed with relief. 'That's the good news.'

Leeson had a hand up for attention. 'The rest is incomplete,' he paused to put paperwork in order, 'and I'm expecting more information. What's here may confuse rather than clarify.'

Murphy sat forward, eyes narrowing, as Leeson went on.

'The traces of soil scraped from Kelly's trainers do not match samples taken where the body was found. That area was in undergrowth, the clay heavily mixed with a peat mixture. Nor,' continued Leeson, 'do the soil patterns on the trainers fit in with how the footprints were disguised.'

He stood up to demonstrate, moving to a corner where his feet could be seen. Five heads strained to watch.

'When you want to scuff footprints in a hurry you tend to sweep the inside of your shoes, or in this case trainers, across the indents.' Leeson swept his right foot along the carpet. 'Soil should collect on the instep. Kelly's trainers don't show that pattern.' He sat down and scanned another page quickly. 'Where the body was dumped cobwebs had collected. The twig samples we received had cobwebs on them as well as fibres not yet identified. Kelly's clothes did not have any cobwebs on them and the cotton fibres of the T-shirt and tracksuit bottoms do not match what was clinging to the undergrowth.'

246

Molloy shifted forward on his seat and slipped his jacket off, the movement momentarily distracting.

'We haven't been able to lift any prints off the knife,' continued Leeson, 'and the hand patterns on the body were too smudged for analysis. There were semen stains on the black skirt the girl was wearing but I haven't got the analysis of that to hand. I'm expecting it through this morning.'

Murphy began running his palms along the table again. 'Conflicting signals there, Arnie?'

'Very much so,' agreed Leeson.

A brief silence descended, broken only by the scraping of pens against paper.

'What about you, Dr Dillon, can you throw any light on this?' Murphy shifted his chair sideways and leaned back on it. 'Could Kelly have murdered this girl?'

Throughout the previous exchanges Patrick Dillon had kept his head down, toying occasionally with pen against blank paper, every now and then making notes in shorthand. As soon as Murphy questioned him he quickly circled the order of importance.

'First of all, Commissioner, I am a doctor and not a forensic investigator. My duty is to help Kelly regain his sanity.'

'We all apprec . . .' Murphy started to interrupt but Dillon cut him short.

'What I will say is strictly off the record,' he continued, 'and probably unethical as Kelly has not agreed that I reveal his medical status.' Fleeting smiles were exchanged. 'However let me tell you what is relevant. Kelly is a chronic drug abuser. His toxicology result alone makes for disturbing reading. The blood sample we took at Rockdale was positive for alcohol, cannabis, heroin, methadone, flunitra-zepam, diazepam, cocaine and LSD. More worryingly he also had high levels of ketamine, an animal anaesthetic also known on the streets as Special K or LA Coke.' Dillon explained further, 'Ketamine is usually mixed with ephedrine and passed off as Ecstasy. When taken it can have profound effects on heart and lungs.' Around the table mouths gaped. 'The side effects of ketamine alone, even without the other cocktail of drugs, include confusion, hallucina-tions and irrational behaviour.' Dillon ticked off his notes as he continued. 'Kelly is also in liver failure with enzymes grossly elevated. He is clinically and biochemically jaundiced.'

Moss Kavanagh decided to sit down.

'Psychologically,' continued Dillon, 'he is even worse. When admitted he was suffering a severe and violent schizophrenic episode, hearing voices and seeing visions. He had paranoid features, distrusting everyone, feeling he was under attack. He thought he could see and hear the devil.'

'Jesus,' muttered Kavanagh.

'And these, eh,' Donal Murphy struggled for the correct words, 'these thought disorders, were due to his drug taking?'

'I feel quite confident of that.'

'Could he have had thoughts driving him to kill the girl?'

'Yes.'

'Could this condition produce any other bizarre behaviour?' Murphy's hands now supported his chin.

'Anything you care to think of,' replied Dillon. 'I was at a conference recently where two cases of metamorphosis were reported.'

'Metamorphosis?'

'Yes,' explained Dillon. 'This is a delusionary state where the patient believes he is turning into an animal. The cases were in young males with schizo-affective disorders, one thought he was turning into a pig, the other into a werewolf.'

'Jesus,' whispered Kavanagh again.

'In terms of bizarre thought processes, anything can happen,' Dillon finished. His forehead creased and he began humming.

Murphy stared at him quizzically.

'Sorry,' Dillon smiled awkwardly as he caught the commissioner's expression. 'I was thinking.'

'Want to share?' asked Murphy.

'Yes, I do. This case bothers me.' He circled his notes again. The others watched expectantly. Dillon settled back in his chair, eyes down, face crumpled. He rested his chin on his left hand. 'What I've heard just doesn't add up.'

'What doesn't add up?' Murphy was now leaning heavily on the table and fiddling with his front collar for a button. It came free and he ran a finger around his neck, tugging the collar loose. The room had become warm and other hands loosened ties for comfort.

Dillon explained. 'The pattern of behaviour in this crime suggests some degree of control, of rational thought. The girl was stabbed. She was then dragged out of sight into undergrowth.' He switched hands to rest his chin. 'The killer searched that skirt seam and didn't find what he was looking for, then turned the body over and cut the back seam. What's important is he was actively looking and going about the most direct way of finding it.'

There was a brief silence while the listeners thought over Dillon's hypothesis.

'What about those blue tablets?' Clarke interrupted everyone's thoughts. 'Any luck, Arnie?'

Leeson flicked paper briefly. 'Nothing. Mightn't have anything on it for a few days.'

'Could Kelly have done any of this?' Murphy asked, hands reaching for his jacket. 'He was covered in the girl's blood, we now have that for fact. What about a sexual motive?'

Dillon came in immediately. 'He could have carried out the stabbing.' He looked directly ahead, voice firm, eye contact held. 'But our friend does not have the balls, literally, to drive him to a sex crime. I doubt whether Kelly has had an erection for the past year, let alone become sexually excited enough to do something like this.' The room was quiet. 'More importantly, the attempt to conceal the body and destroy the footprints suggests a thinking brain.'

'And Kelly doesn't have a thinking brain?' Murphy wondered out loud.

'Kelly's brain is porridge. He is your typical chaotic drug abuser, devoid of logical thought, capable only of raw emotion and the drive to find drugs. He may have inflicted the first two wounds but not what happened after. I have to conclude someone else was involved.'

There was a murmur of noise before Molloy cut across, his usual frown now taking on Mount Rushmore proportions. 'Are we dealing with some psychopath here?'

Dillon pulled at his cuffs, showing a little more white. He tucked his tie deeper behind his jacket.

'Psychopathic behaviour is a rather strange

phenomenon,' he said. 'Many psychopaths never come to the attention of the police, leading apparently normal lives. Indeed some may use their cunning and guile to achieve high positions in society.' He looked around the table, noticing everyone hanging off his words. 'They have a grandiose sense of self-worth with a superficial charm. They are pathological liars, devoid of any sense of remorse. They show lack of insight, incapable of learning from past mistakes.'

'They'd go far in politics,' suggested Arnold Leeson and the table dissolved in laughter.

Dillon pushed his notes inside his jacket pocket. He stood up to leave. 'As far as I can see there's only one man can clear this up.'

Murphy looked up. 'Who?'

'Kelly. He's the only one who knows what happened that night.'

11.37 am

Inside the maximum security ward of Rockdale Hospital for the Criminally Insane, Micko Kelly was sitting on the floor outside his cell. He watched with intense interest anything that moved. He was dressed in long, white, hospital-issue pyjamas. The pyjamas had no buttons or cord, only snap-on top and elasticated bottoms. This reduced any attempts at suicide. Kelly was less agitated and now stronger after eating and drinking proper food. He was also less strung out, the anti-psychotic and drug-withdrawal medicine was claiming his mind back. Some of his mind.

'Watch the little piggy, watch the little piggy. Grunt,

grunt, little piggy.' He was still hearing voices and occasionally hallucinating.

'Waddye doin' on the floor?'

The small, red-haired fellow patient three cells along the corridor tried to make contact but Kelly would not respond. He didn't see a small, red-haired man, he saw a small fat pig. Each time he approached, Kelly smelt pig, heard pig. Once when the pig had come too close Kelly scrunched into a ball, seeing the pig's features change slowly into the face of a devil with horns on head and fire pouring out from the mouth. Kelly curled himself tighter and whimpered.

'Waddye doin' on the floor?' the small, red-haired man persisted. 'Why don't ye get up?'

'Don't answer him, Michael, don't speak back to the little fat piggy.'

Kelly curled tighter and rolled his body along the corridor into his cell. He only stopped rolling when he bumped off the wall.

'Yer fuckin' mad,' crowed the small, red-haired man from the doorframe. He walked back to his own cell, muttering and shaking his head.

Kelly uncurled and sat with his back to the bed. He felt something warm between his legs and looked down to see a pool of his own urine trickle along the tiled floor. He stared at it, fascinated. For a few seconds the trickle turned blood-red and he recoiled in horror. Then the liquid took on a honey colour.

'Bees drink, Michael, bees drink. Buzz, buzz, buzz. Bees drink. Buzz.'

He stretched a finger out and whorled the stream of urine, then licked the fingertip, savouring the sweet honey his mind told him he was tasting.

'Bees go buzz, buzz, buzz, buzz.'

'Ah Jesus, you've wet yourself again.' One of the warders spotted Kelly sitting on his soaked pyjamas. 'Don't drink the stuff, for Christ's sake, don't put that in your mouth. You're sick enough.' He slipped the sopping bottoms off the wasted body and lay Kelly back on his bed. 'Now stay there,' he ordered. 'I'll be back to clean you up.'

Clean the little fat piggy, too. Clean the black ugly face of that fucking pig.

Back at his desk the warder dialled a number and waited. After six rings the phone was answered.

'Is that Dr Dillon's secretary?'

'Yes.'

'I'm ringing from Rockdale. It's about a message he left earlier.'

'Yes.'

'Would you tell him Michael Leo Kelly is still in no fit state to undergo questioning by the police.'

'Certainly. Is that all?'

The warder sighed as he hung up. 'Yeah, that's all.'

2.45 pm

'Would you like a drink, sir?'

Frank Clancy was staring out at distant clouds from the window seat of a Delta Airlines 747. He looked round. A smiling hostess was standing beside the drinks trolley in the galley.

'No thanks. I'll wait until there's food being served.'

'Certainly.'

His gaze returned to the clouds.

'Did you have a fight with the barber?'

Clancy pretended to duck under his own arm. He turned back, face reddening. 'I did it myself, would you believe that?'

The hostess looked closer. 'I'd believe it.' She pushed the trolley ahead.

Clancy started flicking through a complimentary copy of the *Irish Times*. He stopped at page five and read carefully. Then he tore the page out, stuck the rest under his seat, and reread the item. The article took up two columns with accompanying photographs.

REGAN'S FINEST HOUR

By six o'clock next Wednesday evening, Minister for Health John Regan should feel like a wealthy man. A cheque for twenty million pounds will be sitting in his jacket pocket, compliments of the EEC. The money is due to be handed over by German Minister Dr Hans Otto Mayer at a press conference in government buildings. Dr Mayer is chairman of the Euro Medical Fund and this is the largest single grant ever awarded. It will be John Regan's finest hour, a vindication of his drive and effort over the past two years. While the cheque is conditional on results of the first six months' work at the Mercy Hospital's Heart Foundation, government sources say the money is as good as in the bank. Regan's Boston specialists have produced the goods. 'Medical breakthrough' is the spin being put on the event. There may have been days in the past when Regan felt the project would fall apart. There was the initial hostility of the medical profession here, the battle for funds at EEC level, the jealousy and non-cooperation of some Mercy Hospital staff. All could have taken their toll.

But nothing would have prepared him for the biggest setback, the murder of cardiac surgeon Dan Marks' daughter, Jennifer. Close sources say her death has had a profound effect on Regan. He has become more driven, more determined. He is also more easily angered, flying off the handle at the slightest difficulty. Off-the-record comments from senior police officers suggest Regan also wants to end the uncertainty surrounding the schoolgirl's murder. As one unnamed source put it, 'Regan wants his £20 million pounds and Micko Kelly's head on a plate by six o'clock on Wednesday.' Dan Marks has refused to comment on the investigation. 'After the press conference,' he told staff at the Mercy Hospital, 'myself and my colleagues will fly out from Dublin for a well-earned break. We want to put this dreadful affair behind us.' There was no word on where the Dream Team would be heading.

Clancy folded the page into a small square and stuck it in his hip pocket. Have you got the bottle? Are you ready to collapse this house of cards? He ordered a gin and tonic.

5.17 pm

The Goon was waiting.

When Joan Armstrong stepped off the train at Sydney Parade Station she spotted him immediately. He was dressed in denim jacket and jeans, leaning against the second lamppost on Ailesbury Gardens, their usual rendezvous. The tiny road ran alongside the railway track and was usually quiet. Checking no one was following she took the overhead metal bridge to the other side of the tracks.

The Goon seemed more edgy than usual, his brown eyes darting. He licked at his moustache nervously. She walked past him, pretended to drop her bag and fiddled with the spilled books.

'I can't go now. They'll be waiting for me at home.'

The Goon grabbed an arm and started dragging her along the side road.

'Let me go, you big bastard, let me go.'

The Goon was holding firm. 'Mo's waiting,' he snarled, 'he wants to talk.'

With a sudden twist Joan Armstrong broke free and staggered back against a rickety fence. Steps alerted them and the Goon forced himself at ease. An elderly gentleman came past, staring at both. He stopped and looked at the schoolgirl, her eyes frightened, her clothes in disarray.

'Are you all right?'

The Goon shot a warning glare. Joan Armstrong picked up her bag and walked briskly away.

'Fine, thank you very much. Just going home.'

The elderly gentleman waited until she was safely on the overhead pedestrian bridge, scowled at the Goon and shuffled away. As she reached the other platform, Joan Armstrong heard the Goon shout.

'I'll be back. Mo has to talk with you.'

She ran home.

Jim Clarke addressed the investigation team in the incident room at Sandymount police station. Heavy rain clouds had cleared into the Irish sea leaving Dublin city sunny but wet.

'There's a possibility someone else was involved in Jennifer Marks' murder.' His face was taut and drawn; he looked angry. 'Forensics feel Kelly could not have acted alone. I want you back on the roads. Someone out there may be watching every move, delighted to have mad Kelly take the rap.' He directed the tip of his crutch towards a flip chart with scrawled writing. 'Read the points I've drawn up. Most crime happens between people who know each other.' He paused briefly. 'Go back over the girl's lifestyle and ask the same questions we asked the first time. Only this time ask them louder.' He hobbled to the other side of the flip chart. 'What happened that night? Who could have committed this crime? What was so important she had to be killed? Was this guy some psychopath hell bent on killing and she just happened to be in the wrong place at the wrong time?'

Clarke watched as pens scribbled on notebooks. 'The forensic psychiatrist says Kelly doesn't have enough brain cells to know how to conceal the body and then destroy the footprints.' Laughter rippled and died. 'Interview the same people, those at the railings, the school kids who volunteered information, the staff at Balfe's pub. Ask did they see anyone besides Kelly? Rattle their brains.'

As the group filed out into weak sunshine, Clarke continued his instructions. He dispatched Molloy back to Joan Armstrong.

'Find out who else was in that pub. Who was the dealer? Ask about those blue tablets. Find out where she got the money for her drug habit. Go into that more.' Molloy sucked on an antacid as he frowned his way to the door.

Clarke turned to his minder. 'Shift it, Mossy. We're going back to the park.'

The early-evening traffic was light along the quiet side roads of Sandymount Park. Cats threatened refuse sacks while dogs sniffed at anything interesting on footpaths and telephone poles. The warmth of the sun raised steam and insects skated along puddle surfaces. The immediate neighbourhood was a pleasant mix of good taste, expensive houses and decent breeding. The only blot was the heavy police presence. Clarke ignored disapproving frowns as the park was cleared of joggers and strollers. He sat in the back of the unmarked squad car. When the last protesting straggler had been escorted out he made his way back to the murder scene. Kavanagh kept a respectable distance behind. Uniformed officers dispersed to strategic corners and hung around with bored expressions. Clarke stopped at the grassy patch where seven days earlier a young life had been brutally taken. With a twisting movement he forced the crutch tip into the wet earth and leaned heavily on its hand rest. His face furrowed.

A gentle breeze lifted his straggling hair. He tried to conjure up the schoolgirl's final moments. Did she scream? How loudly, how often? Did anyone hear? How could Kelly's clothes be covered in her blood? He shifted position and fixed on the graffiti-covered wooden shelter, thirty yards away. Had someone been hiding there and attacked? Nah! Where did the other person go afterwards? No one saw two leave the park. Clarke remembered Molloy's description of the trail at the far end of the park. On that side there were large trees and heavy undergrowth. As the breeze rustled leaves he noticed redbrick housing on the road behind. The brickwork disappeared as the wind lightened and then reappeared with its next strength.

'Mossy.'

Kavanagh looked over. 'Check that side.' Clarke tugged the crutch from the ground and shuffled towards the undergrowth where Jennifer Marks' body had lain overnight. The uncut grass left wet trails on his shoes. He crouched and inspected the twigs, shrubs and insects. He sniffed at the air, then scooped a handful of wet earth. The spiders had spun fresh webs. Raindrops danced on their mesh.

A sudden movement caught his attention and he turned. The trees were rustled by another faint breath of wind and the brickwork showed once more. The heavy rains had turned dusty earth to mud and leaves showered drops of rain onto Clarke's shoulders as he inched his way along the trodden path connecting Sandymount Park with the road behind. Within minutes he was standing in front of The Palms apartment block and the large granite rocks.

Kavanagh came beside, trying to look interested. 'See anything, boss?'

Clarke shook his head. He hobbled along the quiet road, past the abandoned ESB box that had once held Jennifer Marks' schoolbag. He squinted at doors and windows, trying to decide which house he'd spotted from the park. They were too alike and he stopped after five minutes.

'I want the branches and undergrowth along that trail checked.'

Kavanagh clicked his mobile into action.

'She gave me nothing new and her old man warned he'd want a lawyer present if I came back.' Tony Molloy sat in the back seat of the unmarked squad car with Clarke.

Kavanagh fumed in the front, annoyed at being kept late from his heavily pregnant wife. It was ten thirty and night was closing in. The squad car was parked at the side of Sandymount Park, lights off. Headlights from passing cars moved shadows behind their heads.

'Swore she knew nothing about another man, certain she only saw Kelly with Jennifer Marks.' Molloy was going over his latest conversation with Joan Armstrong. 'She's scared stiff,' he added, squinting out the back window. His stomach rumbled and he massaged his straining belly.

'Scared of what?' asked Clarke.

'I dunno. Maybe it's the investigation, maybe she's

frightened we're gonna spill the beans on drugs to her parents. Maybe,' he paused and wound down the window slightly for air, 'she knows something more she's not sure about telling.'

'Find out anything about the dealer at Balfes?'

'Nah,' grunted Molloy. 'Said she didn't know.'

'What about where they got money for drugs?'

'From Marks' parents. Always says it's the parents who kept Jennifer bankrolled.'

Kavanagh turned around. 'They'd need to be bankrolling her a helluva lot to keep up a heroin habit.'

'Who ya tellin?' Molloy put on his best Brooklyn accent.

'Find out anything about boyfriends,' Clarke pressed. 'Old flames, fellas she may have been screwing?'

Molloy shook his head. 'Nope. Says she knows nothing.'

'What about the tablets?'

'Knows nothing about them either. Acted real surprised when I asked.'

Clarke opened the car door slightly. 'It doesn't add up.' He let the breeze cool his face.

'The semen on her skirt didn't match Kelly's DNA profile, that came through this afternoon. So who *was* she screwing?'

'Not me anyway,' muttered Moss Kavanagh wistfully.

They walked in the dark along the wet grass. Clarke kept checking the trees separating Sandymount Park from the side road. The breeze was gentle, the evening cool. Lights from the red-brick houses twinkled. He made his way to the undergrowth and waited. He felt his hair lifted by soft brushes of wind. He listened to the whispering of the leaves.

'Gotcha, bloody gotcha.' Molloy and Kavanagh looked over. 'Wait a minute.' Clarke was whispering, as if frightened to break the moment. 'Don't move.' The wind disturbed the trees again and the light from a window glimmered. 'I checked the weather reports this afternoon. That night there was a slight breeze blowing, just like now. Whoever's in that house might have heard something. It was a warm evening, the windows could have been open.' The excitement in his voice lifted it. 'We're going there now.'

'Ah, Jesus, boss, it's nearly eleven,' complained Kavanagh.

30

The Delta Airlines 747 touched down at Boston's
Logan Airport one hour late, courtesy of a traffic
controllers' go-slow. Bright sunlight glinted off the
control tower as Frank Clancy squinted through the
window, trying to catch a glimpse of the downtown
city. Inside the main terminal he first rang Springton
Hospital but couldn't get through to his contact. He
made an appointment for the following morning.
Next he went through a hotel reservations agency,
passing up a room at the Ritz Carlton for a more
modestly priced stay at the John Jeffries. 'It's a turn-
of-the-century grand house in the affluent Beacon
Hill district,' the agency explained, 'and it's been
renovated to modern standards without shedding its
original architectural details.' Clancy couldn't have
cared whether it was a steel-and-glass monstrosity, he
just wanted a bed for the night without bankrupting
himself.

He took the subway, got off at Government
Centre T-stop and flagged a yellow cab. It was a
warm, humid day and perspiration formed on his
brow quickly. The John Jeffries was more than

comfortable. It boasted a graceful double parlour with Federal-style New England decor.

'How long will you be staying with us, Dr Clancy?' asked the dark-haired receptionist.

'Just tonight.'

'Seems very short after such a long journey.' His personal details were being entered.

Clancy managed a grin. 'Story of my life, always chasing my tail, always behind time, always rushing.'

The girl smiled and handed back his passport. 'Enjoy your trip anyway.'

He caught her staring at his hair. 'I'm trying a new image,' he said hurriedly.

The girl leaned across the reception counter, looked up and down, then whispered. 'It ain't working.'

Clancy blushed.

In his room overlooking the Charles River he was surprised to find French-country furnishings and spent the first few minutes admiring their detail. But exhaustion from the flight caught up and he finally gave in, slumping down in a deep armchair and staring out at the traffic on the waterway. Young, muscular arms dragged long, narrow oars in and out of the river, their splashes throwing dances of rippling rainbow in the strong sunlight. White-sailed yachts drifted lazily in the gentle winds, disturbed only by high wash from passing motorcraft. On the opposite side of the river the buildings of the Massachusetts Institute of Technology seemed to edge towards the shoreline. Drained with tiredness, Clancy eased himself onto the double bed and soon fell asleep.

He was awakened by the shrill ring of the telephone, maid service wondering could they turn his bed for the night. Groggy and disorientated he squinted at his watch in the unexpected gloom, discovering it had turned eight o'clock, local time. Grunting a reply he showered first to freshen, then changed clothes. An hour later he was sitting comfortably in a small Italian restaurant off Commonwealth Avenue sipping on a glass of deep red Barolo. His hunger was intense and he chewed on the fresh bread set before him, scanning the menu. He ordered a fish starter and pasta, then relaxed back in his seat, watching the world go by outside.

The tables filled with a mixture of college students and confidently underdressed youthful business types murmuring into mobile phones between mouthfuls of steaming spaghetti. The women looked better dressed than the men, even more confident. He felt out of place.

'I'll have the other half of that bottle,' he suggested. 'Dutch courage.'

The waiter grinned. 'Why not, it's gonna be a long night.'

It is indeed, thought Clancy as the cork popped and his glass was topped. He relaxed, the wine easing his tension. I wish Anne and the children were here. If she had the slightest inkling where I am this minute she'd pack and leave. I wouldn't blame her. The uncertainties began edging back. There's still time to cut and run. Grab the first flight out tomorrow, be back on the wards by late afternoon. Nobody need know. He suddenly realised he was the only sole diner and the loneliness became acute. He wished he'd brought a photo of the kids. In the hurry to flee without being tailed he'd forgotten mementoes. He spotted an abandoned copy of the *Boston Globe* and began scanning its pages, anything to take his mind off home. Between mouthfuls of pasta he read about lives and events in Massachusetts that meant nothing to him until he spotted a headline.

BOSTON PHARMACEUTICAL CO MAKING ITS MARK

This year is shaping up like last with strong performances by a number of big stocks and sectors on the NYSE. Among these the pharmaceutical sector has been second only to the banks in investment performances.

Since January the Dow Jones All Share Index has appreciated by approximately fourteen percent while pharmaceutical stock has jumped an impressive twenty-eight percent. The coincidence of political remission, strong demand growth and attractive product development has been accompanied by a period of industry consolidation and drive for global strength. Clients should maintain a reasonable exposure to the sector through our key choice recommendations: SmithKline Beecham; Glaxo; Zeneca and local Boston company, Cynx. Buzz in the industry suggests Cynx is about to release final clinical trial results on a new cardiac wonderdrug and well-placed leaks have driven the share price to $19.59. Wall Street analysts are dismissing talk of a possible takeover of Cynx by one of the multinational pharmaceutical giants.

Clancy set his fork down slowly and reread the article. His appetite vanished. The uncertainties vanished. The final pieces in the jigsaw were coming together. He tore the page out and folded it into his pocket. Quite a little scrapbook you're building up.

Back in his hotel room he flicked through the Boston area *Yellow Pages* until he found the hospital section. Map alongside, he tracked down Springton to an area between Brookline and Huntingdon Avenues where a number of institutions were located. Beth Israel Hospital, Brigham and Women's Hospital, the Children's Hospital, the Massachusetts Mental Health Centre and Harvard Medical School all clustered the same zone. By his reckoning, Springton was about two blocks from the Wentworth Institute, off Ruggles Street.

He climbed into bed but lay awake, tossing and turning. Once or twice he dozed off, only to be woken by the pounding of his heart. I'm getting closer.

11.37 pm, Dublin.

'Who's that?'

Clarke, Molloy and Kavanagh stood in the porchway of number 17 Mercers Road, five houses from the T-junction and cul-de-sac with The Palms apartment block. Two floors above a light burned in a front room.

'Who are you?'

The door had been opened by an elderly man who'd taken one look at his unexpected visitors and immediately slammed it shut. Molloy rang the bell again, pushed the letter box open, and shouted inside. 'It's the police, don't worry, it's only the police.'

The lock slipped and this time an inch gap was offered. A security chain had been dragged across and a set of suspicious eyes glared out. 'How do I know that? Where's your identification?'

There was no mistaking the edginess in the voice. Badges were flashed and inspected.

The suspicious eyes narrowed further. 'Why are you calling at this hour?'

Molloy sighed. 'We're investigating the murder of the girl found in the park last week. You probably heard about it? Jennifer Marks? Daughter of the heart surgeon?'

The suspicious eyes never moved.

'We were in the park just now and noticed the light in the room above.' Molloy looked upwards and suspicious eyes followed. 'We were wondering if anyone was in the room that night and maybe heard something? We don't need to come in. Can you help with that?'

The security chain was slipped and suspicious eyes pulled the door back. 'I'm sorry,' he grumbled, 'since that wee girl's murder nobody feels safe around here.'

The three made sympathetic noises. He was a small man, slightly stooped and bald. He was in a tartan dressing gown and wearing fleece-lined slippers. A pipe stem poked out from one of the side pockets with tobacco stains marking the spot. While the gesture of opening the door confirmed he did not feel threatened, he stood his ground. 'That light's left on every night. It's a deterrent against burglars. No one uses the room, it's empty.'

Molloy kept a fixed smile but behind Clarke cursed deeply.

'I live on my own and I didn't hear or see a thing that night. Didn't even know anything had happened until I read about it in the papers the next day.'

Molloy continued to smile. 'Sorry for disturbing you so late. If you think of anything please let us know.'

The door closed in their faces.

The cursing group had reached the T-junction when they heard the old man's call. He stood at his front gate, one hand clutching his dressing gown to his throat, the other waving for attention.

'There's a young fella in that block of flats who might be able to help. He's a bit simple, but he keeps some sort of diaries and log books of everything that goes on around here. He might know something.'

'Which flat?' shouted Clarke.

'Seven, I think. Yeah I'm sure it's seven. The one at the front with the lights on now. Try number seven.'

'Look, we don't want to disturb him at this hour.'

Molloy had identified the trio, then apologised for calling so late, then pushed his luck by asking about the 'young lad' who spent his time looking out the window. His ring had been answered on an intercom at the bolted front door to The Palms. A woman's voice had quizzed him for almost five minutes. They were then ordered onto the road while she looked them over from a window on the first-floor landing. Finally each was called in turn while a plump grey-haired woman in navy tracksuit inspected. She relented and allowed Clarke in first. Molloy and Kavanagh watched from the darkness while he was grilled. A man of about sixty from the ground floor joined in. He squinted through the door at the two outside, then insisted Clarke phone HQ (which he insisted on dialling) and listened to the exchanges before taking the receiver and directing his own probing questions. Satisfied, Molloy and Kavanagh were allowed inside and up the stairs to number seven.

'He doesn't sleep at night,' wheezed the woman. Her clothes smelled heavily of cigarettes.

'Never?' asked Clarke, anxious to make small talk.

'Rarely. Whatever happened to him at the accident knocked his sleeping routine. Sleeps all day and lies awake all night.'

'That must be difficult,' Clarke said.

'It's a nightmare,' the woman panted as she ushered the three into the living room. There was a small sofa, two high-backed lounge chairs and a large, wide-screen TV in one corner. A small coffee table peeped from underneath a pile of newspapers. Cigarette burns had destroyed a specked blue carpet and the smell of stale smoke hung everywhere.

'Would you like a fag?' Three heads shook. 'Do you mind if I light up? The name's Annie, Annie Carton.' The three didn't mind and thanked her anyway. 'He's twenty-five really, but the clinic say he hasn't moved beyond the mental age of a twelve-year-old.'

Annie Carton drew heavily on an untipped cigarette and coughed slightly before plumping herself down on one of the high-backed chairs, blowing smoke into the air. The three visitors squeezed onto the sofa and immediately regretted the move there was so little space. Kavanagh made a face at Molloy behind Clarke's back.

'He's slow in his speech and body movements. He's not slow at understanding, mind you,' she added unhappily. 'He misses nothing.' The quarter-burned cigarette was ground out.

'What happened?' asked Clarke.

'Every parent's nightmare. Coming home from school on his bicycle and turned out in front of a car. For a while we didn't think he would live at all his head was so badly smashed. But the doctors never gave up and he pulled through.' She stopped as she remembered, then lit up another cigarette and drew deeply on it. 'He was months in rehabilitation, lost his memory completely.' Her gravelly voice rose. 'He couldn't even remember his own mother and father. That's what they gave us back. Sometimes I wish he had died.' She rested her forehead on an upturned palm and stared at the floor, weary and resigned.

Clarke interrupted. 'Does he spend most nights looking out the window?'

Annie lifted her gaze. 'Aye. And writes down everything in one of his exercise books. He's been doing that since he came home. He's got every train, plane and bus timetable under the sun in that room.'

'Could we have a few minutes with him?'

'I suppose the break in routine will cheer him up. Go ahead. Don't tire him out, though.'

Clarke promised.

Annie Carton started to light up another cigarette, stopped, then dumped the packet back on the coffee table. 'Call him Danny.'

Danny Carton sat propped up on a pile of pillows on his small single bed. The bed was positioned to the side of the room, one edge tight beside the only window. Clarke noticed this immediately. The room was tiny, no more than ten-foot square, but furnished for maximum use of space. One wall carried a network of shelves with portable TV, CD player and computer terminal. To the left, another shelf unit held books from floor to ceiling, mostly computer manuals and soccer annuals. In a neat pile in another corner were train, plane, boat and bus timetables. The walls held posters of Liverpool football team.

Danny Carton smiled when his mother walked into the room, then frowned as the three detectives followed awkwardly behind.

'It's okay, Danny,' promised his mother. 'These are policemen. They just want to talk to you about your hobbies.'

A puzzled look spread across Danny Carton's face.

'You know, all the statistics on the area.' Annie Carton winked conspiratorially at Molloy. 'Danny calls his work statistical analysis.' She turned back and grinned and her son's face lit up.

Clarke hobbled over and sat down heavily on the bottom of the bed, making it creak and sag.

'Be careful,' warned Danny. 'The nurse sat on that end one day and the leg came off.'

The voice was slow and laboured with a profound nasal twang. The man/boy had short ginger hair, cut pudding-bowl style, and a heavy freckled face. His eyes were bright and alert and for a moment Clarke could sense the man behind the boy and his heart ached for the loss. One side of the freckled face was slightly weak and saliva collected on the corner of his mouth. Clarke noticed a pile of used paper tissues stuck in a plastic bin. Danny was dressed in denim trousers, cut short above the ankle, and a black T-shirt. In his left hand he clutched a pen. Lying on the crocheted bedspread was a simple lined exercise book. The book was open and out of the corner of his eye Clarke noticed that day and date. It was written in careful, child-like capitals at the top of the right-hand page with a number of further entries beneath. He nodded towards the book.

'Are we in that?'

Danny Carton looked down and poked at the book

nervously with the pen, turning it round and round. Then he picked it up and peered closely, holding it about an inch from his face.

'His eyesight's not that great,' explained Annie as she turned on a side lamp. The room lit up only slightly better with shadows casting grotesque shapes against the walls.

'Yeah,' grinned Danny, wiping fresh saliva away. 'You just got marked in before midnight.' At the doorframe Kavanagh cursed quietly. 'If ma had let yiz in any later I'd have had to make a fresh page.' He laughed, a nervous noisy laugh.

'Do you write everything down, Danny?' pressed Clarke.

'Only what I can see for meself. Me ma sometimes tells me when she sees things but that doesn't count.'

'Could I see the book, Danny?'

'No.' Danny was firm.

'Ah, Danny,' cajoled his mother, 'show the man the book. He's a policeman. Remember you were always asking me to show the police your books on car numbers? Remember? When we lived over in Rathmines?'

Annie explained Danny had spent long hours recording licence plates of cars stuck at the lights outside the old cinema in Rathmines, another Dublin suburb. They'd lived there in a one-room flat.

'Just before me husband died,' she added by way of useful explanation. 'It was the bit of money he left and what we got from the insurance that gave us enough to move here.'

Molloy suppressed a yawn and nodded sympathetically.

'I only want to look at one entry,' Clarke reassured, noticing the boy's anxious face.

Danny Carton looked up. 'Is it the night the American girl was killed?'

Everyone stiffened. Annie Carton made to speak but found the vice-like grip of Molloy restraining. Clarke tried to control his haste and picked at the fluff on the bedspread.

'Well, it would be a big help if you did know something about that particular night.'

'About the man running out from the side of the park?' Danny wiped more saliva from the corner of his mouth and laid the exercise book down. Then with slow, unsteady hands he turned the pages. No one spoke. Outside a car drove past, its headlights catching the group in relief. Danny looked out the window and watched until it disappeared. 'That's a Toyota Corolla,' he announced triumphantly and turned the pages back to the current day. He began laboriously entering the observation onto the left-hand page.

Annie Carton came to the side of the bed and began smoothing the bedspread. 'Danny,' she said, 'show them the page they want to see.'

Danny turned the pages back. 'Monday, 18 May,' he began as a page flicked. 'Sunday, 17 May; Saturday, 16 May . . . I saw three different Datsuns that day,' he continued his laboured search. 'Thursday, 14 May . . . 6.13 pm a big man and a young girl were at the meter box on Mercers Road.'

Molloy interrupted. 'That's correct, Danny. That was me and a friend. We were looking for something.'

Danny dabbed at the side of his mouth. 'That's where the girls hide their schoolbags.'

Clarke looked over at Molloy. He could see the excitement on the other man's face. Danny Carton's diary was now known to be accurate as well as detailed.

Finally. 'Monday, 11 May.' Danny paused and held the pages closer, eyes moving as he read his own writing. '9.47 pm, shouting from Sandymount Park. 10.11 pm, girl screaming.' Clarke's heart began pounding in his chest. '10.23 pm, man ran from side of Sandymount Park onto Mercers Road.'

Molloy cut across. 'Are you sure about that, Danny? It's important. You saw a man running from the park in this direction and down that road out there?'

Danny dabbed at his mouth, squinted at the page, then laid the exercise book down. He seemed very tired. 'That's what I wrote.'

Clarke moved closer and held one of the boy's hands. 'You're doing great, Danny. Can you remember if the girl was still screaming then. Was there still shouting?'

Danny didn't resort to his notes. 'No. Everything had gone very quiet. I remember that well.' He looked again at the exercise book. 'The man drove off in a real hurry. I could hear the tyres screeching.'

Molloy grasped Annie Carton's shoulders, squeezing them tightly. 'You're very good on cars, Danny,' he said. 'You seem to know them all. Did you write down what make it was?'

The exercise book was lifted, the words pored over. 'I didn't recognise it. I'd say it was an American job. It was big and heavy. It was very powerful.'

Molloy frowned. 'Why an American job?'

Danny threw a wet tissue into the bin and looked up, his face excited. 'I looked out. It was a left-hand drive.'

31

31 *8.37 am,*
Tuesday, 19 May.

The Goon was waiting again.

Joan Armstrong sat on a metal seat at the commuter railway station on Sydney Parade Avenue in Sandymount. Early morning sun was filtering through the surrounding trees but it was still cool. Traffic along the side roads was heavy and the smell of diesel hung in the air. The train pulled up on time, dropping off a small group of office workers and businessmen. The girls wore summer blouses, the men pin-stripe suits, trying to look important as they chattered into their mobile phones.

Joan Armstrong climbed on board with three companions. They were engaged in a deep conversation about school, boys, examinations, boys, the summer holidays and boys. One girl started complaining about her acne and the rest took turns to inspect and advise. They were on good form. Even Joan Armstrong. Until she spotted the Goon. He moved into the same carriage and stared at her, his body swaying slightly with the movement of the train. He flicked at his moustache with the tip of his tongue. Armstrong tried not looking. She shifted to the opposite seat, keeping her back to him. She suddenly became intensely interested in a conversation about hockey, a game she didn't play. The Goon walked past, turned and faced her again. He had a slight grin at the side of his mouth, one of the many irritating features Joan despised.

The train pulled in at Blackrock Station, the stop where the convent girls usually got off for school. Armstrong tried forcing her way through the crush but found her left wrist suddenly gripped. She tried shaking it free but the fist held tight. As the passengers walked along the platform, the Goon pulled Armstrong aside.

'Mo wants to talk, Joan. He's sent me to get you.' He suddenly noticed the other girls staring at him and let go. Joan Armstrong ran ahead, false laughter trying to hide her fear.

'What a wanker,' she cried when she reached safety. 'Another reporter trying to get a scoop about Jennifer.'

The girls began crowing at the Goon's retreating back. They didn't see his fists grip and ungrip with rage.

10.12 am

'He's not ready.'

'We have to talk to him.'

'You can talk all you want, I can't guarantee he'll make sense.'

Jim Clarke was on the telephone to Patrick Dillon.

'We've had a definite sighting of a second man,' Clarke explained, trying to contain his excitement.

'Someone ran from the back of the park and drove away in a powerful car. Your theory's making sense.'

'Glad to hear that.'

'He's the only suspect in custody. The way it's looking he'll never get out of gaol.'

'He'll never get out of *hospital*,' Dillon came back immediately.

'Can we just talk with him?' Clarke's exasperation grew by the minute.

'It'll have to be through me,' Dillon began laying down the ground rules, 'and only one of you present.'

'Okay.'

'No pens or paper. If you want to record what he says use a Dictaphone.'

'Agreed.'

'Better still,' added Dillon after a brief pause, 'use one of those concealed microphones. He's so paranoid he'd run a mile if he thought you were recording his thoughts.'

Clarke scribbled the instructions on a pad. 'Anything else?'

'We'll have to play this by ear. He's still confused and disturbed. He might remember something, he might not.'

'Okay.'

The traffic along Dublin's northside was slower than usual with roads dug up for gas-pipe laying. Just before the motorway to the countryside a large JCB was pulled halfway across the road, moving mounds of earth from one hole in the ground to another. In the back of their car Clarke and Molloy watched, fighting to contain their impatience.

'Wouldn't you swear to God they waited until

today to do that just to annoy us.' Molloy was in his complaining mood.

'At least the roads are dry,' Kavanagh shouted over his shoulder against the background of heavy machinery.

The morning had begun bright and sunny. A pleasant warmth had cleared the early chill. It was shaping up to be a fine day.

In his cell in Rockdale Hospital for the Criminally Insane, Micko Kelly sat at the end of his bed staring through the heavily barred windows. He ran his right hand along the spiking hair on his head and felt the early stubble on his chin. He was hungry and thirsty, the first signs of recovery. He was dressed in hospital-issue pyjamas, clean and reasonably well-fitting. He stood on the bottom of the bed to get a better look outside and sighed deeply. He wanted to be get away from the tiny cell. He wanted to pee and old habits took him to the sink unit even though there was a toilet in the corner. He stared at the mirror above the hand basin, fascinated at the changed reflection. He barely recognised himself. His long, dank hair was gone, his face shaven apart from overnight stubble. His eyes were still sunken and yellow. He inspected his hands, astonished at how short and clean the nails were. For a moment he felt pleased, then confused, then suspicious. Where were his nails and hair? Who had taken them? Why had they been taken? He shuffled up and down the tiny space between door and wall, stopping and turning. Keys rattled in the lock and he sat down abruptly.

'Here's your breakfast,' a heavily built warder pushed a trolley inside and lifted a plastic tray onto the bed. 'I'm leaving the door open. You can go in and out as you please. No fucking high-jinks like yesterday,' he added.

Kelly didn't look up. The warder moved on to the next patient. Kelly looked at the tray. The fare was the same as most days. Cornflakes inside a plastic bowl to be eaten with a plastic spoon. A plastic beaker full of milk. Buttered toast on a plastic plate with some marmalade inside a small plastic cup to be spread with a plastic knife.

Hunger urged Kelly to eat but he was frightened. The morning before had been hell. When he'd looked down at the flakes of corn he'd seen a face. Not one face but many faces. Each face was identical. It was the same on each cornflake, the face of a young girl. The girl's mouth was open, as if in a scream. She had dark hair. It was not a face he knew and yet there was something familiar about it. That disturbed him further. He'd ignored the bowl until gnawing hunger drove him to eat. He'd averted his eyes from the flakes and poured the milk. And blood had streamed from the plastic beaker. Warm, bubbling, thick, sticky blood. He'd wanted to scream but couldn't, the sound stuck in his throat. The blood had poured over the tiny faces inside the plastic bowl, moving them around. The dark-haired, open-mouthed screaming faces slowly became covered in blood. Kelly had lifted the spoon and bowl to his mouth.

'Taste her blood.'

He roared and dropped the bowl of cereal and milk over his pyjamas. 'I'm covered in her.' He rushed into the corridor, tearing furiously at the mess stuck to his pyjamas. 'I'm covered in her blood.' He tore the pyjamas off and sat naked in a corner, curled in a ball.

It took the warders forty minutes to calm and sedate.

Kelly now peered cautiously at the cornflakes, half-expecting to see faces again. Only golden flakes rested innocently in the bowl. He forced a darting glance inside the plastic beaker, relieved at the whiteness of the milk. Then he devoured his breakfast, relishing the taste, relieved at the normality. The voices inside his head were less intimidating, less frequent, less frightening. His hallucinations were abating but his paranoia had not settled. When he left his cell, his eyes were averted, always checking over his shoulder.

Conversation was avoided or answers given in short 'yes' or 'no' or 'fuck off'. Fellow patients gave up on him and conversed their mad ideas among themselves. The warders were noticing an improvement and Kelly took his anti-psychotic and drug-dependency medication without question or aversion. He was stabilising. He was looking better.

'I need to talk with you.' Patrick Dillon sat on the edge of the bed trying to establish eye contact. Kelly's eyes darted from side to side, up and down, anywhere but towards the man opposite.

'He's no friend, Michael. He wants your mind.'

Dillon came closer and Kelly recoiled, as if touched by hot steel. He crawled off the bottom of the bed and sat in a corner, both knees tucked under his arms. He tried to squeeze into a ball. 'Fuck off.'

Dillon waited for a moment. 'Michael, I need to talk with you. Something terrible happened and you may be part of it.'

'Fuck off.'

Dillon waited another five minutes. He glanced at

his watch. It was nearly midday. He had suggested a meeting at noon in the outer garden where he'd reckoned Kelly might feel less intimidated. He'd been warned by the warders not to expect much co-operation. They hadn't been happy at the haste to question. A beam of sunlight filled the cell. Outside the morning was a mixture of bright sunshine and great cotton-wool clouds. There was heat in the air.

'Would you like to get out for a while? Get into the sun and move around a bit?'

For the first time Kelly looked over, eyes a mixture of suspicion and expectancy. He said nothing. The psychiatrist stood up, stretched and yawned. He went to the barred window and squinted out. 'There's a grand garden out there. Why don't we have a walk. Stretch our legs and sit in the sun. There's a few benches.' He stepped out of the cell and began conferring with one of the warders.

Kelly checked no one was looking, then padded across to the barred window. He gazed down at the green below. Rockdale Hospital had been built around a central garden. The wards stretched along four wings, north, south, east and west. The single cells looked over the garden, the connecting corridors running along the outer perimeter walls. The garden itself was quite large, almost three hundred square yards of lawn and shrubbery with electrically pumped streams and small waterfalls. There was a bright red footbridge over one stream. The setting had been created to induce a sense of calm and order. The lawns were tended by those patients deemed safe to use tools and mowers. Once, in the early fifties, a sad misjudgement had been made in this regard and a seemingly safe inmate had plunged a pitchfork through the throat of a fellow patient. From then on all tools were of the non-sharp variety.

As Kelly gazed down at the beckoning lawn his will to resist waned. He yearned to be out of the wards and tiny cell, away from his hated fellow inmates. He pulled tighter against the bars to get a better view and sunlight momentarily dazzled. He was confused and angry, uncertain why he was in such a place, unsure he was ever going to get out. He spent long periods trying to remember what had happened, to make sense of his situation. While little glimpses might suddenly light up the darkness, more often he was left frustrated by large blank gaps. It just wouldn't come. Blood was blocking his mind. Thick, sticky, oozing, bright red blood. Kelly could almost smell it.

'Are you coming?' Dillon stood in the doorway.

'He stole your hair and nails. He'll steal your mind.'

Kelly glared sullenly.

'We don't let many out from the wards,' said Dillon. 'This could be your only chance.' He walked along the outside corridor and turned keys in the barred gate. A suspicious and angry Micko Kelly edged out from his cell.

'Wait, ye fucker,' he shouted. 'I'm coming.'

A warder fell in behind, keeping within ten-steps distance. The trio walked along high-walled corridors, through locked doors, past isolation and treatment units. Confused faces stared out at them. They reached ground level. As Dillon walked onto the outside grass Kelly stopped, frightened to move. His suspicious eyes checked what lay ahead. The warder waited patiently. With tentative steps, Kelly finally edged his way into the garden. The warm country air momentarily surprised and he sniffed, savouring the different smells. In the back of his head voices surged but he felt so elated he suppressed their anger.

Dillon strolled lazily towards a small gravel square in the middle where there were two wooden benches. He sat down with a great show of relaxing, his movements casting weak shadows along the lawn. He stretched both hands behind the back of his head and locked them in place. With a satisfied sigh he closed his eyes and basked in the noon sunshine. From the edge a paranoid and suspicious Kelly watched.

'Come on over here. There's great heat in the sun.' Dillon kept a wary eye for any sudden movement behind his back. His protective instincts were never sharper. He'd been cautioned against taking unnecessary chances with Kelly. He was still considered dangerous and unpredictable.

Kelly made his way across the lawn, amazed with the impressions his feet left in the fading dew. He was still in hospital-issue pyjamas and wore a pair of worn sneakers, much too large for his feet. Every three or four steps he stopped and posed as if listening for some distant sound. Then he rubbed both hands along the spiky hair on head and chin and ventured further. His journey was painstakingly slow and erratic. Finally he stood rock still, one ear cocked in the air. He scuffed at the earth with his right foot, like a bull pawing before a charge. Then, lightning fast, he darted to the bench opposite Dillon and sat down. The staccato movements took the psychiatrist by surprise and he jerked to attention, then relaxed as he watched Kelly shove his face directly at the sun and close his eyes.

They heard Jim Clarke approach long before they saw him. The drag of a leg, the crunch of crutch on gravel alerted. Kelly looked over suspiciously. Clarke sat beside Dillon and pushed his leg out.

'Watch that bastard, Michael. He's not one of the regulars.'

The paranoia returned. The voice inside Kelly's head surged forward. He stood up and began walking agitatedly around the bench, stopping and listening. He rubbed at his stubbly hair with the open palms of both hands. The bizarre movements continued for almost five minutes.

'Michael,' Dillon began. Kelly had returned to the bench. 'I need to talk with you. This man,' he gestured towards Clarke, 'is here to help.'

Kelly stared at the gravel.

'Something terrible happened before you came in here. You're being blamed for it.' Dillon leaned across on the bench, both elbows on his knees. He rested his chin on his upturned palms and tried to engage eye contact. 'We're not sure about this. We don't know if you did anything. But you were there, you were definitely there. We need you to tell us what happened.'

Kelly continued to stare at the gravel. He jumped up and stumbled agitatedly around the bench, then sat down abruptly. He looked across at Dillon. 'Fuck off.' There was little strength in the voice, little conviction in the bravado. He sounded uncertain.

Dillon crossed his legs and leaned back on the bench. In the distance a tractor engine started up, scaring crows into the air. From the cells above insane men and women stared down.

'Can you remember anything before you came in here?' Dillon pressed. 'A young girl was murdered. An eighteen-year-old girl was stabbed to death in a park.'

Kelly started shaking.

'You were in the park at the same time. Everyone's blaming you. We need you to help us. We need to make sense of this.' Dillon edged along the bench. 'What happened that night?' He leaned closer. 'What happened to Jennifer Marks?'

'Jennifer, Jennifer. The screamer.'

Sweat began to bead on Kelly's forehead, his limbs shook. He grabbed both legs, trying desperately to control his agitation.

'Who stabbed her? Who else was there? You've got to remember. It's your only hope of getting out of here.' Dillon looked around. 'You'll be stuck in this hospital for ever. You'll never get out.'

Kelly circled the wooden bench. He began talking to himself, a mixture of nervous laughs and angry growls. His eyes darted from side to side. Dillon forced him back onto the bench.

'What happened that night?' He gripped his shoulders tightly. 'Who was with you? Who killed Jennifer Marks?'

Kelly looked down at his hands. They were covered in blood. The blood dripped from each finger and he rubbed at his clothes furiously in an attempt to clean them. But his mind would not allow relief.

'Who killed Jennifer Marks?' Clarke was shouting.

Kelly's mind was in turmoil, his body shook violently.

'Who killed Jennifer Marks?' The shouts echoed along the granite walls and more inmates crowded to their windows to listen. 'Who was with you?'

'Gimme the fuckin' knife, you scumbag!' For a fleeting second Micko Kelly remembered everything. He saw a face, heard the screams of a young girl. He

heard the angry roars of a man's voice. *'Gimme the fuckin' knife, you scumbag!'* He saw a knife flash in the night sky. Then he ran. He ran from one end of the garden enclosure to the other. At the end of the lawn where granite stone marked the boundary walls, he tried scrambling to safety. It took the warders thirty minutes to catch and subdue him.

It took Clarke a lot less to recognise he had problems. Big problems.

12.27 pm

Fifteen miles away in her apartment near Dublin's Mercy Hospital, Linda Speer had her bags packed and set aside in one corner. She checked her flight tickets, made out in a false name, Dublin to Amsterdam. The money tranfer had been arranged once the target of $22.50 was reached. Sell, sell, sell. Cynx shares would be traded like confetti. She had everything worked out to the final detail. Except for Frank Clancy. He couldn't be traced. That worried her. He knew too much. But they were working on it, had a lead. Speer checked her watch, then lit her sixth menthol-tipped in an hour. Seven o'clock tomorrow evening. It would all be over by then. Goodbye Dublin. And fuck you. Frank Clancy, you'll soon be dead meat.

2.32 pm

'We've narrowed it down to this man.'

Back at the incident room in Sandymount police

station Tony Molloy was explaining developments. Kavanagh and Clarke sat on two chairs. They had the room to themselves and were studying three enlarged glossy photographs stuck with pins to a wall. The blow-ups were of the group of spectators gathered at the park railings the morning Jennifer Marks' body had been discovered.

'We've checked names against faces twice. This man,' the tip of a biro pointed to a shadowy figure, 'is the only one unaccounted for.' Molloy picked up an A4 sheet lying beside him and scanned it quickly. 'Two people, a thirty-three-year-old male school-teacher and an eighteen-year-old female office worker, were standing beside and behind him at the time. They're sure he was wearing a black hairpiece and sunglasses. No one else was wearing shades, it wasn't that bright.'

'We've got to find him,' said Clarke. He poked at the side of a chair with his crutch. 'Put the word about. Print another fifty photographs and have them handed out. We must track him down.' He tapped Kavanagh on the shoulder. 'Who's your friend in the *Post*, the crime reporter?'

'Barry Nolan.'

'Ring him. Say we're looking for a second man. Let him know Kelly's not the only suspect.'

'Jesus, boss,' warned Kavanagh, 'that'll stir up a right hornet's nest. The papers will go mad.'

Clarke dismissed the other man's alarm. He hobbled over and stared intently at the unidentified man in the three blow-ups. With enlargement the paper had become grainy, but there was still enough detail. He picked up a magnifying lens and peered through it, moving from print to print, squinting at each angle of the same small group. Molloy watched, an amused smile on his face.

Clarke beckoned him closer.

'Do you see how tall he is compared to the others?' Molloy looked. 'Yeah.'

'See that straight stare.' An index finger moved from print to print. 'Look at the other faces. Notice how they've moved, they're looking around.'

Molloy scrutinised the prints with a different eye. Each photograph captured a single time frame, reflecting movement of the onlookers, position, head turn, hand up to face. Except one. In all of the photographs the unidentified man with the hairpiece and sunglasses had not moved. His gaze was straight and unwavering.

'Let's flush that bastard out.'

32

10.00 am, local time,
Boston, Massachusetts.

Frank Clancy waited for Dr Harry Walters on level six of Springton Hospital. The floor was devoted to haematology disorders and Clancy recognised the familiar set-up as soon as he arrived. There was a large laboratory adjoining treatment wards. Ill patients conversed in hushed tones, some wandered aimlessly while others pushed drip-stands holding blood transfusion bags. He immediately envied the same-level facility, he hated having to chase up and down to the laboratory in the basement of the Mercy Hospital.

'Dr Walters will be with you in a minute.' A petite, dark-haired secretary offered him a seat. 'Coffee?'

'No thanks, I'm not long after breakfast. Maybe some iced water.' Clancy felt underdressed in his jeans, T-shirt and trainers.

Springton came as a shock to a man who thought he knew all about hospitals. It was very different to what he remembered in Chicago. The complex was massive, three ten-storey steel-and-glass blocks cramped tightly on a two-acre site. The energy of the staff and their constant activity was almost unsettling. Nobody

290

walked, they either hurried or ran. Emergency vehicles screeched. Trousers were standard and worn by all female staff with long white tunics over them. Everyone had a laminated identity card dangling around the neck. Faces were grim and set rigid as if everybody had heard bad news. Security guards patrolled and Clancy noticed two spot checks within five minutes. The security staff wore dark grey uniforms, black peaked caps and dark glasses. Those with red stripes on sleeve edges carried handguns.

His attempts to stop these worker ants and ask directions were greeted with surprise and hurried replies. He got lost twice and arrived on the haematology level three minutes before ten o'clock, out of breath and perspiring heavily. He clutched a large brown envelope. While he waited to introduce himself, the dark-haired receptionist was on the phone warning Dr Walters wouldn't have any windows in his diary until late the following week. Clancy sensed his visit might be rushed.

'Good moring, Dr Clancy. Nice to meet you.'

Harry Walters, chief of the haematology department at Springton, was an impressive-looking man. Tall and business-like, he had steel-grey hair and equally steel-grey bobbing, bushy eyebrows over deep blue eyes. His nose was bulbous and red-veined. He was dressed in a lightweight navy suit with red pin-stripe shirt and navy bow tie. In his jacket pocket a crisp white handkerchief peeped out. Like everyone else he carried a laminated identity card around his neck. Clancy estimated he was in his early sixties, though the ID suggested younger. He was all teeth and smiles but his eyes roamed restlessly as he shook hands.

'Did you get my fax?' Clancy asked immediately.

'I did. Can't say it made a lot of sense though.'

The accent reminded Clancy of Dan Marks. Deep voice, New England twang. Heavy emphasis on the 'I'. Walters sat in a high-backed chair behind a wide desk. The office was tastefully furnished, quiet and discreet, pale greens and yellows. A small bunch of dark red roses inside a fluted vase contrasted nicely. Clancy sat opposite in a smaller, maroon cloth seat.

'No, I'm suppose it didn't,' he said. He laid the brown envelope on the desk and began pulling documents out. Walters looked on, his toothy smile replaced by a puzzled frown.

'First of all,' said Clancy, 'let me confirm my identity.'

Walters' frown deepened.

'This is my registration certificate with the Irish medical council.' A heavily embossed document was passed across the table. Walters inspected briefly. 'This is my medical defence licence, confirming I am currently insured against malpractice claims.' A laminated credit card-type identity was offered. 'This is verification of my contract with Dublin's Mercy Hospital confirming full-time consultant haematologist status.' Two A4 size pages with Mercy Hospital heading and official stamp were laid down beside the others. 'This is my passport.'

Walters scrutinised, then flicked to the photograph. He glanced at Clancy's hair and did a double-take on the passport.

'Finally,' concluded Clancy, noticing for the first time the other man's bewilderment, 'my registration with the American Board of Haematologists and

Oncologists.' He stopped, then added for good measure, 'I sat the exams in Chicago.'

Walters held up a hand. He rocked his chair from side to side. 'Dr Clancy, you're not looking for a job. What takes you all this way in such a hurry?'

Frank Clancy had been rehearsing his lines all morning. He didn't want to give too much away immediately, yet wanted to get to the point as soon as possible. He especially didn't want to go in up to his neck without sounding Walters' reactions first.

'Could you tell me if your department noticed an unusual cluster of patients presenting with agranulocytosis in the past few years?'

Walters leaned back in his chair and studied the younger man opposite. 'You came all this way to ask me that?'

'That and a whole lot more.'

'And this couldn't have been dealt with in the usual way? Telephone, fax, e-mail? A search through the medical literature?' Walters began pushing himself from side to side again. 'If I wanted to discuss medical conditions at your hospital in Dublin, do you think I'd turn up on your doorstep on a working day and expect you to open your case files?'

'No,' said Clancy, 'but this is no ordinary request.'

'I'm with you all the way on that,' agreed Walters.

'I couldn't risk anyone else knowing,' Clancy tried explaining, immediately aware he sounded ridiculous. 'And I must have the information back in Dublin before six o'clock tomorrow evening.'

The intercom buzzed and Walters picked up the telephone and listened. 'Tell Dr Goldstein I shouldn't be much longer. Offer him a coffee. Thanks,

Marlene.' He hung up and forced a smile. 'You've got five minutes to make sense of this.'

'Okay,' said Clancy, eyes half-closed, lids fluttering with intense concentration. Please God, don't tell me I'm wrong. Don't let me make a complete fool of myself. 'In my department I see maybe one case of agranulocytosis every year. I've always identified a cause. You know the trigger factors in this disease, I'm not going to call them out.'

'Thank you for sparing me that,' said Walters. His fingers were toying with the intercom button.

'In the past few months I've had three new cases. I've lost all three patients. I haven't been able to figure out why. That's why I'm here.'

Walters looked across sharply. 'You've come to Boston for a discussion on the management of agranulocytosis?'

'No,' said Clancy evenly. 'I've come to Boston to see whether you've had a similar cluster.' He leaned on the table and held the other man's stare. 'And I want to know whether that unusual clustering has ceased.'

Walters crossed both hands and rubbed his knuckles under his chin. He adjusted his bow tie, then buzzed the intercom. 'Marlene, another five minutes. Sorry.' He turned back. 'Dr Clancy,' he said, 'I don't know the protocol in Ireland, I've never worked there. But you trained in the US and must be aware of the standard methods of sharing confidential information.'

Clancy came back immediately. 'I do. But I'm breaking with tradition, I'm prepared to bend the rules to get the facts. I need to know whether this hospital has had an unusual cluster of cases of agranulocytosis and whether that cluster has ceased as mysteriously as it appeared.'

'Why Boston?' asked Walters. His dismissive tone had softened. He was sitting more upright in the chair. 'Why not Chicago since you worked there? Why not New York, LA or even Denver?' He adjusted his bow tie again. 'Why Boston?'

Okay, thought Clancy, here it comes. In at the deep end. Jump. 'I'm trying to establish a possible link between my cases of agranulocytosis and the arrival in my hospital of Dan Marks, Linda Speer and Stone Colman.'

Walters' features suddenly darkened. 'You're way out of line on this, Dr Clancy. Way out of line.' He flicked the intercom button. 'I'm coming out now, Marlene. Apologise to Dr Goldstein for the delay. Give Dr Clancy a coffee and order him a cab.' He paused, 'Where are you staying? Maybe you'd prefer to use public transport?'

Frank Clancy stretched across the table and flicked the intercom button off. Walters looked up, stunned. His face turned puce with anger. He tried forcing the button down again but found Clancy's grip restraining.

'Dr Clancy,' he spluttered indignantly, 'would you let go . . .'

Clancy pushed Walters back in his chair. It spun to one side. 'If I don't leave this office with the information I need I'm going public on this. I've got until this afternoon before my flight leaves. I could give a lot of interviews in that time.'

Walters glared at him angrily. 'What the hell are you talking about? I could have you charged with assault for what you just did.'

'I don't give a damn,' Clancy was leaning across the desk, trying hard not to lose control. 'I haven't come this far to go home empty-handed. I need answers.'

Walters continued glaring. 'I don't know what you're talking about.'

'Maybe this will shake your memory.' Clancy upended his brown envelope and onto the desk dropped a small blue tablet. 'Recognise that?' he asked.

Walters straightened his clothing, picked up the tablet and inspected. He noticed the lettering CYN on one side, XP on the other. He slid it back. 'No. You've got one minute to get out of here or I'm calling security.'

Clancy had decided earlier how any possible confrontation would run. He'd rehearsed all options. He was now in scenario number three. Walters' denial. Time to open up.

'Dr Walters,' he said as he sat down again, 'don't treat me like some fool. Do you think I've flown from Dublin on a wild impulse? I'm as aware as you of the implications of what I'm suggesting. But I have a lot more information, hard facts, more than I've divulged so far.' He didn't. That's why he was in Boston. Bluff time. 'And someone's been following me, ransacked my house, stole important documents. I think my life is in danger. I'm not talking medical mistakes, bad judgement or poor clinical standards. I'm talking murder.' He stopped, suddenly aware he was shouting.

Walters rested chin on upturned palms. His lips moved slightly but nothing came out. He reached for the intercom, then stopped halfway. 'What time are you due to fly back?' he asked abruptly.

Clancy frowned, uncertain what was coming. He

glanced at his watch. It was now eleven thirty. 'I'm on a Delta direct to Dublin at three exactly.'

'Go for a later flight,' advised Walters. He picked up a phone and started dialling. 'If you want answers I'd suggest you come back this afternoon.' At the other end of the line a voice answered. 'Put me through to Ken Foss, please. Tell him it's Dr Harry Walters at Springton. Tell him it's urgent.' He cupped his hand over the mouthpiece as he waited. 'Kenneth, how are you? Good. Look, Ken, something very interesting has come in about our mutual medical problem . . . yeah, the same one . . . exactly, exactly.' He glanced across the table. 'There's a gentleman here in my office right now I'd like you to talk with.' Pause. 'Five this afternoon, that okay?' Walters hung up and immediately buzzed the intercom. 'Marlene, Dr Clancy is booked on Delta out of Logan direct to Dublin at three o'clock exactly this afternoon.' He checked for Clancy's confirmation. 'Find him a flight later this evening, okay? Don't make it any earlier than, say, eight o'clock.' Angry mutterings came across the intercom. Walters ignored them. 'And Marlene, cancel the whole afternoon. Yes, the whole afternoon. Then get me Sam Bawden on the line as soon as possible. Thank you, Marlene.' He flicked the OFF button and stood up. 'I've got a lot of work to do and this discussion has delayed me considerably.' He turned the handle on the door, then paused. 'Your threats disturb me, Dr Clancy. Before we speak again I'll need to take legal advice.' The door was pulled open. 'I'd recommend you do too.'

It was Barry Nolan's exclusive in the *Evening Post* that precipitated a crisis in the Jennifer Marks' investigation. The front-page report was accompanied by photographs and background briefings from police and hospital sources, with further 'startling new revelations' offered on pages five, six and seven. There were a number of 'off-the-record' quotes. The banner headline guaranteed bumper sales. JENNY: SECOND MAN INVOLVED?

Nolan recounted how the police investigation into the 'teen schoolgirl's murder' had taken a dramatic twist. There were insider accounts on Micko Kelly's continuing mental instability accompanied by an old mugshot-style photograph. Unnamed warders at Rockdale confirmed he was being questioned about a 'second man'. Another source added fuel to the fire with 'a definite sighting' of someone other than Kelly running from Sandymount Park. The tabloid had its readers worked up with a final, possible conclusion: IS KELLY INNOCENT?

Nolan added that news bureaux from around the world were following the story closely. TV crews from

Sky, CNN and two major US networks had based themselves in Dublin, filing regular updates while they awaited developments. The *Boston Globe* had three reporters walking the streets looking for new angles. 'America demands justice', was how one cable TV journalist began his account.

Jim Clarke was summoned to an urgent meeting with the police commissioner.

Stuck in a long line of traffic near the city centre, he stared sullenly out a smeared back window, observing his fellow citizens. People were eating hamburgers, improving their cosmetics or fighting with boisterous children. Being driven around allowed him to inspect society at his leisure and the more he saw the less he liked. He had been aware for some time that the constant pain from his damaged leg was making him bitter and easily angered. He'd always said he wouldn't retire early on health grounds, that would only have given the criminal underworld a sense of victory. Recently he'd begun to have second thoughts. When this case is over, he promised, as the car sped into the quadrangle at headquarters, I'll pack it in for good. Spend some time with the family, with Katy in particular. I hardly see her nowadays. She's growing so quickly. That's what I'll do, I'll pack it in after this. I'll tell them this evening.

Commissioner Murphy was in no mood for discussion.

'Sit down, Jim. I'd like to get this over with quickly.'

Clarke was directed to a chair around a wide, dark wood circular table in room eleven. Already waiting and glaring was Minister for Health, John Regan, and his cabinet colleague, Paddy Dempsey, the Minister for Justice. Donal Murphy was in navy slacks with open-neck, short-sleeved shirt. He appeared pre-occupied and studiously avoided eye contact. Dempsey was dressed in ill-fitting tweeds, his bull neck straining at a shirt collar an inch too small. By contrast John Regan's physique made the most of his loose-fitting slacks and yellow jumper over dark blue shirt.

'I've had a complaint about the handling of the Jennifer Marks' murder investigation,' Murphy began. He raised an index finger to stifle any inter-ruption. 'After your questioning of Annie Marks she apparently became very agitated and her husband had to be called from the operating theatre. She is now under sedation.'

Clarke sensed trouble.

'Dan Marks was so angered he made an official protest to the department.' Murphy finally looked over. 'Minister Dempsey contacted me this morning and was most forthright in his criticisms.'

Clarke glimpsed a smug, satisfied smile flicker at the other side of the table. He found John Regan staring at him.

'I agreed to this meeting to review the situation,' continued Murphy, ignoring the look of dismay on Clarke's face. He shuffled paperwork on the desk in front. 'And,' he added, 'I have reassured the ministers the investigation is proceeding apace. Michael Leo Kelly is still our main suspect and we plan to charge him as soon as the medical team in Rockdale give permission.'

Clarke listened with suppressed fury. He gripped at the sides of the table, his nails digging into wood. He wanted to shout to stop the words he was hearing.

'Since the investigation is more or less complete I

feel it would be wiser, Jim, if you took a break.' Murphy looked directly at him. 'I have explained how difficult life has been for you since the bombing and Minister Dempsey has agreed to fund a month's paid holiday over and above your standard leave.'

Dempsey spoke for the first time. He leaned heavily on the table and glanced across, avoiding eye contact. His thick lips mumbled the words.

'I think this inquiry is getting the better of your judgement. The report in tonight's *Post* is ridiculous. Who's leaking that information? This second man theory is no more than the ramblings of some mentally retarded youngster. We've got our man.' He sat back in his chair. It slid on the highly polished floor from his weight. 'Dublin's full of reporters standing beside satellite dishes shooting their mouths off. If this goes on much longer we'll be made to look like fools. Kelly was seen running from the scene, Kelly was covered in the girl's blood. That's it, full stop.'

John Regan interrupted. 'And I'm not impressed with his so-called insanity. That angle came up very quickly. There'll be no pleas of diminished responsibility when he comes to court if I can help it.' He glared at Clarke. 'And no bleeding-heart psychiatrist supporting him.' He stopped, then leaned across the table, the picture of sudden concern. 'Are you using regular painkillers? Maybe you're taking something that's clouding your judgement?'

Clarke almost erupted but was saved by the timely interruption of the commissioner. 'Thank you, gentlemen, I think you've said enough. Superintendent Clarke doesn't have to put up with cheap jibes.'

Regan snarled. 'Superintendent Clarke has nearly brought the Heart Foundation to its knees. The staff were incensed at Annie Marks' interrogation.' He eyeballed Clarke. 'I have a crucial press conference tomorrow night. A twenty-million-pound EEC grant is due to be handed over for the Mercy Hospital project. And in full view of the world press. I will not lose that because of the actions of some small-time knifeman. I plan to disclose formal charges will be laid against that junkie.' He stood up. 'This investigation is finished, the file is closed.' He stormed out of the room, slamming the door after him. A mumbling Dempsey followed.

Donal Murphy started packing paperwork into a briefcase.

Clarke spoke at last. He'd held silence long enough and his anger finally surfaced. 'Commissioner, I'm tendering my resignation as from now. I'll put this in writing and have it on your desk within half an hour.' He was white-faced, his emotions crumbling. He'd been humiliated without an opportunity to reply. He felt betrayed, disgraced. His superior's last-minute support had been feeble. He wanted to be out of the room, away somewhere on his own.

Murphy laid his briefcase on the floor. 'I don't want your resignation. I want this girl's killer. If you think there was someone else involved you better prove it before Regan's press conference.' He stood up to leave. 'Kelly is the only one who knows what happened that night. You're off the case, so get on to that psychiatrist Dillon, it's time he produced results.'

8.12 pm

At Rockdale Hospital for the Criminally Insane,

302

Patrick Dillon was trying to get results. He'd been rung from police headquarters and warned about John Regan's press conference. That had disturbed him. 'Most unhelpful,' he'd commented. Equally he recognised how volatile the media reporting had become. The murder investigation was still the lead story on most bulletins. And international interest was intensifying. His own involvement was being analysed over the airwaves by armchair psychiatrists offering informed opinion. He was now as important as his charge. PSYCHO JUNKIE'S SHRINK was how one US tabloid had described him. He'd laughed at that. He hadn't laughed when a TV lawyer suggested his sole involvement was to get Kelly off the murder charge on grounds of diminished responsibility. Worse was to come. An American forensic psychiatrist previously involved in a high-profile murder was paraded on primetime television. He suggested Dillon could be keeping Kelly in hospital longer than necessary with a view to writing a bestselling book about the case later. 'Just like I did,' he openly confessed. That had rankled. Dillon disliked the media spotlight intensely, hated TV pundits trying to second guess his management. He decided to try to move things along faster.

He faced Micko Kelly across a five-foot-square oak-veneer table in a small 'time-out' room. Outside in the corridor of the maximum security ward halogen lights glared. The 'time-out' room, barely ten feet long and twelve feet wide, was reserved for interviews and management of aggressive outbursts. It was a cooling-off area, strategically situated beside the padded cell. The room was poorly lit by a single central forty-watt bulb and a swivel lamp had been set on the table for better light. Dillon had spread out a range of newspaper cuttings on top of the table. Each was a report of the Jennifer Marks' murder, many with photographs. He slid a cutting across and pointed. 'That's Sandymount Park. Do you remember being there?'

Kelly studied the clipping then shook his head. He ran a tattooed hand across the spiky growth on his head, then against the stubble on his chin. 'Nah.'

Dillon sorted through the collection and pushed another over. It was a front page of the tabloid *Daily Post* with a close-up of Jennifer Marks. The banner headline had been cut away. Kelly looked at the photograph with a seeming disinterest, then squinted closer.

'Gimme the fuckin' knife, you scumbag.' The voice flashed and disappeared. Kelly seemed momentarily stunned. Then he lifted the page and scanned each detail closely.

'Do you know who she is?' asked Dillon.

Kelly dropped the page back on the table. 'Nah.'

Dillon mentally recorded the other man's reaction. 'Think. It's important for you. Try and remember. She was in that park with you that night. Something terrible happened to her.'

Kelly shook his head violently from side to side. 'Nah, nah. I can't remember. I'm tellin' ya, I just can't remember. Stop torturin' me. I can't remember.' He pushed the chair away with the back of his legs and began pacing around the room.

Dillon watched closely.

'You all think I'm mad,' Kelly shouted angrily. 'Well, I'm tellin' ya I'm not.' He pointed a nicotine-stained index finger at his right temple. 'I was all right 'til I came into this dump. Now I'm surrounded by crazies.' His hand movements were jerky, eyes rolling. His lips moved furiously but not always with words. He sat down at the table staccato-like. 'Get me outa this fuckin' place,' he snarled.

Dillon leaned back in his chair and began humming quietly. 'I'd have you out tonight if I thought you weren't a danger.'

'I didn't do fuck all.' Kelly had slumped into a dark corner. 'D'ye hear me? I shouldn't be in here with these fuckin' lunatics.'

Later Dillon recorded his observations in the hospital chart. 'Michael Kelly improving slowly,' he wrote, 'hallucinations abating, physical appearance reflects better nutrition and lack of hard drugs. While his long-term recall is good, memory for recent events is still poor. This confuses him greatly. He is prone to bursts of aggressive agitation. Still exhibiting para-noid schizoid-type symptoms. Impression: progress not sufficiently established to justify discharge to secure unit.'

When he'd finished Dillon sat at the desk thinking. Kelly's disorganised thought pattern could persist for weeks. The loss of short-term recall was the biggest problem, it frustrated him most. If we jog his memory, Dillon reasoned, the truth might come out. Is he a psychotic murderer or a madman being set up as a stooge? There's one way to find out. It's risky. It could destroy my reputation if it backfires. He heard an angry shout. Micko Kelly was being closed in for the night.

I'll do it. Tomorrow. In time for that press conference.

34

3.07 pm, local time,
Boston.

Frank Clancy was a troubled man. He sat on a wire-backed chair in the cafeteria of the west wing of the Museum of Fine Arts on Huntington Avenue chewing a tuna-on-rye sandwich. He had no appetite, the snack tasted like sawdust.

Twenty minutes earlier he'd telephoned his wife Anne from a phone booth in a busy lobby.

'Where are you, Frank?' she'd screamed at him. 'Everyone's looking for you.'

'What do you mean?'

'The hospital administrator has been on asking where you are. He's furious you've taken so much time off.'

'How did he get your number?'

'I rang the hospital looking for you. They told me you were at home.'

Clancy shouted. 'I told you not to contact me.'

'I had to, the children want to go home. I want to go home. We want to go back to our own house.'

'Oh, Christ,' groaned Clancy. He slapped at his forehead.

'Where are you, Frank? What's going on? I'm

306

worried sick, the children are worried sick.'

Clancy went into mental overdrive. 'Are you at the house?'

'No, I'm still at my mother's.'

The relief was overwhelming. 'Anne, I can't explain anything yet. Just make sure you stay where you are and don't go back to the house.'

Silence.

'Frank, what's going on? Where are you?'

Wait for it. 'I'm in Boston.'

Silence.

'Frank.' Anne's voice had dropped. It was full of suspicion. 'What are you doing in Boston? Who's with you?'

Clancy lost his temper. 'There's nobody bloody well with me. I'm here at the haematology department of Springton Hospital trying to find out something.' Even as he spoke Clancy knew the truth didn't sound convincing.

'What are you trying to find, Frank? Why have you been lying to me?'

Oh, Jesus, will this never end? If I tell her the truth she'll call the police. She'll maybe even tell the hospital. My job could be on the line. Speer will get to hear about everything. She'll cover her tracks. I can't say anything.

'Anne,' he glanced around, hoping no one would overhear. 'I love you and I love the children. You've just gotta trust and believe me on this one. I know this all seems very suspicious.'

'It sure as hell does,' Anne cut back angrily.

'I'll explain everything when I come home tomorrow. Just don't say anything to anybody, promise me that.'

307

Silence.

'Anne, you still there?'

Silence.

'Anne, I know you're still listening. Don't tell anyone anything. And don't go back to the house. Do you hear me? DON'T GO BACK TO THE HOUSE.'

Silence.

'I love you, Anne. Tell the children I love them. I'll sort everything out tomorrow when I'm back.'

The line went dead at the other end.

He walked out into the bright sunshine. It was warm and humid and he felt his clothes stick to his back. It was time to go home.

5.03 pm, Boston.

'Dr Clancy, I'd like you to meet Ken Foss.'

The door to Harry Walters' office was opened by the tall man himself. The dark-haired receptionist was nowhere to be seen and Clancy rapped rather than wait. Inside two strangers stood talking, heads close.

'And this is Sam Bawden.'

The handshakes were brief and perfunctory as if all were anxious to get down to business. Clancy noticed neither Foss nor Bawden had laminated name tags around their necks.

'Ken is the legal representative for Springton Hospital,' explained Walters. Foss was a tall, reedy man in a two-piece suit with receding hairline. He half-smiled and sat down in a chair near the window overlooking the hospital complex. 'Sam is our head of security.' Bawden was swarthy and bulky. It seemed he had been squeezed into his ill-fitting light jacket over dark slacks. He wore an open-necked shirt and sneakers. He moved to an empty seat at the side of the room. A soft chair stored behind a coat-stand was produced and offered to Clancy, then Walters sat down in his usual swivel. There was an embarrassed silence as if no one knew where to start. Walters looked briefly at his two companions. 'Dr Clancy . . .'

'Call me Frank,' Clancy suggested.

'Okay,' agreed Walters, 'Frank it is.' He loosened his bow tie for comfort. 'I've explained the reason you're in Boston.' Clancy noticed he was the centre of attention. With his unusual hairstyle and casual clothing he began to feel very self-conscious.

'My colleagues here are very interested in what you have to say. However your line of questioning this morning caught me very much by surprise. I don't know how it works in Dublin but let me assure you we are somewhat legally minded in New England. Nobody's going to give information without a lawyer's advice.'

Ken Foss cut in. His voice was as reedy as his frame. 'Frank, you've made some unusual allegations . . .'

'Not allegations,' Clancy corrected firmly, 'suggestions. I'm very close to making allegations and involving the police. I just need confirmation of my suspicions.'

'That's all very well,' Foss came back, 'but the gravity of those suggestions could be far-reaching. If they're wrong you could spend a lot of your time defending expensive lawsuits. We don't want any involvement, no matter how peripheral, in such a situation.'

'I'm aware of that,' said Clancy. He clutched his brown envelope tightly. The other three kept glancing at it.

'So,' continued Foss, 'before we discuss this any further perhaps you might share the hard facts you mentioned to Harry?'

Clancy hugged the envelope to his chest. 'No.' Assertive.

Foss looked over at Walters and Bawden. 'In that case, Frank, I think we're wasting our time.' He studied his watch briefly. 'Don't let us delay you from your flight.'

Harry Walters interrupted. 'Okay, let's stop circling each other as if this a dog fight.' He stopped his swivel chair. 'You want information from us, Frank. Well, we want information from you.'

Clancy knew at that moment he was on the right track. 'Shoot,' he suggested.

'What,' asked Walters, 'is the connection between your cases of agranulocytosis and Marks, Speer and Stone Colman?'

'Each of the patients had been in the cardiology unit before they developed the blood disorder.'

Walters eyebrows bobbled. 'That's a very tenuous link.'

'There's more,' hinted Clancy.

'Like what?' Foss cut across. Sam Bawden was scribbling furiously on a notepad.

Clancy forced an exaggerated shrug. 'Nothing else from me until I get something from you.'

Walters managed a grin. 'Okay.'

Clancy asked. 'Did you become aware of an unusual cluster of cases of agranulocytosis in the past few years?'

'No.' Walters was emphatic. Clancy was stunned. Foss and Bawden had their heads down.

'No?' Clancy repeated feebly. What's going on?

'No, Frank,' Walters repeated, 'not an unusual cluster of agranulocytosis. We had clusters of a number of blood disorders. Agranulocytosis was one, certainly. But we had a rash of haemolytic anaemias as well.'

Clancy did a mental double take. In haemolytic anaemia the blood cells broke down, leaving the sufferer very weak. Just as with agranulocytosis there were many causes of haemolytic anaemia. An unusual reaction to a prescribed drug therapy was top of the list. He came back before his confusion became obvious. 'Did this grouping of blood disorders surprise you?'

'Very much so,' admitted Walters. The swivel chair was now pushed up against the desk. Walters rested his chin on the knuckles of both hands, his gaze fixed on Clancy. It was as if the Dublin doctor was interrogating him in a witness box.

'Did you come to suspect the blood disorders were connected to the cardiology team working here at that time?'

'Don't answer that, Harry,' advised Foss. He was now standing at the window, his backside resting on the sill. 'What other information do you have?' He looked straight at Clancy.

'Altered medical records,' Clancy dipped into the brown envelope and showed the top of a maroon-backed file. 'An experimental drug not licensed for use in this country or Ireland.'

Foss frowned. 'Anything else?' His reedy voice had deepened.

'Trade-off time,' said Clancy. He had looked at his watch. It was close to six o'clock. His flight out was at eight. He'd have to leave soon. He still didn't have enough information. 'What's been going on at Springton? You know there's a similar development at my hospital. Why don't we cut the waffle and come out with everything.'

'It's not as easy as that, Frank,' said Foss. He had walked over beside the security chief Bawden. 'We have . . .'

Clancy interrupted angrily. 'You all know a certain journalist in this town called Chuck Henning?'

The room went quiet. Chuck Henning was chief investigative journalist on the *Boston Globe*. Clancy had taken his name off the morning edition after reading an article on fraudulent practices in Boston financial circles.

'Well,' he lied, 'I spoke with Mr Henning two hours ago and he's very keen to talk with me again. He senses quite a scoop on his hands.' Bluff.

Ken Foss started to speak but Harry Walters cut across. 'I don't think any of us would care to see our mutual difficulties spread across the papers.' He stood up and walked to the window and looked out. 'Do you enjoy your work, Frank? Do you get personal satisfaction from it?'

Clancy didn't answer.

'Well, I love this hospital,' continued Walters. He opened the window slightly and an ambulance siren whoo-whooed in the distance. 'I've been working here for over twenty years now.' He turned round, shoulders slumped, a look of defeat. 'I know it's not an architectural wonder and I know it's not a perfect institution. No hospital is and I've worked in many.'

He walked back to his desk and sat on the edge. Clancy tried to sense if this was a man unburdening his soul or a careful act. 'But it's my hospital and I do a lot of good work here. My patients need me to make them better but, equally, I need them. Their hopes and dreams, their lives and families are as precious to me as my own life and my own family. I share their misery when they fall ill, I rejoice when they recover.' He undid his bow tie and ran a finger around his shirt collar. 'When their illness is an act of God, or an accident, or some unusual infection, I can cope with that. But when someone creates disease for no other motive than financial gain, I get very upset.' He stopped and turned to Bawden. 'Tell him our side, Sam. It's time to end this sorry business.'

Bawden closed his notebook. 'Dr Clancy,' he began, 'there's an ongoing investigation in this institution about a cluster of patient deaths.' He spoke with a slight guttural accent. 'It's gone past the stage of medical management into possible criminal intent.' Clancy shifted excitedly in his chair. Pay-back time.

Ken Foss cut in. 'I'm sorry if this sounds a bit vague. I've urged caution in anything said here.'

Bawden went on. 'The hospital is under the threat of eight massive litigation suits. There may be more for all we know.'

It's finally coming, thought Clancy. He took his watch off and kept it in his left hand. It was now six ten. Speed up or I'll miss the flight.

'Someone conducted drug trials here on patients without their consent or knowledge.' Bawden was now reading from his notebook. 'Between April 1996 and January 1997 we had eight deaths recorded from blood disorders, mainly agranulocytosis. Each of those patients, unknown to them and this hospital, was being treated with an experimental drug. Each died from reactions to that drug.' He looked over at Clancy. 'The blue tablet you have is not the one used here. However the marking CYN confirms it has come from the same company.'

'Cynx pharmaceuticals?' asked Clancy. More jigsaw pieces.

Foss coughed slightly. 'How did you know that?'

Clancy ignored the question. 'What do you know about Cynx?' he directed the question at Bawden.

'Cynx is a small pharmaceutical company based here in Boston,' Bawden explained. 'It's been unimpressive and uninspiring, very much a minnow in the industry. About five years ago it was bought over by an ambitious consortium from New York who planned to turn it round.' He stopped and looked across to Foss. The other man nodded. 'Dr Linda Speer was one of the investors.'

I knew it, thought Clancy. I bloody knew it. He squirmed in his seat as he listened.

'We believe Cynx became focused in the area of new cardiology compounds,' continued Bawden. 'That's where the big money lies. The company put all its research and development money into one product. But it didn't have the financial muscle to fund standard clinical trials.'

'Which is where Speer's know-how came in,' suggested Clancy.

'I can't state that for definite,' warned Bawden. 'We were looking at all three of those specialists when they suddenly upped anchors and left Boston.'

'We think they were running away,' Walters offered. He was back in his swivel chair, bow tie off.

'The investigation was closing in after I became suspicious and informed our legal advisors. It's my personal belief Springton Hospital was becoming too hot for them.'

'So they were going on with these trials,' Clancy said angrily, 'in the full knowledge some patients were dying from side effects?'

'From what you've told us that would seem to be the case,' said Walters. 'I think they were constantly modifying the molecular structure of the compound, trying to find the right formula to give clinical benefits but none of the deadly side effects.'

'And how many patients would have to die before that ideal compound evolved?'

Walters rocked from side to side in his swivel chair. 'I don't know the answer to that, Frank. But your arrival here suggests they're no closer.'

'And,' added Ken Foss, 'Cynx finances must be running out. There's talk in the trade of a takeover bid from one of the bigger multinational pharmaceuticals. My guess would be they're showing false research results to boost the sell price. Certainly Cynx shares have been driven upwards on the NYSE recently.'

Clancy squinted at his watch. It was six forty-five. He'd have a helluva race to catch the flight. He turned to Walters. 'Can you explain why Speer assists at specific heart operations? Like, what's the connection between drug trials and these operations?'

'My understanding,' explained Walters, 'is that this compound was being tested on diseased arteries in the laboratory as well as on humans in the wards. I believe Speer was harvesting the damaged blood vessels. That's why she assisted at operation. She could assess them as they were being removed ensuring they had ideal pathological specimens to work on. She recovered them from the theatre sluice, iced and couriered them to the labs at Cynx overnight for testing.'

'With Dan Marks' approval?' asked Clancy.

Walters shook his head. 'Can't say that for certain, Frank. Certainly Marks and Speer had a very hot sexual relationship going on when they were here.'

Clancy's eyebrows shot up.

'You know yourself, Frank,' Walters was smirking, 'these surgeons are powerful men. Big egos, strong sex drives. He was married to an invalid. It was inevitable he was going to stray.'

The plot was becoming complicated. Frank Clancy noticed he was perspiring and wiped at his forehead with the shoulder of his T-shirt. 'What about Stone Colman?'

'We've nothing definite on him,' Bawden cut across. 'Speer's involvement seems without doubt. We can't be sure of the other two.' He put away his notebook. 'Linda Speer has been trying for years to make her name in cardiology. She resented bitterly being passed over in career moves. Maybe she decided on a different route to the top. Thought she could produce the heart drug of the future.'

Ken Foss spoke. 'You see, Frank, unlike you we have little physical evidence to confirm our suspicions. The paper copy medical records were changed, we're certain of that, but we don't have the originals. There's confusion about the tablets. We only recovered one and it's currently undergoing biochemical analysis.' He tugged at his jacket to straighten its creases. 'More disturbingly, someone accessed our back-up database. The back-up database is the power house of any hospital's records system. If information is altered there, all original observations, treatments and drug reactions are lost for ever.'

Clancy's brain went into overdrive. Had that happened already in Dublin?

'You'll have a difficult job proving your case if whoever's involved destroys the trail,' Foss finished.

Sam Bawden slipped of his jacket and rested it over his seat. He turned towards Clancy. 'We've been following the murder investigation of Dan Marks' daughter.' The words were spoken casually but the room fell suddenly silent. Clancy looked from one to the other, noticing the intense stares.

'And?'

'It's a terrible business,' Bawden offered.

'Yeah,' replied Clancy slowly. What the hell's coming next. 'Real terrible.'

'You don't think there's any possible connection?' Bawden sounded embarrassed at his own suggestion.

Clancy's mouth dropped. 'Do you?'

'No, no, no,' Bawden hastened to reassure. He didn't sound reassuring. 'Maybe it's my suspicious nature.' He tried to smile to hide his discomfort. It didn't work. 'Forget what I just said.' He looked at his watch. 'You're gonna miss that flight.'

Frank Clancy leapt to his feet. It was three minutes before seven o'clock. He prayed his plane might be delayed. He knew he had to confront Linda Speer before the press conference. He knew the EEC grant hinged on results from the Mercy Hospital Heart Foundation. But to Clancy everything coming out from that top level now stank. No result could be trusted. Everything was tainted by greed and manipulation. And murder.

Harry Walters booked a Springton Hospital emergency car to rush Clancy to the airport. 'Be careful, Frank,' he warned as the door was closed. 'The stakes are high in this game. Whoever's behind this is in too deep to pull back. Keep looking over your shoulder. Play safe.'

Clancy played safe and looked over his shoulder all the way to Logan. As far as he could make out the car wasn't being followed.

'Where are they?' he screamed at his mother-in-law. He was in a call booth at the airport. He'd missed his flight but had rebooked on a Virgin Atlantic to London, with a connecting Aer Lingus from London to Dublin.

'Frank Clancy,' he was rebuked sharply, 'don't you dare shout at me like that. Do you know what time it is?'

Clancy mumbled his apologies. He'd forgotten about the differing time zones. His heart was pounding, from excitement or effort or both he couldn't be sure. He thought it would lift right out of his chest.

'They went back to their own house.'

Oh no, Clancy groaned. 'When?' He couldn't stop himself shouting.

'After you rang.' The mother-in-law was working herself up to some righteous indignation. 'And I may as well tell you, Frank, judging by your behaviour recently you may not be allowed join . . .'

Clancy hung up and dialled his home number as fast as his trembling fingers would allow. In the background he heard the final call for the Boston/London flight announced. It was now nine thirteen.

'Hi, this is Frank and Anne's number. We're sorry we can't take your call right now but . . .' He hung up as soon as he heard the answering machine, thought furiously, then redialled.

'Hi, this is Frank and Anne's number . . .'

'Anne, Anne,' Clancy screamed into the mouthpiece. A lady waiting in line for the booth moved away. She kept staring uneasily at the shouting man's back. 'If you're listening Anne please pick up the receiver. PLEASE!'

'. . . if you'd like to leave your name and number . . .'

In the department terminal the PA clicked into action again. 'Would passenger Frank Clancy booked on Virgin Atlantic to London please go immediately to boarding gate seventeen. This is the last call for passenger Frank Clancy. Please go to gate seventeen immediately. Passenger Frank Clancy.'

A last, desperate throw of the dice. Clancy tried reaching administration at the Mercy Hospital. The switchboard operator apologised. 'I'm sorry but there's no one answering from admin. It is very early in the morning you know.'

His heart sank.

'Are you Frank Clancy?' Clancy spun round. One of the Virgin ground staff was looking at him. The girl's expression suggested she was dealing with a madman. Clancy forced himself to relax, trying to put on some façade of normality.

'I'm coming.'

He sprinted towards gate seventeen.

35

2.37 am,
Wednesday, 20 May.

As Frank Clancy boarded the Virgin Atlantic jet, back in Dublin events were moving to a climax. Two miles south of Mercy Hospital and across the blackness of the River Liffey, the Goon was working into the early hours in a lock-up garage. His metallic black Lincoln had been clipped on the left rear bumper when he'd reversed angrily away from the railway station after the failed confrontation with Joan Armstrong. That had upset him. When he'd returned without the girl, Mo had been very disturbed. Mo had warned the Goon how worried he was about Joan Armstrong. And the Goon so hated to see Mo annoyed. And Frank Clancy was making life even more difficult. The Goon couldn't find him. And he didn't like that. Mo didn't like it either. At all. The Goon decided enough was enough. Time for action.

Now he filled and carefully touched up the dent. In the light of a two-hundred-watt bulb dangling from a beam he admired his handiwork. Perfect. He opened the boot and checked his trade tools. Binding tape: black, heavy-duty, thick and strong. Four rolls. Enough, he reckoned, to secure struggling legs and arms and cover mouths. Black leather gloves, tight, conforming. Two pairs in case he lost one in the encounters. Walther PPK .38 double-action automatic handgun with full magazine. He unclipped the magazine, checked it was full, then clipped it back onto the main frame. He pressed a side panel in the car boot and a recessed area lit up. He slipped the gun and rolls of tape inside. From his hip pocket he produced a flick knife and released the catch. A thin, razor-edged six-inch blade shot forward. The Goon admired its steel as it glinted in the light. Satisfied, he eased the blade back. He'd already decided only to use the handgun in an emergency. It was too noisy. The Goon preferred the silence of the knife. He looked at his watch. Mo had said everything would be over soon. Mo had told him to take care of all loose ends. Joan Armstrong. Frank Clancy. Clancy's family if necessary. The Goon was happy to agree, easy meat. Like taking candy from a baby. Except he'd lost track of Clancy and his family. Until a few hours ago when he'd spotted lights back on in the house. The loose ends had returned. Tidy up time. He unrolled a heavy-duty, extra-wide black plastic bag and laid it carefully along the bottom of the boot making sure enough of the edges were turned up. The Goon hated it when blood leaked onto the upholstery. He'd also modified the back seat so it could be split and moved forward easily. For long bodies that didn't fit easily into the boot. Finally he hid a baseball bat and two sealed cans of petrol behind the passenger seat.

The Goon was ready for the final push.

3.02 am

Sweat poured off the face and forehead and body of Joan Armstrong. She was prostrate on her bed at home, staring at the ceiling, then at the digital clock on her locker, counting the minutes away. Her body ached, she was trembling. She slumped back on the soaked sheets and tried to sleep. Sleep wouldn't come. She rocked backwards and forwards, then doubled up and grasped her knees tightly against her chest. She needed a hit badly. She rubbed at the entry tracks on the bends of her elbows, trying to imagine the sting of the needle, the rush to the brain. She needed Mo. Mo would give her whatever she wanted. She would give Mo whatever he desired. In her desperation she even wished the Goon would turn up.

4.47 am

The Goon snipped the telephone wires to Frank Clancy's house. He'd parked the Lincoln behind the two other cars in the paved driveway. It had been a tight squeeze and almost four feet of the metallic black car jutted onto the footpath. Still, he reasoned in the gloom, it's only for about ten minutes. He disarmed the burglar alarm, cut through the back door glass and slipped the bolts. Four minutes later he was inside the house. He stood still and listened. Nothing. Slowly and stealthily he padded into the front hallway and stopped. And listened. Nothing.

He unrolled the binding tape and cut off three slices. Two were of equal length, one was a shorter strip. Tip-toeing gently to the first bedroom he lifted child number one, eight-year-old Martin. The sleeping body barely stirred as binding tape was wrapped around ankles. When the Goon started prising the Manchester United soccer team scrapbook from the boy's hands, he woke up. In the gloom Martin tried warding off the enveloping tape and was caught on the side of the head by a closed fist. Fifty seconds later he was lying on his side downstairs, bound hand and foot, mouth taped. The soccer scrapbook was caught up in the strapping. Three minutes later Frank Clancy's struggling four-year-old daughter Laura was laid alongside her brother. The little girl's terrified eyes flitted as she rolled her head from side to side, trying desperately to free her face from the binding.

The children watched with horror as the tall shape sprinted back up towards their sleeping mother. Tears streamed but the sobs were muffled. Anne Clancy was half in and half out of the bed when the Goon pushed the door open. She started to scream. A closed fist across the side of her head stunned and stopped her dead. The flick knife was sprung, the steel blade glinting in the darkness. The Goon came closer. CUT, CUT, CUT. Three strips of tape were produced. Anne Clancy's hands and feet were bound. Groggily she looked up to find the black band coming closer. She started to scream again but it was stifled. The tape was forced across her mouth.

5.06 am

Anne Clancy and her children lay trussed up in the kitchen, squirming in a frantic attempt to free

323

themselves. The Goon was pulling the house apart looking for her husband.

'Where's the fucker?' he snarled into the young woman's face, the flick knife waved threateningly at Laura's throat. He released the tape to let her speak.

'At work,' Anne lied through terrified sobs. 'He's at the hospital.'

The Goon kicked the back door angrily, breaking more glass. 'Well, you're coming with me 'til he turns up.'

He sneaked outside, checking he wouldn't have to deal with some public-spirited neighbour. The road was deserted, the nearby windows still curtained off from the breaking dawn. He opened the car boot and right back door.

5.09 am

Laura first, into the boot. Pushed up against the rear seats. Martin next, struggling. A threatening fist stopped the boy's movements. Terrified eyes watched the boot close down.

5.11 am

The writhing body of Anne Clancy was pushed onto the floor space between front and rear seats. She lashed out desperately as door engaged on lock but succeeded only in breaking her left big toe against the panel. She winced with pain.

The Goon started the engine as softly as he could

and eased the Lincoln onto the road. He checked for activity. Nothing. He looked along the upstairs windows of adjoining houses. No movement. He smiled, then flicked on a tape to drown out the dull thuds of kicking feet. Seven minutes later he was on one of Dublin's main traffic arteries, speeding away. The roads were relatively quiet. The Goon stopped at every red light, taking care not to go too fast or lane hop. Mo had cautioned against drawing attention to the car. As he crossed the River Liffey, past early-morning news-vendors setting up their stalls, the Goon felt good. Everything was going to plan. Mo would be pleased. And it would all be over soon. A hint of early-morning sun danced off one of the buildings in the steel-and-glass International Financial Centre. It might be a nice day, thought the Goon. This could turn out to be a very good day.

6.07 am

Anne Clancy and her children were lifted one by one and laid on the basement floor of Mo's residence. The Goon was panting from the effort and sweat beaded along his brow and moustache. He set twelve plastic beakers full of bottled water on the floor near them. Each beaker had a long straw sticking out. Then he checked that nothing could be used to free strapped limbs. Satisfied, he ripped the masking tape from the children's mouths, ignoring the terrified faces wincing at him.

'You can scream and shout all you fucking well want.' His perspiring face was stuck up against Anne Clancy. 'No one will hear.' He flicked at an edge of tape, then slowly peeled it away from the young woman's mouth. Anne Clancy spat at him. Surprised, the Goon backed away, then grinned. 'You want to be careful,' he warned. 'I could break your neck right in front of your kids.'

He paused at the basement door. It was made of reinforced steel. He dragged it shut, plunging the small room into blackness. 'See ya later.'

9.00 am

Forensic psychiatrist Dillon informed Jim Clarke he was planning to roll the dice. 'This could drag on for weeks,' he explained over the telephone. Clarke was up and dressed and halfway out the door when Dillon made contact. Maeve hovered in the background, trying to eavesdrop. She had wanted to stop her husband going to work after she'd heard about the confrontation the previous day. Clarke was having none of it. 'This is one case I've got to see through,' he growled over breakfast. He ignored the disapproving frown at the other side of the table. 'It's got to be decided by six this evening. Kelly's either in or out.'

Still, the call from Rockdale took him off guard. 'I've set up a reconstruction in Sandymount Park,' Dillon informed. 'Three o'clock this afternoon.' Clarke checked his schedule and agreed. 'This could fall either way,' the psychiatrist warned. 'There are no guarantees. It's a gamble, but I'm going to run with it.'

Clarke mumbled his uncertainties.

'What other choice do we have?' asked Dillon. Clarke said nothing. 'Regan's going to condemn

Kelly to the world this evening. This is our last chance to find the truth.' By ten minutes past nine the outline plan was agreed.

Clarke cancelled the morning and elected to wait at home and rest. It's out of my control now, he thought. It's up to Dillon. And Kelly. He sat down at the kitchen table and poured a fresh mug of tea. Maeve smiled at him and he even managed a weak smile back. 'It'll be over tonight,' he promised. He unclipped his personal revolver and hid it in a biscuit tin in the crockery cupboard. I won't be needing that today.

It seemed to Frank Clancy the gods were conspiring against him.

'This is your captain again.'

A loud groan erupted from the passengers aboard the Virgin Atlantic jet. The estimated time of arrival at London's Heathrow Airport was ten that morning. For the last hour of the flight updates on difficult weather and traffic control conditions ahead had been announced over the PA. A thick blanket of fog covered much of southern England. Spanish air-traffic contollers had called a lightning one-day strike. The combination produced major delays and re-routing of flights in and out of the airports at Heathrow, Gatwick and Stansted. There was a tailback of aircraft awaiting clearance to land.

'I'm afraid the news from Heathrow isn't good. There's still a lot of fog and control have informed me it's showing no sign of lifting. I've been advised to circle for a little longer. I'll get back to you as soon as I have anything new. In the meantime please try and relax. I've asked the cabin crew to play the in-flight movie again.'

This only brought louder complaints. Everyone sensed the delay was going to be longer than had been hinted. In his seat near the back of the aircraft, Frank Clancy fretted. He was chewing on his nails. Everything's going to be okay, he reassured himself. When we get off, I'll ring home. I just know everything will be okay. The optimistic half of his brain wasn't making much impression on the pessimistic side. Something's wrong, I know it. He drank his fifth cup of coffee inside forty minutes. His bladder irritated. He excused himself and waited in a queue for the toilet. Through a porthole he could see the morning sunlight bathed on swirling banks of clouds. Inside the tiny lavatory he inspected himself. His hair was bedraggled and sticking up, his face drawn from worry and lack of sleep. His T-shirt was sweat-stained. He smelt unwashed. Dark stubble made the overall picture most unattractive. I look like a madman. He returned to his seat and waited impatiently.

Thirty minutes later. 'This is your captain again.' Heads craned forward to catch every word, headphones were pulled away from ears. 'I'm afraid we've been diverted to Bristol airport.' Loud groans, frustrated shouts. 'Air-traffic control at Heathrow can't guarantee a flight path for another two hours and we don't have enough fuel for that length of time. We've been advised to land at Bristol. Ground staff will help organise onward connections. On behalf of my crew and Virgin Airlines I apologise for this inconvenience but as you can imagine it's due to circumstances well beyond our control.'

Story of my life, thought Frank Clancy. Situations beyond my control. God, I hope Anne and the kids are okay.

In the basement darkness, Anne Clancy was trying to keep her children's spirits up. She'd stopped the first panicking shrieks in her usual calm, controlled manner.

'Come on, Martin, you're the big boy here,' she'd coaxed. 'You've got to be brave for all of us. I don't want Laura to hear you crying, so stop that.'

It was an approach that had proved successful with previous temper tantrums. It was working again. Laura couldn't see her brother's fear, it was too dark. She could sense it though. And she sensed it in her mother. She wept uncontrollably.

'I want my daddy.' This only added to the sickening terror.

'Daddy will be here soon to rescue us,' Anne lied bravely. 'And then that bad man better look out for himself. Daddy'll punch him straight in the nose.' The children giggled at the suggestion. 'Let's sing a song.' They began singing 'Jingle Bells'.

Only Laura didn't sing as loudly as her brother.

'Mummy, I feel hot.'

12.37 pm

'I'd suggest you take the train. There are connections to link up with the express to Holyhead. You could then get the ferry to Dublin.' The arrivals terminus at Bristol Airport was bedlam. It seemed to Frank Clancy that every flight into London had been diverted to the small airport in the west of England. People were scrambling for advice on regaining their journeys. He stood at the head of a surging queue leading to travel information and explained his predicament to a harassed young brunette in a blue uniform.

'What time will that get me in?'

The brunette pored over train and ferry timetables. 'Looks like the earliest would be about seven or eight this evening.'

Clancy swore. 'That won't do,' he complained. He stuck his bottom out to give himself more space from the pressing bodies.

The brunette dropped the train and ferry time-tables and turned to her PC. She began typing. Five minutes later she offered a different route.

'There's a flight to Paris leaving here in fifty minutes. I could get you on that. You could then . . .' tap, tap, tap on the keyboard . . . 'get an Air France into Dublin leaving Orly Airport at four ten, arriving Dublin sometime after five.'

Clancy didn't even have to think. 'I'll take it.'

Tap, tap, tap. His details were entered. The flights were booked. He rushed to the phones and waited in another frustrating queue where tired and thwarted passengers from Europe and North America rang friends and relations and business colleagues to explain where they were. After an agonising ten minutes behind a wildly gesticulating Italian who'd lost his flight connections and baggage and a multi-million-lira business deal, Clancy finally reached the front. He slipped his credit card into the phone set and dialled home. The line was dead. There was no ringing tone. Panicking, he pressed redial. No ringing tone. Redial. No ringing. Redial. No tone. He contacted directory enquiries, ignoring the angry grumblings building up behind.

'I'm sorry, sir, that line appears to be out of order. Are you sure you have the right number?'

Clancy's heart sank to depths he had never before experienced. 'Yes, yes. It's my own home number.'

The operator offered to try again. 'Sorry, sir, still no connection. I'll try going through your local exchange.'

Clancy pulled his T-shirt up and wiped at his forehead. 'Great, thanks.'

The queue was becoming more agitated. The grumblings had gone past the muttering stage to angry shouts. Clancy tried ignoring.

'Sorry, sir, the local exchange can't get through either. They say there's no recorded fault on that number either. They're sending out an engineer later today. Is there any other number you'd like me to try?'

An aggrieved voice shouted into his left ear. 'Hey, buddy.'

Clancy turned to find an angry face squaring up to him. A tall, swarthy looking young man with tight crew cut had had enough. He'd left the middle of the queue to speed things along.

'We're all in this fucking jam so don't start ringing the fucking world. Two calls each, maximum. Your time's up.' He snatched the receiver from Clancy's trembling hands and passed it to a woman behind. The rest of the queue cheered.

Clancy stood back. He was tempted to smack his challenger in the mouth but desisted. He needed to get to another phone fast.

He sprinted towards the departure gates. His flight to Paris was due out in twenty-eight minutes.

'Laura? Are you okay?'

In the basement Anne Clancy sensed her daughter's unusual stillness. She squirmed closer, the binding around her wrists and ankles still holding them tightly together. The only movement forward and back was like a snake curling and uncurling. She nuzzled her face against the little girl, feeling the heat from the child's body immediately.

'Laura, are you all right? Speak to me, Laura.' For the first time Anne Clancy's voice cracked. Her son recognised the change.

'Mummy, are we going to die?' He began sobbing.

'No, Martin, we are most certainly not going to die. Your daddy will be here very soon. I just know it.'

Anne side-winded to the beakers and lifted one in her teeth, then wormed her way back. The precious water spilled as she crawled. What little was left she tipped over Laura's face.

'Don't, mummy,' the child whimpered. 'I'm too tired. Leave me alone.'

Anne Clancy lay down beside her daughter and began crooning. She felt the little heart racing, sensed the chest rise and fall rapidly. Too rapidly.

'Martin,' she ordered. Her voice was controlled again, firm, commanding. 'Try and grab one of those beakers with your teeth and edge yourself carefully over to me.' In the dark she sensed the boy listen obediently. 'Then tip the water over Laura. Can you do that?'

Martin rose to the occasion. 'Yes, mum.'

He started wriggling. Anne Clancy began praying.

Frank Clancy was on the telephone again. He was inside the departure lounge of Bristol terminal, at the gate for his flight to Orly Airport. He rang his mother-in-law first. There was no reply. He tried furiously to remember the names of his neighbours where he lived in Greenlea Road, north Dublin. He couldn't think of one. His wife's rebuking voice echoed in his mind.

'Frank, you're so caught up in work you wouldn't know if the house was on fire. You've made no attempt to make any contacts around here. You just work, work, work. You've no interest outside of that hospital. I'll bet you don't even know the names of the next-door neighbours.'

It was all coming home to roost. He went through directory enquiries once more and finally scribbled the number of his local police station in Clontarf. He dialled.

'Clontarf police station. What can I do for you?'

Clancy took a deep breath. He explained where he was and his difficulties contacting home.

'Are you sure it's not the telephone company you should be ringing?' suggested the officer.

'I've done that,' said Clancy. He was trying desperately to sound controlled. He didn't want to come across like a crank. 'It's just that I'm very worried something's happened to my wife and children. Could you get someone to call round and check the house out?'

The officer waited. Then, 'And what do you think could have happened to them?'

Clancy suspected he was talking to a man not

particularly interested in his rather far-fetched query. 'I dunno,' he admitted. 'I'm just very worried, that's all.' In the background his flight was being called. Come on.

'And who are you again?' asked the police officer. Clancy rattled off his name, address, hospital appointment and estimated time of arrival in Dublin.

'And you're flying in from Paris?'

'Yes.'

'But you're ringing now from Bristol?'

Oh, Jesus. Can you not just shift your arse and go and look? What difference does it make if I'm flying in from the moon?

'Yeah, I've been diverted from Heathrow. There's huge disruption at the airports over here. The only way I can get home is through Orly.'

The officer now sounded interested. 'Did you not think of trying the train and ferry. There's great connections for that new Seacat boat, you know. It takes only an hour from Holyhead.'

Clancy wanted to scream. Through gritted teeth he explained all the difficulties. Over the PA he was named personally, yet again. 'Last call for passenger Frank Clancy on board British Airways flight to Orly Airport.'

'Look,' shouted Clancy, 'I gotta go. Can you check the house out?'

'Will do, Dr Clancy. Give us a call when you get to your next stop. I'll have something for you then.'

'Thanks.' Clancy grabbed his holdall and sprinted.

Micko Kelly was taken from his cell just after lunch on the afternoon of Wednesday, 20 May. He was dressed in fresh casual clothes, navy blue tracksuit bottom, white T-shirt, bright red tracksuit top, white socks inside new white trainers. His stubble hair now looked like a respectable crew cut, his stubble beard was gone, shaved that morning. His tall, lank figure carried more flesh than the day he had first arrived at Rockdale Hospital for the Criminally Insane. His eyes were somewhat clearer and he even managed to smile at his fellow inmates.

'Where ye goin', Micko?' asked the red-haired multiple murderer three cells up.

Kelly shook his head as if in wonderment. 'Fucked if I know.'

Dillon was in overall charge and issued the orders. He was wearing light slacks, short-sleeved, open-necked shirt and light shoes. Two warders in navy tracksuits approached with a set of chains and cuffs. Well used to such manoeuvres, Kelly offered his wrists and within seconds they were manacled. A separate set of chains and cuffs were attached to ankles, barely allowing normal walking pace. Strong yellow-orange rays filtered through the barred windows along the corridor.

'Ye lucky fucker,' growled one inmate. 'Yer gettin' out.'

A black stumped grin was the only reply.

The small group shuffled past open cells towards the iron gate that barred the maximum security unit. Keys jangled and locks clicked as door after door was opened and shut.

'Jaysus,' muttered Kelly as he looked on, 'there's not much chance anywan gettin' outa this kip.'

Dillon smiled slightly. 'Not unless you're well enough.'

Kelly stopped and turned back. 'I don't know what I did to be put in here but I gotta get out before it drives me fuckin' mental.' The warders smirked. 'I don't wanna come back to this fuckin' hole.'

Dillon ignored the outburst. Chains clanked as Kelly was pushed forward. The group stopped at another locked door. Keys jangled, the lock clicked. Kelly was urged through and entered the white-tiled reception area. One of the warders selected an extra large key and glided it into the lock of the front door. With two quick turns it was pulled open and sunlight streamed in. Kelly tried to shield his eyes from the unaccustomed glare but the manacles restricted. He dropped his head and ambled towards the brightness. The warmth of the air, the farmyard smells, the buzzing of insects, all swamped his senses and he stood still, savouring the moment. He was nudged in the back. 'Shift it.' The chains jangled again.

Parked a short distance from the front entrance were three unmarked police cars, each with driver and armed detective. All eyes fixed on the lonely figure in the tracksuit. A black transit van drove over and its side panels were slid open. There was a long bench inside with attachments on the floor for chained wrists and ankles. Kelly stiffened. He eyed the scene suspiciously.

'They're going to take you away for ever. They took your hair and your nails and your clothes. They want you, Michael.'

The voice zipped through his brain like a startled rat. For a split second Kelly heard it, then it was gone. It left him agitated and nervous. He didn't want to go inside the van. It reminded him of another day. A bad day, a very bad day.

'I'm not goin' in there,' he shouted and backed away. Two sets of restraining arms held him fast.

Dillon came beside and talked him down. 'Relax. It's okay, nothing's going to happen.'

Kelly snarled at the watching policeman. The heat of the day was making them perspire and they fanned with their peaked caps. Car doors were open to let air in, windows were wound down. Whispered comments drifted in the still air. Dillon allowed ten minutes, then checked his watch. It was twelve minutes before two. Kelly was due in Sandymount Park by three o'clock. Depending on the traffic the journey would take at least one hour.

'Michael,' he said, 'if you want to get out of here you're going to have to get into that van.' No movement. Dillon sidled up beside his patient. 'I'm giving you three minutes. After that you're back on the wards.' He swivelled the other man's head around so he could see the grey intimidating walls and peaked roof of the hospital.

Kelly looked for only a minute. With a nervous shake of his wrists he finally struggled inside. The chains were released and connected to bolts on the floor. The two tracksuited warders sat beside him on the bench. Dillon climbed into the front passenger seat. He looked around, double-checking the security.

'Okay, move it.' The dice was rolling.

2.08 pm

Two uniformed police officers stood outside Frank Clancy's house in Greenlea Road, Clontarf, in north Dublin. They were in short sleeves and open-necked shirts with peaked caps held under their arms. Both were young men, tall with short hair, neatly combed and parted, regulation style. The sun was high in the sky with only the occasional cloud threatening. Birds chirped happily from nearby trees. The two were in a relaxed mood. Business was quiet, the level of criminal activity at a lower than average level. They felt unrushed and were glad of the leisurely drive from the local police station along the suburban roads. It broke up the tedium of the day.

Greenlea Road was a row of mainly red-bricked terraced houses on both sides along a wide, tree-lined avenue. The road was quiet, safe even for children kicking football. There were no kids around at that time, most still at school.

One officer rang the front doorbell, the other rested his backside against a front windowsill. They admired the streetscape as they waited. There was no reply. The bell was pressed again. No reply. The letter box was pushed open and one shouted in. No answer. The two ambled around the back and discovered the broken glass. They noticed the rear door lying slightly ajar, its panes shattered.

Gingerly, one pushed the door open and peered inside. Nothing. He shouted. No reply. Quickly they scouted the ground-floor area. Nothing. No sign of any disturbance. One sprinted upstairs and came upon the unmade beds. He shouted. Nothing. There was no reply. He picked up a family photograph from a shelf and studied the smiling faces. Then he took the ten steps to the attic study in three giant lopes. Empty. He shouted again. Nothing.

He punched at the buttons on his mobile phone. He knew his quiet day was over.

2.58 pm

Jim Clarke hobbled up and down along the outer railings of Sandymount Park. Tony Molloy sat in an unmarked squad car parked beside. A white film of antacid flecked his lips; he massaged at his straining belly. Molloy was listening to anxious reports coming down the police waveband about a missing family. An Anne Clancy and her two children aged eight and four. The details and descriptions were being repeated and transmitted throughout the Dublin metropolitan area. Molloy sensed there was a lot of concern about this missing family. He mentally logged the report.

The road alongside Sandymount Park was sealed off by two squad cars skewed across at both ends. There a posse of reporters, photographers and TV crews fought for vantage positions. The perimeter fence and furthest edges were patrolled by uniformed officers, walkie-talkies moving to and from mouths. They looked edgy, as if expecting some imminent attack. Three cars were stopped near an open park gate. They were empty, their doors hanging open. Armed detectives, handguns bulging under jackets, paced up and down. They mopped at their brows in the afternoon heat. There was a brief diversion while Moss Kavanagh was given clearance at one checkpoint and drove up. He wound the driver's window down and beamed out at Clarke.

'Caroline had the baby,' he announced gleefully.

Clarke stuck a hand forward. 'Ah, Mossy, that's great.' He was elated, then suddenly annoyed. He'd been so preoccupied he'd neglected to ask about Kavanagh's wife. 'When did it happen?'

Kavanagh couldn't stop grinning. The words tumbled out. 'Three o'clock this morning. She felt the pains about six last night. Her waters broke just before eleven and wee Alexander was born at three. Very quick the doctors said.'

Clarke shook his hand again with delight. 'Mossy, I'm thrilled for the two of you. I know it's been a long wait, but sure isn't it worth it all now?'

The excitement was infectious and both men were grinning. Kavanagh shrugged slightly. 'Well, it's third time lucky. The two miscarriages, nearly broke our hearts. She's clean made up with this wee baby.'

'I'm sure she is, Mossy, I'm sure she is,' Clarke enthused, remembering the day he'd first brought brought Katy home. 'What was the weight?'

'Nine pounds seven ounces.'

'Ouch,' Clarke winced, 'I'm glad she was having him and not me.'

The exchange was interrupted by Molloy. 'We better shift it, the floor show's about to begin.'

A black transit van had stopped at one of the road blocks. A head was half in and half out of the passenger window, a hand gesticulating. One of the blocking cars was moved and the van drove slowly into the controlled zone. Clarke, Molloy and Kavanagh watched. Only the background hum of Dublin's traffic disturbed the relative calm. The van's side door was slid open from inside. Patrick Dillon climbed out of the passenger seat and stretched. He looked at the media pack and shook his head. Micko Kelly's escort stepped out, tugging at their sweat-stained clothes. Camera shutters whirred.

Dillon leaned into the van, rocking the vehicle slightly, then stood back. A white trainer touched the pavement, followed by the red and blue tracksuited frame of Micko Kelly, wrists chained, ankles now free. There was an intense and prolonged whirring of camera shutters. Some of the brasher photographers shouted out, urging Kelly to look in their direction. He started to turn but was pushed ahead and stumbled past open gates into Sandymount Park. The sky was now clouding over. There was a smell of rain in the air. The wind had picked up. It was becoming cooler, less humid.

'Moment of reckoning,' muttered Molloy.

Dillon called an immediate conference, those he wanted were pulled closer, the rest ordered well away. Kelly stood between his minders, head jerking as he watched. He tried brushing at his forehead with an elbow, the only movement possible with the restraining chains. Within minutes four had grouped. Dillon and Kelly, Clarke and Molloy.

'When the chains come off everyone moves to the railings,' announced Dillon. Tiny beads of perspiration were forming on his brow. 'Nobody's to come near until I give the word.' He paused. 'He is still officially under my care. He is a patient, not a prisoner. Is that clear?' The voice was emphatic, firm.

Clarke glanced over at the red and blue tracksuited figure. 'Absolutely.'

Dillon wiped at his brow with a white linen handkerchief. 'When this is over,' he added, 'I want him taken back to hospital without being hounded by photographers.'

Clarke immediately waved towards Moss Kavanagh, beckoning him closer. 'You have my word on that,' he promised.

Dillon slipped a microcassette out of his side pocket and checked the batteries were working. 'I'm carrying my own recorder for a verbatim report. I'm also wearing a listening device.' He patted a side pocket out of which a tiny red-tipped microphone poked. 'There are earphones for you to listen in on.'

Two sets were handed over. Clarke stuck one in his right ear, twisting until it fitted comfortably. Molloy followed suit. Leads from the earphones connected to small Walkman-sized antennae which were snapped onto waistbands. Dillon fed a thin black lead through his shirt, clipped a microphone to a buttonhole and turned it out of sight. The lead was plugged into the microcassette and the ON button pressed.

'Right,' he said, 'let's start.'

Clarke and Molloy moved back ten yards. The manacles connecting Micko Kelly's wrists were unlocked and released. He rubbed at his skin where steel had dug in, then looked around. He seemed uncertain, bewildered. Cameras whirred in the background. Dillon rechecked his microcassette, then guided his patient towards the wooden shelter.

'This is it,' he said. 'This is our last chance to find the truth.'

Molloy and Clarke adjusted the volume on their earphones.

The shelter had been prepared according to Dillon's instructions. It looked much the same as on the night of Tuesday, 12 May. The rotted wood, the graffiti, the peeling paintwork was untouched. Empty beer cans, cider bottles and cigarette butts had been dropped, apparently at random. A blood-red stained syringe had been strategically placed under the chipped and cut seat.

'Sit there,' Dillon directed. Kelly moved awkwardly onto one edge of the semicircular seat. Dillon waited, then sat on the other side.

'Like a fag?'

Kelly's eyes lit up. 'Fuckin' sure.'

Dillon produced a prepared roll-your-own. Kelly stuck it in his lips and puffed at the offered match. The end glowed. He drew on it hungrily.

'Fuckin' brilliant.' He lay back and smoked contentedly.

'Do you remember this place?' Dillon asked as the cigarette burned to a butt. He offered another. Kelly inhaled deeply, found a trace of tobacco leaf on his tongue and spat it out. He looked around the shelter with total disinterest. 'Nah.'

'You've been here before. The night Jennifer Marks was murdered, you were in here with her.'

Kelly adopted a look of bemused astonishment. He pointed a finger at his chest. 'Me? Here?' He found another leaf of tobacco on his tongue and lifted it off with a finger, inspecting the result closely. 'Jennifer Marks?'

'That was her name.'

On the green Jim Clarke fidddled with his earpiece. He turned sideways and found better reception.

'With me? In here? Ye sure?' Kelly sounded indifferent.

'I'm certain. You were seen with her.' Dillon adjusted the microphone on his buttonhole where it had begun to irritate. He looked outside. The policemen had gathered in small groups and were talking quietly among themselves. The sun moved briefly from behind a cloud, dazzling with its brightness and casting sudden shadows. 'The two of you had scored a deal and were lolling about. Drinking and maybe shooting up.'

'Was I smashed?'

'That's what we want to find out. Just how smashed you were that night.'

Kelly inhaled deeply and looked around.

'Gimme the fuckin' knife, you scumbag.'

The voice disappeared as quickly as it sounded.

'Jennifer Marks? That the girl in the pictures you were showin' me?'

'Yes.'

'No, Mo, no. No. I wasn't going to do anything.'

The voices returned. Kelly could distinguish two. Someone was shouting angrily. Viciously angry.

'Dark-haired girl, wasn't she? You told me she was a dark-haired girl?'

'She was. Long, jet-black hair. Very pretty girl.'

345

'Gimme another fag.' Kelly's hands shook as Dillon lit the tip. He inhaled, coughed slightly, then drew deeper again. 'What happened to her?' Over the listening devices the change in his voice was obvious. Kelly was becoming agitated.

'She was stabbed.' Dillon edged closer. 'She was in this shelter with you. What happened? Was there an argument? Maybe she said something that annoyed you? Was that it?'

Kelly shuddered. Sweat dripped off his head and forehead and he wiped at it nervously.

'Gimme the fuckin' knife, you scumbag.'

'I tried to help her, honest to fuck, I did.' His head was slumped, tobacco leaf and saliva dangled off his lower lip.

'Tell me what happened?' Dillon's voice was calm and controlled. He glanced at his watch. It was three thirty-five. He had been inside the shelter for almost fifteen minutes.

'I can't remember,' Kelly shouted suddenly. 'It won't fuckin' come. Quit annoyin' me.'

'There was someone else here, wasn't there? Was it one of your cronies?' Dillon had edged closer again. He could feel the heat from Kelly's breath. 'Who else was here?'

'Gimme the fuckin' knife, you scumbag.'

Words returned, angry, threatening words. Vicious words. Kelly began pacing anxiously. At the perimeter fence one of the tracksuited warders started forward, then stopped. Dillon had raised a reassuring hand.

'Why did you stab her? Did she do you out of a deal?' Dillon's voice was now louder. 'Why did you kill her?'

346

Kelly looked over. Froth was forming on his lips. 'I didn't mean to do anything. It was the big bastard that started it.'

Clarke and Molloy almost fell against one another. Excited hands cupped earpieces.

Dillon sat back on the seat. 'What big bastard?'

'Gimme the fuckin' knife.'

The exact words came back.

Kelly stopped pacing. He dropped his head, moaned, then wrapped both hands around his body and squeezed tightly. Sweat poured off his face, dropping from chin onto T-shirt, soaking his body. He tore off the red tracksuit top and threw it to the ground. 'Lemme outa here.' He made for the park, as if to run away, to escape.

Then he saw it.

'Jaysus Christ,' he roared. 'Waddid you do to her?'

Lying on the green grass of Sandymount Park was a bloodstained body. The body was clothed in a short black skirt with a red-stained T-shirt. White trainers over navy blue ankle socks were on the feet. The face-up body with dark hair and red lips was sprawled on the exact spot where Jennifer Marks had lain when first struck ten days earlier. It was a mannequin, assembled and dressed according to Dillon's instructions.

Kelly tried backing into the shelter but was grabbed from behind by Dillon.

'What happened to the girl? Who killed her?'

Kelly whimpered with fear. He tried looking away from the body.

'Why did you kill her?' Dillon was shouting. 'You've been lying since the very beginning. You killed that girl. DIDN'T YOU?'

'Gimme the fuckin' knife, you scumbag.'

The voice sounded like a pistol shot in Kelly's brain. 'I didn't mean to hurt her.' His voice dropped to a broken whisper. 'I didn't mean no harm.'

'What happened?' Dillon pressed. He pointed towards the mannequin. 'What happened to Jennifer Marks?'

The voices returned like a babble. A cacophony of curses and vicious roars crowded Kelly's brain.

'No, Mo. I wasn't going to do anything.'

Then it came back. Kelly's mind cleared and he saw again the dreadful scene. 'There was two of them.' He slumped onto his knees. Yards behind, Tony Molloy checked his watch. It was four fifteen. He knew schools in the area and beyond had discharged their pupils for the day. He knew many of the students used the road alongside the park and would now be held up at the checkpoints. He worried they might start shouting, might distract. Come on, come on.

'Who were they?' Dillon forced.

'No, Mo, no. Please, no'

'I dunno. I never seen them before. She knew them, she fuckin' knew them.' It was as if a veil had been drawn back from Kelly's mind. A thick, blood-wet veil. He sounded calmer. 'We were in that shelter and they came in. She knew who they were.'

'What happened?'

'I stayed on. Didn't know who they were and didn't give a fuck either. She took them outside to talk.'

'What happened then?'

Kelly shook his head. 'I don't know. I heard these shouts, she was shoutin' for me.'

'Go on,' encouraged Dillon.

'I sorta staggered out to see what the fuck was

348

goin' on.' He paused as the image faded then returned. 'Wan of them told me to fuck off. The big bastard, that wan. Even in the dark he looked fuckin' huge.'

'What were they doing?'

'They were arguin' about somethin'.' Kelly made a shadow-boxing gesture. 'She was screamin' at them to leave her alone. "I didn't mean no harm." Some sort of shite like that.'

'No, Mo, no. I wasn't going to do anything, honest.'

'What did you do?'

Kelly ran a hand through his stubble hair, feeling the wetness there. He rubbed the sweat off on his T-shirt. 'I had a knife.'

Dillon froze. Ten yards away Clarke and Molly froze.

'What did you do with the knife?' Dillon was trying to keep the questions calm and clear. He sensed he was breaking Kelly's insanity.

'I ran at the big fucker.'

'No, Micko, no.'

'What happened then?'

'She tried to stop me.' Kelly shook his head angrily from side to side. 'The fuckin' stupid bitch.'

'Then what? I need to know everything.'

Kelly saw the movements in the dark, the scuffling, the flailing hands. 'She started hitting at me. I wanted to get at the big bastard but she was in the way. She tried grabbin' the knife from me.' Kelly shook violently. 'I lost me fuckin' rag and stuck her. A coupla times.' He began to heave and clutched at his stomach. 'I didn't mean to hurt the little bitch. She just got in the fuckin' way.' He brushed at the wetness on his face. 'I tried to lift her but she was covered in blood and slipped outa my hands.' He crumpled onto the grass, shoulders heaving, body shaking.

Dillon sat beside. 'What did the other two do?'

Kelly dragged his knees to his chest. 'They took her away. They wanted her. The big bastard came back at me.'

'Gimme the fuckin' knife, you scumbag.'

'What did you do?'

'I ran. I dropped the knife and I fuckin' ran.' He remembered the final moments. He was scrambling at the railings, wet bloodstained hands clutching for support. He looked back. The shadowy figures were dragging the young girl's body. He heard loud, angry shouts and curses. Then he saw his own knife flash. The blade swung in a vicious downward arc. 'They stuck her while she was on the ground.'

Dillon wiped his brow. He sat down on the grass beside Kelly, hands behind knees for support.

'Who were they?'

'No, Mo. I'm not gonna do anything.'

Kelly wiped at his face. 'She kept shoutin' Mo, that's all I can remember. Mo, Mo, fuckin' Mo.' He blew his nose on the T-shirt. 'That other bitch would know.'

Dillon looked over. 'What other bitch.'

'That other bitch in the pub. She was talkin' with that big bastard. She knows him.'

Molloy quickly pulled Clarke aside. 'That's Joan Armstrong. That's who he's talking about. She's known all along.'

Clarke waved furiously at Moss Kavanagh. 'Where would she be now?'

Molloy looked at his watch. 'Coming off the train at Sydney Parade Avenue.'

Clarke hobbled towards the approaching Kavanagh, ushering him back to the gates. 'Organise Kelly,' he shouted over his shoulder, 'then follow me. If Armstrong knows anything I want it out of her immediately.'

As Molloy feverishly issued instructions, something in the back of his mind crowded forward. He tore at his trouser pockets until he felt a crumpled slip of paper. It was his own scribbled report of new evidence phoned through from the forensic science laboratory that morning. The fibres taken from the crime scene had finally been identified. Mohair.

Mo. Mohair. He didn't dare believe what he was thinking. Mo. Mohair. Never. Crazy. Too dangerous. He sprinted towards his car to follow Clarke.

38 4.34 pm

The Goon had got there first.

Joan Armstrong stepped off the train at Sydney Parade Avenue. She fiddled with her schoolbag, dropping books, picking them up, taking her time. She watched until her fellow pupils had left the platform. All the time she was looking for the Goon, even praying he'd be there. She didn't know how she'd got through the day. She'd shivered and shook in every class, was edgy and irritable. Her mind was fixed on white powder, glass ampoule and clean syringe. How she ached for a hit. She spotted the Goon. He was dressed in black. Black jacket and jeans, black T-shirt and trainers. Hair slicked back. As usual he was leaning against the second lamppost on Ailesbury Gardens.

Making sure no one was following she took the overhead metal bridge to the other side of the tracks, walking as nonchalantly as she could fake. This was the usual arrangement with Mo. The Goon would wait at the lamp-post, then the girls, herself and Jennifer, would walk to wherever Mo waited in the parked car. They understood why Mo could never be seen, he was such an important man.

'Where's Mo?' She walked straight past the Goon, apparently ignoring him. He let her get a few yards ahead, checked no one was watching, then followed.

'He couldn't come. I'm to take you to the house direct.'

Joan Armstrong turned. 'I can't, I'm telling you, I can't. I have to be home by six at the latest.'

The Goon made a show of looking at his watch. 'No sweat. I'll have you a hundred yards from your front door in plenty of time.'

'Where's the car?'

'Round the corner.'

Joan Armstrong began to feel uneasy. The black car with its opaque black windows was usually parked nearby. 'Where around the corner?'

The Goon grabbed her roughly by the arm. 'Round the next corner. Now move for fuck's sake.'

The metallic black Lincoln was parked at the end of a quiet cul-de-sac, boot facing backwards. The Goon frog-marched Joan Armstrong the last twenty yards, his grip digging deeply.

'You're hurting me,' she protested.

'Come on, come on, we'll be late. You said you wanted to be home by six.' In the distance a police siren sounded. 'Come on.'

The Goon pressed a button on his car alarm pad and four indicator lights blinked twice, then stopped. The door locks clicked, the boot lid opened slightly. Gripping the young girl's arm, he twisted her round, back towards the boot.

'You can put your schoolbag in here.'

Joan Armstrong looked up, fear in her eyes. 'Why do I have to put my bag in the boot?' Her voice was strained.

One-handed, the Goon flipped the lid open. Joan Armstrong turned. The moment she saw the black plastic she started to scream. The Goon hit her hard and she dropped, half slumped. With one swift movement he grabbed her ankles and forced her inside. He looked around. The road was empty, not a movement. He quickly scanned the windows. No one. The siren was coming closer. He pressed the recessed compartment and snatched one roll of binding tape. Within seconds he had the young girl's ankles bound. She moaned slightly, too dazed to know what was happening. The tape was sliced with the flick knife. Wrap, wrap, wrap. Her hands were strapped together. The Goon stuck an edge of the wide tape along the boot lid, roughly measured and sliced a short strip off. It was stuck down across the groaning mouth. The knife was closed, the tape stuffed back in the recess. The Goon looked up and down the road. Nothing. He turned back to see the frozen-eyed stare of Joan Armstrong. He grinned and slammed the boot closed.

The Goon climbed into the left-hand side driver's seat. The siren had stopped. The clock on the dashboard said four fifty. There was plenty of time. He would drive to the secluded underground car park he'd checked out earlier and slit the girl's throat. Then he would douse the car inside and out with petrol and light a match.

Easy.

Like taking candy from a baby.

4.57 pm

Frank Clancy was a nervous wreck. He stared out at

354

the clouds from his window seat aboard an Air France commuter flight from Paris to Dublin. His heart was pounding. He was sweating. He felt like getting sick. He hadn't eaten since the breakfast on the Virgin Atlantic Boston/Bristol trip. His hair was sticking in all directions, his T-shirt was wet through from perspiration. He now knew something had happened to his family.

'What time's your flight due in at Dublin?' Clancy had telephoned earlier from Orly Airport. The duty sergeant in Clontarf police station made a big effort to sound calm.

'Five ten. Why?'

'We'd like to meet you as soon as you arrive.'

'Why? What's happened?'

'Now we're not sure if anything's happened at all, Dr Clancy.' The duty sergeant didn't sound convincing. 'It's just that your wife and children aren't at home.'

Clancy almost collapsed. He gripped the telephone receiver. 'There's more, isn't there?' he shouted. 'You're not telling me everything.'

'Now don't be jumping to conclusions,' the sergeant advised. 'There's probably a perfectly simple explanation for everything.'

'They're missing, aren't they?'

'Well, they're certainly not at home.'

'Oh, Christ, they've got them. Jesus. They've got them.'

There was a pause at the other end. 'Now who exactly would that be, Dr Clancy? Who do you think's got them?'

Clancy slapped at his forehead in frustration. How am I going to account for everything? If I start talking conspiracy this man'll have me arrested and taken away by men in white coats. I'll bet he suspects me in some way. Crime in the family is usually between family members.

'It'll be easier if I explain all when I get into Dublin,' he suggested. 'I'm chasing my tail here. I'll miss this flight.'

'Very good then, Dr Clancy. I'll have a squad car waiting for you on the tarmac. You needn't go through arrivals. My men will collect you at the plane.'

That worried Clancy even more. Either they're going to detain me for questioning or they really do know something more than they're saying. Jesus. Dr Harry Walters' parting words in Boston echoed ominously. 'Be careful, Frank. The stakes are high in this game. Whoever's behind this is in too deep to pull back. Keep looking over your shoulder. Play safe.' I did play safe. But not with my family. If anything's happened to Anne or the kids I'll kill that bitch Speer. With my own bare hands I'll twist her neck 'til I hear the bones break. He tried two last desperate calls. His mother-in-law was in but most unhappy.

'No they're not here, Frank. I've been trying to reach them all morning. The line's down or something. Anne was very upset when she left here. The children were very tearful.' Go on, twist the knife. 'I don't know what you're playing at, but . . .' He hung up. Then he dialled administration at the Mercy Hospital.

'No I'm afraid there's no one here, Dr Clancy,' he was told. 'Half the hospital's taken the day off for the big press conference tonight. Everyone's expected to be there to hear the minister.'

Clancy swore loudly, then apologised.

'There is a message for you though.' His spirits rose sharply. It's from Anne. She's taken the kids somewhere and left details.

'Oh yeah? What's it say? Quickly.'

The girl at the other end coughed nervously. 'You're to present yourself tomorrow morning for a disciplinary hearing. Nine o'clock exactly. It says you should bring your legal advisor. The meeting will be held in the hospital boardroom.'

Frank Clancy felt his world crumble. I'm gonna lose my job. My wife and children are missing. He seriously contemplated a long swim in a deep pool. End it all with one simple dive. Then he gritted his teeth. Not yet. I'm not beaten yet. He sprinted through the departure gate and his flight home. I'll see you in hell first, Linda Speer.

39 *5.15 pm*

Jim Clarke spotted the Lincoln first. Moss Kavanagh had screeched away from Sandymount Park at breakneck speed, siren blaring, beacon flashing. He broke red lights, overtook on pavements, caused traffic chaos as he criss-crossed lanes. He finally skewed to a halt beside the railway station on Sydney Parade Avenue. Clarke knew immediately they were too late. The platform was deserted, the nearby roads quiet. He was climbing out to check with the ticket collector when he noticed a black, powerful-looking car edge out ahead. The car shot dangerously across the main road, forcing a motorcyclist into a hedge. Everything about the car fitted Danny Carton's description. Clarke knew he had his man at last. 'Quick, Mossy, move.'

They caught up with the Lincoln in a long queue on Merrion Road in south Dublin. It was no more than ten cars ahead, dodging and weaving, lane-hopping. Horns were being sounded by angry drivers, fists shaken. Kavanagh contacted headquarters, describing the target.

'We'll get him, boss. He'll get stuck somewhere.'

Suddenly the Lincoln veered sharply onto a smaller side road. Kavanagh pressed the accelerator and flicked on the siren, whoo-whooing the immediate traffic away. He turned right in time to see the black tail veer over a small hump-backed bridge. It then spun left towards the big football stadium on Landsdowne Road and out of sight.

'There he is.' Clarke had pushed against the front seat. He shook Kavanagh's shoulder. 'To your left.'

The Lincoln had found a parallel road and was scorching along, forcing oncoming traffic onto the pavement.

'Take a left, for Christ's sake. He's spotted us.'

Siren blaring, Kavanagh overtook on a narrow stretch and grabbed the next left turn before a coal truck. He ignored the startled white eyes behind blackened faces. The squad car was hemmed in by a struggling '91 registered Toyota, smoke bellowing from the exhaust. 'Fuck it, we've lost him.'

By the time a space opened up the Lincoln had disappeared. Kavanagh skidded the car to a halt. Clarke shoved the back door open and struggled out. Kavanagh started to say something but an angry wave silenced. They were along a quiet side road. The area had been recently developed, new expensive apartment blocks cheek-by-jowl with old red-bricked terraced houses. An ugly multistorey car park offering cheap all-day rates was to their right.

Clarke listened, every sense pinging. Then he heard the screech of tyres, an unusual engine. 'He's in the car park.'

Kavanagh gunned the engine and arrived at the entrance ramp. A red-and-white striped barrier blocked until a time-stamped ticket was pulled. Beside the barrier was a green portacabin booth. Inside a bored youth stared at a battery of TV monitors.

Kavanagh swerved the car to a halt and leapt out. 'Police,' he shouted, flashing his badge. The young attendant stuck his hands up in the air. 'The big American car that just came in?' The youth shook his head vigorously. 'Where'd he go? Quickly, which level?'

The attendant turned to a row of monitors and began pressing buttons. His hands shook, he was speechless with fright. Different views of the parking lot flashed. Kavanagh took over and flicked faster. Breathless and agitated, Clarke looked on. One view flicked up, then disappeared.

'Go back.' The grainy grey-black image showed a row of cars, some front end forward. There was no movement along the rows. 'Can you close in on any of those?' Kavanagh snapped.

The attendant pointed towards a joystick. Twisting and turning, the camera was directed towards an awkwardly parked car near the end of one row. Kavanagh zoomed as close as the lens allowed, then steadied the view. Nothing seemed unusual, there was no movement. He was about to shift again when the merest hint of a shadow appeared, then disappeared. Clarke stuck a finger at the monitor and Kavanagh squinted closer. The car rocked slightly, the shadowy figure moved again.

'We've got him.' Kavanagh drew his handgun and ran towards the ramp. 'What level is that?'

'Basement, two down.' The young attendant's eyes were out like stalks.

Clarke grabbed the phone in the booth and ordered a back-up team. Then he followed.

In the time it took to call headquarters, the two men lost contact. Clarke hobbled down one ramp and spotted a large white-on-black sign: LOWER GROUND. He stopped and listened. The only sound came from his thumping heart. He started towards the next ramp and reached for his revolver. The free hand searched one side of his waistband, then the other. He suddenly remembered he'd left it at home in the biscuit tin in the crockery cupboard. Fuck. He leaned against a car bonnet. I'll wait for the back up. No point risking your life with no firepower. They'll be here in minutes. I'll wait.

He wiped at his brow. Then he heard a sickening thud. Without thinking he followed the noise. His leg dragged badly, his crutch tapped against concrete. He stopped and listened. Nothing. He moved another few feet down the ramp, now almost halfway. Stopped and listened. Nothing. He was about to move again when he heard a bumping, rocking movement. Crouching on both hunkers he peered into the gloom. The American car was obvious. He wanted to shout 'Mossy', but knew that was senseless. Kavanagh could be chasing ahead two levels up, even out on the road. I'll go back. The young fella must have seen it on the screen, he'll know what's happened.

He made to stand when the rocking movement came again. Apart from a distant dripping it was the only noise in the basement. Back on his hunkers, Clarke squinted at the car. Nothing. Suddenly the 'looney-tunes' jingle of Kavanagh's mobile phone broke the silence. It rang and rang. Clarke slipped his jacket off for a freer movement. He felt along the crutch handle for twin bolts, pressed and turned. The handle moved. He turned until he sensed another

361

quarter-inch would disengage it from the main frame, then checked. The mobile phone stopped, plunging the basement into an eerie stillness.

Clarke held his breath and listened. Nothing. He took two hesitant steps and reached the last level. He spun left and right, as if an attacker was upon him. Nothing. He let his eyes drift along the cars until they reached the large dark model. No movement. He was about to turn when the rocking started again. He twisted in time to see the Lincoln shift slightly. Sweat formed on his face and forehead, dripping so fast it blurred his vision. He wiped it away. An unusual scraping, rustling noise sounded. He started slowly towards it, looking over his shoulder. He was within ten feet when he spotted a fresh pool of blood. He knew it was fresh, knew the blood was still oozing. The pool was widening as he watched. It curled around the tyre of a grey Mercedes. When he reached the gap between it and its neighbour Clarke discovered Moss Kavanagh. The big man was slumped awkwardly between the vehicles, one arm jammed in a door handle. His legs had crumpled, his head lay on his chest, motionless.

The Lincoln moved again, this time with a thud. Clarke looked straight at it, hardly daring to breathe. He limped closer, clutching his crutch hand grip firmly. Two steps and he was right behind the metallic black monster. He glanced along both sides. Nothing. The boot thumped, this time two dull thuds. He heard a moan. He eased himself along the right-hand side where there was more space. The doors were locked, the buttons firmly down. The back rocked slightly. He sensed movement between the vinyl of the back seats.

He bent closer, rubbing at the window. The tip of a

finger was wedging itself through. It wiggled, like a worm emerging from earth. He moved his head staccato-like to the right and felt a sudden rush of wind. The side window shattered and a heavy, thickening blow hit off his right shoulder. Staggering from the impact, he struggled to keep upright. A boot crashed into his leg, the searing pain making him screech. He tried to turn and face his assailant but couldn't move. He slipped, one hand desperately groping, the other grasping the crutch hand grip.

'You just don't give up.' The Goon was standing over Clarke, a bloodstained baseball bat swinging in his right hand. He let it drop heavily on Clarke's leg, the pain boring up to hip level. 'You're a real fucking nuisance.' Clarke tried to push himself back but found his strength ebbing. The Goon kicked out viciously. 'You're trying to ruin my big day . . .' kick '. . . you miserable . . .' kick '. . . bastard.'

The pain suddenly eased in Clarke's tortured leg, only to be replaced by a warm wetness. He was half in and half out of consciousness. He turned the hand grip a final quarter inch, freeing it from the frame.

The Goon spun the baseball bat in the air and swung it down. Clarke moved his head and the bat thudded an inch from his right ear. He felt the vibration along the cold concrete.

'Missed that time.' The Goon spat into both hands, preparing for a better grip. 'But I won't miss again.' He lifted the bat.

Through the pain and gloom Clarke could still make out the bulky frame above. Smash. The base-ball bat swung into Clarke's leg. Bone and cartilage splintered. The pain scorched. The bat was in the air again, twirling. The Goon's face was twisted with rage. He swung it downwards in a vicious arc.

'You can go to hell, you bastard.' Clarke pressed the buttons on the hand grip and lunged upwards. He heard the 'shush' of steel as blade shot out, heard a startled grunt as it pierced flesh. He felt a sudden wetness, warm and profuse, against his face. As his own blackness swamped, Clarke twisted the knife inside the soft opening, forcing it deeper with every fading ounce of strength.

Blackness caressed his pain. He slumped back and welcomed it.

The multistorey car park was swamped by armed detectives. They crawled along ramps, between automobiles and over trucks, down air shafts. Tony Molloy lead the pack, revolver drawn, panting from the effort. They knew exactly where to go, everything had been followed on the security cameras by the startled attendant in the portacabin. They found Clarke moaning and barely conscious. The heavy frame of the Goon lay motionless beside. Blood pooled in patches beneath him. Moss Kavanagh was in a coma. They laid him in the recovery position and loosened his clothes. They were all stunned at the scene of carnage and gabbled excitedly. Molloy cursed at being too late. In the distance an ambulance siren came closer. The young attendant had kept his wits about him enough to order one.

In the agitated babble the group almost missed the muffled shout from inside the Lincoln. Molloy held up a hand. The basement was plunged into silence once again. The big black car rocked slightly. Dull thuds came from the boot. Another moan escaped. Three UZI submachine-guns and four .459 Smith &

Wesson barrels trained on the back. Molloy searched the Goon's bloodstained pockets and found the car keys. He pressed the alarm pad and the door locks popped. The boot lid opened slightly. Inching closer, revolver held in front with both hands, he tipped up the lid. Joan Armstrong's terrified eyes stared out at him. Molloy stumbled back. 'Jesus Christ.'

As soon as the girl's tapes were cut she started screaming hysterically. It took five minutes to calm her. The ambulance came screeching down the ramps and skidded to halt. Four white-coated paramedics leapt out and began fussing. Molloy wrapped Armstrong in a blanket and lead her away. Her body shook violently, she was still sobbing. Her shoulders heaved. Molloy was double-checking the boot of the Lincoln when he spotted the Manchester United soccer scrapbook. It was wedged in one corner. He flicked it open, then stopped at the inside front cover. Even in the gloom of the car park he could make out the childish scrawl:

Martin Clancy aged 8 years
14 Greenlea Road
Clontarf
Dublin
Ireland
Europe
The World.
DO NOT TOUCH UNDER PAIN OF DEATH.
ARSENAL STINKS.

He stopped and thought. He looked around. The body of the Goon lay where it had been discovered. Yellow incident tapes were being set up to protect the scene. The paramedics had Clarke and Kavanagh in the back of the ambulance and were connecting drip sets. Joan Armstrong was crumpled inside the blanket, supported by one of the detectives. She was shivering. Molloy read the address again, remembering the earlier alert about a missing family. He connected the names.

'Where was he taking you?' He stood squarely in front of the trembling schoolgirl.

She looked up. 'To Mo.'

Molloy inspected her closely. She looked like someone who'd been to hell and back.

'Where does Mo live?' He knew already. He just needed to hear it confirmed.

Armstong's lips started quivering, her eyes brimmed with tears. She began to shiver.

'Where does Mo live?' The ambulance siren started up, deafening everyone in the basement.

'Where does Mo live?' shouted Molloy.

He stuck a pen and notebook into her hands. Shaking fingers scribbled three lines. Molloy checked them, then stared at the girl. She was crying again. Molloy couldn't decide if the tears were for herself or Mo.

5.48 pm

Frank Clancy was in the back of a squad car en route to Clontarf police station. He'd been detained at the bottom of the steps of the Air France when it landed at Dublin Airport. The three officers in the car were giving nothing away. 'We're to take you straight to the station,' one of them said. 'Everybody wants to talk to you.' Clancy pleaded for more information. 'Is

there any news on my family? Are they still missing?'
His questions were met with a stony silence. The car
was caught in a tailback of traffic trying to negotiate
past a broken-down bus blocking two lanes. The radio
suddenly crackled into life. Clancy couldn't make out
what was being said over the static. He noticed one of
the policemen crouch forward and pick up a headset.
He could see the man squeezing it tightly against his
right ear. A hand tugged the driver and the car was
swerved to a halt. The front-seat passenger leapt out
and immediately stopped all movement on the road.
The driver did a three-point turn and criss-crossed
two lanes. The passenger door slammed shut, the
siren was switched on. The car sped forward, tyres
sreeching. 'What's wrong?' he asked.   He felt
frightened. 'What's happening?'

No one answered. The car swerved past trucks and
buses, careered along bicycle tracks, lane-hopped and
broke every red light. Frank Clancy had a sense of
foreboding. He wanted to vomit from fear and wound
down the side window for air. He hadn't eaten for so
long he felt weak. As he leaned his cheek against the
ledge, blurred images flashed by. People were going
about their daily chores, sweeping streets, selling
newspapers, window-shopping. Life was normal for
everyone except Frank Clancy.

They're dead, I know that. Anne, Michael, little
Laura. They've been killed. All because of me. He
looked up, noticing the car had crossed the River
Liffey and was heading eastwards along the quays.
'Where are we going?' he shouted. The passenger-
seat police officer turned slightly. He was grim-faced.
'You'll know in a minute, we're nearly there.'

Tony Molloy stood outside the two-storey-over basement, end-of-terrace house in Fitzhill Square. The square was three miles from the fashionable southside centre of Dublin and close to a major business district. It was a small group of Georgian houses cramped around a central green. There was a mixture of residential and office use. The pavements were tree-lined and in full leaf, the central green sealed off by ornate railings. There was on-street parking, disc display for residents only. Molloy waited anxiously outside number five. It was painted bright yellow with a red Georgian panelled front door. A clematis in full bloom twined itself along an outer corner.

Molloy had rung and knocked. There was no reply. He'd then contacted the police commissioner, Donal Murphy, and explained where he was and why. The commissioner was stunned. He'd already heard of the bloodbath at the multistorey car park. Molloy's information rocked him totally. 'Go in,' he ordered finally. 'I'll take full responsibility.'

But all the basement and ground-floor windows were protected by security bars. The only way in was through the front door, and it was massive. It seemed reinforced. There had been a delay while a 'break-in' team was summoned. They arrived just as Frank Clancy's squad car pulled up. Clancy was taken out and bundled across to the group collected at the front door.

'Who's this?' asked Molloy. Clancy was identified. Molloy looked him up and down. 'You're the guy with the missing family?' Clancy nodded. His mouth was so dry he couldn't speak. 'Wait in the car. And keep your fingers crossed. I think they're in here.' Clancy was thunderstruck. He stepped back to get a better look at the house.

A transit van pulled up and four heavily built men in black tracksuits leapt out. They carried a battering ram. Residents and office workers crowded nearby windows to watch. With five powerful back and forward thumps the red Georgian door crashed off its hinges and six armed detectives scrambled into the house. Molloy was at the lead. Within minutes they discovered the basement door. It was bolted from the outside but not locked. Inside they found Anne Clancy curled up against her two children. All three were shivering and freezing cold. They were whimpering from fright. Beakers lay scattered around, pools of water along the floor.

Molloy left men with them and rushed upstairs. The team had scouted every room until they reached the top floor. There they came upon another locked door. Molloy noticed three Chubb bolts protecting. The battering ram burst through them with four strong thumps. Molloy clambered over the splintered wood, revolver at the ready. He waved away those following and they stood outside.

It was a large room, about twenty-foot square. In the middle and pushed tight against a wall was a king-size bed. It had an old-fashioned brass bedhead, rails top and bottom. At the foot of the bed was a tripod with video camera. Two arc lights were pulled back and rested in a corner. There were handcuffs hanging from the top headrails, black silk thongs tied to the bottom. In another corner a wide-screen television and video recorder were secured to a bench top.

Beside was a collection of video tapes. Molloy pulled at drawers and discovered a selection of syringes and needles inside their sterile wraps. He found a box of ampoules of sterile water and a methylated spirits wick burner. Finally he uncovered twenty individual clingfilm wraps of heroin.

He sat down heavily on the bed, stunned and shocked with the revelations. He spotted the video tapes again and sorted through them. He noticed one with the letters J.M. scrawled in red biro on the front. He slipped it into the VCR and turned on the television. There was a delay as zigzagged blurred tape ran through. Then images flashed. The camera picked up the bed Molloy was sitting on. He turned to check, recognising the headrails immediately. Sound came through with the voice of a young girl, giddy laughing. Onto the bed rolled the naked body of a black-haired girl. She seemed to be moving very slowly, as if drugged. One arm waved at the camera, beckoning. Molloy noticed what looked like a sticking plaster in the crook of the elbow. The girl turned towards the camera and gave a come-on leer.

Molloy's mouth dropped. It was Jennifer Marks. Suddenly a man's body entered the frame, tall and slim. He had his back to the camera and was in denim jeans but stripped to the waist. The man sat down on the bed and began dragging one of the girl's arms up to the handcuffs. The hand was secured. Then he fastened the other. The man ran his hands slowly along the naked body and parted the ankles. In the fleetest of moments he turned and faced the camera. Molloy froze the frame and stared. There was no mistaking the face.

He ejected the tape and punched at his mobile

phone. Within two minutes he was put through to the police commissioner.

'It's him,' he said grimly. 'It's definitely John Regan. I even have him on tape.'

6.15 pm

Frank Clancy clutched his wife and children. He squeezed them so tightly his eight-year-old son started complaining. His wife Anne clung to his neck, covering him with kisses. Laura lay stretched across his lap, subdued and sweaty. She seemed limp but struggled to life as she looked up at her father. They sat together on a couch in the ground-floor front room of John Regan's house covered with blankets. Anne was still only in her nightie, the children in their pyjamas, dressed as the Goon had taken them. The door was closed to give them privacy and intimacy for a few minutes. After that they were to be taken to hospital for a thorough check-up. The questions flew and Clancy couldn't answer them all. He was so relieved to see his family alive he couldn't focus on anything. He just wanted to hold them for ever.

'What happened to your hair, daddy?' Laura finally piped up. Despite her fever and lack of food and restricted movement she was rallying. She stared at her father as if he was from another planet.

Martin stood and inspected. 'Yeah, what happened?'

Anne sat back and checked, noticing for the first time the straggling strands, the dark stubble, the haggard face. 'What *have* you been up to?'

Clancy's eyes danced with delight. He looked from

one to the other. 'I had a fight with a dragon.'

His wife managed a wry grin. 'Well, whoever she was, she won.'

The door was rapped and Tony Molloy entered. He was ashen-faced. He called Clancy aside and explained what had been discovered. 'We're going over to lift him now.'

Clancy didn't hesitate. 'I'm coming with you.'

There was an immediate cry of protests from his wife. 'No, Frank, no,' she pleaded. 'This is not your territory. Leave it to the police.'

Frank Clancy clutched his family to his chest again. He kissed them one by one, then turned his wife's face towards him. 'This is my territory, Anne. They were my patients. I've come too far now and there's too much at stake to stop.'

Laura forced herself up, one hand tugging at her mother's nightie for support. 'Mummy,' she said out loud, 'you told me daddy would punch that bad man in the nose. Well, I think he should go and do it right now.'

Frank Clancy glanced at his watch. It was almost six thirty. The press conference would have started.

'Disneyland,' he promised, 'Disneyland. As soon as I've sorted that bad man out I'll go straight out and book the tickets.'

The children cheered. Anne Clancy heaved a resigned sigh.

41 6.51 pm

'Good evening, ladies and gentlemen, thank you again for coming along.'

John Regan addressed the gathered media from a podium. The large hall in government buildings was full to overflowing and Regan glanced around, assessing the turnout. He was well satisfied. There were six TV crews including two major US networks. The national station, RTE, was carrying the press conference live. He knew they had already agreed deals for edited highlights with Sky, CNN, the BBC and a number of European networks. A TV crew from Boston had forced itself close to the podium and the cameramen were checking angles. Print and radio reporters lounged in various chairs near the rear. The front rows were filled with Mercy Hospital staff, mainly from the top-floor Heart Foundation. All were wearing their best suits and dresses for the occasion. The hospital administrator, a tall rake of a man with tight-curled grey hair, sat in an aisle seat at the middle of the front row. He had a satisfied smile on his face.

The government propaganda was back in place. *A

New Government For A New People. Images of John Regan shaking hands, looking concerned, head thrown back and laughing, wiping away tears, kicking a football. Strong, positive images. Behind Regan sat the Dream Team. Linda Speer was looking stunning in a linen trouser suit. Stone Colman was in a simple navy jacket over grey corduroys. He wore an open-neck shirt. Dan Marks was in trousers and short-sleeved shirt, his jacket hanging behind his chair. Marks was chatting to Dr Hans Otto Mayer, the German minister responsible for distribution of EEC medical grants. Dr Mayer was a small, tubby man in an ill-fitting suit. His hair was thin and slicked across his head, he wore thick-rimmed glasses. He was smiling contentedly. Every now and then he reached inside his jacket pocket, fingering the EEC cheque for twenty million pounds.

For the previous half-hour he and the rest of the audience had been bored to distraction with bar charts, graphs and discussions on mortality rates from ischaemic heart disease. John Regan had blinded with a dazzling display of the first six months' results from the Mercy Hospital's Heart Foundation. Even to those remotely unconcerned with medicine, the findings were remarkable. Deaths from heart attacks had been halved, the number of early bypass operations more than doubled. The waiting time for heart operations in children under one year of age had been reduced from ten to two months. More astonishingly came the announcement of a new compound for use in heart disease.

'While I cannot say very much at this stage,' Regan teased, 'it is no exaggeration to state we are looking at a major pharmacological breakthrough.'

The audience had politely clapped, the first applause coming from Regan's PR advisor, Louis Flanagan. He had positioned himself in the middle of the auditorium, leaning against a wall, monitoring every response from the assembled media.

'I'd like now to introduce a very important guest,' Regan announced, 'who has something for us all to celebrate, I believe?' Regan turned to the German minister who beamed in response.

Flash lights lit up the room. Dr Mayer stood up. As he did the doors at the back of the hall opened noisily.

'Minister Regan,' began Mayer, 'may I first of all congratulate you on the wonderful first results from the Heart Foundation you fought so hard to establish.' Mayer's English was perfect, if a little clipped. 'Speaking as a doctor myself . . .'

Along the side aisles marched grim-faced uniformed policemen. They pushed past anyone in the way.

Mayer stopped. A look of consternation flickered crossed his face. Then he continued. '. . . I can confirm the data you presented so succinctly this evening . . .'

The policemen forced their way to the podium and stopped. John Regan looked down angrily, furiously waving at them to go away.

'. . . confirms the highest international medical standards . . .'

Along the central aisle marched Police Commissioner Donal Murphy. He was dressed in full uniform, his peaked cap pulled firmly down. Behind followed Tony Molloy. He had his personal revolver drawn. Taking up the rear was Frank Clancy. His head bobbed over the two in front, trying to catch a glimpse of those on the podium. He noticed the door at the side swinging. He jumped to see clearly. The chair Linda Speer had been sitting in was empty.

Dr Mayer watched as the policemen came right beneath where he stood. He looked nervously towards Regan and tugged the EEC cheque from his inside pocket. 'Well,' he said hesitantly, 'without further ado may I now present this . . .'

'Stop please.' Commissioner Murphy was on the podium squaring up to Regan. Four other officers stood behind Stone Colman and Dan Marks. The heart specialists looked around in astonishment, they struggled to stand but were forced back into their seats.

Donal Murphy grabbed Regan's left shoulder. The other man's face crumpled. 'John Regan,' Murphy announced loudly. The cameramen below fought to capture the moment. 'I am arresting you on suspicion of involvement in the murder of Jennifer Marks on 11 May. I must inform you, you are not obliged to say anything unless you wish to do so, but anything you do say will be taken down in writing and may be given in evidence.'

Behind Tony Molloy couldn't stop grinning. The hall erupted in chaos. Cameramen and reporters fought their way to the front, screaming at one another. Chairs were knocked over, bystanders pushed aside. Mobile phones were forced into action as journalists tried furiously to contact their editors.

The Mercy Hospital staff sat like stunned mullets, shocked and disbelieving. Only Frank Clancy kept his wits about him. He was still looking for Linda Speer. He scouted the building, inside and out. She had disappeared. Clancy ran from room to room, bursting open doors. He sprinted along the car parks, squinting into each vehicle. Nothing. Speer had slipped the net.

Clancy ran back into the auditorium. It was in uproar. John Regan was being lead shouting and red-faced down the central aisle. He was in handcuffs. Dan Marks and Stone Colman were being pushed along a side aisle, policemen ahead and behind. Dr Hans Otto Mayer still stood on the podium, the twenty-million-pound EEC cheque hanging in his hand. His mouth was open and closing but nothing was coming out.

Clancy spotted the hospital administrator. He was slumped in his seat, head in hands, rocking backwards and forwards as if in pain. Clancy grabbed him by the lapels. 'Where's the hospital database?' he shouted.

The administrator looked at him as if he had fallen from another planet. 'You're . . . you're . . . you're supposed to come to the boardro . . .' The words were stammered and Clancy shook him violently.

'Where's the fucking hospital database?' he snarled. 'Do I have to rip your fucking tongue out at the roots?'

The administrator shook his head. He was terrified. 'N . . . n . . . n . . . no . . . no. It's in the annexe, beside the old records department.'

Clancy dropped him like a hot potato.

7.43 pm

The hospital back-up database was located in a large brick and perspex room adjacent to the records annexe at the back of the Mercy Hospital. It had its own entrance, steel slide doors opened only when a swipe card was inserted into a panel. The walls on each side of the doors were made of reinforced perspex so that anyone inside could be seen immediately. The room was lit twenty-four hours a day with seven halogen bulbs. The database stored computer information from all activities in the Mercy Hospital, clinical and non-clinical. If material was entered in any PC within the institution, on midnight of that working day the information was backed up separately in the database. In addition a separate disc was prepared automatically. In this way if someone altered the medical or laboratory records, there was still an original information storage facility. The discs were created daily by technology within the massive computer and stored in a separate sealed container. Each was date-stamped.

Linda Speer now was looking for the sealed container. She'd used a stolen swipe card, one she'd managed to sneak from administration months previously. She'd been planning this moment for some time but never had the right opportunity. The security presence had always been too heavy. Tonight with everyone at the press conference, it was light. She'd left just as Dr Hans Otto Mayer stood to deliver his congratulatory address. She hadn't seen the policemen enter the auditorium, hadn't seen John Regan and her Dream Team colleagues lead away. As usual she was pursuing her own agenda. She stood inside the room and looked around. The steel doors had glided shut behind her. She quickly checked through the perspex windows. Nothing. No activity. Easy. Over in a few minutes, all evidence destroyed.

She walked around the huge machinery. It was floor to roof, outer doors red. There was colour coding: clinical, laboratory, administration, stores, et cetera. She opened the clinical doors. For a moment she couldn't believe her eyes. It was totally different to what she'd been used to in Boston. There the dials and switches had been simple, easy to become familiar with. Here there was nothing. Just plastic casing behind which whirring and buzzing could be heard. She stood back to think. How do I get at it?

7.52 pm

Frank Clancy had grabbed a police motorcyclist. 'Take me to the Mercy Hospital, as fast as you bloody well can.'

The officer had almost thrown him off there and then except Clancy had forced him to double-check with Tony Molloy. They then sped through Dublin's traffic, blue lights flashing, siren blaring. Clancy was still dressed in his sweat-soaked T-shirt, denims and trainers. He almost froze on the pillion seat. The motorcycle screeched to a halt outside the hospital front doors and Clancy leapt off. He stood for a moment to get his bearings.

The Mercy Hospital was a large complex, he didn't want to get lost going down some blind alley. Then he spotted the sign. RECORDS ANNEXE. He ran towards it.

7.58 pm

Linda Speer had found how to log in. She'd discovered the sealed container with the back-up discs. Her swipe card had opened it. She was feverishly flicking through, trying to get the exact days she knew contained the damaging information. Her fingers shook and she dropped disc after disc as she checked. She started to sweat.

Inside the room was becoming unbearably warm. The heat from the machinery, the closed, stifling atmosphere caught at her lungs and she coughed. At last she found them. The five discs with the dates she was most concerned about. Five discs that could prove everything. The five discs that would bring her down. She slipped them into her jacket pocket. Done it. Beat the system again. Fuck you, Frank Clancy.

She flicked open a packet of menthol tips, desperate for a cigarette. She looked around, checking she'd left no traces. She began wiping her fingerprints off all surfaces, then swiped the card. The steel doors glided open.

8.02 pm

Frank Clancy was pounding at the wrong door when the security guard rugby-tackled him from behind. Thinking the database was in the records annexe, Clancy had been crashing against the locked door, trying desperately to break down the hinges. He suddenly found himself forced to the ground, two strong arms wrapped tightly around his knees.

'Let go, let go,' he shouted desperately, 'This is an emergency.' The security guard twisted him onto his stomach and struggled to pin his arms. 'I'm a doctor, let me go.'

The guard only saw a stained T-shirt, denim-clad

thug with hair sticking in all directions. 'And I'm the fuckin' man in the moon,' he snarled back. He reached for his walkie-talkie.

In that split second Clancy swung round with all his might and hit out with a closed fist. He connected with a nose and the guard swore. He loosened his grip momentarily, long enough to allow Clancy escape. He heard an alarm whistle blown as he rounded the corner to the database storage depot.

8.05 pm

The steel doors were open. The darkness beckoned. Linda Speer had all she needed. She planned to slip out the side exit from the hospital, grab a taxi and flee to the airport. Her false documents and suitcases were already in the left-luggage department there. She reckoned she'd be sipping champagne in first class within two hours. And a millionaire many times over soon.

She glanced around one last time and spotted a disc lying on the floor, one she'd dropped in her hurry. The menthol tip dangled from her lip. She lifted the disc and looked to see where she might hide it. She decided to take it as well rather than waste time opening the sealed container again. Without thinking she flicked her gold cigarette lighter on and puffed hungrily at the flame. Suddenly a red light above the steel doors flashed on and off, a klaxon sounded inside the room. Speer stood rock still. Then she dropped the disc and rushed towards the steel doors. As her hand touched the edge, they snapped shut. A hissing of gas filled the room. Speer pounded at the doors desperately. She felt an acrid taste in her mouth, her lungs stung and she coughed violently. She tried swiping the doors open but they wouldn't budge. She stumbled, the air in her lungs felt like fire.

She staggered to the perspex windows and looked out. She pounded at the glass. 'HELP! HELP!' The hissing of the gas filled her ears and she slid to her knees. Suddenly the glass was being pounded from the other side. She looked up to find Frank Clancy staring in at her. She felt the room darken, she coughed violently again. Her every strength was ebbing. Clancy was down on his knees outside, scratching desperately at the perspex. Speer crumpled onto the floor, her eyes still looking longingly at the darkness outside. The halogen lights inside the database seemed to slowly dim. She closed her eyes. The windows were pounded again. For the last time Linda Speer looked up. For the last time she came face to face with Dr Frank Clancy. He was crying, great blobs of tears streaming down his face. Linda Speer reached a hand across and let it fall on the perspex. The room went completely black. The hand fell lifeless. Outside Frank Clancy crawled into a ball and wept. The waste of life. The terrible, terrible waste of life. And all for greed.

42 *Six days later.*

Tony Molloy inspected a pear. He squeezed at the middle, decided it was too soft, then returned it to the fruit bowl. He twisted off a cluster of green grapes and began nibbling. He sat in a chair too small for his bulk in unit twenty-six of the private wing attached to the Mercy Hospital. It was a decent-sized room, fifteen-foot wide and twelve-foot long. There was a small colour TV in one corner, two bedside lockers and a closed door leading to an en suite bathroom. Lying on the only bed was Jim Clarke. He was having his stump dressed and wore light pyjamas.

When he'd been transferred to the Accident and Emergency department of the Mercy Hospital after the blood bath in the car-park basement, he'd been in poor shape. A decision had been made to amputate his damaged leg. He'd been taken to theatre immediately. While he was being anaesthetised, across the same corridor in the neurosurgical wing, Moss Kavanagh was having a depressed skull fracture repaired. The Goon's baseball bat had shattered the big man's head bone, but fortunately caused no brain damage. Both he and Clarke were now off the critical list and convalescing.

On the bed lay piles of newspapers. Irish, British, European and US editions. Tabloids and broadsheets. Clarke had been flicking through the headlines earlier. GOVERNMENT COLLAPSE! . . . GOVERNMENT SHAME . . . IRISH GOVERNMENT RESIGNS . . . The international media had had a field day. The tabloids lapped it up. SEX SCANDAL BRINGS DOWN GOVERNMENT . . . MY NIGHT OF HELL WITH MONSTER REGAN. A lot of young girls had come forward with their own tales of involvement with John Regan. MINISTER IN DRUGS FOR SEX SCAM. Dublin was full of reporters following the story. It had every ingredient: greed, corruption, sex and drugs. The banner headlines guaranteed huge sales.

'Will I start?' Molloy asked when the nurse had finally left the room.

Clarke massaged at the stump. 'Do you know,' he said, 'it's great to be free from pain at last. I wish to God they'd taken that bloody leg off ages ago.'

Molloy grinned. 'You actually look better too, Jim. Not as haggard and drawn. You always seemed to be in discomfort.'

Clarke pulled the bedclothes over the stump and settled himself. 'Okay, tell me all.'

Molloy unpeeled a banana. 'First off it was Linda Speer who persuaded that Dream Team come to Dublin. Apparently things were getting so hot in Boston she was desperate to get away. She'd been doing secret drug trials. Some guy over there got suspicious and told the authorities. They were closing in on her.'

'What about Marks and Colman?' asked Clarke.

'Colman was an innocent bystander. He's clean,' said Molloy. 'Marks and Speer had this hot thing going on between them at the time.' He spat a piece of banana out. 'She had him by the balls sexually, stringing him along. Also Speer knew all about the trouble he was having with Jennifer.'

Clarke looked over. 'What trouble?'

'Jenny was running her own little scam in Boston. Sex for drugs. She even had three of her school friends on the game.'

'Jesus,' muttered Clarke. He threw the blankets back to cool himself.

'Now,' went on Molloy. He was eyeing a green apple. 'Speer met Regan at some heart conference before he went into politics. She was bitching and whining about never advancing in the States, always being passed up at interviews. Claimed it was because she was a woman. Sexist thing, that sort of crap.'

'And it wasn't?'

'Nah, not a damn bit of it. Speer was being passed over because no one trusted her research papers. Apparently she had a reputation for fiddling results, always putting a glow on her work where no glow existed.'

A nurse came into the room and the conversation stopped. She checked Clarke's temperature, blood pressure and pulse. Molloy watched. When she left he closed the door firmly behind her.

'Nobody ever takes my blood pressure,' he complained. 'What you gotta do to get a check up round here?'

Clarke grinned. 'Have your leg amputated. Get your skull bashed in.'

386

Molloy scowled. 'I'll leave it then.' He started into the grapes again. 'So, anyway,' he went on, spitting out a pip, 'Regan knew all this and later approached Speer. He wanted to make a big impression on the international medical scene, he knew she wanted to go to the top. They both knew they'd use any tactics, fair or foul. They were the perfect team. Speer could fiddle results if necessary to get that EEC money, Regan would allow her to continue her drug trials.'

'Where did it all go wrong?' Clarke was watching his fruit bowl slowly disappear.

'With Jennifer Marks. That kid was too streetwise.' Molloy flicked at grape juice on his shirt. His belly seemed more strained than usual. He fiddled for an antacid. 'She knew Speer and her father were at it hammer and tongs. She kept a close eye on them, according to Joan Armstrong. One night Jennifer overheard this almighty row. Annie Marks was laying into Dan about Speer. Armstrong told me Jennifer said her mother was drunker than usual. She let fly with all the dirt she knew, and she knew a lot. Jennifer overheard everything. She made a copy of her father's key to Speer's flat and went in one day. Discovered all the tablets.'

'What the hell use were they?' wondered Clarke. The room was getting warm and he asked Molloy to open a window.

'They were Jennifer's bargaining card.' Molloy was struggling with a catch. Finally it came free and Dublin's traffic hummed in the background. 'Jennifer wanted drugs. She'd learned very early on about Regan's reputation, knew he liked young girls, knew he often paid for them to come to his house. I meant every dog in the street knew about this. Just Regan was so powerful and dangerous no one was ever brave enough to say anything.'

Clarke shook his head. 'And to think that bastard challenged me.'

'Forget it, Jim,' said Molloy. He chewed on an antacid. 'You'll be out of here very soon. Regan's going down big time. He's yesterday's man.'

'So how did Jennifer Marks cross Regan?'

'Tried bribing him,' replied Molloy. 'She took a handful of the tablets Speer was using at the hospital. Sent them to him, one at a time, anonymously. One every day for three in a row. On day four she sent a note saying she wanted a million pounds in cash to shut up.'

'How do you know all this?' Clarke was impressed at the detail.

'Mainly from Joan Armstrong. She and Jennifer were in cahoots. Both were into heroin, really addicted. Both paid for their habits the only way they knew, with their bodies. Both wanted an easier way, and faster supplies.'

'So they got greedy?' Clarke suggested.

'And stupid.'

'So what did happen that night in Sandymount Park?' Clarke opened up his pyjama front to catch the breeze from the window.

'Regan had this heavy minder. He called him the Goon. Same guy who nearly brought the election campaign crashing down with his aggro.'

Clarke sat forward. 'Yeah, I remember something about that.'

'That's the one,' said Molloy. He opened a button on his shirt to ease the pressure on his belly. 'Regan sent the Goon into Balfe's pub to get Jennifer Marks.

Only Jennifer's already spaced out of her mind and hanging out with that knifeman, Micko Kelly. Joan Armstrong says Jennifer told the Goon to fuck off. And that poor sap Kelly squared up as well.'

'A dangerous scenario,' suggested Clarke.

'Dynamite. Regan and his henchman followed Jennifer and Kelly to the park. Regan tried to make her see sense, talk her round. She started arguing. Kelly came out to see what was going on.'

'Then all hell broke loose,' interrupted Clarke. He lay back on the pillows, exhausted. Molloy sensed he'd had enough. He stood up to leave. 'I'm told you knew it was Regan even before you went to the house. How come?'

Molloy sat down again. He perched himself on the edge of the chair. 'The fibres at the scene. They were mohair. Micko Kelly could only remember one name that night. Mo.' He looked over. 'D'ye get it?'

Clarke shook his head.

'Mo. Mohair. Mo. John Regan. Everybody knows him as Mo Regan. Our champagne socialist. He only ever wears mohair suits and sweaters. It was his fibres clinging to those twigs in the park.'

'The bastard,' muttered Clarke. 'The miserable bastard.'

Molloy was on his feet again. 'I'll call in again tomorrow. I was talking with Maeve and Katy. They're on the warpath for you to resign and I ain't getting in that firing line.'

Clarke grinned. He slid further down in the bed and made himself comfortable. 'Before you go.' Molloy had the door partly open. 'Who's this Frank Clancy I read about all over the papers? And what happened to Speer in that database room?'

Molloy grinned. 'That guy Clancy deserves a medal. He's the one who was doing his own detective work in the hospital. He's being fêted the length and breadth of the country like some war hero. The media are going mad looking for him.' He buttoned up his midriff. 'Speer got caught with a new fire-sensor system installed in the computer database. Apparently it's super-sensitive to heat and smoke. She lit a cigarette, the alarm went off, the doors shut and the room was flooded with neon gas.' He noticed Clarke's puzzled frown. 'Neon deprives the room of oxygen and snuffs any fire within seconds. Snuffed Speer as well.'

Clarke grimaced, then pulled another pillow under his head. 'And where's Clancy now?'

Molloy tapped the side of his nose. 'This one's between you and me.' He closed the door tightly. 'He's in Disneyland.'

Epilogue

John Regan was charged with a wide range of offences including murder, narcotics, procurement and fraud. He is currently in gaol on a twenty-year stretch. Within an hour of his arrest in Dublin and news of Linda Speer's sudden death, trading in Cynx Pharmaceuticals on the New York Stock Exchange was suspended and fraud detectives raided its Boston offices.

Jim Clarke retired from the police force on health grounds. He now works as a security advisor to a number of Ireland's multinational pharmaceutical companies. He uses a walking stick and has adjusted well to his prosthetic limb.

Moss Kavanagh recovered from his severe head injuries and is based at police headquarters.

Tony Molloy was promoted to inspector and continues to work the Serious Crime Squad.

Dr Frank Clancy returned from Florida to a hero's welcome. He was wined and dined by the Mercy Hospital board of governors and offered substantial inducements to develop his department within the hospital. He was also invited to sit on the board. For such a young man this would be rapid progression in medical politics. He declined gracefully, didn't even need to think about the offers. Frank Clancy was a doctor first and foremost. He loved his work, cared for his patients. He did not want to be side-lined, no matter how attractive the position might be. He is back on the wards of the Mercy Hospital, but home every evening no later than seven. He and his wife Anne are expecting their third child. Martin and Laura are delighted.

Dan and Annie Marks returned to Boston. He works in a private hospital and has retired completely from public hospital duties and medical research. He has sued for divorce from his wife.

Dr Stone Colman was given total clearance at the subsequent investigation surrounding the Dream Team appointments to Dublin. He continues to work at the Mercy Hospital.

Patrick Dillon discharged Micko Kelly from Rockdale Hospital for the Criminally Insane into secure accommodation at the beginning of July 1998. On 30 July Kelly was formally charged with the murder of Jennifer Marks. Dillon confirmed he was fit to plead. Three days before his first court appearance Micko Kelly wet the sheets in his cell and tore them into strips. He waited until he had been checked and the prison warders were settling down for the night.

At 11.37 pm on 31 August he was found hanging from the bars on his cell window and pronounced dead at three minutes before midnight. The cell was occupied the next day by a seventeen-year-old male arrested at Dublin Airport carrying three kilos of heroin. It was business as usual.